This is
FALLING

A novel by Ginger Scott

For Mom

Chapter 1

Rowe

I was feeling brave when I picked McConnell. It was one of those afternoons where everything was suffocating me, and the college packet was just staring me in the face.

Two years of being homeschooled by a woman who taught economics at the state university would prepare anyone for a stellar performance on their SATs. The test was actually easy. I finished quickly and didn't even spend time checking answers like all of the prep books told me to do. I turned in my booklet to the campus proctor and got the hell out of the testing room. Three weeks later, it showed up in the mail—a 2390, near perfect. That meant scholarships. And scholarships meant options.

For months, I fought the idea of going away to school. I'm not ready to be out, to be *on my own*. I don't think I'll ever be ready. Two years of homeschooling also left me a little out of practice when it comes to social interaction. And college is *all about* social interaction.

My parents were pushing me. I don't think they thought I'd call their bluff and pick a school a thousand miles away. But I was hoping they'd call mine when I slid the McConnell acceptance across the table to them.

They didn't. My dad smiled and looked at my mother, both of them breathing deeply, ready to take this step. I wasn't. I'm still not. I'm not even remotely close to ready. But I want to be. I'm desperate to be ready. I've spent the last seven hundred days of my life seeing everyone else live from my self-imposed bubble. My biggest romance was watching some couple fall in love on a reality TV show, and the only prom I attended was in a movie. It's like I'm caught in an internal tug-of-war with myself—my heart begging to beat from thrill, but caged by fear.

But somehow I've gotten myself this far—a map in my hands leading to my room at Hayden Hall on the McConnell campus. My parents made it a road trip. It takes fifteen hours to drive from Arizona to Oklahoma, and my dad powered through the entire trip—I think worried that I would back out if he stopped. I thought about it. I almost broke down at a gas station in New Mexico, bawling my eyes out in a Texaco bathroom. But as badly as I didn't want to leave the safety of home, I was more afraid of what would happen to me if I stayed.

It's clear I was dying there. Well, maybe not *dying*, but certainly not *living*. I was crossing off days on my calendar, putting one foot in front of the next, living a routine and getting to the next. How could I? My mind was swarmed with guilt that made living impossible.

Now, standing here, my hand gripping the handle of my giant roller trunk and my parents hauling suitcases behind me, I'm not so sure I chose right.

"Rowe—are we almost there, honey? I think I've lost a gallon of sweat. This humidity is brutal," my mom says, fanning her face with one of the programs they handed out during orientation.

Being from Arizona, I thought the heat would be bearable, but I guess I'd never felt real humidity. My tank top was plastered to my back with sweat, and in front of me, my father's T-shirt was doing the same to his skin. I'd be embarrassed, but everyone on campus looked exactly the same—like we were all trying to win a game of *Survivor*.

I finally see the marker for Hayden Hall on the walkway and turn to smile at my mom, nodding my head toward it.

"Thank God!" she says, a bit melodramatically. I let it roll off me. In less than an hour, I know Tom and Karen Stanton will be long gone—and I will be completely alone. So as mental as my mother has made me for the last two years, I hang on to every last drop of her personality, terrified of how I'll manage when she's actually gone.

We take a small elevator up two stories and find my room at the end of the hall to the right. Three thirty-three—I remember thinking it felt lucky when I got my boarding placement package in the mail. Lucky. I feel so far from *lucky* now.

The door is open, and I can see that two of the three beds have already been claimed. The only one left is closest to the door—obviously my last choice, and my mom can see the anxiety attacking my face.

"Maybe you can move the beds, move yours more to the corner," she says, giving my shoulder a small squeeze and sliding one of the suitcases next to what will be my bed for the next eight and a half months.

All I can do is nod. My dad is sliding the rest of my belongings into the room and lifting the case to my bed so I can start unpacking. I brought everything I own with me. I think somehow I thought surrounding myself with my *stuff* would make this place feel more like home, and maybe I could just tough it out in my bubble and not have to venture from my room much.

"I haven't met her yet. God, I hope she's not a total bitch or something!" one of two blondes says as they enter our room. My mom coughs a little to get their attention, and when they look up, one of them is embarrassed—unfortunately, not the one who wished publicly for me not to be a *bitch*.

"Oh, good. You're here!" the confident one says, walking over to me with her hand outstretched, almost like she's welcoming me into *her* home. This is not going to be good; I can tell.

"Hi, I'm Rowe," I say, my voice barely a whisper. I don't talk often, so sometimes it takes me a while to warm up my vocal cords, but I know I was loud enough for her to hear, which makes her reaction that much more offensive.

"I'm sorry...did you say Rose?" she says loudly, her face all bunched, like I just fed her stale broccoli. Everything about her is harsh and abrasive.

"Rowe," I repeat, and she just continues to stare. "Like...like a boat?" I actually start paddling in the air.

"Ohhhhh. Cute," she says, turning her attention to her bed, which is layered with piles of clothes. "I'm Paige. And that's Cassidy."

"Cass," the other one pipes in, shaking her head with her lips tight and gesturing toward Paige. I think she's telling me not to take her personally. Not a problem, I've already filed her and this room into the how-fast-can-I-get-out-of-here category. "I like to be called Cass. And *Paige* and I are glad to meet you."

Paige isn't even listening to our conversation anymore, already more interested in whoever just sent her a text on her phone. I'm in a freshman dorm, but nothing about Paige says freshman. Her body is tall and curves in all of the right places, and her skin is a warm bronze, like I'd imagine a lifeguard in Florida looks. Her blonde hair is long and layered, and every strand sits in the perfect place, like a golden frame around her crystal blue eyes.

Cass is blonde, too, but she seems more like a real person. Her hair is pulled back in a ponytail, and I can tell she had light makeup on at one point today, but the humidity has worn most of it away.

It's clear my role here will be the oddball, the one who doesn't fit. Honestly, that's what I expected. Two years ago, I was doomed to never fit in again—like a wounded superhero tattooed by kryptonite. And standing here, no makeup, brown eyes, a plain shirt and denim shorts, my walnut-colored hair twisted in a bun, still crunchy from my shower almost a full day ago, only makes the differences between me and *everyone else* that much clearer.

"Paige and I both got here yesterday. We sort of picked beds; I hope that's okay?" Cass says, sitting down on her mattress, which thankfully is the one closest to mine.

"It's fine. I'm good with whatever," I say, knowing my mom will be happy to hear me going with the flow. Internally, I make a note to check with the front desk the second my parents leave, hoping like hell there's a bed open somewhere on this campus that isn't steps from the door.

After an hour of unpacking and small talk with Cass, my parents finally leave. I couldn't mask the tears building up in my eyes when my mom hugged me goodbye, and my dad only waved from the door, knowing he's the weaker of the two of them and that he'd cave in if I asked him to take me home.

Disappointment only continued when the front-desk girl told me every room on campus was full. She told me to check back after rush week because a lot of students end up moving into the Greek dorms. But that would be a month from now. A month—I could survive a month. Couldn't I?

Paige disappeared almost the minute I met her, which was a relief. I'd have to work my way up to her personality. Thankfully, Cass had a lot of unpacking of her own to do, so I've spent the rest of the late afternoon with my ear buds pressed into my ears and my music turned up loud enough to drown everything else out.

I could probably find a way to keep myself busy with my clothes and music and silly pictures for the rest of the night, but Cass is waving her hands animatedly, pointing to her ears and mouthing her lips to get my attention, so I finally relent and put my headphones away. "Sorry, I had it up kind of loud."

"Yeah, I could tell. You have good taste in music, by the way." I like Cass. Her smile is genuine, and she reminds me of the friends I used to have at Hallman High. Plus, she recognizes things like the greatness that is Jack White and Broken Bells. I bet Paige is more of the Katy Perry sort.

"Thanks." I don't know how to carry on a conversation, so my eyes dart around her things, looking for something to reciprocate the compliment. "Your quilt is pretty."

It's possibly the most ordinary quilt on earth. It's gray and there's a tag on it, so it's not even homemade. The second I say it, I feel ridiculous, but the way Cass smiles and laughs doesn't make me feel stupid or small, so I join her. For the first time in two years, I feel like a teenager again—the normal kind that doesn't wake up with nightmares and hear screaming in her dreams.

I notice things most people don't, like that Cass is wearing a purple shirt with a V-neck cut and white shorts that cuff on the bottom. Her toenails are blue, slightly chipped, and she has a rope anklet on her right foot with a few dark-blue beads. I've been this way since the day my world came crashing down. It's like I'm trying to make up for failing to notice things when it counted most.

"You like it?" It takes me a minute or two to follow what Cass is talking about, but I eventually realize she caught me staring at her anklet.

5

"Yeah, sorry. I was just looking at the beads. They're beautiful," I say, hoping that Cass's mind isn't mulling over the idea that I might have a foot fetish or something.

"Thanks. My mom owns a bead store, so I make a ton of things like this. I could make you one, if you want?"

To her, the gesture is probably small and insignificant. But I smile and nod at her offer, and my stomach flutters a little with excitement, first-date kind of butterflies. Somehow, I may have done the impossible. Somehow, I proved myself wrong. Somehow...I made a friend.

Chapter 2

Rowe

This late at night, the bathrooms are dark, minus a few panels left on so students can find their way in and out. It's all part of cutting down on energy use—being *green*. There are suggested hours, but I'd rather be alone. The hallway lights are dim, but bright enough I can see if I use the stall closest to the door. This is the part that worried me most—showering in public. Most of the girls will probably shower in the morning, though, so I plan on taking mine late at night—in the dark.

Cass and Paige went out for the evening. Cass tried to get me to join them, but I convinced her I was exhausted from our trip. Not everyone is on campus yet, but a lot of the freshmen have arrived, and there are a few parties at the apartments on the outskirts of town. I'm not ready for parties.

The water doesn't take long to warm, so after looking around the room once more, and peeking out the door, I decide it's safe enough to undress. There are a lot of showerheads in the open, and I can't imagine being comfortable enough in my own skin to actually walk around naked. Even if my side wasn't riddled with scars, I don't think I would be the kind of woman who could show everyone her goods and bits.

I stack my clothes carefully on the small bench right outside the shower stall and step inside, pulling the curtain closed behind me. My heart is racing so fast I have to remind myself to breathe—long and deep—just to slow it down. I miss my shower at home, in my parents' bathroom, behind two doors that locked. I miss the hum of the fan, and the way it interrupted my thoughts. It's quiet in here, and it makes me shower fast, rushing through the shampoo and conditioner, barely running the shower gel over my skin before twisting the shower handle to *off* and wrapping myself in my towel.

I quickly pull my sleep-shirt over my head and let the towel drop; I'm stepping into my underwear when I notice the sound of the water pipes still vibrating. The thought that I'm not alone sends a wave of panic through my veins; I feel light-headed. I sit on the bench and clutch my dirty clothes and towel to my body, leaning forward enough so my eyes can scan the other stalls in search of feet.

But I'm alone. The pipe sound stops seconds later; I figure the water was probably coming from the floor above. I finish getting dressed, pulling on my cotton shorts and slipping my feet into my flip-flops before I enter the hall.

"Evenin'," he says, scaring me so badly I drop all of my things and push myself flush against the wall. I look like a jailbird in one of those old black-and-white movies, trying to step out of the spotlight during a breakout. "Sorry, didn't mean to scare you, but I figured if I didn't say anything, and you just saw me in the dark, it would be worse."

He's picking up my things for me, and somehow I manage to calm my pulse down enough to realize he's manhandling my underwear. *Oh god!* I grasp at my belongings, but my hands get tangled with his, which only makes me panic more and drop everything again.

"Boy, I scared you good, huh?" he chuckles. All I can focus on is gathering up my things and making my way back to my room—that, and the slight southern accent when he talks. "Hey, are you okay?"

It's not until his hand is gripping my arm that I finally look up at him. I'm not prepared for my reaction at all, and I'm sure I'm amusing him, because I blush so quickly I would have a better chance playing off a can of paint being dumped over my head. He's cute. He's *more than cute*; he's the exact boy I fantasized about when I was fourteen and dreaming of going off to college with my best friend Betsy. Brown hair just long enough on the top to flop over his forehead and eyebrows, blue eyes that hide under dark lashes and a half-shaven look that reminds me instantly that he isn't a boy at all. No, I'm standing in front of a man. It's been so long since I've been in the presence of a male; I somehow skipped over that moment in-between. He's like one giant, walking, shirtless symbol of my life before everything I loved went away. Before Betsy was gone. And before my first—and only—boyfriend left with her.

I have to speak. He clearly lives on my floor, and if I walk away from this without saying a word, it's only going to be more awkward when I run into him in the elevator, at the stairs, in a class.

"Sorry, adrenaline still working its way through me, had a hard time getting my words out," I say, reminding myself to fill my lungs. That's what Ross, my counselor, tells me to do when I feel the world closing in on me. Stop. Breathe deeply. Ross is a thousand miles away, but I'm supposed to call him twice a month. I'm starting to think twice a week might be necessary for a while.

"Understandable." Southern accent. Dimples. Smile. "So, you live...down there?" he asks, gesturing down the long hallway that leads to my room.

"Room three thirty-three," I say. Why in the hell did I tell him what room I'm in? That's completely unlike me, and it feels...*unsafe.*

"Ah, well...nice to meet you, three thirty-three. I'm three fifty-seven." He gives me his hand, and I shake it, feeling every cell of his fingers spark against mine. The feeling is foreign, and scary, and amazing all at once.

"You going to any of the parties tonight, Thirty-three?" I like it when he calls me by my number, and the fact that he's suddenly given me this nickname makes my stomach feel warm, regardless of how trivial and meaningless it probably is to him. It also makes me realize that I never gave him my name. I should do that. Shouldn't I do that?

"No, I'm pretty exhausted. We drove straight through from Arizona. And you can call me Rowe," I say, my heart racing just to get through this part of the conversation. I don't know why, but for me, every interaction causes the same internal struggle others feel while giving a speech. Only for me, it's the tiny speeches, the one-on-ones, that strip me completely.

"Rowe." He smiles after saying my name, and my god do I want to hear him say it again. At the same time, I keep looking toward my room in my periphery, the other part of my brain— the dominant part—trying to convince me to go back to safety and hide. "I'm Nate. And I'm really glad I decided to take a shower tonight."

This is flirting. I remember it, vaguely, as he smiles and walks backward to his room on the other end of the hall, his eyes lingering on me just long enough to send a rush down my spine. I mimic him, and don't turn away immediately either, willing myself to keep my smile in place, to leave the night on this high, to burn the look on his face into my memory—a new face, brand new to my life, and worlds apart from the demon that haunts me every night in my sleep.

I take advantage of my roommates being gone and push my bed a few more feet away from the door, almost flush to the window. Cass will notice, but I'm pretty sure I can convince Paige that the bed was always this way. And for some reason, I think Cass will back me up on it.

Getting my bed ready is always a process. I have four pillows and two blankets. Not because I'm cold, but because I've learned my mind rests easier if I have some sort of barrier pushing against my body. I know that the foam and cotton of the quilts will do very little to protect me in reality, but for some reason, they make sleep come easier. So I go to work, rolling and folding until I've built a fort of sorts along the side of my mattress—something to lay against so I can feel hidden while I sleep.

If I sleep.

Then come the medications. There's the first dose I took a few hours ago—melatonin. I take the Ambien now. I fought taking pills for a long time. I didn't want to go through life being *drugged up.* But I wasn't sleeping. Like...at all. And it turns out not sleeping messes with your brain, and you start seeing things—things that you should only see in your sleep.

Even three stories up, I can hear the chirp of the crickets outside my window. I like their sound. It's even and steady—something to focus on. So I keep the glass open, letting the warm air mix with the air conditioning as it spills in through the screen. I pull my laptop into bed with me, cross my legs, and log into Facebook. Writing to Josh has become a ritual, and my string of messages to him is more of a diary now. I never read them again once I hit send, though. I just pick up where I left off each time, starting a new thought but never going back.

So I made it. I'm a college girl. College. We were supposed to do this together, remember? And I sure as hell wasn't supposed to end up in Oklahoma. I know, I know—my fault totally on that one. I picked it. It's actually a pretty nice campus. The buildings are all made of red brick, and the trees here are enormous. Everything is so...green. I have two roommates. I like one of them. I guess I can live with the other one. It's orientation week. I'm not sure I can hide in my room the entire time. I don't want to. This is my great test, what I've worked toward for two years. But my courage diminished with every mile we trekked on our way to Oklahoma, and I fear my tank's close to empty. One of my roommates, Cass, the one I like? She fought hard to get me to go out tonight. I think I'm going to have to give in on some of the social things, so it might as well be the school-sanctioned ones.

I went to see your mom before I left. My mom took me to the house. She looks good. Your dad wasn't around, so I didn't get to say goodbye to him, but I'm sure I'll see him during my fall break. That was part of the deal with my parents. We pre-booked every single one of my flights home for the semester. I get to come home four times. The first one isn't for about a month, so that's going to be hard. Of course, I also have to get on an airplane. Alone. I know I don't have to explain any of this to you. I guess that's why I write.

Wish you would write back.

Love, Rowe

He won't write back. He never does. But that won't stop me from writing him. I move my curser to log out when the sound of a new message startles me. My mom is really the only other person I connect with on Facebook anymore, but that's not whose picture I'm looking at right now.

It's a picture of Nate, on a beach somewhere, without a shirt. I don't think that man ever wears one. I click it open, my hand shaking with nerves, and my brain starting to slow from the effects of my dose of sleeping medicine.

So the first message I sent went to a girl named Row. She was twelve, and that was awkward. And I'm pretty sure her parents have now put me on a block list since her mom was the one to intercept. Anyhow, found you. Rowe, with an e...at least, I think this is you? Wanted to see if you wanted to check out the area with me tomorrow? Take a walk, around 11? Let me know.
-357 ;-)

I don't know how to do this. I don't know how to do *any* of this. And I'm not in a good place for this. Flirting is one thing. It's harmless. I could make that a hobby. Not that I'm good at that either, but making plans? Plans lead places. And I can't go places—places feel like relationships. And I definitely don't know how to do relationships, having had an entire *one* in my life. Besides, I would just be someone's poison.

I shut my laptop and push it away from me, like a child does to a plate of vegetables. The crickets are still chirping outside, and in the distance I can hear the music pumping from someone's apartment balcony. If I listen closely, I can almost make out the sounds of girls giggling and guys celebrating. Maybe it's all in my head—the soundtrack I've imagined for college, based on all of the movies I've seen. Or maybe it's real. I'll never know because I've kept myself on the periphery, too afraid to be in the middle. I hate myself for being so afraid.

My hair is still damp, so I reach under my bed for a dry towel to cover my pillow. When I catch my reflection in the window, it gives me pause. Nothing about me is extraordinary. My hair is long and straight—the color of a pecan, just like my eyes. I used to be good at sports; I was on the tennis team before I left the school system, and I continued to play with my dad, so my body is lean. I'm nothing like Paige—things on me don't curve, and there is *nothing* voluptuous happening. Taking my personal inventory has me laughing at myself now, and laughing hard.

Nate probably won't remember me in the morning, and here I've gone and imagined some crazy scenario where we're a couple, leaps and bounds away from reality. I'm one of a handful of girls to arrive to the dorm so far; a pleasant waste of time until something better comes along. And if anything, he's a potential friend, and maybe my only hope of upping my number in my inner circle from one—if Cass even counts yet—to two.

I know that in about two more minutes I'm going to become so sleepy that I might accidentally agree to donate all of my organs to Nate, so I open the screen on my computer and type fast, using this strange mix of rationality and courage that has suddenly taken over my body.

Sounds great. I'll meet you at the elevator.
-333

Chapter 3

Nate

I know the second he finds out Ty is going to give me shit. She's totally my type. I know I have a type. People have types for a good reason, to help weed out all of the jerks on earth. And my type looks exactly like her.

I have pretty good instincts. It's why I'm a catcher—I can anticipate the bad pitches, the short swings, and what the batter is going to do. But my instincts run deep. I can read people off the field, too. And Thirty-three? She's not the kind of girl that spends an hour getting ready to go out for the night. She's blue jeans and T-shirts. Burgers and fries.

Her fingers were bare—no annoyingly long fake nail shit or sparkly colors. She was wearing an old T-shirt to bed, not some special outfit that probably costs more than everything in my closet. And, while I know this would probably mortify her that I noticed, her underwear was simple—plain-white, cotton. Not granny panties. They were tiny and delicate and *far* from granny panties. In the slight seconds they were in my hand, I imagined them on her, and believe me, that fantasy is going to haunt me for the rest of the night.

Even her name was perfect. *Rowe.* No room for bubble letters and hearts. Just four letters that cut right to the chase. Okay, so I'm probably still a little buzzed from the party I bailed on an hour ago, and her personality could totally blow it tomorrow. But tonight, I'm deciding to believe this girl is perfect, and I get idealistic and romantic after I drink, so I'm going with it.

I've dated lots of chicks, and some have come close to perfect. But somewhere along they way, there's always that one *big issue.* Sadie, my ex from high school, was really close— all the way until she slept with my best friend at our graduation party. That was her big issue, and apparently it had been her big issue for a few months. I just hope I don't uncover Rowe's tomorrow, because I'd like to enjoy this for a while.

Thank God for Facebook. I promise I'll do something good for the world later this week, because people are supposed to thank God for things far more important than some geeky billionaire computer-developer's invention. But, right this minute, I'm giving the grand ole mighty shout out to Facebook.

She doesn't seem to post much on her page. Maybe it's private? I feel lame sending her a friend request, but I guess I already sent her a message, so what's one more level of stalking? I wish like hell she had a picture posted. Probably would have spared me my first attempt that went to some pre-teen in Arkansas.

"What's that smirk on your face for? Are you watchin' porn?" Yeah. Here comes Ty's shit.

"No, asshole. I do that on your bed." I'm not even surprised when his notebook flies at my head. I duck just in time, but he gets me with the follow up of his hat.

For a guy who can't move his legs, my brother is pretty nimble. He's lived with paralysis for almost six years now, and he's half the reason I decided to come to McConnell. He's here for grad school—an MBA. And part of the deal when I committed to play here was that we'd get to room together.

Ty is the good in me. For some, it's hard to see that, because my brother can be blunt and crude, and he's a real asshole to women. But he's also exactly who he is—no apologies, no pretending. The day he woke up in the hospital and the doctors told him he wouldn't be able to walk anymore, he asked them what he *could* do. And he's been putting all of his energy into those things ever since. It's probably why he's so damned good at school.

I tried harder in baseball because of him. He was better than me, and even as a junior in high school he was being scouted. But then he tore his spinal cord. Baseball became *my* dream then. At first, I did it because I felt like I owed it to him, like a tribute or something. But he slapped me around over that more than a few times, so now I play for me. And like Ty, I don't apologize for who I am or what I want out of life. And right now, all I want to do is find out more about Rowe.

15

"Are you cyber-stalking girls? Fuck, man. That's creepy." Ty's chair has me pinned to my desk, so no use hiding this now.

"Met a girl," I smile.

"Oh God. You're going to get all sappy and shit. Man, we just got here! All right, who is she. Show me who we're stalking."

I tilt my computer, and Ty slides it over to his lap. I get nervous when he smirks at me, and it only gets worse when he starts to click on things. When I reach to grab my computer back from him, he just twists away, jamming my leg into the side of my desk and pushing me away with his massive forearm.

"She wrote you back, dude," he teases. I'm somewhere between wanting to punch my brother and dying to know what Rowe said. "Rowe, huh? That's cool. You know who she looks like, right?"

"Yeah, yeah. I know; I have a type. So sue me." I reach again, and he turns completely away, pushing off to the other side of the room and holding his arm out to block me again.

"She says she'll meet you at the elevator. Oooooo, whatcha doing in the elevator? Have you been reading my *Penthouse*?"

"Don't be a dick," I grunt, kicking his wheel enough to twist him toward me so I can get my laptop back. Ty can tell he's pushed me far enough, so he eases up…for now.

"You know you have workouts tomorrow, right?"

"Fuuuuuuck!" It's like I thought I was on vacation or something. I completely forgot about workouts.

"It's not mandatory," I say, hoping he'll corroborate my plan to play hooky.

"Right. Yeah, you could skip. It's just one workout. It's not like you're a freshman fighting for a starting spot or anything. I mean this *elevator* appointment is really important. It could determine your future with…what was her name?"

"Rowe," I say, my lips pushed tightly as I try to hold in my frustration with Ty. I'm frustrated because he's right. And I might still be a little drunk. And I might just be imagining how I felt when I ran into her in the hall.

I mutter a few swear words under my breath and take my laptop back over to my bed to write Rowe back.

16

I forgot I have something in the morning. Won't be back until after lunchtime. You free in the afternoon? Or maybe going to the mixer? Let me know.

- 57

"Asshole," I say, tossing my closed laptop down by my feet and pulling my pillow up over my eyes to block out the light...and to block out Ty.

"Just your angel of responsibility, my brother. That's what I'm here for," he chuckles; I give him the finger before I fall asleep and dream about Rowe and those damn cotton panties.

Chapter 4

Rowe

I feel like an idiot. I've been sitting in the hallway next to the elevator for twenty minutes now, and I've watched about a dozen more students move their belongings in. Almost every room is full, and parents are nagging their sons and daughters and some are crying about leaving. The whole thing is making me appreciate how fast my parents were with this process. But they had different motives—if they stayed too long, we all would have bailed on the plan. And I would never grow up.

Paige and Cass were dead to the world when I woke up. That's another element of the sleeping medication—when it's done doing it's job, my eyes are wide and ready, no matter how badly I'd like to keep them closed.

I woke up a little after seven. My hair had dried overnight, so I just put on some eyeliner—to make myself look older than twelve—and slipped on my running shoes to go exploring. Being outside makes me nervous. Ross says I have a slight agoraphobia brought on by my trauma, and the best way to overcome it is to push myself a little more every day. I have four days until classes start, and if I want to show up to any of them, I have to push myself out the front door of our dorm. So that's what I spent the first three hours of my morning doing. I paced the area around the front desk. Then I sat in the lounge. Eventually, I went outside and stood on the steps, forcing myself to count to fifty. By the time my breathing slowed down, I did a full lap around the building, and soon it was almost eleven. I've been sitting here ever since.

He isn't coming. What has me upset is that I'm surprised he isn't coming. I'm starting to think I dreamt the entire thing. The Ambien makes me do that sometimes—and the dreams feel so real. I pull out my phone to check my Facebook messages and see if that conversation is even in there, but while I'm waiting for it to load, a folded up paper airplane lodges itself under my knee.

"Hey, mind throwing that back?" I look down the hall and my eyes are met with a face that's oddly familiar. He looks just like Nate—or what I imagined Nate to be? But this guy is older, and he's in a wheelchair. His smile is disarming, and I'm starting to feel like someone is pulling a trick on me.

Getting to my feet, I bring the plane into my hands and look it over for bends in the folds before squinting my eyes to line it up in his direction. I give it a push, and it sails several feet past him, which for some strange reason makes me really happy. Yes, if airplane throwing were an Olympic sport, I would surely take home the gold.

"Hey, nice toss. Thanks," he says, wheeling back to pick it up again. I smile and nod, tugging down my shorts and the back of my shirt, which have crumpled from sitting in the corner by the elevator for so long. I'm about to slump back to my room when Nate's mystery twin stops me.

"You're Rowe, right?" It's strange how my heart speeds up just by his question. Maybe I didn't dream any of this at all?

"That's me," I say, folding my arms around myself and squeezing my stomach for strength.

"You must not have gotten Nate's message." He's coming closer to me now, and the closer he gets, the more familiar his features are. His face is almost an exact replica of the one I saw last night, but his eyes are a little different, and his cheeks are fuller. All I can do is shrug in response.

"Nate had workouts this morning. I think he sent you something on Facebook," he says, and I'm unable to stop myself from swiftly pulling out my phone to check. I'm sure I look desperate, but whatever—I'm not good at this. No sense in pretending. When I tap on my Facebook app, his message alert is the first thing I see.

"You know what? Why don't you come out with me? We can see where our classes are, and then I'm heading to the gym. Maybe Nate will be done by then," he's already heading back to his room with his keys out. I can't get my voice to work, so I just look from him to my room and back again, constantly calculating if I have enough time to run. Cass squashes that

19

plan, though, when she's suddenly next to me in her full workout clothes.

"You missed a hell of a party last night. You're coming to the mixer with me tonight, no excuses," she says, looping her arm through mine. I don't have time to answer her either, because suddenly the mystery man is back.

"Hey, I think I met you last night," he says, a smile tugging at the corner of his mouth when he looks at Cass. It's the same face Nate made when he introduced himself, and I recognize it—he's full-on flirting with Cass.

"Yeah, we hung for a bit I think. I got pretty shit-faced," she laughs, and I'm a little surprised. I don't know why really—I know it's normal for college kids to party and drink. But the thought of it all scares the hell out of me. I've never been drunk. I've barely had a drink. I mean you don't go from missing your prom and hiding in the house all the time to life of the party. And just listening to these two people, whom hours ago were strangers, bond and laugh and flirt in front of me, is making the scars on my side hurt and my head is getting dizzy.

"What was your name?" he asks, and I can tell he's faking the expression he's making. He doesn't know her name at all, but this is his way of finding it out.

"Cass," she says, and an actual giggle escapes her. Every second ticking by in this interaction, I'm learning more about my roommate.

"Cass. That's right. I'm Ty," he reaches his hand in front of me to shake hers, and I notice the toned muscles of his arm. I can tell Cass sees them too, and when we make brief eye contact, she looks almost like she's trying to signal something to me. "Rowe and I were just heading out to the gym. We were going to stop by a few of the buildings on the way. You know, scout out our classes? Wanna come? You look like you're heading that way."

Cass bunches her brow, clearly confused at how I know Ty, and why I'm making plans with him. I'd love to give her an answer, but I'm not even sure how I got here and into this situation, so I just smile and stuff my hands deep into my pockets, my thumb rubbing obsessively over the grooves on my room key to keep myself calm.

"Sure, sounds great," she says, tugging on my arm again to walk closely alongside her.

The elevator ride is quiet and uncomfortable. Several others join us on the next floor down, and we have to wait for everyone to file out when we get to the ground floor. All I can focus on is the front door of the building, the one I practiced walking in and out of all morning. It's always easier to venture outside when I'm not alone. And Cass makes me feel comfortable, so I take in my deep breath and move my feet forward until we're finally outside. I must be squeezing Cass's arm too tightly, because by the time we make it to the next building, she leans into me to ask if I'm all right.

"Sorry," I say, letting my arm hang loose from hers. "Not good with strangers."

"You don't really know him?" she laughs, keeping her voice quiet and tilting her chin forward toward Ty, who is a few feet ahead of us on the walkway.

"I just met him this morning," I say, shaking my head. Cass laughs and tugs on my sleeve so we can catch up to him.

"So, ladies. Where are you from?" he asks, his eyes really focusing on Cass when he asks that question, and for some reason, I'm relieved that she has to go first.

"Me and my sister are from Burbank," she says, and I can tell he's trying to figure out how I'm related to Cass but look nothing like her, so I stop his question before it comes.

"Oh, no. We're not related. Cass and I are roommates. I'm from Arizona," I say, turning to Cass, now wondering whom the hell she's talking about.

"Oh, yeah. Sorry, my sister's our other roommate. You met her last night, too. Paige?"

I'm so stunned by this revelation I'm unable to keep my thoughts inside my head. "What?" I literally stop walking when I speak, and Cass can't help but laugh at my response.

"I know, we couldn't be any more different, huh?" she says, shrugging and smiling back at both of us. "We're twins. Nobody ever believes it."

"And why would they! You're polite and smart and Paige...seems to have other qualities," I try to change the course of my words midstream, realizing a little too late that I'm calling her sister rude and stupid. Probably a little soon for me to assume that's okay to do, and I inwardly curse my lack of social skills. Thankfully, my rant has Cass laughing even harder now.

"I know, right? My sister's a real bitch!"

My eyes almost pop out of my head, and I look at Ty for assurance that I heard her right, but he's just staring at her and smiling even harder than he was before. I wonder if she knows he likes her? And I wonder how much they got to know each other at the party last night?

"So where are you from, Ty?" Cass asks, biting her bottom lip a little. She notices his stare, and I think she likes it.

"I'm from Louisiana originally, though I just transferred here from Florida. I'm in grad school, but my brother's a freshman. We thought it'd be cool to live together, so we both settled on the same school. They have a great business program here, and a hell of a baseball team, so it worked out."

"Nate's your brother," I nod and mutter quietly to myself. I feel like I'm trapped in an episode of *90210,* and I'm just grateful that I'm getting all of these revelations out of the way early rather than having to wait for the season to end to put the puzzle together.

"Oh yeah. I think I saw him last night, too. My sister was *all over* him," Cass says, and I'm suddenly overcome with a rush of jealousy. I'm embarrassed by it, and I'm sure they both can tell, so I turn my gaze to my feet and start to look for cracks in the sidewalk.

"Oh I remember her. She's cute," he says, and I tilt my head up just in time to see the same emotion I was just feeling wash over Cass. "Not my brother's type, though."

Ty's gaze switches to me when he speaks, and he holds his stare long enough to make me feel uncomfortable and look back down. Was he trying to tell me *I'm* not his brother's type? Was that a warning to get out before I'm disappointed? Or just confirming my assumption last night, that Nate's just looking for friends. Nothing more. I hope that's it, because the more I get to know people, the less sure I am that I'm even ready for friends.

We walk along the main path up the middle of the campus, and I'm able to spot every single one of my buildings along the way. I have mostly general-studies classes. I still haven't declared a major, and the advisor said I could wait a semester or two before I figured it out. I'm not sure that's enough time, though—I have no idea what I want to do with my life. Before everything changed, I used to think I wanted to be a designer. No real reason why, and I've never been great at computer programs, so that dream sort of dissipated the less attention I paid to it. Unfortunately, nothing stepped up to take its place.

"Nate's in there. I know the coaches, so I can go in with you if you want. He'd like to know you're here," Ty says, and I can't help but notice the look Cass is making behind him. She wants to know more, and I know I'm going to have to tell her about my run-in with Nate.

"Oh, okay. I guess so, if you think it's okay that I go in? I can wait out here, too. I don't want to interrupt something." I start fidgeting and I can feel my skin tingling with discomfort. Ty smiles and winks while he passes me, urging me to follow.

"You're fine. Come on," he says, so I look to Cass, who's still waggling her eyebrows my way.

Deep breaths. Take deep breaths.

We head through a long hallway to a separate area of the gym, and I can tell this is where the school's athletes train. It's football season right now, so almost everyone in the room is four times my size.

"Oh my god, Rowe. Paige is going to be so pissed when she finds out we were in here without her. This is like her own personal supermarket full of jocks." We both stay back near the door, but let our eyes wander the expanse of the room. There's a slight tinge of sweat-smell in the air, but it's not gross at all, and I can't help the way my body is reacting to it. I blush when one of the large, shirtless men walks by me and says, "Excuse me," brushing his arm against the front of my body slightly while he passes. Suddenly, I'm standing straighter, and sucking in my stomach, pushing out what exists of my chest.

"There he is. Hang on, I'll let him know you're here," Ty says, moving toward the back of the room. I see Nate's profile in the far distance, but my eyes zero in on his features immediately. He was not a dream. Everything I thought I saw and remembered is exactly as it should be, and when his gaze flicks up to mine, I'm catapulted back to the hallway and the way he looked in the dark, holding my underwear.

"You are like seven shades of red, girl," Cass says, leaning into me.

"That bad, huh?" I used to think I would be the kind of person that would lie when people called me on my emotions. But there's something about Cass that makes me comfortable. It's either that, or I'm just too tired of hiding everything else to give a damn about getting gushy over a boy right now.

"Suck it up, chickadee. He's on his way over here."

I draw the air in slowly through my nose the entire time he's walking my way, so by the time he's standing in front of me, I don't have to panic for a breath.

"Hey, so I'm totally sorry I blew our plans. I forgot about workouts this morning," he says, and his words come out like butterscotch candies. I've never heard someone talk like him, and I'd give anything for him to read me a story at night. I bet I wouldn't even need to take Ambien to relax.

"That's okay, I understand." My heart is thumping wildly and erratically, and I'm worried it's making my voice quiver.

"She's lying, bro," Ty says suddenly, knocking the wind from me again. "I found her waiting by the elevator. Some asshole stood her up."

I. Want. To. Die. My eyes dart from Ty to Nate to Cass, who only shrugs since I haven't been able to bring her fully up to speed on my late night run-in yet.

"No, really. It's my fault. I didn't check my messages this morning," I explain, giving Ty a look that I hope sends a warning. I'll have to practice those faces, because I'm not really sure how to make them. This one seems not to be very intimidating, because he just laughs softly and backs away.

"Damn, that guy *is* an asshole. And so is his brother," Nate says, scratching under his chin and flicking his hand at Ty. He turns to me—dimples, smile. "I was going to stop by your room this morning, but I didn't want to wake you up. Hey, I'll make it up to you. You hungry? Want lunch?"

My stomach is growling, and I'm starving. But the thought of sitting in a crowded cafeteria makes my body break out in an instant sweat.

"Rowe, I've gotta go. I have an appointment with a personal trainer in ten minutes," Cass says, pulling her watch from her wrist and tucking it in the small workout bag she's carrying. "I'll see ya back at the dorm."

I smile and wave, scrunching my hand closed, and stuffing it back in my pocket.

"Yeah, so...it looks like I'm her trainer, since I have a noon appointment. I fucking love today," Ty says, looking up and smiling, which makes both Nate and me laugh. "I'll see you later, dude. Oh...and *this one*? Yeah, she's totally your type."

I. Want. To. Die.

Chapter 5

Nate

If he weren't my brother, I would kill him. I might kill him anyway. I can tell she's embarrassed. Her body is now bright pink, and I can practically feel the heat radiating off of her.

I don't like the way he showed it. But I do like that my brother approves. He never liked Sadie; said he didn't trust her. But I didn't listen. Seems my brother's instincts are a shitload sharper than mine. And if he thinks Rowe has something, then I'm definitely making this girl go to lunch with me. I have to figure her out before the rest of the school shows up and I have to compete for her attention.

"So, what do you say?" I ask. She seems nervous, and I feel like she might back out. Maybe if I can find a way to stick with the original plan. "If you're not hungry, we could just walk around town?"

She's tugging on her bottom lip with her teeth and hugging herself with her arms, like she's not sure what to do with herself, and I catch her eyes searching for her friend who's walking away. Damn. She's trying to get out of this.

"Or whatever. If you're tired, I get it. My fault for missing our date." For some reason, that last word catches her attention, and her eyes meet mine quickly, flaring open a little wider. Shit, she didn't like the word *date.*

"No, I...I could eat, actually. It's just," she starts, and her eyes fall to her feet, looking over her arms that are still folded tightly around her and down to her shuffling shoes. "I'm kind of a picky eater. So, maybe we could go somewhere in town? Is that...okay?"

I try to play it cool, but inside I'm glad she's up for my back-up plan. It's going to take us a good twenty minutes to walk into town, and I already know I'm going to make her go to Sally's. It's good food, but the service is slow as heck. That gives me at least a couple of hours with her.

"That's perfect. There's actually this place I've been dying to try. Mind?"

She just nods and smiles, still fidgeting with her feet locked to their place. I notice she's not wearing socks with her running shoes, and I don't know why, but I can't seem to take my eyes off the line along her calf muscle and the way it stretches deep into her ankle. It's weird how a girl can look so soft, but so strong at the same time.

"You play sports?" I ask, my eyes still locked on her leg.

"A little. I used to, I mean. I was good at tennis," she says, finally relaxing her upper body. "Ty says you play baseball?"

I love that she has no idea who I am. Not that I'm *that* big a deal, but I did turn down a lot of Division 1 schools to come here. The chick at the party last night sure knew who I was. Or, at least, she knew that I was an athlete at the school. She was sloppy drunk and kept telling me how she just wants to hook up with a jock this week.

Some guys love that shit. *Easy.* Ty kind of likes it, at least in the moment. But usually he's pissed at himself that next day when he has to face a girl he really has no interest in. I'd rather wait around until I find someone worth it, someone I'd like to see in the morning, not just the night.

"Yeah, I'm the catcher." I sort of wait to see how she reacts, and when she doesn't, I keep going, suddenly feeling like I have to work a little to impress her. "So, I pretty much play every game. I'm stepping in for a senior this year, and it's kind of awkward, because I think they'll probably play me more than him."

"Are you good?" Her bluntness is adorable, if not intimidating.

"Huh. Well, I was good enough for them to ask me to come here. I guess I hope I'm good enough for them to want me to stay." All I can do is smile at her, the way she's crinkling her nose while she thinks about what she needs to know about me next. Anything...I want this girl to ask me *anything.*

We're walking to the front lobby now, so I nod to my coach that I'm heading out, and he just waves me off. I'm about to place my hand on her back to lead her outside—both because I want her to know what direction to go and because I want to feel her shoulder blades under my fingers. But I notice she pauses when we get to the door; I can see her breathing pick up, so I pull my hand away before it grazes her. She's nervous.

"Did anyone else ask you?"

"Huh?" Her eyes are staring at the metal grate that divides the outside from the inside, so I can't even get a clue from her expression as to what she means.

"Baseball. Did anyone else ask you to play?"

"Oh." For a second I thought she was asking me about other girls, and other girls is the *last* thing I want to talk about in front of Rowe. I spent my summer forgetting all about Sadie with my brother's help, and let's just say that's how I know I'm not meant for one-night stands and good-enoughs. For the last three months, I've felt like a major asshole, which is exactly why I left the party last night. Fate rewarded me by running me into Rowe.

"Yeah, I had a few other offers."

"How many?"

She still hasn't brought her eyes back to me, but we're walking again, so at least she's not trying to run away anymore. "I don't know. Ten or twelve."

I know exactly how many schools asked me to play—*sixteen*. And there was also an offer to get into the Indians organization. But I didn't want to trade a free ride through business school with my brother for a year or two in some shit-splat town making a teacher's salary.

"So, you must be pretty good, huh?"

"I'm all right."

It takes us about fifteen minutes to get into town, and we make small talk the entire way. I don't have any classes with her—probably because she's still figuring out what she wants to do. I can tell she's stressed about the topic, so I don't grill her on it for long. She talks about her parents a lot, which for some reason makes me like her even more. Ty and I have a great relationship with our mom and dad, and it's a turnoff when a girl wants to bag on her mom over stupid petty things.

When we walk into Sally's, I wince. The guy behind the bar recognizes me, and he's going to blow my cover. "Nate! Hey man, how's it hangin'!"

28

"Hey, Cal. Things are good. Good to see ya." I raise my shoulders and hold up my hands when Rowe snaps her gaze to me. Her brow is lowered, and I can tell she's suspicious.

"So, whatcha having, the usual?"

Goddamn. Of all things that man could have said. My brother and I are probably keeping him in business, and I'm pretty sure I ate every meal here for the two weeks I came for summer ball. I thought it was safe, because Cal doesn't work days. Though, it seems I have that wrong now.

"I'm not alone, Cal, so maybe give us a few minutes to look over the menu," I say, sliding into the booth near the jukebox. I'm prepared for Rowe to look like she wants to kill me; I hold my breath when I turn to look at her. When I see the smirk on her face, I'm ecstatic.

"You've been here before," she says, her lips curling tightly like she's trying to hold in laughter.

"Yeah. I'm not even going to try to fix this one. This is sort of my place. Been coming here since summer ball, and Cal never works during the day, so kinda thought I could get away with it."

"Why not just tell me you wanted to come to your favorite place?" she asks, and I close my eyes I'm so embarrassed.

"Because the cooks are extremely slow, and I wanted to act like I was surprised when it takes an hour for us to get our order." I crack open a lid and she's still smirking, so I open all the way, and grab the salt shaker, spilling a little of it on the table to swirl around and give my hands something to do. "Yeah, so...this was all one big ruse to spend a shitload of time with you. Hope you're not too hungry."

Rowe's smile never wavers, but for a few seconds I see worry flash across her eyes. There's a story to her, but I know it's going to take time for her to warm up enough to be willing to tell it. I think I'm alright with giving this some time, though.

"So, how do you feel about burgers?"

She finally breaks her eyes away from me and pulls the torn paper menu from the rack on the wall.

"Burgers are good," she says. "I don't eat out much. I usually just eat something at home. I kind of like things that are plain. What do you suggest?"

"Can't go wrong with the classic cheeseburger," I say, waiting for her to tell me she doesn't eat bread or cheese, or to ask if they have a veggie burger instead. She never does though, and instead, refolds the menu and pushes it back against the wall.

"Sounds good. I'll have one of those," she says, pushing her way out of the booth. "Mind ordering for me? I need to find the ladies' room."

"You got it," I wink and nod to the back, letting her know where the restrooms are. She doesn't look back when she walks away, so I indulge and lean completely out of the booth, watching every inch of her long, golden legs walk down the aisle.

"Looks like you've gone and made yourself a new friend, eh?" Cal teases.

"Yes, sir. I believe I have. And she'll have a cheeseburger."

Rowe

Once I lock the bathroom door, I break down. I'm not sure where the tears are coming from, other than the sheer stress of this entire situation. Nate seems nice. He seems *more than* nice. And I think I trust him. I must, otherwise I wouldn't have been able to leave the safety of the gym and walk along the open road with him.

Somewhere, deep inside, I know this is serious flirting. And maybe a little part of me hopes I'm more than just a distraction for Nate. I'm being so boring, though. One-word answers, surface questions—it's like I don't even know how to be real. Our conversation sounds like the dinner table with my parents.

I think it's because my back is to the door. I can't think clearly, or even think at all, because I keep waiting to see who walks in next. Maybe we can move somewhere else. Would it be weird to ask him to move somewhere else?

30

Someone's knocking, so I run my hands in the hot water and then splash some of it against my neck, patting myself dry with a paper towel. I exit and trade places with an older woman, and our bodies touch when she passes. The exchange practically knocks the wind out of me because I'm so involved in my stupid panic attack—so I stay hidden in the darkness of the hallway, just staring at the back of Nate's head.

His arm is stretched along the top of the booth and his body is tilted slightly to one side while he talks to the man he called *Cal* when we walked in. Nate's arms are long. Like, really long—I'd like to measure them. He has dents and lines that define muscles just like the guys I see on TV, and his T-shirt hugs tightly around his chest and biceps. His clothes don't drape on his body like Josh's always did—probably because he isn't some skinny sixteen-year-old who hasn't met the weight room yet.

Cal notices me standing in the darkness, so I remind myself to breathe again and force myself forward. *I'm not good at this. I'm not good at this. I'm not good at this.* The closer I get, the more comfortable and convinced I become with the fact that Nate and I are just friends, so once I reach the edge of our table, I decide to test out honesty.

"Do you mind if…if we moved to a booth in the corner?" I can tell he's confused, but he doesn't seem to be against my request because he's sliding both of our water glasses forward and holding them in his enormous hands while he leaves the booth. I lead him over to the corner, the one seat that I think gives me a view of the entire restaurant, and I settle in, already breathing easier.

Nate never asks why I need to move, and I never tell him. Instead, he picks up the conversation, and starts to tell me about his family and growing up in Louisiana, and I listen—at first, splitting my attention between my heart rate and breathing as well as Nate's words, until eventually all of my focus is on him.

"You and your brother are close," I say, not really needing to ask it. He smiles and nods at my question.

31

"Ty's my best friend. Always has been. I had friends in high school when he was gone and at college. But Ty, he's the only guy I ever share my secrets with."

For some reason, the second he says it, all I want to do is become the second person he shares secrets with. Maybe it's because I don't have anyone to share mine with, and the thought of getting some of *this* out is so inviting.

"How about you. You have any brothers or sisters?" he asks.

"Just me and my parents. I spend most of my time with my mom, because her office hours are at home. We live near the campus she works at—she teaches economics at State. She homeschooled me the last two years, so I guess that would make her my best friend." And that would make me...pathetic.

"It's nice that you're close to your mom," he says, and I smile and look down into my lap. Am I close to my mom? I guess I am. I don't really hide much from her, but I don't really have much to hide either. She knows my issues. She's more like my doctor—my live-in, enabling-and-disabling doctor. But Nate's not ready to hear all of that yet. I wouldn't even know how to begin to articulate it without telling him everything.

"So, tell me something about yourself," I say, wanting to get the focus away from me for a while. "Who is Nate—" I panic for a moment when I realize I don't remember his last name. Instead of asking, I hold up a finger and pull my phone from my pocket to look up his Facebook message. "Preeter! Who is Nate *Preeter*?"

The way he laughs sets me at ease, and at that moment I realize I can no longer hear my heartbeat rattling in my own head.

"Ouch! I made like...no impression on you at all, did I?" he chuckles, and I flush a little, embarrassed that I forgot his last name.

"That's not true. You made an impression. We just met, though, so that's not fair. I can't be expected to remember everything. I know your room number! That one stuck! Besides, I bet you don't remember my full name."

As soon as I issue that challenge, he leans forward on his elbows, and I get a good look into his eyes. They were mesmerizing in the dark, but here—in the full light of day—they are breathtaking. There's a grayish hue to them, and when his brown and golden hair drapes over his forehead while he talks, I can't help but awe at the contrast of the light and dark. I could get lost in his features, but suddenly his voice captures my attention.

"You're Rowe Stanton, a freshman from Arizona, and you're here with honors. You haven't picked a major yet, though I can tell from the small things you said during our walk over here that you really like art. You should think about that. You used to play tennis, and I bet you could still kick my ass, and you don't wear socks with your sneakers. I like that. It's hot."

He sits back when he's done, and takes a long sip of water, the smirk on his lips peeking out from the sides of the glass. I feel naked in front of him. Granted, he didn't really pull out anything very personal—except for the art comment, that one was pretty intuitive—but the fact that he's locked away every fact I've given him makes me feel...*something.* And my heartbeat is suddenly pounding again in my eardrums, but for an entirely different reason.

"So, art, huh?" I say, trying to build a little distance from the fact that he just called me hot.

"Yeah. Art...you seem to be interested in it. You should think about that. And yes, Rowe."

"Yes, what?" I gulp.

"I think you're hot. *You* made an impression."

Nate

Something tells me that if I put a pencil in her hand, Rowe would draw me a picture, and it would probably be the prettiest damn sketch I've ever seen. I wish there was a fast-forward button somewhere I could hit to get to her secrets. She keeps everything so guarded, and I feel like we're playing a game of chess, the way she detours our conversation away from herself.

Our food is coming out—just my luck, the one time that kitchen is fast. Rowe doesn't waste any time, and normally I'd love the fact that she doesn't pick at her food. She wraps both hands around the bun of her burger and takes a bite that makes a serious dent. At this rate, she'll be done and ready to go in about ten minutes.

"Hey, you know that gallery building we walked by at the end of campus?"

She shrugs, covering her mouth with her napkin while she chews, because her bite's too big. She tries to get the word "yeah" out, but her speech is muffled by the fullness in her cheeks. She might be awesome.

"Right," I laugh lightly, smiling at her and taking a giant bite of my burger so I can talk with a full mouth too. "They hab a arrrr show neck weeeeek. Wah a go?"

She completely stops chewing, shirks her shoulders up, and bunches her brow at me, staring. "Wha?"

I finish chewing and laugh more—when I do, she blushes a little, finally getting that I'm teasing her. She's turning so red I start to feel bad, but then she surprises me, grabbing a handful of fries and taking a giant drink of her soda, chewing with her mouth open and looking me squarely in the eyes.

"Yah, arrr showwwww. I'll gooooo," she can't quite finish her sentence without giggling uncontrollably and covering her mouth again with her napkin to keep her food from flying out. But I heard enough—just the right words. She'll go. That means I've got her attention for at least another week.

34

Chapter 6

Rowe

I managed to finish lunch without having another freak out. And the more we walked and talked, the more comfortable I became with Nate. He felt familiar, like we had known each other since we were kids or something and were just catching up.

Maybe that's because I kept the spotlight on him. I asked about his baseball playing, and I found out he started with tee-ball at three. His brother used to play, too. In a few of the stories he told, he mentioned his brother running and playing with him, and I know something must have happened to put him in the wheelchair, but I didn't feel comfortable enough to ask about that.

He talked about his childhood home, and he asked about mine. Louisiana and Phoenix don't sound so different, only his summers sound more humid. My past stayed on my childhood, talking about my embarrassing first-day meltdown in kindergarten where I protested the coloring exercise and made the teacher call my dad to take me home...and my first slow dance with a boy, where he blew a bubble with his gum and it got stuck in my hair, leading to my first short haircut.

He seemed to soak up everything I said, and I found myself wanting to keep talking, telling him more. And a few times, I thought of stories I *could* share. But they were stories about Betsy and Josh. Nate doesn't need to hear those, and I'm not ready to give them away.

His brother was waiting for him at the elevator, so I came upstairs alone. All it took was a few seconds in my own head for me to second guess everything—promising myself I'd distance from him after today, making sure he didn't have the wrong idea or think I could give him more than I can. I need to remember that Nate isn't any different from Cass—a new friend. No matter how he makes my insides feel.

Cass and I have been swapping music for the last two hours while Paige gets ready in the bathroom. The freshman mixer is tonight, and I saw them setting up for it in the gym when I left with Nate earlier. Cass is making me go, and I think if I refused she would throw me over her shoulder and carry me.

I really like her. I think we have a lot in common, at least, the few things about me that are left. Our music libraries are almost identical, and she wants to go to Austin for South-by-Southwest this year. I've always wanted to go to a music festival, too, but that's just not in my cards. I've spent the last forty-eight hours talking myself out of dropping out of college. I don't think a road trip will be possible until I can master a semester or two.

"So, how was your...*lunch*," Cass asks, making air quotes around the word lunch, which I don't really understand.

"It was fine. He seems nice," I say, noticing Paige is paying attention to us now.

"Riiiiight. Nice," Cass teases, and I just shake my head.

"We're friends. That's all."

"Hmmmmm, yeah. Same with Ty and me. Of course, I still kissed him," she says, standing to her feet the second she speaks and covering her mouth while it hangs open in a big *O*, her eyes wide.

"You slut," Paige butts in, "I knew you liked that guy. But he's in a wheelchair?"

Cass shrugs a *so what*, but I kind of want to kick Paige. I'm not sure I'll ever be able to understand how she and Cass are sisters.

"Yeah, well, you can have that guy. Just keep your hands off his brother," Paige says. My body fires up defensively, but I keep my eyes down, thumbing through my music on my iPod. I can feel Cass looking at me, and I'm forcing myself to control my breathing.

"Maybe Rowe can help you out there," Cass says. "She and Nate are *friends*."

My stomach is thumping with my own pulse, and I feel heat roll over my spine. I decide to keep my eyes down, because I know looking up will give something away. This is jealousy. I remember this emotion, too.

"Oh. My. God! You're friends with Nate Preeter? He is so fucking hot! How can you even stand it?" Paige continues to gush about Nate, his perfect abs, his eyes, his ass—she's the female version of a Hooter's patron. The more she talks about him, the more I wish I never met him at all, because then I wouldn't have to be in this situation, feeling...*gah!* I don't know what this is I'm feeling, and that's part of the problem.

"I don't know him that well," I say, trying to get her to drop it.

"That's okay. Just introduce us. He'll remember me from the party when you do, and I can take it from there."

I don't answer her, but it doesn't matter. She goes back to the closet, stripping out of the short dress she had on and opting for an even shorter one. Cass is looking at me again, but I can't tell if she's smiling or showing sympathy, because I won't bring my eyes back up to deal with anything else that happens in this room tonight. Putting my headphones on, I turn up the volume on my iPod and close my eyes, lying back, and pretending to rest while my mind conjures up pictures of my fist in Paige's face. And I hate that I feel this way.

Katy Perry is blasting from the speakers in the gym, and Paige is singing along loudly. *Check*—one more assumption confirmed. Nothing against Katy—she's on my iPod, too. She's just followed up by the Kings of Leon and The National. Maybe I'm a music snob, and it's probably from two years of social isolation, but I just feel like a person who sings along with Katy Perry...in public, for attention...doesn't have much else to offer.

Of course, the fact that I can see Paige's nipples through the fabric of her dress begs to differ. Yes, she has two more things to offer, and she's serving them up tonight. I just hope Nate's not interested. Or maybe I don't care. Maybe I hope he is interested so that way I can sum him up nicely too, and go back to putting my life back together.

"Thirty-three." Nope, I definitely hope he's not interested in Paige. His voice is deep and perfect; I couldn't make his southern accent up if I tried.

"Heinz," I say, instantly wishing I owned a dress like Paige's. Not that I could ever fill it out like she does. Once again, I'm in denim shorts and a tank top. I pull the bottom of my shirt down to my pockets, making sure it covers my scars underneath.

"Heinz?"

"You know, Heinz Fifty-Seven?" My joke doesn't feel as clever now, and I can see Paige rolling her eyes next to me, just waiting to steal the spotlight. Nate smirks and chuckles quietly; I feel pretty confident it was a pity laugh.

"So, this is my roommate Cass, you met her yesterday?" Nate smiles and nods toward her, quickly moving his eyes back to me. I can feel Paige kicking at my feet just waiting for her turn. "Oh, and this is my other roommate, Paige. They're sisters."

"By blood, but really, we're nothing alike," Paige says, stepping in front of both Cass and me to make sure she's the first thing Nate sees. And I know he sees her breasts, because I watch both his and Ty's bodies tense as their eyes zero in exactly where Paige wants them to go. She's like a bloody hypnotist! She may be a genius.

"They're tits, boys. Get over them," Cass says, walking over to the check-in table and leaving me both mortified and in awe all at once.

When I turn back around, Nate's eyes are back on me. He's rubbing his chin, laughing because Cass caught him.

"Sorry, nothing to see here," I say, grabbing my chest and squeezing. It's like an out-of-body experience, and I can't believe I said something so bold and brave, but the way he smiles makes me feel proud.

The program director starts calling everyone into the main gym for activities, so we all follow Paige through the doors. The crowd is a little overwhelming, and my feet feel stuck to the carpet. Paige is far ahead of me, and Cass and Ty are close behind her. I can feel my chest crackling, fighting to breathe, when suddenly Nate's hand rests on my back. His touch makes my eyes blink rapidly, and it feels like a thousand volts into my heart. And then...calm.

"Come on, we'll survive this together," he says, his breath hot against my neck and ear. Despite the dozens of strangers packed in the small space around me, I'm still standing...and breathing. And I think that's because of Nate.

For the next hour, we break into groups and meet new people based on the various things the moderator calls out. The first grouping is based on the middle initials. Mine is Anne, so I go to the A group, and I go there slowly. *Breathe. Breathe deeply.* Nate is with me again, and instantly I relax.

"Andrew," he says, shrugging.

"Anne."

While in our group, the moderator reorganizes us by birthdays, first asking for months—Nate is still next to me for February—and then by dates.

"What's yours?" he asks, his fingers out like he's calculating.

"I'm the fifteenth," I say, hearing someone next to me say they're the fifteenth, too.

"Sixteenth," Nate says, and he puts his hand flat along my spine again, keeping me close.

"Now I'd like everyone to turn to your right, and put your hands on the shoulders of the person in front of you," the moderator calls.

Nate is in front of me, and there's a small, quiet girl with curly hair behind me. I still feel my muscles tighten when she puts her hands on me, but I'm able to endure it. I think it would be worse if it were one of the other guy's in the group, but I'm comfortable here between this girl and Nate.

The moment my fingers connect with his shoulders, I feel it again—it's that heart-speeding-up kind of feeling. I know I should forget about it, bury it, and stuff it away deep inside—because I only have enough energy to focus on being a human. I don't have the capacity to focus on being a *girl.* But I can't help this reaction. His muscles are hard, and I feel every curve of his shoulders and the grooves along his back.

"That's it, Thirty-three. Dig in right there," he jokes, while I massage and work his muscles. The girl behind me can barely be felt, but I'm letting my fingers and thumbs rub all along Nate's broad shoulders and back.

"Switch!" the moderator calls, and I turn quickly, knowing that Nate's hands are seconds away from my bare skin. I'm both thrilled and worried that I wore a shirt with spaghetti straps. I try to put my focus on the shoulders of the small girl in front of me, doing my best to stare at the words on the back of her shirt, but I don't give her near the attention I gave Nate. I'm more patting her shoulders in circles.

Nate's fingers sweep my hair over my shoulder first, and I hold my breath the entire time. I can hear him breathing behind me, like I've tuned out every other sound in the gym, and I flush when I realize my arms are covered in goosebumps. I know he sees it, and for a moment, I think I feel him blow gently on my neck. His fingers finally find my shoulders, and my lips part and let out a sigh. Thank god he can't see my face right now.

His touch is slow and deliberate, his thumbs circling gently along my back and his fingertips feeling every inch of bare skin on my shoulders. My eyes are locked on the moderator, and internally, I'm begging her to forget about the next announcement; when I see her pull the mic to her lips, I almost cry.

"Okay, now freeze right where you are. Slowly, I want you all to sit on the lap of the person behind you."

I'm not ready for this. I'm not ready for this. I can't be a girl. Maybe I can dazzle Nate again with Paige's blatant nipples. I'm looking for her, actually wanting her distraction, but she's a dozen circles away. Cass seems to have bailed out completely—instead, sitting along the wall with Ty, and they're both watching Nate and me, giving each other commentary. She catches me looking at her and lifts her hand from her knee for a small wave.

"I got you," Nate says over my shoulder, sending the goosebumps I just got rid of right back along my arms. Without warning, I'm suddenly sitting back, his hands firmly on my hips, guiding me onto his legs. Everyone is giggling—everyone...but me. My body is starting to shake, and I know he can feel it.

"You won't fall, I've got you," he says over my shoulder.

I'm not worried about falling, I'm worried about not being able to get out once I'm tangled with other bodies. And maybe

I'm worried about how sitting on Nate's lap is going to make me feel.

His legs are just as strong as his shoulders, if not stronger. They're solid, and long, and warm; I can feel my back pressing against his chest, which is also solid and strong—unlike anything I've ever felt. I don't even notice the girl in front of me sitting on my lap; I keep my hands along her shoulders for support. Sparing a look downward, I see Nate's hands still along my waist—and for just a few seconds, my mind fools me, and I see Josh's hands instead.

Squeezing my eyes shut tightly, I wish my vision away. *Josh is not here.* When I open again, I see the differences. The last time a boy touched me here—anywhere—his hands were soft and young, the hands of someone who's barely lived. It's only been two years, but it seems eighteen is so very far from sixteen. Or maybe it's just the way Nate is built. His hands are rough and weathered, and large enough to wrap completely around my midsection if he wanted them to.

I must have been holding my breath the entire time, because it seems minutes have passed without my knowledge, and I'm on my back with Nate's perfect, dusty blue-gray eyes staring back and forth from one eye to the other. His lips are moving, but I don't hear any sound. *I don't hear any sound!*

It doesn't take long for my heart to react, and suddenly I'm sitting and fighting and punching to break free. Exits, where are the exits? Why are Josh's hands on me again? Why is he stopping me?

"Rowe! Rowe! Breathe!"

Breathe. That's right; just breathe.

I blink. It's like one of those sand drawings where slowly everything falls into place, and I can see the entire picture. Most of the other students are leaving the gym, and the music comes back into focus. I see Cass standing over Nate's shoulder. And Nate—Nate is holding me at my shoulders and looking with concern into my eyes.

"Wha...what happened?" I ask, wondering why the room is no longer filled with freshmen sitting in circles.

"You fainted," Nate says, moving his hands from my shoulders to my face. The way he's squeezing my cheeks makes me feel as if I'm making a fish face, and I scoot away from him. "You hit your head. I want to make sure you're okay."

"I'm fine. Just...just a little confused is all. How did I get on the floor?"

His hands are back on my face, and he's looking at me closely. I'm not sure he has any qualifications to be giving me a concussion test, but I let him look this time, mostly because I like the way my head feels in his hands.

"You were on my lap, and then all of a sudden, your entire body went limp. The girl that was balancing on you fell, too. She hit her head hard!" He cringes, and I feel terrible; all I want to do now is find that quiet, curly-haired girl I took out with me.

"Is she okay?"

"I think so. Her friend was with her and took her to the health center. She was walking though, so I'm sure she's fine," Nate says, lifting me up to a stand by pulling under my arms. His hand quickly finds its way to my back again, and despite the cold sweat covering my body, I feel a rush of heat.

During our walk back to the dorm, Ty invites everyone to hang out in his and Nate's room; I notice Paige perk up at that thought. She's standing on the other side of Nate, asking him question after question—about baseball and what position he plays, and what his number is, and what time his games are so she can watch. He's giving her clipped answers, which strangely pleases me.

"I know sometimes practices are open. I'd love to come watch you play," Paige says, grabbing ahold of his other arm and looking at him with the most annoying doe eyes I've ever seen. Something inside me snaps; I shirk away from his side and wrap my arms around my midsection, squeezing.

"Yeah, maybe you can come watch and analyze his swing, tell him he dips his shoulder too much, and that's why he doesn't get the pop he should off the bat," I mumble to myself, rolling my eyes while I look out at the buildings leading up to our dorm. I barely finish my sentence when Nate's hand finds my shoulder again, and he spins me to look at him.

"Say that again," he says slowing us down enough, Paige has to continue with Ty, Cass, and a few of the other students who live on our floor.

"Nothing." I'm squeezing myself tighter now, wishing I didn't just throw a baby fit because I was jealous.

"That was not *nothing*, and you know it. How do you know I dip my shoulder? And how do you know what *dipping a shoulder* means?" he asks, his eyes squinted, a hint of a smile tugging at the corner of his mouth. He looks at me while we continue now, well behind our friends.

If I could have one super power, I would want the ability to enact re-dos in life. Because right now, all I want to do is relive the last two minutes and keep my damn mouth shut. But since that's not going to happen...

"I Googled you." I feel like an idiot.

"You...*Googled* me?"

"Yeah, I Googled you. After our lunch, I wanted to see how good you were, because I could tell you were being modest. *And you were being modest, by the way. The Indians wanted you!*" This is called diarrhea of the mouth.

"You...*Googled* me," he says again, his accent making that word sound so much better than it does when it leaves my lips.

"Yeah, well...your on-base percentage is impressive. So I found a video and watched it. Noticed your swing. That's it." I actually feel angry now, and I don't know why.

"You watched my swing. And...*on-base percentage?*" He seems shocked that I know what I'm talking about, and for some reason, it pisses me off.

"You're being kinda sexist, don't you think?" I say, picking up my step to catch up with the others.

"I'm sorry...you're cyber-stalking me, and I'm the one being creepy?" he asks, half laughing.

"First of all, I didn't call you creepy, I called you sexist. And I wasn't stalking you. I just like to do a little background checking on people before I trust them. And you stalked me first, mister *Rowe with an E* on Facebook!" I actually huff that last part out and am somehow able to hear how crazy my rant sounds. I look at him from the corner of my eye and catch his snicker. Soon we're both laughing.

"Fair enough," he says. "Okay, just tell me this. How do you know so much about baseball?"

"My dad coaches for a high school. I'm a bit of a sponge for knowledge. And when you're homeschooled, you end up watching a lot of day games on television," I say, my mind trying to block out all of Josh's games I used to watch.

Nate's stare is intense, and he doesn't say anything for a while, which only makes my discomfort grow. By the time we reach the dorm, my head is pounding—partly from my fainting spell, and partly from the stress now rolling over and over inside me. When the elevator reaches our floor, everyone turns toward Nate and Ty's room, but I stop.

"Aren't you coming?" Nate asks. I catch Paige's eyes looking at me over his shoulder, begging me not to. A defining moment—and I know that if I went, this flirting thing I've been doing with Nate would only continue. And where could that possibly go?

"I can't. I'm still not feeling so well. I'm going to go to bed. But you guys have fun. I'll catch up with you later," I say, the strange tinge of regret eating away at my insides.

Nate doesn't respond, but his smile fades, and he sucks in his bottom lip while he studies me with his eyes. I raise my hand and hold it up with a still wave before turning down my hall to head to my room. It takes me a minute or two to finesse my key from my pocket, and when I finally have it in the lock, I feel my heart actually sting. I just gave up on something because I'm *afraid*. And it hurts.

Chapter 7

Nate

Everyone crashed in our room last night. One of the hazards of being the room that sneaks in alcohol—everyone sort of stays for the party.

Cass and Ty seem comfortable, cuddled up in the corner of his bed. She's different for him. Normally, he'd be hot after her sister, who is completely wrapped up in the blanket on my bed, her dress hiked up enough that I'm literally staring at the underwear hugging her ass.

We all did shots last night, but I stopped after one or two. No one noticed; I think that Paige chick thought I was just as lit up as she was. I let her crawl into my bed, and I even entertained the idea of making out with her. But she had this giggling fit over dumb shit she was saying, and it was so damned annoying, it helped me keep my head on straight.

If I ever want to curl up in my bed with Rowe, I can't entertain myself with her roommate. So I let Paige lay on my chest until her giggling stopped and she passed out. Then I crawled over her and slipped out of the door to the study lounge and slept on that miserable-ass sofa for a few hours.

I need my shoes. That's the only reason I'm back in this room right now. And I think I can get to them. I just hope Paige doesn't wake up while I'm in here. I can barely stand her on two shots of tequila. I think sober me would want to run from this room screaming.

"Pssssst." Ty's head is lifted from his pillow, and he's motioning for me to come closer.

"Hey dude. I have workouts. Just gonna grab my shoes and take off. I'll be back around noon. Wanna grab lunch at Sally's?" I try to keep my voice in a low whisper so I don't wake up Cass.

"Yeah, I'm fucking hungry, yo," he says, rubbing his stomach.

"You were pretty much on the liquid diet last night," I say, patting him once on the shoulder while I sit on the edge of his bed and slip my foot in my shoe. "All right, I'll see you later. Maybe...let's meet there? I don't want to have to run into..."

I nod my head to my bed where Paige is still deep asleep. Ty lifts an eyebrow at me and I shake my head *no*.

"She passed out. I slept in the lounge," I say, finally standing.

"Hey," he whispers just as I'm about to go. I look at him, and he lifts his head a little more, looking over at Paige again and then back at me. "Why'd you lie about your middle name and your birthday?"

I was wondering when he'd give me crap over that. I lean over to make sure Cass is asleep this time. When I look back at him, I just wink, and he chuckles softly, slapping his hand to his forehead.

"You're a hopeless romantic," he says. "I'll make sure Cass knows you slept in the lounge. Don't want any of *that* getting misunderstood."

"Thanks, man," I say, giving him knuckles.

I wait at the elevator for a few extra minutes, and then I decide to take the stairs, which are closer to Rowe's end of the hall. The closer I get to her room, the less I breathe, trying to listen for any sign of her being awake. But the bottom of her door is dark. She's either still asleep or long gone. Either way, she's going to realize her roommates never came home. And I hope like hell my brother keeps his word.

Rowe

I woke up early since I never showered last night. I figured most of the dorm would be asleep, so I could take my shower alone. Seems anytime after eleven and before six is good.

Paige and Cass were both gone, or they never came home. I suspect it's the latter. I spend my entire shower wondering where Paige slept, wondering if Nate paid any attention to her. Since she's not here, I'm guessing he did, and I hate that my mind keeps conjuring up visions of her sitting on his lap, kissing his neck, making out with him. Jealousy is the theme of the day, I'm afraid.

My laptop keeps staring at me. I haven't written him in two days. Ross says it's good for me to write to him, but he also says I shouldn't make it a ritual; I should make it something I do when I need it. When I want to feel better about things. And I want to now. But it feels wrong to write to Josh about another boy.

I flip my laptop open anyway, and go right to my Facebook messages to read the few sentences Nate sent me. Then I click into his profile and sift through his pictures. There are a lot of him with his brother, and a few of him with his family. He looks just like his dad—sharp, angular jawline, and the clear grayish-blue eyes. His mom is beautiful, dark black hair, blue eyes, and a tiny frame.

I decide to keep going, flipping through some photos from his high school. There's a girl in a few of them, mostly the ones that look like they're from some dance or something, and she's pretty too. She looks like an athlete, her arms are muscular and there's just something about her smile that looks strong—fearless. Her hair is close to the same color as mine—almost a muddy brown. From the number of photos of them together, I would guess they had been together for a while.

There are a few more photos that are more recent, and those are the ones I'm obsessing over. They look like they were taken this summer, and there's a different girl in every one—and a lot of them look like Paige. Each time I click to a new scene, I see Ty and Nate, holding a beer in one hand and a girl in the other. Sometimes the girl is on Nate's lap, and other times he's carrying her around on his back. His stupid charming smile is the only thing that stays the same.

I click my message button and start to type:

I've survived two days, but I don't know about this college thing. To be fair, I haven't gone to class yet. That part will probably be easy. But...

I stop and stare at the screen, because I'm about to veer in a new direction with Josh. Closing my eyes, I hear Ross's voice in my head—"write to him when you need it."

I need Josh. And I need him now.

...there's this boy. There, I said it. I know it's weird for me to write this to you, but I don't have anyone else. I think he likes me, but I don't know. I think I like him, but...you know? I've only known him for about 48 hours, but I've thought about him for 47. He's a baseball player, like you. Well, except he's really good (no offense).

I totally Googled him—I didn't tell him this, but I've seen every tape of his games posted on his high school's website. Dad would love him—he's a catcher. You know how my dad feels about catchers. "They're the heart and the soul of the team, Rowe."

I know, so what's my problem, right? Well, I'm just not very good at this...this...boy-girl thing. I don't even know what to call it. When I was with you, though, it was just easy. You wrote me a note in class one day, told me you liked me, and asked if I liked you back. I told you I did, and then boom! We were boyfriend-girlfriend. Up until we weren't.

With Nate (that's his name), there's no note. Yeah, he said I was hot. Or, he sort of said I was hot. He actually said the way I wear my shoes is hot, and I'm not sure that counts, but then he hung out with my roommate in his room all night. Not the cool one, he hung out with her too, but she was there for his brother. Long story. Anyhow, I could have gone, too. I was the one he invited, but then I just froze.

I'm frozen, Josh. And I don't know how to get unstuck. I know you won't answer. I know you don't have an answer to give me. But I wish you did.

Oh, and I think Ross might be full of shit. Because I don't feel any better. Like, at all.

Love,
Rowe

What I need to do is be more like my friend Betsy. Betsy wouldn't think—she would just act. Maybe that's the new mantra I need to follow: "What would Betsy do?"

I know what she would do right now. She would march over to Nate's room and barge right in just like she belonged there.

Be like Betsy. Be like Betsy. I tip my head over my knees and run my fingers through my wet hair, fluffing it out into waves.

Be like Betsy. Be like Betsy. I stuff my feet into my sneakers, grab my wallet and keys, and shove them into my back pockets after I pull my door closed behind me. The hallway is quiet, because it's still painfully early. I'm careful with my steps, like I'm sneaking up on someone. All I can hear is the thump of my pulse in my ears, and I'm worried it's distracting me—keeping me from hearing someone coming.

I lean against the wall next to Nate's door, and for minutes I just listen. The less I hear, the more my heart races, until I'm either going to pass out or choose to be strong.

More than a few times, I turn to walk away, but I keep pausing at the elevator and walking back. Finally, on my last trip, I shut my eyes at his door and turn the handle slowly, stepping carefully into his room, which looks like a smaller version of mine. It's dark in here, so I leave the door slightly cracked to let my eyes adjust. At first, I don't quite know what I'm staring at. But then the blonde curls of Paige's hair register with me, and she rolls over, twisting her body into the blankets even more—unfortunately not enough to cover her underwear. Panties that are nothing like a single pair in my drawer. Victoria Secret panties, made of barely anything at all.

"Hey," someone whispers, and I just back to the door a little. "Hey, it's Ty. Rowe? That you?"

Ty is lifting his chest up from the other bed, and I blush when I recognize Cass is cradled next to him.

"Oh god, I'm sorry. I was just...they didn't come home. So, I...I don't know. I'll just go," I fluster, hitting my knee with the door when I pull it open. God, could I be any louder?

"If you're looking for Nate, he had workouts this morning. He's out on the fields," he whispers, lying back down and moving the pillow over his face to block the little light I'm letting in.

"Okay. Thanks," I say, with no intention of doing anything with that information other than going back to my own bed to fume over Paige and where she slept last night.

"Oh, and hey. When you see him, make sure you ask him when his birthday is," Ty says, and within an instant, I swear he's sleeping again.

I shut the door behind me, and before I can talk myself out of it, I go to the elevator and push the button for the first floor. *What would Betsy do? Be like Betsy.*

It's getting easier to leave the building on my own, which is promising for my first day of classes the day after tomorrow. But right now, I'm grateful for ulterior reasons. I keep telling myself that every act I'm doing is an amazing achievement in my own recovery. But really, it's just an act of bitter jealousy—and so will be the embarrassing fit I throw in front of Nate after his practice, when I rip him apart for being predictable and hooking up with Paige for the night.

Unless...unless it's not just for the night? Maybe they hit it off? Maybe he decided he likes her after he got to know her. And maybe she's more than just Katy Perry lyrics and G-strings.

As much as the doubt is there now, I can't convince myself wholly of the idea of Nate and Paige as a couple. Not that I want to be a couple with Nate. I just don't want anyone else to be. *I think I may need to write Josh again.*

The ball fields are easy to find. When I climb onto the bleachers, my back against the solid corner in the back, I'm transported to my life two years ago. The way the ball sounds when it's struck by the bat—I think it's a similar effect some people have with wind chimes. Over and over, that repetitive *crack!* The sounds of gloves catching balls, of boys shouting plays, random swear words, and laughing. It's every practice my dad ever held. It's every tryout I went to with him. It's watching Josh play summer ball, and staying late to watch his practices after tennis would end.

I'm so lost in my own nirvana, I almost forget why I came. And then I see him pull the mask from his face, propping it on top of his head. He's standing next to another catcher, and Nate completely dwarfs him. I used to have a thing for the pitchers. That's why I first had a crush on Josh. But seeing Nate stand there—his hair tussled in different directions, wet with sweat, and his face smudged with dirt from the field—has now become my favorite memory. And I'm finding it harder to hold on to that raging, jealous anger that got me here in the first place.

When his eyes snap to me, I jolt. *Crap!* I really didn't want him to see me, but I kind of thought he would have an equal look of panic when he did. Instead, he's all dimples and teeth. He's saying something to one of his coaches, and I can see his head nod in my direction, which suddenly has me on my feet, scrambling my way down the bleachers. I think I might just make it, when he pops out of the back of the dugout, cutting off my path.

"Hey, how's your head, Thirty-three?" Dimples. Accent. Damned irresistible charm. He's looking at my eyes with concern still, worried about my head after last night's faint.

"Oh, it's fine. I'm fine, I mean. I was just...tired last night?" I say it like a question, like I'm trying to sell myself on my excuse. I wasn't tired at all. I took Ambien like I always do, and then I had messed-up dreams augmented by the drug that only left me feeling worse about everything this morning.

"You didn't miss much. Your roommates did a bunch of shots and passed out," he says, kicking his feet into the dirt on the ground and swinging his catcher's mask at his side.

"Yeah, I saw them," I say, gritting my teeth hard, forcing myself to smile and not delve into what else I saw. I don't want to leap with my assumptions, because I still have hope that I'm wrong.

"You...stopped by my room?" His head is tilted when he asked, and I can tell he's being guarded.

"Yep. Saw Paige made herself nice and comfortable in your bed." My mouth! Maybe I need to revise the *what-would-Betsy-do* campaign, because snarky and biting just doesn't sit well with me.

"Yeah," he says, still looking down, his hand rubbing at his neck. "Made it kind of hard for me to sleep there. For the record, that couch in the lobby is miserable."

My heart is thumping again, and I think it's actually jumping up and down in my chest, it's so excited by his answer. Which is bad, because it's only going to make it harder for me to tame my heart into stopping at *friends.*

"Hey, Preeter! Ass back on the field, son!" one of the coaches yells. I don't want him to get into trouble because of me, so I just nod him on.

"You'll stick around? Yeah?" he asks, pushing his mask back over his head. I don't believe in signs. If signs were real, then surely I would have gotten a few of them to stop my life from crumbling. But for whatever reason, my eyes center on the small scratched letters etched on the side of his metal mask—N.J.P. And Ty's voice runs through my head.

"That depends," I say, still looking at the letters on his mask.

"On what?" he asks, his feet starting to shuffle backward toward the field.

"What does N.J.P. stand for, and when's your birthday?" I ask, my heart now in my stomach, begging and hoping for the right answer.

Nate's lip pulls up on one side, and he tucks his lower lip under his teeth as he backs away, and inside I'm willing him—"Say it, just say it," I'm thinking.

"My birthday's in October, and the *J* is for Jackson. What can I say, beautiful girls turn me into a complete and utter fraud."

I turn back to the bleachers without saying a word, and I can feel Nate's eyes on me the entire way—watching me climb back up to my seat, lean back, and cross my legs, making myself comfortable.

This is still flirting, and it's going to make being *just friends* damned near impossible. But right now, I don't give a shit.

52

Chapter 8

Nate

She stayed for the entire practice. She even walked with me through campus, back to the workout room. It's fall, so we only have a few tournaments to play—exhibitions. The real work starts in a month or two, but I still have a pretty full schedule. It makes it hard to squeeze in extra things...*Rowe.*

The weekend is free, though. The dorms are all full, because classes start on Monday, and everything about this place feels exactly like I thought college would feel.

"Hey, douchebag!" Ty yells when he comes through the door, throwing his rolled up dirty socks at me. "Think fast!"

"You are such an asshole sometimes," I say, brushing them from my lap to the floor. Seriously, Ty's feet stink.

"Yeah, well. Tell Mom," he laughs. "Speaking of, I talked to them this morning. They're coming to visit in a couple weeks. Taking us to dinner, and all that. I'm bringing Cass."

My brother's infatuation with Cass fascinates me. He has never held onto a girl longer than a week, but she seems to have found his weakness. What's more amazing is how absolutely normal she is. Girls have never been a problem for Ty. He was homecoming king in high school, and that was after his accident. The local paper thought it was this cool story, about how our student body elected a guy in a wheelchair. Then the reporter interviewed Ty, and his quote pretty much summed it up.

"The chair might make people notice. But this face is so pretty, girls just can't help themselves," he said, right there in print. Mom told him he shouldn't be so cocky, and Dad just high-fived him. That's Ty. I wish I had an ounce of his confidence.

"You should ask Rowe," he says, his back to me. That's how I know he's being serious, and not just teasing. If he were giving me crap, he'd be in my face, relentless and crude about her. But he likes her; he likes the idea of *her and me.* And I like that.

"Yeah? You think she'd go?"

"Bro, I *know* she'd go," he says, turning around and throwing his dirty boxers at me now.

"Fucking asshole!" I get him back when I stand up and push his underwear on his own head as I leave the room.

"That's right, you better run!" he yells as I swing through the door.

Their door is open, and for some reason that makes me nervous. I can hear music blaring as I get closer. It's not the kind of stuff I'd expect to hear from a girl's room. I knock on the door, but I know they can't hear it, so I step slowly around the corner. Rowe's back is to me, but Cass sees me right away and winks. Rowe is singing "Sex Is On Fire" by the Kings of Leon, standing on a chair in the middle of her room, her arms pumping in the air as if she were actually on stage. It's the single cutest thing I've ever seen in my whole life. I quietly slip all the way into the room and slide my back along the wall, pulling my knees up so I can sit and just look at her for a little longer.

When the chorus comes around, Cass jumps onto the bed and sings along with her. They sound terrible, but I'd watch an entire concert of this just to look at Rowe. She spins around once, but her eyes are closed, so she doesn't notice I'm here, and it gives me such a good idea.

I put my finger to my mouth, motioning to Cass while I sneak up behind Rowe; Cass grins and nods. I wait for a few seconds for them to get to the chorus again, and when Rowe lifts her arms up, I wrap my arms around her waist and lift her up from the chair into my arms.

Rowe has a hell of a right hook. It's amazing how fast my nose is bleeding. I've been hit in the face by ninety-mile-per-hour pitches, and I've never bled like this. "Ohhhhh fuck!" I say, embarrassed that my eyes are tearing up as much as they are.

"Oh my god! I'm so sorry. Hold on, I have a towel," Rowe says, running to her closet and pulling out a giant bath towel and handing it to me. I hold it to my nose quickly because the last thing I want to do is bleed all over their floor.

"My fault," I say, raising a hand and sitting down on the chair Rowe was just dancing on.

"No…oh god! I'm so sorry. I just…I scare really easily."

"Yeah, I can see that."

Cass turns the music down so we can hear better, and Rowe kneels next to me, putting her hand on mine to pull the towel away from my face. It's the smallest gesture in the world, but for some reason, the way she's looking at me takes my breath away. Her eyes are so concerned, and her hand is trembling against mine. I'm unable to stop myself from reaching up to hold her hand with my other one. As soon as I do, her gaze jumps to our hands and she jerks away.

"I should get you ice," she says, standing and hugging herself.

"No, really. I'll be fine. I have a brother, and I've been punched…*a lot*! It will stop in a minute."

Rowe keeps her arms around her stomach and moves backward until she sits on the edge of her bed. Cass reaches under her own bed for a duffle bag, pulls it out and goes into the closet to fill it with laundry. "I'm going to go do a load. Rowe, you need me to wash anything?" she asks.

"No, I'm good. Thanks," Rowe says, her eyes watching her friend walk out the door, and her breath stops the second the door closes behind her. Cass may just be my new best friend, because I know she did this so Rowe and I could be alone. But for some reason, her leaving has Rowe acting even more nervous and uncomfortable; she stands and walks over to the small corkboard by her bed, arranging some photos, and pushing in a few pins.

"So, you ready for Monday?" I say, pulling the towel away from my nose to check that the bleeding has stopped.

"Yeah, I guess," she says. Her voice is distant, and she doesn't sound sure.

"Ty says the first week is always easy. Just syllabus review and expectations…all that," I say, getting back up to my feet and walking over to stand behind her. Rowe's entire body gets tense as soon as I get close. She's moving the same picture to different spots on her board, like she's not quite sure where this picture fits or belongs. "May I?" I ask, reaching my hand out to look at the photo more closely.

She hands it over and makes a tight smile. The picture looks like it's a year or two old, because Rowe looks younger. I'd guess she's maybe sixteen in the photo. She's sitting on some guy's lap, her arms around him, and her nose tucked into his neck. He's smiling one of those genuinely happy smiles, and I'd make the same damned face if I were in his position. He's wearing a baseball hat, and I can tell he's just left practice or something because he has baseball pants on and they're covered in dirt.

"Boyfriend?" I ask, just getting right to the point. Not really ready to know if that word is in the past or present tense.

She nods *yes* and takes the picture back from me, pinning it to the bottom of the board and leaving it there.

"One of your dad's players?" I ask that, hoping she'll answer the rest without me asking. But she doesn't. She just nods again. The silence in the room is suffocating now, and I feel like an intruder, so I hold my towel up and suck in my bottom lip, giving myself some time to think.

"I'm gonna wash this for you. I'll bring it back, okay?" I say, my feet slowly backing out of her room.

"You can keep it," she says, but there's something about the way her lips move that makes me feel like she wants to say more, so I pause. I'm standing here, in the middle of her room, looking into her eyes, and they make me want to cry. After a few long seconds, when she doesn't speak, I turn and leave.

Rowe

The second he's gone, the tears come streaming down my face. I hate these pictures. I hate them, but I love them. My mom told me not to bring them. "These things were best left at home," she said. But I wanted them with me. I wanted Josh and Betsy with me, and not just in my head.

I hate you.

That's all I write to Josh; I slam my laptop closed again and fall to my bed, curling up into a ball with my covers. When I hear Cass come in the door, I hold my breath, stopping my cries, until she believes I'm sleeping; she gets her keys and leaves me alone.

I slept the entire Saturday away. Of course, I only slept in fifteen or twenty minute fits. I wasn't really tired, but my emotions were exhausted. Paige was out all weekend, which was a blessing. But when she rolled into our room on Sunday afternoon, she made up for all of the peace and quiet I enjoyed in her absence.

"I'm thinking of rushing Delta or Sigma. I like them both. Cass, what do you think?" I can tell Cass isn't listening, and I know Paige is only going to ask again, but louder, so I decide to play defense.

"I think you should pick Sigma," I say, not really having a clue what Sigma or Delta or any of the other goddamned annoying letters she's been spewing for the last thirty minutes mean. Frankly, I want to set up appointments with every single one of McConnell's sororities to warn them not to accept her, to let them know what a *step down* they would be taking in terms of their own personal standards. But I don't. I don't because I also would give anything for Paige to move out and leave Cass and me here alone.

"I think I'll pick Delta," she says, just to spite me. *Whatever.*

There's a light knock on the door, but I'm the only one who hears it. It's Nate. I know it's Nate. I actually recognize his knock, which is dangerous and scary, and makes my heart feel panicky things that I don't like. He knocks again, this time a little louder, and Cass stands up from her bed and walks over to let him in. Ty is with him, and I'm relieved.

"Hey, ladies. Your heroes have arrived," Ty says, tugging on the loops of Cass's jeans and pulling her onto his lap. She giggles when he does, and just watching them makes me smile. Everything is so...*easy.* I look at Nate, and he's smiling just like I am when looking at his brother and Cass, and I wonder if he's feeling the same longing and reservations.

"Took you long enough. I'm starving!" Cass says, grabbing her purse and looping it across her body. "We're going to grab dinner at the cafeteria. You coming, Rowe?"

"Oh, no. I'm fine. I'll just eat something here." My excuse floods from my mouth quickly, maybe too quickly.

"You don't have anything. Come on, just come," she says, reaching for my hand and pulling me to a stand.

"I'll go," Paige says, pulling the extra layer of shirt off of her arms to make sure the one-size-too-small tank top is squeezing her boobs enough to make part of them spill out. I don't want to go. I don't do public places well, especially cafeterias that are crowded with people. But Paige is already positioning herself close to Nate, and she's making excuses to touch him, pointing to something on his shirt and lifting the back of his shirt to "look at the tag on his jeans to see what kind they are."

"Okay, I'll go." I don't know what I'm doing, and I don't know how I'm going to survive this. But thank you, jealousy, for being a force to be reckoned with, perhaps the only emotion strong enough to conquer fear.

We're walking out the door, and my heart is pounding so fast I honestly think I might have a heart attack. I try to keep my arms out to my sides because my armpits are sweating profusely. I've never been so nervous in my entire life.

"Whose phone is ringing? Cass is that you?" Paige says, tugging at her sister's purse. She's on the other side of Nate, and has to reach across him to reach Cass, which is the only reason she is doing that, and I know it. I know it because it's my phone that's ringing, and every single one of us knows it. It's obvious, and Paige is pathetic.

"It's mine. You guys go ahead. I'll catch up," I say, pulling my phone out and seeing my mom's contact info.

"I'll wait. We'll catch up," Nate says, leaning against the wall and nodding to me to take my time. He's waiting. For me. And I'm so glad, but also mortified that he's going to hear me talk to my mom. And she's going to ask questions. Personal ones— ones that I don't want to answer in front of *him*.

"Hi, Mom," I say, trying to sound just the right mix of positive and neutral.

"Well, you sound good," she says, already analyzing. My mom is an economist. But somewhere along the way she decided she's also Dr. Phil.

"Yeah, just going to get some dinner. What's up?" I say, trying to urge her to be fast, but also not encourage too many questions.

"You're going out?" *Shit.*

"Yeah, I've made some friends. My roommate is really nice. We're going to eat." I spare a quick glance at Nate, and he's grinning at me. I'm so embarrassed that he's listening, because I know my mom is about to go on and on about how important friends are, and how proud she is of me for trying hard. And there she goes.

"Honey, you're doing so well. This is only going to get easier, too. Friends are an important part of the healing process..."

I tune the next part out, because I've heard this speech before. Friends equal healing, yeah...got it. Ross said this to me once in a joint session with my mom, and she clung to it. I don't think she even knows what those words mean anymore, she just repeats them to me over and over—like it's a cheer—until I reach the invisible finish line.

"Look, Mom. I'm sorry, but they're waiting on me. I don't want to make them wait," I say, staring right at Nate, who's the only one really waiting.

"Okay, well, call me tomorrow. Let me know how classes go," she says, not hanging up right away.

"Right. Okay, love you," I say, suddenly really dreading the idea of going to the cafeteria full of people. But there is some truth to what my mom says—friends are part of healing.

"Ready?" Nate says, kicking off from the wall and holding his arm out for me. I don't take it—not because I don't want to, because *god, do I want to*—but because I don't like what it means if I do. I used to take Josh's arm. He used to sprint from his class to mine, waiting for me outside my door just to walk me to my next class. It was *our* thing, and I think that means it can't be a *thing* I do with anyone else.

I can tell I've made him uncomfortable by the way he's standing in the elevator, like he's afraid of offending me. He's all the way in the opposite corner—giving me space since I refused to touch his arm. I like Nate. And I want to be his friend because I like being close to him. And that has to be enough.

We stop on the second floor, and two girls get in. They notice us standing at opposite corners. "He farted," I say, partly wanting to see how uncomfortable it makes these two girls—because, like, who the hell takes the elevator for one floor? And, I want to bring back Nate's smile, which I seem to have done. Teeth. Dimples.

"Ooooooh, yeah. Sorry ladies. I think I may have sharted," he says, and I cover my mouth with an actual snort-laugh while my cheeks burn with the brightest shade of pink. The two girls just stare ahead, eyes wide, leaning their arms into one another, waiting to discuss this elevator ride. When the door opens, I slap Nate on the arm, pushing him off balance a little.

"I cannot believe you said that!"

"Hey, you left me little choice. You should know—I don't lose the embarrassment game. If you think you want a piece of this, consider this fair warning. You're going to lose, every time." He's so sure of himself that it stirs another feeling in my belly. I used to be competitive—I was even that way with Josh, always having to one up his test scores, and run my mile just a little faster in PE.

"Oh yeah? You think I'm scared off by that?" The look in his eye and the way he smiles—biting his tongue with the back of his teeth while he listens to me—is enough to pull me all the way in. "I just felt bad for you. Those girls think you're a sharter. You're never getting in their pants now."

"I don't *want* in their pants," he says, the same look on his face, and I feel like there is a double meaning to his words. My lungs feel tight with hope I shouldn't have.

"It's on," I say, turning to look back in front of me, my eyes focused on the two doors leading into the cafeteria. This step is so amazingly huge—I wish someone in my inner circle were here to witness it. I know that distracting myself with Nate is the only reason I'm now pushing the doors open and stepping inside the noisy room full of tables and chairs and strangers.

My lungs grow even smaller and tighter when I do, but my feet keep moving.

Yes, friends help you heal. But Nate is stronger than that. And he's bringing back pieces of me that I thought were dead for good.

"Hey, guys. Sorry we're late. Rowe got a phone call that her ointment was ready. We had to go pick it up. That's the one that helps with the...*burning*...right?" Nate fake-whispers, holding my gaze to see how I handle his challenge. I fight against myself, knowing how badly my eyes want to show shock, and my cheeks want to flair up with embarrassment. I used to be good at this. And I think I can do this again. I remember *friends*.

"Yeah, it's way better now. That stuff works really fast," I say, and his lips tick up at the corners into a tiny smile. "Too bad about your pants, though."

I leave everyone hanging, because I know if I wait long enough, someone will take my bait. It won't be Nate. He's too good, and he knows exactly what I'm doing. He even sees me grab the bottle of water in line and slowly pull off the cap. I'm pretty sure I can count on Paige, though, and when she's the one to ask, a little tiny part of my world feels right again for the first time in months.

"What happened to your pants?" Paige asks. *Check.*

"Oh, I thought everyone knew. Nate's incontinent. He pissed himself on the way over here," I say, tipping the water bottle enough to spill down the back of his jeans, but behind him, so no one really sees while we're standing in line. He doesn't flinch, but instead, stands there perfectly still while I soak his pants. *Checkmate.*

"Yep, totally pissed myself. Just gonna have to sit in my urine all day I guess. Who's hungry?" he says, flipping up an apple and lodging it in his teeth while he grabs a tray and moves down the line in his dripping wet pants. Cass and Paige stare at him, completely lost over what just happened, and Ty laughs and shakes his head, grabbing a tray to follow his brother.

Nate is the challenger I always wanted, and I like him more than I thought I did. I like him more than I should. And a little part of me is okay with that.

Chapter 9

Nate

"Cass, pleeeeeeaase just trust me. Rowe will be totally okay with this. Just let me do it." I've been pleading with Rowe's roommate for the last twenty minutes. I loved seeing that side of Rowe, the side that jokes and smiles, and doesn't take things seriously. I went to bed thinking about it. I woke up thinking about it. I thought about it through my two morning classes. And now I'm here, standing in her room with her dresser drawer in my hand.

"Uuuuuugh! Fine! But don't get me involved in this stupid war you have going with her. If she asks, I had nothing to do with this, okay?" Cass grabs her backpack and slings it over her shoulders to go to class. I salute her and cross my heart; she sighs again before she turns around.

"You love me, and you know it," I shout over my shoulder as she's about to leave.

"She better not!" I hear Ty's voice a second later.

"Hey, what's up?" I say to him as I start flipping over every single one of Rowe's drawers. It's a tricky prank, because I have to hold her clothes inside with one arm while I slide them in. I spend a little longer than I should on her underwear and bras, which Ty points out immediately.

"This is a new level of creepy, bro. Even for you," he says, stopping right next to me, but reaching his arms over to help me hold her clothing in.

"Just a little prank," I smile.

"Oh, that's a good one. I'm in. This one Cass's?" he asks, pointing to the dresser next to Rowe's. I just shrug because honestly the only things I've ever noticed in this room all belong to Rowe.

Ty slides the top-drawer open and pulls out a bra, holding it in front of him and squeezing the cups. "Yeah, this is hers. I recognize this lovely little thing," he says, and I roll my eyes at him. "What? Just because you can't close a deal like I can, don't give me shit."

For some reason, what he says makes me start to think about how I feel about Rowe. And yeah, I want to kiss her. And yeah, I want to remind myself what those cotton panties look like again. And there are probably a million other things that involve her that I would never say no to. But I'm not in a hurry. And for some reason, I feel like Rowe is holding back with me, sort of glad I'm not pushing.

"Hey, you really like Cass, huh?" I say, flipping over her bottom drawer and pressing my arms up to hold in the heavy jeans.

Ty just sighs, never answering, which is enough for me. He really likes her, and that's kind of a first for him. I just hope he doesn't do something stupid to make it impossible for me to come to this room again.

I'm about to push the last drawer in all the way when I feel a pile of something slide out onto my foot. I push the drawer in just enough so I can let go and feel my hands along the floor. At first I think they're playing cards, but then I pull them out to look at them and realize they're photos—photos of Rowe...with the *boyfriend*. I slide the drawer in the rest of the way and sit back on her bed to flip through them.

The first one is of her and him in what looks like her parents' driveway, and they're dressed in formal wear, like they're going to some dance. Then there are a couple of pictures of them at a swimming pool. He's lifting her, and threatening to jump into the water. She's laughing in the photo, and it strikes me that I've never seen her laugh like this.

"Hey, dude? Do you know if Rowe...does she..." I'm almost afraid to ask, so I just flip the last picture over and hand it to him. It's a picture of the same guy, kissing her on the cheek, and she's literally squealing with happiness. "Does she have a boyfriend?"

Ty takes the photo in, looking at it for a long time before finally shrugging and handing it back to me. "No idea. You should probably ask."

It's the last thing on the planet I want to ask. Mostly because it's the last answer on the planet I want to hear...unless the answer is *no*.

I help Ty with the last couple drawers, and we lock their door from the inside to bring it back to a close. When we pass the elevator, I hear Paige laughing while she talks on her phone, and she holds a finger up to try to get our attention, but we both keep moving, pretending not to see it. Ty's eyes turn sideways to catch mine, and we both laugh quietly.

"Dude, I can't stand that chick! How is it that I'm crazy about her sister?" Ty says, and I know he just answered my question from earlier, but he doesn't want me to make a big deal out of it. So I don't. And instead, I focus on the first part.

"She has great tits!" I say, waiting for him to respond.

"Ah, that's a good point. Way to focus on the positive. She does indeed have great tits," Ty says, grabbing the remote and turning the TV on to *Sports Center.*

Rowe

I call my mom on my walk back from class. I don't like talking to her in front of other people, so I try to time our conversations for my walks. That, and the distraction helps me focus on something other than the wide-open spaces, and cars, and people milling around.

After filling her in on my first day's schedule, and running through my list of professors to see if there's anyone she knows, which she knows two of them, I move on to the regular litany of questions. Am I sleeping? How are my roommates? Am I really making friends? Have I called Ross?

I called Ross right before I called my mom, but I don't tell her that. I slipped up once, telling her I called Ross first for something and her feelings were hurt. I can't handle guilt trips—I have enough. So I just lie instead, and tell her I'm calling Ross next. I feel like if I ever have to stand before some supreme being who gets to decide if I get into heaven and he brings up this lie—it was warranted. I'd like to think the ultimate judge in this case would understand.

I never bring up Josh. My mom found my messages to him once, so I told her they were old messages and that I don't write any more. I just changed my password though. Okay, so two lies. This one might not be as easy to explain away.

The hallway is eerily empty when I exit the elevator, which always makes me nervous. It's the middle of the afternoon, so I guess most students are in their classes by now. I've learned there are only a few of us who prefer morning classes. I happen to have a pretty full schedule—what with trying out a little bit of everything—so my day starts at seven and goes until three thirty.

After jiggling the door handle, I start to feel silly. The door is locked, and I am safe. There's a constant string of reassurances running through my head at all times.

I make my way into my room and drop my book bag to the floor. One drawback to having a back-to-back kind of schedule is the pressure it puts on my spine. One philosophy class and one art history class alone add up to fifteen pounds in books. But those two were definitely my favorites, and I think Nate might have pushed me in the right direction with art. Today was all about looking at pictures of famous paintings, and everything I saw inspired me.

When my socks and underwear spill onto my feet, I immediately know that Nate was here. Son of a bitch! I pull the next drawer out and the same thing happens. Again and again, until all of my belongings are in a pile at my feet and my drawer bottoms are staring me in the face.

"That mother..."

"Hey, watch what you're about to call the guy standing at your door," Nate says, and my heart kicks.

"That motherly, wonderful, down-the-hall neighbor of mine. What's wrong with saying that?" I smile, flipping my top drawer over and sliding it in. I get to my knees to start picking up my delicates first, mostly because I don't want them out for display. Nate, though, is quickly by my side, helping me.

"Oh! Hey, don't touch those," I say, grabbing the silky black pair of underwear from his hands. They're the only girly pair of panties I own, and I bought them with a Victoria Secret gift card my aunt sent me. She wanted me to buy nice bras, but I hate the foo-foo ones they have at that store, and I can't stand the idea of spending forty bucks on a bra. So I bought underwear—six boy shorts and one fancy panty. I was saving those, but lord knows for what.

Nate just sits back on my bed and watches me piece back together my dresser. "Real funny there, Preeter. But you better watch your back," I say, my mind already spinning in a million directions with what I can do to get back at him. I'm reveling in the ideas when he brings everything to a screeching halt.

"Oh, I also wanted to give you these. They, uhhh," he swallows hard handing me a stack of pictures that I recognize instantly. "They fell out of one of the drawers. I didn't want them to get lost."

I don't turn them over to look at them, and instead just shuffle them into a neat pile and tuck them back under my jeans. I don't like looking at the girl in those photos. It's hard to see Josh, but it's even harder to see me—who I used to be. "Rowe? Can I ask you something?" Nate says, and my pulse begins that racing thing again, and my breath gets shorter and shorter.

"Depends," I say, not looking him in the eye and just pushing on each drawer until they are all lined up and shut neatly again. I sit on Cass's bed when I'm finished, and keep my eyes at his feet and then his hands. He's nervous and fidgety, and I know what he wants to ask, but I don't know how to answer it.

"That guy? The one in the pictures? You said he was your boyfriend. Is he...*still* your boyfriend?"

Speechless. This is the same question I've asked the universe a million times. I asked Ross just an hour ago. I asked my mother before I left to come here. And I asked Josh's parents, too. But nobody gives me a goddamned answer when I ask. So I'm not giving one to Nate.

"I have to go," I say, grabbing my heavy bag of books and racing through my door to the stairs so I don't have to wait for the elevator. I stop at the top of the first floor and I sit down on the steps, tucking my head between my knees and reminding myself to breathe. *Breathe deeply, Rowe.*

I don't know how long I hide there, but when I come back upstairs, my door is open and Cass is home.

"Damn it, Rowe! I didn't want to be a part of this war, but looks like I'm in it now!" she's kicking around the pile of clothes at her feet and flipping over her own drawers. "Tell me what you need me to do. I'm all in. You don't mess with an Owens sister!"

"Who's messing with you?" Paige says, kicking her shoes off under her bed and hooking her backpack over her desk chair.

"Ty! And Nate! They flipped our dresser drawers," Cass says with a huff, stuffing her clothes back into her drawers without folding. Paige rushes to her dresser next, biting her lip and waiting for her clothes to spill out. When her drawers are fine, I see the disappointment flood her body, and I feel sad for her.

"Okay, tell me what you girls need me to do. Let's get those assholes back," Paige says. I don't know if she's just mad that they left her out of the practical joke war or if she's just trying to put on a brave face, but for the first time since I've met her, I feel a connection with her, so I hold onto it.

"Okay, I have an idea. We're gonna need a hardware store," I start, and they both pull up their chairs to listen.

Chapter 10

Nate

Staying away from her room was harder than I thought it would be. I never brought up going to the art gallery, and I avoided accidental run-ins when I could. I didn't have workouts during the first week of school, but I found myself in the gym anyhow. Coaches liked seeing me there, but I wasn't there for them. I didn't need to make an impression—I was their guy, and I knew it. With me on the roster, McConnell was in the mix. Without me, they were a decent team but not good enough to make the series.

Whatever, though—me being here on a non-workout day made me look like a team leader, and I did want to fill that role for the other guys. Even if the only reason I was here was to keep myself busy and away from Rowe.

Ty was with Cass every night. She came over to watch *Sports Center* with us after dinner, and she'd drop these totally obvious stories about Rowe, taking extra care to say her name nice and clear for me to hear.

It's not like I was angry with her. Damn, I'd have to *understand* her for that to be a part of the equation. I guess I was angrier with myself for being so intimidated by her, and those pictures. She couldn't even look at them, and the way she ran out of her room when I asked her about them made me start to think that she might just have some emotional baggage I'm not equipped for.

"Hey, you about ready to head back?" Ty says, popping his head in while I finish up my last set. Ty does personal training at the campus—he was hired on to work with some of the disabled students initially, but he's so disciplined that others started requesting him, too. My brother took his rehab seriously when he got out of the hospital, and the dude is probably in better shape than I am.

"One more set. I'll meet you out front," I say.

He just nods and leaves me to finish my workout, alone with my thoughts. I could lift a thousand pounds and it still wouldn't be enough to distract me from thinking about Rowe.

She takes her showers late at night. I heard her in there yesterday while I was taking mine, and I thought about running into her again. But she'd see right through that. Instead, I sat on the locker bench quietly, listening to her sing lightly under her breath. She was putting on an act when she was singing with Cass in her room the other day because I can tell she has the voice of an angel. I bet if she really let herself go, she would surprise the hell out of a lot of people with her voice—she'd probably surprise herself a little, too.

It's late by the time Ty and I get back to the dorm, and I can hear both of our stomachs rumbling. "Dinner?" I say, turning my key in our lock.

"Yeah. Let me just text Cass. She wanted to come. You mind?"

"Nah," I say. Honestly, I don't mind. I like Cass's company, and I like having the small connection to Rowe. I still want to invite her out with my parents next weekend, but I just feel strange talking to her after the whole *picture* incident. I think I just need to know what the guy in that picture *is* to her first.

"What. The. Fuck!" Ty sees it first. It takes me a few minutes to make sure my eyes aren't tricking me. Our entire bedroom, every square inch of the walls, is pink. The back of the door—pink. The ceiling—pink. And it's not a subtle pastel. No, our dorm room is Barbie-princess pink!

I have to hand it to her. Rowe is good. I mean, like, *really* good. This took effort and time, and I know she had help—Ty's fault for flipping Cass's dresser. Ty is fuming, but I just start laughing, tossing my gym bag on my bed.

"Dude, this isn't funny! I fucking *hate* pink!" My brother is more worked up over his room color than he was about losing a grand in a Super-Bowl bet last year.

"Rowe." I say, sitting down on my bed and taking everything in. This must have taken three gallons to get it covered so well, and they must have worked on this *all day.* The paint smell was still fresh. I have to admit, I am pretty damned impressed.

"Dude, I know you like that girl or whatever, but this shit is unacceptable," Ty says, flinging open our door and heading down the hall to their room. I catch up with him, my smile growing bigger with every step.

The door is shut, and Ty has his hand up ready to pound, but I grab it to stop him. I hold up a finger and tell him to stay quiet, then I go to the room two doors down and ask the quiet girl who lives there to do us a favor. I bring her back to the door, and she knocks while Ty and I hide to one side, out of the view of the peephole.

"It's Molly. I'm out of printer ink, and I need to get this paper done. Can I borrow yours? It will only take a few seconds," Molly says, selling it so well that I think I may have underestimated her too.

"Thank you soooo much," I whisper back to her. It's scary how willing she was to help Ty and me out, but the Preeter brothers have always been good at getting girls to do things. Every girl but one, it seems.

"Hang on." It's Cass I hear, so I ready myself low to sneak past her into the room so I can get to Rowe. I can tell she's looking through the hole, and Molly just stands there, smiling. The door is barely open, and I push it the rest of the way. Cass starts laughing hysterically and screaming just a little.

"Rowe, run!" she says, and I see Rowe's long legs fly up from her bed and leap over Cass's in an effort to lock herself in the closet. Paige is standing on her bed, too, laughing and pointing at Rowe.

"This was all her idea!" Paige screams.

"Oh, I know exactly whose idea this is," I say, my fingers reaching just enough of her shirt to tug her to a stop and grip at her waist. She's strong, and she's wiggling and laughing, and still trying to get away from me. But she's no match. I finally get my arms completely around her body, and I lift her over my shoulder, locking her squirming arms and legs in before I take off in a run.

"No! Nate, don't you dare. What are you doing? Where are you taking me!" She's kicking like hell, but she's still laughing, so I keep going, all the way to the stairs.

71

"You tell me, Rowe. Elevator or stairs?"

"Huh?" she asks, her voice muffled from the blood rushing to her head.

"I'm not letting go of you, but I'm taking you outside. You're lucky I'm giving you a choice—elevator or stairs? Me? I'd pick elevator. Because I'm not so sure I can balance down three flights with your long-ass legs kicking at me."

"Elevator," she says, her body going limp.

"Good choice," I say, marching her over to the button and waiting for the elevator to open. There are a few people inside, and they all move out of the way when I get in with her.

"Chick painted my room pink. Payback. You know, they're a bitch?" I say, hitting the button to close the door.

"What do you mean payback?" Rowe asks, her head behind me and still upside down.

"Oh, you're going to find out sweetheart. Just you wait," I say, not really sure where I'm taking her, but just out-of-my-mind excited to have her in my arms, even if it is a bit like kidnapping.

"Nate? No...you're making me nervous," she says, but she's still giggling, so I push on. The elevator opens, and I walk quickly to the main door. As soon as I get it open, I take off in a sprint, and her arms and legs start kicking and slapping at me again.

"You're going to make me drop you!" She's lifting up the back of my shirt, and I swear I feel something wet. "Did you...did you just *lick* me?"

And oh my god the mischievous laugh she lets out when I ask her that. I know she thinks she's being a badass and sneaky, but fuck me! That laugh? Her tongue on my skin? She's being sexy as hell, and she doesn't even have a clue. I slow to a walk, but I keep carrying her. The ball fields are only a few hundred yards away, which gives me an idea.

"Rowe, I feel I have to tell you this. We're close enough that I think you deserve honesty. Putting your tongue on me is in no way, whatsoever torture. It's pretty much the shit I've been dreaming about since the night I ran into you in the hallway. So unless you're prepared to follow through with what your tongue suggests in my mind, I'd encourage you to keep it in your pretty little mouth."

I feel her body stiffen a little when I finish, and she's no longer laughing. But I also don't think she's mad. Her muscles finally relax when I cut through the back gate at the ball field. I can hear it, but I don't think she can because she's upside down. I probably only have a few more minutes to catch it, so I tell her to hang on and I jog with her over my shoulder into centerfield.

When I hear it stop for a second, I pull her back over my shoulder and let her feet touch the ground. Immediately, she tries to run, so I pull her into my chest, her face away from me, and I lock her arms in tightly.

"Uh uh. Time to face the music," I say, and on the perfect cue the outfield sprinklers kick on, soaking her body, hair, and shorts with every pass. I'm soaking wet too, but I don't care. I would walk through fire to hold her in front of me like this. And then, a remarkable thing happens.

I let my arms loosen their grip, and Rowe slips away from me, but she doesn't run. She just stretches her arms out to her sides and looks up, her hair dripping wet, and her face glistening from the water beading up on her skin. She starts spinning slowly in a circle, laughing. And then it's there—*the* smile. The same look she had on her face in that picture. It's joy. And I just gave it to her.

My god, do I want to give it to her again.

Rowe

The water is so cold that I start to shiver, but I don't care. I keep spinning and laughing. Maybe I'm having a nervous breakdown. Whatever this is, I don't care—I feel free and honestly happy. A real moment of happiness, uninterrupted, and Nate just stands there watching me and waiting.

His smile is spectacular. He's like those faces I see in my magazines, when I flip through ads of people in love. The way the man looks at a woman in the perfume ads—that's his face, right now, for me. I don't want it to go away, but I know it has to, and the second I start to let my reality creep in, my happiness fades.

I stop spinning, but I force my smile to stay in place, because I don't want to go back to those other feelings just yet.

"You're beautiful; you know that?" My breath is gone with his words. Nate can't think I'm beautiful. I'm not—I'm scarred and ugly.

"Don't do that."

"Don't do what?" I ask, my posture dipping, and my hands coming back to that familiar place around my waist, squeezing tightly.

"Don't refuse to listen to me," he says, stepping closer. I step back, but with every two I take, he takes three, until he's touching me, his hands gripping my elbows. "You're freezing."

"I'm fine," I say, not wanting this moment to end. I'm so terrified of it—so unbelievably afraid of this conversation continuing. But I haven't wanted anything in so long. And right now, all I want is *this*—this time right now, alone with Nate.

His hands slide up my arms to my neck, and soon his hands are cradling my face. My teeth are chattering, but I'm begging them to behave. I can feel Nate's breath he's so close to me, and for a moment, I think he might kiss me. Instead, he steps back and pulls his long-sleeved shirt over his body and slips it around my head, holding it out for me to tuck my arms inside.

"Thank you," I say, my lips still quivering, partly from the cold and partly from my desire to be kissed.

"Well, it is sort of my fault. I ran you through the sprinklers," he says, reaching his arm around me and pulling me into his side. We walk through the field, our feet squishing in the grass.

"Are we supposed to be out here?" I ask, noticing the deep feet prints we're leaving in our wake.

"Oh god no. I'm going to get my ass chewed, too. There are cameras all over the place. I bet security is on it's way right now."

I start to pick up my pace, my heart thumping with panic now. But then his laugh registers, and I stop. "Not nice," I say.

"I know. I'm kidding. There are no cameras. We're probably not supposed to be here, but no one will know."

74

We climb over a small pony wall into the dug out, and Nate reaches for my hand to help me down. His hands are somehow warm, despite everything on my body feeling so cold. I want to hold his hand, feel my fingers intertwine with his, but his touch leaves me as soon as my feet meet the ground. And I can't ignore the sharp pain it causes in my heart.

The dugout bench is wide; I sit sideways on it, pulling my knees up to hug them closely to me. I tuck my legs into his shirt for a bit, trying to warm the rest of my body. Nate sits in front of me, crossing his legs and tugging at my shoelaces.

"I meant what I said, you know," he says, looking up at me with one eyebrow raised. "That you're beautiful?"

Sucking in my bottom lip to hide the smile on my face, I nod once and whisper "Thank you."

"Oh Nate, and by the way, I find you incredibly handsome," he says, putting on his best female voice to imitate me. I laugh and stare down into my lap, not knowing what to say next.

"You're...*not bad*," I say, shrugging for emphasis. "I mean, you're kind of big and gangly. And I bet your knees crackle and pop from catching, so you're probably going to suffer from massive arthritis. But, you're all right."

He pushes up my feet without warning, tipping me over on my back. "Damn, and here Ty and I thought Paige was the bitchy one," he jokes.

"Nope. It was I all along. In fact, this isn't even what I look like. If I ripped off this layer of skin, underneath I would smell like sparkly body spray, and my skin would glitter, and my hair would feel like wire from all of the product I put in it."

"Wow! Now *that's* what I was *really* hoping you looked like. Go on, baby, rip it off. Show me the real you," he says, laughing and reaching for my hand to pull me back up to sitting. This time, though, he leaves his fingertips on mine, shifting his touch from one finger to the next, like he's not sure if it's a good idea to hold onto me too tightly.

"You don't want to see the real me," I swallow, and look away.

"Sure I do," he says, and I can feel his eyes on me. They're burning, and I know I can't wait this one out.

"Tell me about Ty. How'd he get hurt?" His hand drops from mine, and he grips both sides of the bench underneath him, lifting his entire body up a few inches from the seat, like a gymnast. He lets out a big breath when he rests his arms again, folding his hands together in his lap. His gaze stays there the entire time.

"Ty was sixteen. I was twelve. We were at this big lake, near New Orleans. My grandparents owned some land there. Ty taught me to swim in that lake when we were real little. I mean, that place was like a second home. *So many* memories."

Watching him remember his youth is incredible. The way he talks about his brother just gushes with affection, and I'm envious he has something in his life that feels like that.

"Well, this one year, we were both feeling a little adventurous. There was this big ledge that I had watched some teenagers jump off of the year before, and the entire year after, all I did was talk about that ledge to my brother, begging him and making him promise to take me back there so we could jump off together. Only, when we climbed up on the ledge, I got really scared. I'm not really good at heights, and I started crying. Now, keep in mind, while twelve sounds kind of young to you right now, it's not that young for a boy who's crying. I felt like a loser, and my brother felt bad for me, so he said he'd go first and show me how easy it was. He, uh...he didn't come back up."

I'm covering my mouth because I don't want Nate to see the complete reaction on my face. I know I can't mask my eyes, and I can feel the tears pooling already, threatening to fall down my face.

"He injured his L2 and L3. No, I'll be blunt—he smashed them to pieces. I ran down the hill and screamed bloody murder. A few fishermen heard me and helped me pull him out. Getting to the hospital is all one giant blur, and I remember my thinking the entire time that my parents hated me. I hated me. Because I made my brother do something so stupid."

"But it wasn't your fault," I say, reaching for his hand on instinct. His breath pauses when my fingertips touch him, and he hooks his fingers into mine a little more this time.

"I know that now. Ty snapped me out of it pretty quickly. You may have noticed, my brother doesn't really do pity," he says, his eyes still watching our hands as they fight to hold on harder to one another.

"You're brother is pretty awesome," I say, waiting for his eyelashes to flick up and for his gaze to reach mine. But he keeps his eyes down, at our hands.

"Yeah, he is. I'm good at baseball because of him. He always wanted to play professionally, or at least in college. When he couldn't anymore, I made it my dream. I wanted to get here for him," he says, a faint smile pulling up at the corner of his mouth.

"I can't wait to see you play," I say, and his eyes finally meet mine, piercing my heart the second they do.

"You can come to practice. You know…if you want. Anytime," he looks down again, biting at his lip. I can tell he's embarrassed about asking me to come.

"I will," I say, and his smile grows bigger and he nods.

"Good, that's settled then." Nate's expression starts to change after that; soon his brow furrows, and he's chewing at the inside of his cheek. "I have to ask you something. But I'm scared of your answer."

My heartbeat stops completely when he says this. I know what he's going to ask, and I know I have to start to let my story out for others to hear. If I ever want friends—real friends—the kind that help you *heal,* then they need to see every part of me. "You want to know about Josh," I say, and his fingers stop moving with mine, his hand becoming strong and rigid. Nate just nods once and looks up at me, his mouth in a tight, flat line.

Deep breath. "Josh was my high school boyfriend. I guess you could call him my high school sweetheart or whatever. He was the only boy I ever…*you know,*" I can feel my face grow warm, but when I look at Nate he just smiles, urging me on. "Anyway, Josh played for my dad. He started on varsity as a freshman. He was tall and pretty strong. He was a pitcher."

"Typical pitcher," Nate says, rolling his eyes and laughing lightly. He lets go of my hand and leans back on his hands; I miss his touch instantly. "Sorry, I was just kidding." He pushes his foot into mine, letting me know he's sorry for the joke, and then he leaves it there.

"We dated for a year and a half. I mean, that first year, it wasn't really much. When you're fifteen, you pretty much kiss all the time, and that's about it."

"Yeah, you can skip the kissing part," Nate says, pushing his fingers in his ears. "La la la la." His little act makes me smile—I love that he's jealous, even if it's only pretend jealous.

"It was the last day of school our sophomore year, and we were all in the cafeteria, signing yearbooks. All of a sudden, there was shooting. There was a man in all black, wearing a ski mask. He was in his twenties, and he didn't even go to our school—never did. People were screaming and climbing over one another to get to the exits, but we were right in the middle. We always sat in the middle—it was *our* table."

I'm crying now, and my body is shaking a little. I haven't told this story out loud to anyone other than the investigators, my parents and Ross, and at this very moment, I would give anything to rewind time and take it all back. I want to share it with Nate though. I need to, so he'll understand why I am the way I am, and why I'm not the kind of girl you think is beautiful and that you flirt with on a baseball field in the middle of the night.

"You can tell me," he says, reaching for my hands again, holding them tightly within his, his grip on my wrists unwavering.

I close my eyes, and when I squeeze them shut, the last of my tears slide down my cheeks, coming to rest on my collarbone under the warmth of Nate's shirt.

"The man, his name was Thomas. He was suffering from a psychotic break—thought there was a plot against him, and somehow it involved our high school. Josh...he...he put himself *over* me. The man shot Josh in the head, and he ended up with severe brain damage. My best friend died right in front of me. Her name was Betsy. She was the first one Thomas shot, and she was one of two people who didn't survive. The other was a teacher, Mrs. Sharring. She was going to retire."

Nate doesn't speak any more. He doesn't ask any more questions, even though I know he must have dozens. He just reaches up to touch my face, and slowly slides the remainder of my tears away, then he tucks the few strands of my hair that are blowing across my face behind my ear.

"That's why I never know how to answer that question," I say, looking away from him, because I know if I look in his eyes I'm going to fall in love.

"What question is that?" he says, his voice soft and gentle.

"Is Josh still my boyfriend?" I say, my eyes letting the lights in the distance blur together out of focus. "He stopped being *Josh* the second the bullet cut through part of his brain. He's on feeding tubes, and he can't talk or do anything for himself. Even his parents are ready for him to die. I know that sounds awful, but he's come close so many times that they're just there now. You know, mentally?"

"I'm so sorry, Rowe," Nate says, and I turn to look at him, his face so honest and forgiving. I can tell with this one look that he would give anything to take what I'm feeling away from me.

"Thanks," I say, allowing myself to stare long into his eyes, the next round of tears lining up, but my will holding them in. And it happens all at once—just looking at him, I fall in love. But it doesn't matter—because I can belong to no one.

Chapter 11

Rowe

I told him.

Miss you,

~ Rowe

Chapter 12

Nate

For an hour, we sat there in the dugout—completely quiet. I wasn't going to go home until she said she was ready. And I wasn't going to ask her anything else until she was ready to tell it.

When the groundskeepers started showing up, we left, not wanting to have to deal with *breaking in*. We were quiet all the way back to the dorm, but somewhere during the walk, her fingers found mine again, and I held them tightly until the elevator opened to our floor.

Then—it was like she disappeared. Cass says she's been in the library all week. But I don't know. Knowing what I know about Rowe's past now, I get the feeling places like libraries are hard for her. I understand why she wasn't hip on eating in the cafeteria, why she likes to sit in corners, why she's skittish and nervous all the time.

My parents are coming up for the weekend, and they have extra tickets in the nice seats—the expensive ones—at tonight's football game. Cass is coming, and there's one more seat open. I really want Rowe to fill it.

"Dude, I am so sick of your moping around. Come with me," Ty says, grabbing one of my shoes from the end of my bed and throwing it into the hallway.

"Awe man, I was comfy. Why'd you do that?" I say, pulling myself up from my bed to a sitting position, slipping the one shoe still in my possession on my right foot.

"Because I know you. You like things in order, and your shoe hanging out there in that hallway is going to drive you bat-shit crazy." His smile is smug, but he's right. I've always been a neat freak. And I hate only having one shoe on my foot now. I follow him into the hall and reach for my sneaker, but before I get there, he blocks me and scoops it up, cradling it like a football.

"Come on. Give it to me," I beg.

"Oh you can have it. Down there," he says, tossing it to the other end of the hallway. With a *clunk!* it hits the wall near

Rowe's room. I roll my eyes at him and limp on one foot to their door. Ty is behind me, so the option of turning around is not an *option* at all.

Cass opens the door and smiles at Ty. "Why Nate, what a surprise. Please, come on in." She's acting weird, but when I see her wink at Ty and notice Rowe's legs folded up, and her face looking down while her ear buds are tucked in her ears, I understand.

I'd hate them both for tricking me, but I'm really glad they trapped her in one place for me—finally. I take a deep breath, walk over to her bed, and jump onto it so my legs are stretched out long and I'm sitting next to her. She startles, covering her heart, and pulling the headphones from her ears—which instantly makes me feel bad. Rowe is not the kind of girl you startle, and I get that now.

"Sorry, didn't realize your music was up so loud. Thought you heard me," I say, hoping my stupid grin will earn me forgiveness. "Whatcha listening to?"

"The Black Keys," she says, her ear buds still clutched in her hands, and her arms stiff.

"Mind?" I ask, reaching my hand toward hers. She hands me one of the earpieces, and I tuck it in, at first a little surprised by how loud it is. Damn, it's a wonder she isn't deaf. She watches me with her brow pinched for a few seconds before finally putting the other end in her ear.

"What are you working on?" My voice so loud that Ty and Cass turn to look at me and then start laughing. "Sorry. Apparently Rowe is hard of hearing, because she has this thing set to, like, seven thousand."

"It only goes to thirty. You're being hyperbolic," Rowe says, a hint of her smile creeping in.

"So vocabulary, then? That's what we're working on?" I ask, challenging her sass with my own.

She holds my gaze for a while, her eyes shutting until she squints at me. I think she's trying to intimidate me, but I just mimic her face, squaring myself with her until our noses touch. When I do, her lips twist into a smile.

82

"I'm working on art history. I had to pick a painting and write about how it made me feel," she says, scooting her notebook over to rest part of it on my leg. She wants me to see her notes, and I've never wanted to read an assignment more.

"Okay, which one did you pick?" I ask, reaching for the full notebook and bringing it to my lap. My hand grazes hers when I do, and the feel of it almost makes me want to hand it back to her—just to reach for it again.

"I picked this one." When she leans forward, her shirt lifts a little; I notice a few deep red scars along her side. They surprise me, but I don't want her to know I see them. I move my eyes to the notes on my lap before she turns to face me. She opens her book to a painting of a woman wearing a pearl earring. I recognize this one, and it feels like it fits her, not that I know a damn thing about art.

"That's pretty," I say, and she laughs. "What? I mean...the dude—it was a dude painter, right?" She nods, still laughing. "Okay, well, the dude picked nice colors, and her eyes are all symmetrical and crap. She doesn't look like a stick figure, but a real person. Sort of. Yeah, so I'd hang it up."

She's laughing harder now, and it's beautiful. Ty and Cass are lost in their own world, cuddling on Cass's bed. I take a risk, and lean in, kissing her quickly on her cheek. Her laughter stops immediately, and her eyes go wide. "Don't, Nate," she says, her smile completely gone now. *Well, shit.*

"Sorry. You're really pretty when you laugh, and a man can't be held responsible for how he reacts to you laughing. You should be mindful of that. You could end up getting kissed by waiters at restaurants, professors, frat guys. No, wait. No frat guys. Just ugly waiters and *old* professors."

She's smiling again, not as big, but she's not putting a wall up. *Phew.*

"Do you want to read why *I* like the 'pretty' painting?" she says, quoting the word *pretty* just to mock me. I love that she does it. I suck in my bottom lip and study her, just like she did to me moments before.

"Yeah. I do," I say, flipping her notebook over, and scooting down to lay my head on her pillow. Her breath stops when I settle in, but eventually she moves down too, so she can look along with me while I read. Every single hair on my arm is stretching to touch her. But my kiss went horribly wrong, so I'm content to *almost* touch her for now.

The Girl with a Pearl Earring, by Johannes Vermeer.

"Right! I remember this one. They made a movie about it or something." I sound so uneducated. My mom's an artist—which, you'd think would make me more attuned to art, but instead, I just blocked it out. It just wasn't in my wheelhouse. I'm more numbers, finance, and marketing. Our dad runs an accounting firm, and I take after him, so the creative side of my brain was sort of stunted.

I look to my right to see her lying next to me, smiling, and I have to take a deep breath to remind myself what I'm doing here. "Sorry. Reading now," I grin, and then she nestles in closely, her chin on my shoulder while she watches my eyes follow the lines on her paper. I feel every tiny breath she takes, and time actually stops. My god, I have never wanted to kiss a girl more in my life.

I know she feels my chest puff with air when I have to take a deep breath just to calm down, because she backs away a few inches to give me space. But now that I know what that feels like, I'm not sure my shoulder will ever feel complete again.

"You're not reading. Is it that *bad*?" she asks.

"No. I uh. You were. I'm reading," I finally say, and I shuffle the notebook against my chest for a better view.

I'm the girl in this painting. Not literally, but I identify with her. It is the only painting that stopped me completely, and I know it's because when I look into her eyes, I see myself. She's hungry, but she's bound by duty. Every part of her body is cloaked, at least from what you see. Her head is covered, and her bodice as well. But she bothers to put on this one pearl earring, sort of a rebellion to the path she's on, almost like a warning flair for someone. She's begging to be saved. And her eyes are looking right at me, like she's asking me to save her. And her mouth is barely open, about to tell me her secrets, but there is never enough time. Instead, we're stuck—the girl and I—at this juncture. I have to decide if I want to break her free. And she has to decide if she wants to let me. And every time I open the book and look at the page, we do the same dance all over again.

Rowe is staring at me. I may not know art, but I'm pretty sure there's a reason Rowe made me read this. I'm just not sure if she wants me to *break her free* or if she's warning me—if I pursue her, I'll be stuck in a circle that never ends.

"It's good," I say, pulling myself to sit up, just needing to break the electricity firing from my arm to hers.

"Yeah?" she says, closing her book and reaching for the notebook, her fingers staying clear of mine this time.

"Yeah, I mean, it's probably like a B. You didn't really talk about the pretty colors and choice of oil versus acrylic, but it's all right," I tease, and she purses her lips, fighting against her smile before finally smacking me in the chest with her notebook.

"I can live with a B. I'm considering it done then," she says, standing and putting her folder and book into her backpack. I notice she's putting physical distance between us, and it makes me uneasy.

"So, my parents are here this weekend. They're taking us to the football game tonight, and we, uh…we have an extra ticket. Cass is coming. Maybe…you wanna come?" I ask her when her back is to me, and I'm still a stuttering mess.

"You're such a pussy," Ty says, reminding me he's still in the room. "Rowe, Nate wants you to come with us. He's been a mopey douchebag all week because he was afraid you'd say *no*. Please, for the love of all that is holy, come with us and meet my parents so I won't live in hell for another day."

I'm blinking and staring at my brother's back as he goes right back to whispering with his girlfriend. Once again, I wish I had an ounce of his confidence. I shift my focus to Rowe next, and catch her chewing on her lip, her hand on her hip. Crap! A football game is a pretty big deal for her. I didn't think, and when she looks at me, I wince and mouth, "I'm sorry."

"I'll come," she says, her smile tight, and her arms hugging her body. I notice she does that a lot. I think it's her tell, her signal that she's uncomfortable. She doesn't really want to do this, but she's going for me. If I were a good person, I'd let her off the hook. But I'm selfish, and I want her with me.

"My parents have box seats, so we'll be in a suite," I say, standing from her bed and leaning against her desk. She relaxes at that news, and I'm glad it helps.

"What time?"

"We'll walk over around six. Does that work?" I say, checking my watch, which says three thirty.

"Ugh, I guess that'll do. But you have to go now. I mean, if I'm meeting parents, I need time to make myself all glittery and shiny," she smirks.

"Oh, and make sure you put a lot of shit in your hair so it's all crunchy and tangled," I laugh. Cass and Ty just stare at us like we're insane, but we don't break our character and hold in our laughs. *This* is one of those jokes just between us—something that's *ours.* And I'll take it, however small and insignificant it may be.

Rowe walks me to the door, and I keep my hands in my pockets, not able to look her directly in the eyes, because every time I do, I feel like I should be kissing her. But she's made it clear that I can't—at least not today. I'm pretty sure I'll keep trying though.

Rowe

"I blame you," I say to Cass, who is sitting on the edge of Paige's bed, directing me into the closet to try on a few of her outfits.

"Blame me for what? No, I hate that one. Go try the blue one," she says, shoving an orange sundress in my arms, and turning me back to face the closet.

"For *this.* For me having to go to a football game and meet parents." I can hear her laughing behind the door. Every dress I try on looks like I'm trying too hard. And nothing covers me quite enough.

86

"This one looks ridiculous," I say, as I open the door. Cass studies me for a minute, and then nods in agreement.

"Something's not right. Why don't you just wear jeans and a shirt, like you always do?" I know she doesn't mean for that to sound the way it does, but what she says sort of gets my own point across. *Jeans...*like I *always* wear. I'm so tired of it all. Tired of wearing the same clothes that have been in my closet since I was a sophomore. Time stood still the day that gunman came into everyone's life, and my clock never started ticking again.

Letting my shoulders frump to my sides, I sigh, and slouch down on the bed next to Cass. "I'm not good at this," I say.

"What do you mean? Paige would *kill* to be the one to get Nate's attention," she says, just as Paige walks in, and my gut twists wondering what she heard and what she's going to say.

"Paige would kill for what? For you two chickadees to get your asses off my bed?" I stand immediately, smoothing out the wrinkle left behind on her bedspread. But Cass lies down, spreading her arms to the side, wallowing. She actually *wallows*.

"Your bed is always so much more comfortable than mine," she says, rolling to one side and smelling Paige's comforter. "And your sheets are softer. What the hell?"

"Mom and Dad like me better," Paige says, sticking her tongue out. Normally, I would think someone was kidding when they did that, but for some reason when Paige does it, she seems serious.

"Sure they do," Cass says, rolling her eyes while she lifts herself back to sitting. She keeps her eyes on her sister, watching her touch-up her makeup, until finally Paige can't stand her attention any longer.

"What?" she says, twisting to face her sister with her hands on her hips.

"Rowe, I'm afraid we're going to need her help," Cass says, looking at me. *Oh god no!*

"My help with what?" Paige asks, turning her attention back to her own reflection.

"First, you have to promise me you're not going to get pissed," Cass says, and I feel like I'm watching the world's most cautious tennis match. And I'm the ball.

Paige puts the lid back on her lip-gloss and slides her lips together, puckering closely to the mirror while her eyes move to look at Cass in the reflection. "Pretty sure I can't promise that. Just a hunch," she says, holding her sister's gaze and gripping the edge of the sink.

"Nate invited Rowe to come to the game with me and Ty tonight...to meet their parents. She doesn't have anything nice to wear, and I'm not good at makeovers, so we've pretty much just been flailing in our attempts for the last two hours, and we have to leave in like thirty minutes," Cass says, letting out an exhausted sigh when she's done.

Paige doesn't say a word. She doesn't even blink. But her eyes slowly move from Cass to me in the mirror. I let her study me, lifting my shoulders into a tiny shrug and sucking my top lip in against my teeth. Paige and I are worlds apart, and I can't say I've warmed to her. But I wasn't trying to win some contest over Nate. I can't even *truly* be with him.

The longer she looks at me, the more uncomfortable I get, and I keep waiting for Cass to break the silence. But she doesn't. Finally, after seconds that felt like minutes, Paige pushes back from the sink and spins around.

"Stand up," she says, her chin in her hand. "Jewel tones. You're definitely jewel tones."

She spins around, and starts thumbing through the overstuffed hangers on her side of the closet. I look at Cass when she does and mouth "Jewel tones?" Cass just shrugs and nods toward Paige, telling me to pay attention. "She's good at this," she whispers.

"How do you feel about jumpers?" She's holding up a one-piece cotton...*thing*...that is like a tank top and shorts sewn together. I scrunch my nose at it, and she drops her posture with a heavy sigh. "Fine. No jumpers."

She works through several more hangers, but I notice there's one she keeps coming back to. Finally, she just stops and looks down, her hand on a deep-blue cotton dress. "Come here," she orders, so I slide my feet toward her. "Turn," she says, flipping me so I'm now facing Cass, my back to her.

If I weren't so shell-shocked from her helping me, I might have seen it coming. But without warning, Paige unzips the back of the dress I'm wearing, and the garment falls to the floor. My mother, my doctor and the surgeons who fixed me are the only ones who have ever seen my scars. Cass and Paige are both seeing them now. They're too big to conceal—running from my hip, up to my right ribcage: deep divots, where bullet fragments penetrated my skin and lodged themselves into my body, and cuts where emergency surgeons had to go in and remove them. I can't bring myself to look Cass in the eyes, and their silence is making me start to shake.

"Here," Paige says, turning me to face her head on. My eyes are glued open, wide, as I turn; when I finally square myself with her, I'm expecting to see the disgust and judgment on her face. Paige is, perhaps, the *last* person I would ever want to see this. I try to keep my gaze focused on the clothes beyond her shoulder when I face her, but she reaches her hand up to my chin and tilts my eyes to meet hers.

"This..." she swallows hard, and then her lips curl into a soft, tight smile—her eyes sympathetic, and, for the first time since I've met her, real, "this is my favorite dress. It's long enough that you can sit at a game and not have to worry, but it will show off your shoulders and really accentuate your legs and the color of your eyes. Arms up."

She slides the dress along my arms and over my head, pulling the draping of the skirt down quickly over my scars without ever once mentioning them. There are a few small snaps along the back, and she pushes them in place before she reaches her hands into my hair and starts to gather the waves into her hands. She moves me closer to the mirror as she does this, and then she meets my eyes. "You should wear your hair up. Like this. It's pretty," she says, giving me a quiet but reassuring face. I'm unable to stop my eyes from watering, so I wipe the palm of my hand up both cheeks and sniffle.

"Thanks," I say, and she reaches for my hand with her free one, squeezing it once before letting go.

Chapter 13

Nate

"Yeah Mom, we'll just meet you there. You're already parked. It would take you and Dad a long time to walk over here...Okay, love you." My parents wanted to come see our room, but it's still pink. In fact, Ty and I decided just to leave it pink—and, just to show Cass and Rowe how much it *doesn't* bother us, Ty went to the Target in the city and bought Barbie comforters and pillows for our beds.

I am actually nervous about tonight...and Rowe. I can't help but feel like maybe I bullied Rowe into going to the game tonight. Ty won't let me talk about it anymore though. He says I'm turning into a girl, and I kinda am.

September in Oklahoma is strange. It's pretty damn hot all day—and then at night, it's super cold. I'm usually okay with being cold, so I keep my shorts on with the black long-sleeved shirt Rowe wore the other night. It smells like her, and I may never wash it again. Fuck, I am a girl.

We're walking from our end of the hall to theirs when they walk out their door, and my god...

"Pick up your chin, bro. Your girl is smokin'," Ty says, and I just smile because yes, she is. She's wearing this blue dress that hugs her body and sways around her legs when she walks. Her feet are in flip-flops, but her hair is up, drawing my eyes to her bare shoulders and neck. I want to be a vampire.

The closer she gets to me, the more she blushes, and her hands are clinging to the wallet and thin sweater in her hands. She's going to get cold later, and I should probably tell her to grab something a little warmer. But I don't. *This* is a strategic move on my part.

"Hi," she says, almost a whisper, her eyes looking down. My heart is pounding so loudly—I'm convinced everyone around me can hear it. Rowe and I haven't talked much since the night on the ball field, and it feels like we're starting over a bit. I want to hold her hand in the elevator, so I make it my challenge.

We step in, and Ty pulls Cass down on his lap; Rowe smiles when she watches the two of them. I wonder where Cass has been my brother's whole life, because watching them just seems right. They've been dating for three weeks, but it feels like Cass has been a fixture with him for forever.

As the door closes, I slide my hand along the bar in the back until it bumps into Rowe's, and when she doesn't move away, I loop my pinky in with hers. Sparing a glance at her, I see her lip twitch into a faint smile. That's a relief, because I'm not letting go now until I have to.

Rowe and Cass look more like sisters than Cass and Paige. Both are wearing their hair pulled high on their heads, and even though they're both in dresses, they look like they just rolled in from the beach. "You look pretty," I say, leaning closer to Rowe as we walk through the main lobby, and I take advantage of my nearness by threading my next finger through hers.

"You're not going to believe this, but this is Paige's dress," she says, grinning and pulling up the side of the dress to hold it out a little.

"Wow. I didn't think she had anything without bling."

"I can't believe you know what bling is," Rowe says, smirking at me and raising her eyebrows.

"Oh, you haven't seen what Ty and I have done to the place. We've gone full *bling*," I say, making her laugh. I love it when she laughs—even her teeth are freakin' hot. I bet she had braces growing up.

"Full bling, huh? I'm gonna need to see this," she says, and I tuck that to the back of my mind for later, reminding myself that Rowe wants to see my room.

Other than the fact that their sons have decided to come to this school, my parents have no association with McConnell whatsoever, But looking at their tailgate set-up as we walk up—and the crowd that's hanging out with them—you would think they were alumni super-boosters with buildings named after them.

"What is all this?" I ask, tugging on the McConnell fold-up chairs, sitting under the McConnell canopy, and next to the McConnell plates and napkins.

"We thought we'd leave the chairs and tent with you guys. Just something fun," my mom says, leaning in to kiss me and noticeably eyeing the girl standing behind me.

"Your mother just likes a reason to shop. We couldn't even fit the tent in the damn rental car. I had to tie it to the roof," my dad says, reaching over to shake my hand, and eyeing Cass and Rowe behind me just as mom did.

"Mom, Dad, this is Rowe and Cass," I say, reaching back to regain the fragile grip I had on Rowe's hand. She grips me a little harder now, and I can tell she's nervous.

"Cass, we have heard absolutely *nothing* about you," Dad says, pushing his sunglasses into the pocket on his shirt, and for a moment, Cass looks mortified. "That must mean you're pretty special. We only hear the breakup stories, and we used to get one of those a week."

"It was touch-and-go there for a while," Cass says, and Ty's face looks panicked. "I painted his room pink." And Ty's smile is back quickly.

Dad laughs, reaching over to shake Cass's hand, our mom waiting her turn behind him. "Ah, so that explains why you didn't want us to come up to the room."

"It was Rowe's idea," Cass says, shifting Dad's attention to Rowe, who is manically snapping and unsnapping the button on her wallet she's so nervous to meet my parents.

"Remind me to consult you when these two short-sheet my bed over the holidays. And fill my car with packing peanuts. And paint my fingernails with red Magic Marker while I'm napping." Rowe laughs lightly when she shakes my dad's hand, and I can see her relax just a little.

"I'll make you a manual on how to deal with them," she says, and I can't help but move closer to her and put my arm around her. At first, I'm afraid she's going to shrug me away, but instead, she reaches for my fingertips with her hand and holds on.

92

"Rowe, so nice to meet you," my mom says, giving me a wink from the side, letting me know she approves. My mom likes *my type* too.

"Thanks for inviting me, Mr. and Mrs. Preeter," Rowe says when she shakes my mom's hand, her voice wavering; I can actually hear her pulse racing through her vocal cords. My mom holds onto her hand and covers it with her other one, looking Rowe right in the eyes.

"Please, it's just Cathy and Dave. And it's our pleasure," Mom says. I see Rowe whisper my parents' names to herself when they turn away, like she's trying to memorize them, and I almost lean in to kiss her on the cheek when she does, but I catch myself.

McConnell is more of a *baseball* school, it would seem. By the third quarter, the McConnell Bulls were trailing the Miller Pirates by four touchdowns, and the stadium was only a third of the way full. I sat next to Ty, and the girls sat in front of us. I was stuffed—one of the nice things about sitting in the box was free food, and good food, too. Not the cafeteria shit I've been eating.

I can tell Cass and Rowe are arguing about something. Not a *serious* fight or anything, but Rowe definitely seems unhappy. I nudge Ty and nod toward them; he just shrugs. I'm trying not to eavesdrop, but I hear bits and pieces.

"Where am I supposed to stay?" Rowe whispers. Cass says something back, but I can't tell what it is.

"Cass...*pleeeeease?* Can't you go there?" More whispering, and Rowe turns to look behind her—just enough, that I jump and quickly pretend I'm intensely watching the blowout happening on the field.

When the third quarter ends, Cass gets up from her seat and Rowe slumps down in hers. I watch carefully as Cass walks to the other side of Ty, whispering in his ear, and soon he's backing up in his chair and Cass is grabbing her purse from a table.

"We're heading back. Mom, Dad—see you guys tomorrow at dinner?" My mom leans in and kisses Ty on the top of his head and shakes Cass's hand again, walking them to the suite door before returning to her seat. Rowe is sitting alone directly in front of me, and she's getting smaller with every second.

"This seat taken?" I climb over the back of the seat Cass left open, feeling like an idiot, but just dying to get closer to her. She just smiles and looks to the field. "We don't have to stay you know. My parents don't care. My dad's firm has a branch here. That's how they got the seats. They didn't pay for them."

"I want to stay 'til the end," she says, her smile fake and stiff.

"Sure," I say, sliding my feet up to rest on the bar in front of us. I keep my hands in my own lap, because Rowe is hugging herself again. I'm pretty sure I know what she and Cass were fighting about, but I want her to say it. I don't want to be the jerk who pushes her to spend the night in my room when she clearly doesn't want to.

"Paige called. She's staying at the Delta house all weekend. She's probably going to move out in a week or two. They like her." Rowe keeps her eyes on the field when she talks. I try to keep mine there, too, but I slip every few seconds to catch a glimpse of her fidgeting hands and shaking leg.

"Oh. Well...I guess I'm glad Paige has found her people?" I don't know what to say, and I can't even make a funny joke.

"Ty is spending the night in our room." I gathered this much, and I am doing cartwheels inside at the thought of Rowe coming home with me. But I want her to *want* to be there. This forced feeling emanating from her body feels really sucky.

"Well, there's always my friend the lounge sofa," I say, finally turning to her so I can see how she reacts. When she doesn't, I'm even more confused—either I've offended her by not offering my place or she's genuinely indifferent about the lounge sofa.

"Can I borrow a blanket? And maybe some sweat pants or something? I don't think I want to go back to my room if I can help it," she says, her lips twisting and her eyes still not quite on me but looking down.

"Sure. You can borrow a blanket. And I have some clothes." This sucks.

Rowe

We walk back to his room, and the entire time I battle myself internally, trying to get the courage to ask if I can stay with him. My body wants to be there, and part of me was actually a little excited when Cass put me in this position. But the other part of me feels sick at the thought, unsure of what it means if I spend the night with a guy. And I wonder what Nate would expect.

"Here, come on in. You can use my new blanket," he says, flipping on the lights and reminding me that his room is still pink. It makes me smile. I round the corner and move to his bed, where he gathers up a sparkly Barbie blanket.

"Ahhh, *bling*. I get it now," I say, pretty damn impressed.

"I told you. Preeters don't do embarrassed. We embrace," he says, reaching in the crack between his bed and wall to pull out a fluffy, purple, heart-pillow. I take it in my arms and hold it, and he smiles proudly. I keep waiting for his flaw, something to make me *not* want him. But everything he does has the opposite effect.

"Here, you can wear this. You can change in our closet if you want. I promise, I won't look." He covers his eyes but leaves cracks between his fingers, which makes me laugh.

I take the stack of clothes from him and flip on his closet light, shutting the door. He gave me a long-sleeved gray McConnell baseball shirt, which I slip over my head first, pulling the dress straps from my shoulders underneath. I was hoping the dress would slip down my waist, but the two snaps are holding it snug in place, and no matter how many ways I bend and stretch, I can't reach them.

"Everything okay?" I've been in here for several minutes now, and my pulse is racing so fast that I'm starting to sweat.

"Uhhhhh," I say, laying my forehead flat against the door. *Breathe, just breathe.*

"Sweat pants throwing you for a loop?" he chuckles.

My entire body is shaking and my fingers are numb as I twist the closet door handle and crack the door open. When I look out, he's sitting on the edge of his bed, but he gets up quickly and comes closer, putting his hand back over his eyes, not cheating this time.

"It's my dress. I can't reach the snaps."

"Oh." He stands still for a few seconds, still averting his eyes, and I love that he doesn't want to take advantage of me. He's like a straight-A student in the college of gentlemen.

"It's okay. I have your shirt on. If you can just...I don't know, maybe lift up the back and pop the snaps?"

I can hear him swallow, and then he slowly pulls his hand from his eyes, careful to keep his stare on my face. "Yeah, I can do that."

I turn around and move my ponytail over my neck. A few seconds later, I feel his hand carefully lift the bottom of the shirt, dragging it slowly upward. When he gets to the snaps, he stops, not pulling it any further. It's impossible for his fingers not to touch my bare skin when he reaches in and tugs the fabric apart, and that small, gentle caress sends my heart into overdrive.

The dress starts to slip; I try to catch it, but its weight brings it down my legs quickly. Nate backs away, moving his hands to his side; I turn to face him, pulling the bottom of his long shirt down to cover my upper thighs. He's not looking at my eyes any more.

"Thanks," I say, kicking the dress back into the closet and shutting the door again. "I'll be right out."

I pull the sweatpants on quickly when I shut the door, and I reach down to gather Paige's dress, folding it as best as I can. Everything feels urgent. Getting out of this closet feels urgent. Getting out of this room feels urgent. Forcing my eyes to close...*shit!* I don't have my Ambien.

When I open the door, I do my best to put on a grateful face. But just having realized that—not only will I be lying for hours on a sofa out in the open near the place people come and go freely all night long—but any hope of falling asleep tonight is moot, because I haven't slept without the aide of medicine for more than seven hundred days.

I pick up the rolled comforter and small heart-pillow from his chair, stuffing them under one arm and Paige's dress under the other. "Thanks. I'll…just bring these back in the morning, I guess?"

"Whenever. I mean, not sure how I'll sleep without Barbie, but…I'll manage," he smirks just enough to show a dimple on his right cheek.

I walk through his door and focus on putting one foot in front of the next, angry at myself for putting myself in this situation. The lounge door is closed, but not locked, so I slip inside, shutting it behind me again. The wall is completely windowed, but there is one sofa that is more in the corner, away from direct view. I breathe in deeply and head for it, first setting the pillow and dress on the study table, and then spreading the blanket out on the couch so I can climb inside and fold myself up—like a taco.

The couch is hard, and even Barbie can't soften it. There's a TV hung on the wall, but I don't see a remote sitting out anywhere, so eventually I give up and tuck myself in with the purple heart-pillow against my chest for protection. My eyes are wide, and my heart is miserable. Normally, when I feel like this, it's because I'm remembering Josh and how he looked when he picked me up for homecoming, or when he ran out to the baseball field, or when he waited for me by my locker. But right now, I'm thinking about Nate, and the feather-light touch of his hand on my back—and how it lit my body on fire.

"Come on," Nate says, hanging on to the open lounge door.

"Oh no, it's okay. I'm fine," I lie.

"No, you're not fine. You're stubborn. Now pick up Barbie and follow me, Thirty-three."

It feels different when I walk into Nate's room the second time. It's dark in here, just a small light from the barely-opened closet. I notice that Ty's blanket is now on his Nate's bed, which makes me wonder if he planned to just go to sleep—or if his motive was to wait me out until he had to come and get me like he did.

"You can sleep on Ty's bed if you want. I took his blanket. You know, save you from his cooties?" Dimples.

"Thanks," I smile, spreading Barbie out on Ty's mattress, and setting Paige's dress down on Nate's desk-chair. "Can I keep Hearty?"

"Oh. My. God. You named the pillow. Yes, you can keep Hearty," he says, rolling his eyes, but laughing enough that I know he's teasing.

"Says the man who calls his blanket Barbie," I tease back.

"If you're going to make fun of Barbie, you can sleep without a blanket, missy," he says, feigning to get up and pull the blanket from Ty's bed. I leap on the bed and gather the blanket in my arms quickly.

"No! No. I was kidding. I love Barbie. She and I are friends," I say, giggling. Since when do I giggle?

"Hmmmmm," he grumbles, laying back down, and pulling Ty's blanket up to his neck, his long legs hanging out of the bottom because it's too short. "I don't know how I feel about you and Barbie being friends."

It gets quiet after that, and I'm glad the room is as dark as it is. But I can still see his eyes. They're open, and they're watching me. I'm watching him. He's wearing the short-sleeved version of the shirt I'm wearing, and a pair of black basketball shorts, and everything about him has me wanting to be touched by him, a feeling that I fight and ignore, albeit poorly. We lie here in silence for almost fifteen minutes, each taking turns closing our eyes, trying to trick the other one into thinking we're asleep, and a few times we laugh quietly when we catch each other.

"You ever make wishes?" he says, out of nowhere. His voice breaks the thick silence, and it makes my heart jump. I think it would have jumped at hearing him anyhow.

"All the time," I say, thinking of the number of times I wished those bullets hit me instead of Josh and Betsy. "You?"

"Nah," he says, and I start to laugh, but I realize he isn't. "I just made my first one in years."

Breathe.

"Oh yeah? You want Barbie back?"

"No," he smiles. "I wished you were over here instead of there."

98

Oh.

More seconds pass, and I let them slip into minutes, my eyes unable to leave his. He didn't ask. He didn't come up with some transparent scheme. He was just honest—perfectly, beautifully, terrifyingly honest. We lie there for fifteen more minutes just looking at one another, this new *feeling* swallowing us both up whole, until Nate finally rolls to his back and then his other side, facing away from me.

More seconds. More minutes. I watch his body rise and fall with every breath, and it's constant and regular, but I know he's still awake. Being Cass's friend, being Paige's friend, even being Ty's friend—that's all part of healing. But what I'm about to do right now has nothing to do with my own personal growth and overcoming my trauma. Being Nate's friend was a level I left in the dust the second I made his acquaintance. And *right now* is about me, and the pounding in my chest, and the voice in my head telling me to take what I *want.*

"Nate?" I speak, my eyes shut tightly.

"Yeah?"

"Can I come over?" I open my eyes as soon as I speak—amazed the words left my lips.

He rolls back over to face me, lifting his blanket open, and I somehow find my balance and tiptoe to the other side of the room, lying down next to him, in the most amazingly safe place I've ever felt.

He's slow with his arm, pulling the top of the blanket over my shoulder and then reaching around the front of my body to pull me in close. He slides his other arm under my head for a pillow, and my head rests heavily on his bicep. I reach up and pull the tie from my hair, dropping it to the floor. Nate's hand reaches along my arm when I do, and then he runs his fingers up my neck and into my hair, scooping my heavy strands into a pile along my skin. He continues to run his fingers from my hairline to behind my ear, each stroke like a wave crashing over me, making my eyes feel heavy.

"Hey Nate?" I say, my voice barely a whisper.

"Mmmmm," he says, his nose pressed against the back of my head while he pulls me in closer, continuing to wind my hair through his fingers.

"You should make more wishes," I say.

"I just made, like, about twenty. But don't worry. I'm patient."

Every nerve in my body is tingling from whatever it is we're doing. *This* is no longer just flirting. This is *levels* beyond flirting. And I am about to fall asleep without the help of Ambien for the first time in months.

Chapter 14

Rowe

Even your favorite song in the entire world gets old when it's your ringtone and your mother keeps calling your phone—over and over and over. The first time, I reached to the floor and hit *ignore*. The next time I let it play through, and just kept my eyes on Nate's eyelids, waiting for him to wake up. When she called again, this time waking him completely, I knew I had to answer.

"Hi, Mom," I say, my lips pressed together tightly, and every nerve in my body firing with the realization that I am now talking to my mother while lying in the arms of the boy I met in college. I almost giggle because it's such a typical, normal thing to have happen. It's also one of those things I never thought would happen to me.

"Are you all right? You didn't answer right away," she says, her voice delving into that tone that says "I'm concerned about you, are you eating, should I book an appointment with Ross?"

"I'm fine, Mom. I was just away from my phone," I say.

When I roll my head over on Nate's arm to look at him, he mouths to me, "Liar," and starts to poke my ribs, trying his best to make me lose control.

"I wanted to go through the flight details with you for next weekend," she says. Somehow, I've already been away for three weeks. Those first few nights, I was obsessed with this date, knowing it was my reward for a milestone—my first trip home, a chance to back out of everything if I didn't think I could make it. Yet now, I don't want to go.

"Dad will pick you up when your flight gets in. I'll try to sit up so I can see you, okay?"

"Sure, that's fine." Everything that was seconds ago amazing and wonderful is now tense and uncomfortable and sad. I force myself to keep up the appearance of happy for the few minutes my phone conversation with my mom lasts, and I manage to end it without her questioning me again.

"Figured if I wanted to make a good impression on your mom when I meet her, I should probably not make sex jokes in the background of your phone call," Nate teases. All I hear is the word *sex*.

"Oh, you probably won't ever get to meet her," I say, trying to hide my reddening cheeks. I notice Nate's arms fall flat along his sides, and his smile fades. His playfulness suddenly is gone as he turns away from me, his jaw muscles flexing.

"I need to get my workout in. You can hang out here as long as you want," he says, pushing himself to the end of his bed and standing at the foot of it, his eyes never once landing on me.

"Something wrong?" My question comes out soft and timid, and I'm desperate to know what suddenly thrust so much distance between us.

Nate just stops at his closet door, his hand holding at the frame while his back is to me, and he takes a deep breath. "Nothing's wrong, Rowe. Really," he says, turning back to smile, but his lips not quite stretching the full distance of his face, and his eyes still not quite meeting mine. "My parents are taking me and my brother out to dinner tonight. You can come if you want. I'm sure Cass will be there."

The way he asks has me confused on how to answer. It almost sounds as if he feels obligated to invite me, and I don't want that. Maybe he's just worried about how I'll cope with a new restaurant.

While he's in his closet, I pull the blanket over his bed, smiling at the way it looks—pink frills and rainbows everywhere. I gather up the rest of my belongings and sit at the end of his bed, waiting for him. I don't mean to be looking, but when his body passes in front of the slightly open door, I can't help but see more of him than I'm probably supposed to—his abs just as defined as I remembered them from the first night I ran into him, and the muscular line of his torso diving deeper into a low-riding pair of sliding shorts that leave very little to the imagination. Seeing him—so much of him—is intimidating and has my pulse quickening.

"So, see ya later?" he says, finally standing at the door, his workout shorts on and a gray T-shirt in his hand. I blink, probably longer than I should, and the longer it takes me to respond, the more nervous I become. "Unless you're not up to it…"

"No, I'd love to. Sorry, I was…" I was just putting the finishing touches on my mental portrait of your body, like a pervert, that's what I was doing. Nate just smiles, but still not the complete smile from before. He comes closer, and when his feet are almost directly in front of me, I close my eyes, expecting the kiss that never comes. Instead he pats my head, like a little sister, and heads out for his morning workout.

Cass and Ty finally woke up around noon. I was hungry, and Nate didn't have anything to eat in his room, so I forced myself to visit the cafeteria alone. My body didn't react nearly as badly as I thought it would, but I still had to sit in the far corner, with my back pressed to the wall. I ate cereal, the box kind that you fold into a bowl, and I saved the box when I was done—my trophy for taking such a big step.

When I got back, my room was finally open, so I walked in and put my cereal bowl on the shelf by my desk.

"Saving up to win the prize?" Cass asks, pointing to the empty Sugar Loops box.

"Something like that," I smile.

"So, how was *your* night?" Cass wants details, and I know she's expecting my night to have been similar to hers. But I know it wasn't. It probably wasn't even close. But in many ways, I think it was probably a million times better. "Does that smile on your face mean what I think it means?"

"Noooooo," I say, tossing Paige's dress at her. "We just…*slept.* But it was really, really, *really* nice."

"Hmmmmmm, sounds really, really, *really* boring," she says, over exaggerating her frown to emphasize her disappointment. "Wanna hear about my night?"

"Oh god no!" I must be completely distracted by this new experience of having a girlfriend, because for some reason I start to change out of Nate's clothes right in front of her, not even attempting to hide the hideous marks on my body. It's not until I work my own pair of shorts up my hips and button them that I turn to face her and notice her staring. It would only make it worse to grab Nate's shirt or my blanket and cover myself quickly, so I don't. Instead, I just freeze, letting my arms drop to my side and turning even more so she can truly see.

"They've gotten better," I say, the strength in my voice surprising even me.

"What happened?" she asks, folding up her legs to sit comfortably on her own bed. I think that's one of the things I like most about Cass, the little I know of her so far. She's blunt—in a way that cuts through the bullshit in life. Most people would dance around the questions, not wanting to hurt my feelings. But I'm starting to realize all of the hiding in the shadows does far more damage to my feelings than just showing the world who I really am.

I run my fingers over the deep divots a few times, sucking in my lips to keep myself together while I let the memories flood through me. Picking up my tank top, I slide it over my head slowly, pulling the bottom down to meet my shorts and hiding the proof of my story again.

"Two years ago, there was a shooting at my school. You ever hear of Hallman High?" This marks the second time I've told this story *ever*. With Nate, I was more cautious and emotional. But things are different with Cass. With her, I'm seeking an ally, someone who can explain away my weirdness when it comes unexpectedly—and it will come. It will come in droves.

"I think so. This sounds awful—but there are so many school shootings, I sort of get them mixed up," she says, her face showing an apology that she doesn't remember every detail of mine.

"It's okay. Mine wasn't one of the remarkable ones. I mean, it was to me of course, but not the rest of the world."

I reach into my bottom drawer and grab the photos I hid there the other day, then join Cass on her bed. Just as I did with Nate, I recant the basics—mental illness, man with a gun, our cafeteria, Josh and Betsy.

"This is Josh and me at the winter formal," I say, showing her my favorite picture of the both of us. I like this one because we look so much older than 16. Maybe I like pretending we got to grow up together after all.

I have fewer pictures of Betsy, but I show her the few I've kept. Betsy was my other half, the girl who *really* knew me. We met in kindergarten and were inseparable ever since.

"So Betsy didn't make it?" Cass asks, handing the small stack of photographs back to me. I shake my head *no* and look down at them in my lap—all that's left of the two most important people in my life summed up in seven pictures.

"Wow. Well that's..." she pauses for a few seconds, bobbing her head side to side while thinking of the perfect word. "Sucky. That's just sucky."

Her choice makes me laugh, and laugh hard. Because yeah, it is sucky, and that's really the only perfect word there is for my story. "Oh my god, it is *soooooo* sucky!" I say, putting on a Valley-Girl tone. Mocking my own tragedy feels good, and I wish I had done it sooner.

"Riiiight? I mean, like, oh my god, what a lame way to start your summer!" Cass is speaking Valley Girl with me, and I'm laughing so hard my stomach hurts.

"Totes!" I say back to her in between laughs. We're rolling on our backs, tears falling from the creases of our eyes when Paige comes in.

"Oh my god, so like, Paige, do you totally want to hear my sucky story?" I say, barely able to finish my sentence, I'm laughing so hard.

"Uhm, I guess?" Paige says, moving to the closet to hang her sweater on the hook on the back of the door.

"Like, when I was sixteen, this guy came to my school and shot my boyfriend and best friend. I mean, right? *Who does that?*" Cass is holding her stomach she's laughing so hard, her face turning red, and I'm almost gurgling in between my speech.

Paige steps out from the closet, her eyes wide and centered on me; I realize she's not really *in* on the same joke Cass and I are, and then I realize that yeah, I'm probably being really insensitive and maybe a little bit crazy right now. But I don't fucking care.

"Rowe, if you're making this up, I swear to god I will smack you. That's not nice, and it isn't funny," she says, her hand on her hip, which only makes my laugh break through again.

"Oh, Paige. If only this were a joke," I say, my tears half from laughing and half from the truth, and the escape feels euphoric.

Once I calmed myself down, I shared the photos with Paige, too. She was a lot more serious in her response than Cass, more like my parents and others from my hometown. She was sympathetic and kind, but I think I kind of liked Cass's response better. I need more people to treat me like that— *normal.*

Paige told us she was moving out next week to the Delta house, and I could tell Cass was happy about that. I think she relished the idea of *not* being a twin for a while, not that there was anything remotely similar about her and her sister. Surprisingly, though, Paige's departure made me feel a little sad. She was more than her appearances, and I felt like I was just getting to know the real her.

Paige left in the late afternoon for a date—apparently she moved on quickly from her crush on Nate to a member of the football team. For the last hour, I've been sitting still, watching Cass try on outfits for the dinner I was half-invited to, and when Cass realizes I'm not getting ready, she questions me.

"Are you just going like that?" She motions to my shorts and plain blue tank top.

"I'm not sure Nate really wants me to go. He was sort of...I don't know, weird about it," I say.

"Hmmmm," Cass says, reaching for my hand to pull me up to a stand in front of her. When I'm fully up, she slings my arm forward, pushing me toward my clothes in the closet and slapping my butt while I pass by. "Here's the deal. I don't know what you mean by *weird*, but Nate had about a two-hour prep conversation with Ty and me the other day trying to get up the balls to ask you to dinner. So if you don't show up, we're going to feel like failures. Now put something pretty on, and hurry, we're late."

I love Cass. It's decided; she is now my best friend.

Chapter 15

Nate

Usually a really hard workout helps me get rid of the desire to punch something, but not this time. It's still here, a sense of balled up energy stemming from my bicep and rolling all the way through my fist. I don't know why I care so much and so fast, but I do.

When Rowe said she didn't think I'd ever meet her parents, it was like an emotional car wreck went off in my chest. It was a nothing statement to her, but to me it had been so damned significant.

I'm just not that guy, the guy who keeps things in compartments and satisfies urges and doesn't get them tangled with the rest of the shit going on in his heart and his head. I tried being that guy for a few months, and it sucked. I felt like an asshole. I *was* an asshole. My tour through the world of asshole-ness was brief—nope, not for me.

"Rowe coming?" Ty asks, holding his arm out for me to button the cuffs on his shirt. We always dress up for Sunday dinner with my parents. My mom always insisted on it when we were kids and at home, and it just sort of became the tradition—even if we're dining out.

"Don't know, don't care," I say, not lifting my eyes to meet his and just focusing on the button in front of me. There's a soft knock on the door behind me, and her voice soon follows.

"Okay to come in?" Rowe asks, her words pushing the corner of my lips up into a smile against my wishes.

"Don't care my ass," Ty whispers, leaning forward. "Rowe, I know this probably isn't appropriate, but *damn* girl. You look hot!"

Her giggle pushes my lips up the rest of the way. I haven't turned to see her yet, and part of me wants to put it off, knowing it will do me in completely. I finish the last few buttons on my own shirt, a plain white fitted one that I leave un-tucked, and then turn to see if my brother's right.

This is how a girl steals your heart. Rowe's hair is down in waves, the front swept to the side with a tiny braid holding it in place. Everything about her face is simple and plain— absolutely kissable. She's wearing a long black dress with black flat sandals that somehow still make her look like she's six-foot-seven thanks to the slit along the side of her leg showing off what is quickly becoming my favorite part of her body. I'm inching closer to her without even realizing it, and when I reach her, I touch the tips of my fingers to her chin and turn her face so I can kiss her cheek. "May I?"

She only nods; her eyes looking away and her shyness making her face burn red. I tuck her hair behind her ear, letting my fingers indulge in a slight graze along her shoulder, coming to rest along her neck. When my lips meet her cheek I'm instantly charged with a need to kiss her more, but I don't. I wouldn't, unless she gave me permission.

"Ty's right," I smile. "You look hot."

"Well, you're just used to the ideal woman because of your new Barbie obsession. You're just projecting," she jokes, and I can tell it's because she's uncomfortable with the attention.

"Yeah, well, you can turn her head completely around on her body, so that's kinda hard to top," I say, trying to set her at ease again.

"Oh, mine does that too," she winks. Yeah, heart...stolen.

My parents meet us at the only semi-nice restaurant near campus. My mom says it's not a fancy dinner unless the place serves you bread before you eat, so she always insists on places like this. It's a steakhouse called Morgan's, and I'm just excited my parents are picking up the bill.

"Rowe, Cass, so glad you both could join us," my mom says, reaching around to hug both of the girls. I pull out Rowe's seat next to me, and she slides in, her fingers gripping at the side of her dress.

"So, Cass. Ty tells us you're studying physical education? Do you hope to teach?" my dad asks. I notice Rowe's hands flex and tighten even more as Cass responds to my dad's question. She's waiting for the question to come to her next, and she's worried because she doesn't have an answer. We're also sitting in the middle of the restaurant, and I can see her eyes darting from side to side, sneaking in glances at her surroundings. Without even thinking, I slide my hand to her leg and reach for her fingers. She startles at first, and I give her the tiniest shrug, hoping she'll use me for strength—just for tonight. Her hand moves to mine, and soon she's holding my hand tightly.

"I'd like to get into rehab work," Cass finishes explaining. I watch as my mom looks over to Ty, nodding and smiling with her approval. Ty rolls his eyes, but I know he likes Cass a lot.

"How about you, Rowe? What are you studying?" my dad asks, and I feel her grip somehow get even tighter. You'd never know the exertion happening under the tablecloth by the look of complete calmness Rowe is showing up above, and I'm actually pretty impressed.

"Well, I haven't really decided yet. But I'm thinking about philosophy or art." Her voice trails up at the end, almost like she's asking a question, so anxious for my parents to approve. Rowe has no idea how perfect her answer was, but she's about to find out.

"You know, Cathy's an artist," my dad says, always the first to brag about my mom.

"I have a small studio," my mom says modestly. The truth is my mom has three small studio galleries in New Orleans and California, and she sells a lot of her work. She does sculpture and metal work, and I don't know much about her world, but I know people pay her a lot of money when they commission a piece.

"You should check out my mom's website," I say, getting Rowe's attention. "She does metal sculpture. I bet you'd like it." Rowe bites at her lip and smiles, her grip on my hand loosening with every minute that passes.

"Here...I have a card." My mom reaches into her purse and pulls out a bent card with her website listed on it, and Rowe studies it closely.

"Thanks, I will," she says, her smile somewhere between wonder and relief. She leans down to tuck the card in her purse.

Rowe relaxes even more when the waitress shows up, cutting her interview with my parents short. Minutes later, we're all picking at the loaf of bread dropped off at our table, too interested in the garlic butter and toasted edges to pay any more attention to conversation.

I let Rowe's hand go, but only for a few minutes while we place our orders and take our drinks. And as soon as the waitress leaves our table, I reach for her again, and her hand is actually waiting for mine.

"Oh, we ran into the Maxwells," my mom starts, sucking all air from my lungs. I don't know why she thinks this is a good direction for dinner talk, but I'm rapidly trying to get Ty's attention, hoping he can help me make a conversational U-turn somehow. But no, he only makes it worse.

"Yeah? Was that slut Sadie with them?" Ty has a way with words, and those just made sure Cass and Rowe were completely dialed in on whatever my mom says next.

"Ty, your mouth," Mom says.

"Oh, right. Sorry. I guess the appropriate term is *hooker*. Is that the nice way to categorize your brother's cheating ex-girlfriend?" I kick Ty's chair under the table, and he finally looks up. "What? That's what she is!"

I keep trying to motion my eyes to Rowe sitting next to me, and finally he gets it and just mouths *sorry*, returning his attention to the salad now in front of him.

"*Anyway*," my mom continues. "We didn't see Sadie, just her parents. But they said she took the scholarship to Oklahoma State."

Great. My cheating ex-girlfriend, the first and only girl I said I loved, is playing basketball for a college less than ninety miles from me. And I find this out while desperately clinging to the fingers of the girl sitting next to me. The girl I want. The only thing I've thought about since I met her almost a month ago. The girl who says I'll probably never meet her parents because we'll never be anything more than whatever the hell it is we are right now. And all I can do is be okay with it all, because her problems are a hell of a lot heavier than mine.

"Ha, I bet you run into her," Ty says, and this time I throw a piece of lettuce at him, like I'm four. When my mother isn't looking, he just gives me his middle finger, and Rowe lets go of my other hand.

Rowe

Everything changed when Nate's parents brought up Sadie. His posture was different, his breathing was different, the way his hand felt in mine—different. Nate's mom told a few stories about him and Sadie, talking about how they won prom king and queen in high school, and how Nate had this secret crush on Sadie his junior year and used to go to all of her basketball games and leave before the end of the fourth quarter, afraid to talk to her.

I had a hard time imagining Nate being anything other than confident, which made me start to wonder about how different he is with me. Sadie had his heart, as far as I can tell. At least, she did until she betrayed him—Ty wasn't shy about sharing that part, about how Nate walked in on her with his best friend at their graduation party.

The walk home with Nate, Cass, and Ty felt strange now that I had all of this new information, too. And I couldn't help but think that maybe hearing about Sadie had brought up old feelings.

"Wanna hang?" Nate says, bringing me back to the present. Ty and Cass are ahead of us, already heading down the hall to my room. When the door closes behind them, I know I have nowhere to go, at least not for a while.

"Thanks," I say, feeling much more like a burden than I would have a couple of hours ago.

Nate flips the TV on to "Sports Center," and part of me thinks he just wants to fill the quiet in the room. I sit on the edge of Ty's bed, my purse in my lap, and watch a montage of amazing baseball plays.

"That guy's awesome. The shortstop for Colorado?" Nate says, sliding back on his bed and propping his head up on a pillow, the awkwardness still very much alive between the two of us.

"I bet I'll see you up there someday," I say, instantly feeling gushy and stupid, like a fan girl.

"You coming to my tournament next weekend?" He still hasn't looked at me. He hasn't put his eyes to mine since the Sadie conversation.

"Oh, uh...I can't. I'm going home for the weekend." For whatever reason, that seems to get Nate's attention, and his eyes move immediately to mine. I hold his stare as long as I can without breaking, but eventually it becomes too intense, and I look back down to the floor.

"How come I can't meet your parents?" he asks, and I'm so perplexed by his question that I can only respond with one of my own.

"Are you still in love with Sadie?"

Nate holds my stare again, just like he did before, only this time he's the one to break. He reaches along the side of his bed for the television remote, pushing the mute button so we're forced to fill the silence between us. He slides forward on his bed until he's on the edge, right across from me, and then he squares his long legs to the side, facing me completely.

"Sadie was my high school girlfriend. She's the first girl I said I loved and was the one to take my virginity. Before graduation, we were planning on going to the same college. She plays basketball, and she's really fucking good." There's a bite to his tone, and it makes me uncomfortable.

"When I caught her with my best friend Seth, I fell out of love with her—in an instant. There was no thinking about it, no wondering what I did wrong. I woke up that morning in love and I came home that night out of it. So no, Rowe. I'm not in love with Sadie. Her parents are still friendly with mine, but I'm so incredibly out of love with Sadie that I don't even get angry or bitter when my family tells me stories about her. The only thing that made me upset tonight was having to hear those stories in front of you."

It's so quiet in his room that I'm afraid to swallow the gigantic lump that is choking me, but I do. And when I do, Nate leans forward even more, his elbows on his knees while he brings his hands together in front of him to crack each knuckle, again, his eyes never leaving me.

"Why Rowe?" He just leaves his question in the air. Two words that could mean anything, and I know they mean everything.

"Why what?" I sound combative and snarky, and I don't mean to, but I don't know how to cross this line with him, and I don't even know if my heart is mine to give. But I know that I don't like hearing about him and Sadie, and I know I'm relieved he's not in love with her anymore.

"Why do you care about how I feel about Sadie?" His eyes intensify on me. "I mean, if I'm not the kind of guy you introduce to your parents, why does it matter who I hook up with? What are we doing here, Rowe? What is *this*?"

"I don't know!" I stand and bring my purse to my body, wanting desperately to leave, to run back to my own room and hide. But there's a part of me that also wants Nate's mouth on mine, and that part is hungry and forceful and begging to be heard. And then I close my eyes, and I see Josh's face, and everything feels worse.

When I open my eyes again, Nate is standing in front of me, his arms to his side and his fingers threatening to connect with mine, but just coming close enough for me to feel his heat. His chest is inches away, and slowly he reaches up to put his thumb under my chin. I close my eyes tightly, and my fingers cling to my purse, hoping my heart can survive whatever is about to happen.

"I don't play games, Rowe. I'm just...I just don't," he says against my ear. "I will wait, but I won't wait forever."

I hear his door open, and when I open my eyes again, I'm standing in his room alone, my breathing almost that of a heart attack victim. My eyes want to cry, and so does my heart, but all I can seem to do is stand there under the flickering light of Nate's TV while I wait for my roommate to unlock our door again.

Chapter 16

Rowe

He had disappeared. I know he still went to class and to practice, because I caught glimpses of him, but he was never there for long. My flight leaves tomorrow, and I haven't talked to Nate since those few minutes alone in his room.

It's almost as if the universe was on Nate's side. Today's philosophy lecture was all about self-determination, and every example my professor gave was as if he was plucking it from the pages of my own life. I love Josh with all of my heart, but I also blame him for every twist my path has taken. I'm stuck between wanting to let go and wanting to honor everything he was to my life, wanting to prove that I was *his* until the very end.

Last night, I purchased a few items from the corner grocery store, tired of being the third wheel to Cass and Ty in the cafeteria. I packed a small lunch today to eat between my two classes. I knew it would save me time and let me get some reading in before my art-history class, but I also knew that if I could manage—if I could find the courage to sit under a tree on the main campus lawn—then Nate would have to see me. He walks this path every day on his way to the math building. I've seen him from afar, and I hope putting myself in his way makes him notice me again.

My sandwich is dry because I made it in such a hurry, and I have to chase it with most of my soda just to get it down. I went a little overboard on the bag of pretzels, packing enough for a Boy Scout troop, mostly because I wanted to be sure I was still eating something when Nate walked by. It has to seem authentic, and I need to be distracted, or else I will just look desperate.

I sense his legs crossing the street without even turning my face up, and I sneak a look from my periphery just to be sure he's walking this way. For a moment, I think he's not going to stop, and my gut feels heavy. But at the last second, I hear his feet pause along the small gravel path that winds through the trees and grass, and my heart skips a beat.

"Picnic for one?" He's standing next to me now, and I know when I look up at him his face will give everything away.

"Just trying to conquer my demons," I say, honestly. Nate kneels down and picks up the book lying open in front of me, thumbing through a few pages. I allow myself to glance up at him, and when I do, he catches me and holds my gaze. His lips are a faint smirk, almost like he can read my mind, and he knows every thought I've had of him since he left me standing in his room.

He folds my book closed but holds my page with his finger. "When do you leave for Arizona?" He's still studying me, and I can tell that right now—right this minute—he's nervous too.

"Tomorrow, around three. I'm taking a taxi to the airport," I say, my voice wavering at the thought of everything I have to survive tomorrow. "I...I don't really like flying."

"What, flying? Nah, that's easy," he says, handing me my book but careful not to touch his hand to mine. The lack of contact hurts. "Want my secret?"

I nod *yes*, but the truth is I want all of him, the parts I'm afraid to ask for, and the parts I'm afraid will break me.

"Put Neil Diamond on your iPod. It works with almost every song, but 'Sweet Caroline' is the best, because you can't help but want to sing along with it," he says, standing and pulling his backpack up along his shoulder. "Neil's got your back."

He winks when he walks away, and I spend the next fifteen minutes wondering if I've lost him before I even had him to lose.

Nate

"This sucks," I say, throwing the book I've been reading for my English class across the room against the wall.

"That's why I picked business bro. Once you get out of those under-grad classes, every book you read is about money, and who doesn't like to read about money?" Ty rubs his fingers together for emphasis.

"No, the book's fine. Actually, I wouldn't know. I've read the same sentence a hundred times because I can't get my goddamned mind to focus on shit. I sucked it up at batting practice today, too." It's almost eleven, and I know Rowe hasn't hit the showers yet, because I keep checking.

"Girl's messing with baseball now. I was willing to let things slide when she was just messing with you, but now she's fuckin' up my favorite sport," Ty says in a serious tone. I know he's joking, but I also know he's a little frustrated on my behalf. I told Ty about Rowe's past, and I know he'll keep it to himself. But my brother has a different perspective on life—he's all about seizing the moment and not living with regrets. When I told him about Rowe, he tried to encourage me to give up my pursuit, saying that if she's been stuck for two years, then nothing's ever going to break her pattern. But I can't give up yet. Even if I wanted to, I don't think my heart would let me.

"I'll be back," I say, grabbing my keys and heading to the showers again. It's been fifteen minutes since the last time I checked.

"You're kind of pathetic, just so you know!" Ty yells after me.

"Thanks, I know," I say back, shaking my head at myself.

I can hear the humming from a few doors away, and I know she's in there. I don't even know if she realizes she does it, but when Rowe showers, she hums, sometimes actually singing words. I think it's a subconscious thing she does when she's nervous, but her voice is amazing. Tonight she's singing that Maroon 5 song "She Will Be Loved." She doesn't know all the words, so when she gets to a part that she's unsure of, she makes up lyrics, and it's cute as hell.

The water cuts off, and I know she'll be walking out in two minutes. She hurries every time, and I understand why now. My heart is pounding so hard that I can actually feel it in my temples. Damn, how does one girl make me so unsure of everything? Two hours ago, I was determined, and an hour ago, I still thought this was a good idea. I don't know anything anymore though. I take a deep breath and walk out of the men's locker room, moving a few yards away from the women's exit, where I lean against the wall. I'm sure I'm going to scare her, but I hope she gets over it fast. And I hope she doesn't punch me!

I'm actually bouncing on my legs, like a boxer ready to enter the ring, when I see her shadow around the corner.

"Don't get scared," I say, picking probably the worst moment, the worst tone, and the worst phrase to utter when someone runs into you in the dark. This is confirmed when she flattens herself against the wall, dropping all of her things, just like she did that first time we met. Her hair is wrapped in a towel on top of her head, though it's sliding off now that I just scared the crap out of her. She's wearing the same giant T-shirt and shorts she was that first night, too. And my heartbeat is literally doing a drumroll.

"Holy hell, I think I just swallowed my tongue," she says, her hands pressed to her chest. "For the record, yelling 'don't get scared' in a dark hallway to a girl with some serious post-traumatic-stress issues is a sure fire way to make her think she's dying."

"I'm sorry," I say with a wince. I reach down to grab her towel, which has now completely slid off her head. When I stand back up to hand it to her, I'm struck by how absolutely drop-dead gorgeous she is. There isn't an ounce of makeup on her, and her hair is sopping wet, twisted along the side of her neck and dripping down the front of her white T-shirt. She's not wearing a bra, and I'm careful not to draw any attention to that fact, because I don't want her to shift her arms and cover any of that up. I'm a good guy, but I'm not *that* good.

"Were you...waiting for me?" she asks, her eyes sad and hopeful. This moment, the way she looks *right now*, makes every frustrating second from the last four days worthwhile.

"I was." Her eyes widen, just the smallest amount, but it's enough. "So, you have your Neil ready?"

"I do. I took your advice, 'Sweet Caroline.' I'm not so sure it's going to work though. I don't really know the words," she bites her lip, like she's actually embarrassed that she doesn't know the lyrics to a Neil Diamond song. Though, I really can't believe she doesn't know this one.

"It's easy. And you'll know them after you hear the chorus the first time. It's one of those songs," I say. I loop my thumbs in my pockets because at this very moment, if I don't, I'm afraid I won't be able to stop myself from touching her. Her shirt is now completely soaked on one side, and her nipple is peaking through the material. It's *all* I can focus on, that and her lips, which I am fighting not to taste.

She can't seem to hold my gaze long, and I start to make a challenge out of it, dipping my knees to look at her lowered head when she breaks our connection to concentrate on her feet and the floor. This makes her giggle, and *God* do I love that sound.

"There she is," I say, when she takes a normal breath finally and holds my stare long enough to shake her head at my teasing. "You packed yet?"

I'm stalling. I want to stand here in this darkened hallway and have conversations with her about absolutely nothing important for as long as it takes for me to get enough balls to make a statement. That, and I just love listening to her voice. I love looking at her body. I love watching her come out of her shell. And I want to make her whole.

"Is it weird to pack dirty laundry? I was going to do it, but then that just seemed like a waste of time," she shrugs.

"No, moms love it when we bring home dirty laundry," I say.

"My dad does the laundry, you sexist pig." She's feisty again, and I love the way she's now standing with her hand on her hip and her head tilted to one side like she just put me in my place. I also love the way her posture stretches her T-shirt across both of her breasts. I no longer need to imagine what they look like because in the ever-so brief glances my eyes make, I am committing every curve to memory. She bends down to pick up her small bag of shampoo and conditioner, and somehow when she stands, the fabric clings to her even more, and I'm no longer able to hide my reaction.

I stare, and I stare long and hard at the perfect roundness and the small pink tips that are poking through the cotton, almost as if they're trying to reach me. I swallow, and start to lick my lips when I realize how obvious I'm being. I catch my breath, and quickly move my eyes to hers. She doesn't look upset, but she does look embarrassed, and within a fraction of a second, she looks down and notices her wet shirt and everything it's revealing. She pulls her towel up in a clump in front of her and squeezes it to her chest, almost ashamed, and I feel like a dick for making her feel so insecure.

"Don't worry. I...I didn't really see anything," I lie, gritting my back teeth together and forcing an apologetic smile. Fuck, I'm making this worse, and she's starting to look upset.

"Oh my god, I'm pretty sure you did. Oh man..." She's starting to breathe heavier, like she might pass out. "I...I'm so sorry. I didn't realize my shirt was that wet. And you must have...*uhg!*"

Now she's hiding her face in her towel too, and she holds up her other hand, the one clutching the bag, and does her best to wave. "I'm going to go put in my strip-club applications now. Nice talking to you. See you when I get back," she says, walking away quickly.

I stand there for a few seconds and try to figure out my next move, but all I can focus on is how damned embarrassed she was, and how unbelievably beautiful her body is. "You really shouldn't be embarrassed. I mean, I liked it...what I saw? Or, what I *think* I saw..."

"Not helping!" she yells from the safety of her door. She opens and shuts it quickly, and I slap my forehead wondering when the hell I turned into a junior-high boy.

Ty is watching ESPN when I get back to the room, and he waves me out of his way with his arm when I stop in front of the TV. "Well, how'd the grand master plan go?" he says, only half interested in me. Clearly more focused on the highlights from last week's Saints game.

"Oh, you know...I pretty much blatantly stared at her tits for about ten minutes until she realized what a perv I am and ran away," I say, flinging myself backward on my bed and covering my eyes with my pillow.

"That sounds like progress to me, bro. Nice tits?" Ty asks. I stare at him for a few seconds, at first wanting to throw something at him for his dumb-ass question, but eventually I realize I'm no better than he is.

"Yeah. They're pretty fantastic tits," I say, laying my head back again and burying it deep under my pillow.

The sounds of *Sports Center* lull me in and out of a sleepy state for the next half hour, and I'm almost ready to give in completely and just let this shitty day come to an end when my phone buzzes next to me with an alert.

When I pull the pillow from my eyes, the light in the room is almost blinding, and it takes me a few seconds to focus on my phone screen. When I realize I have a Facebook message from Rowe, I find my bearings quickly and scoot up to sit with my back against the wall and open the message section.

Hi Josh.

Shit! This isn't for me. I set the phone back down and click the screen off. I sit up all the way at the back of my bed, out of Ty's view, and I run my hand through my hair about a thousand times hoping some sort of sign comes to me. She writes to him. This...*this isn't good.* Rowe sends messages to her ex-boyfriend who, from what I understand, is damned near brain-dead. I just called him her ex-boyfriend, but that's not even true. He's her boyfriend, or at least that's the last thing he remembers them as—if he even remembers.

Fuck!

"I'll be back, dude." I grab my phone and slip my feet back into my shoes and head out the door. Ty says something when I leave, but I can't even focus on his voice. I head to the stairs and just keep going, my feet gaining speed until I hit the front doors of the dorm. I start a slow jog, and I get faster and faster, until I'm actually sprinting all the way to the baseball field.

The lights aren't on, but I can see enough to find my way. The equipment is all still out, so I slip though the side gate and through the small space at the front of the batting cage. The bats are all hanging still from our practice this afternoon, and I know I'm not supposed to be in here, but goddamn do I need to hit something right now!

I flip the switch on the machine and it takes it a few seconds for the wheels to gain speed. It's dark as hell, but in a few minutes, I should be able to see enough. I pull my phone out from my pocket and look at Rowe's photo and name. I know I shouldn't read it. I should just delete it or not look at it and write her back quickly, letting her know she sent me something meant for someone else.

Someone else.

Fuck! That's the problem. There's always going to be someone else.

I grab the wooden bat because I want to feel the sting in my hands. Sometimes I use it to warm up before games because it makes swinging metal even easier. But tonight I want to feel the pain and stress of the wood—to pull this feeling from my heart and push it into my hands.

Crack!

The vibration hurts like hell, and I step back and let the next two pitches smash into the hard plastic behind the plate. My eyes are starting to adjust, so I step back in and hit three more, swinging harder than I normally do, punishing the ball for everything I'm feeling. One more ball fires my way, and I swing and miss, which just pisses me off.

"Stupid goddamned machine!" I throw the bat across the cage and smack my hand against the emergency shut-off and the motor slows until the only thing I hear is my rapid breathing and the crickets in the grass.

I hold my phone in my lap while I slide down to sit with my back against the chain-link of the cage. My weight sends up a small puff of dirt when I hit the ground. I pull my knees up and pat the dust from the legs of my jeans and let out a tiny laugh at how futile it is. I'm filthy, and I just picked a fight with a decade-old pitching machine.

I'm slow at first, clicking the phone screen on and hovering my thumb over Rowe's profile picture on Facebook. I don't even have her number. I never asked, but she never gave it to me either. This is the only way I can contact her, other than holding her hostage in her own dorm room. And neither method was from her choosing. I sought her out on Facebook, and heaven gave me a break when they put us together on the same floor of Hayden Hall. But never, not once, did Rowe come for me.

I'm reading before I can stop myself, and I'm reading with anger in my heart. I'm not angry at Rowe, I'm angry at myself for falling for her—for falling for a girl who can't let herself be mine to love.

Hi Josh.

Haven't written in a week, lots to catch you up on. I told two more people about you—my roommates, Cass and Paige. I know, I know...but I was wrong about Paige. She's actually pretty nice, once you get through all of that fake crap. I've been wrong about a lot. I didn't think I could do this without you. But here I am, almost a month in, and I don't want to go home, Josh. Please don't take this the wrong way. I miss my parents, and there's a part of me that wants to crawl back into the cocoon I lived in for two years, the one where I hid from the world because you're no longer in it. There's a reason I don't go into your room when I visit your parents. At first, I thought it was because I couldn't— because I was too afraid of hurting and seeing you unable to speak or move. But I don't think that's it anymore. I don't come see you because I'm selfish. I'm selfish, Josh, and I feel so awful about it, but I am. I want to forget about you. I want to remember you on that last day, moments before that man walked into our lives with his gun, but I don't want to remember you after. I don't want to know what you look like now, because I don't want that vision in my head making me feel guilty for being alive. And I want to be done with you. I am cold and callous even writing this, but oh god Josh, I want to be done with you. The more I think about it, the more I know we probably would have broken up by now anyway, because as good as you were, we were young, and the me I'm growing into wants to experience more in life. There's this guy, and he's all I can think about, and Josh I want to love him. I'm so close to giving in, and I think if I could just let myself, he would love me back. But I can't, because you're always there...in the way of my life. I'm probably just angry. And I'm sorry I'm taking this out on you tonight. But it's not like you'll write back or see any of it. I'm not writing you any more. Not because I don't love you, because I always will. But because I'm letting you go. I let you go, Josh. Please...please let me go too.

At some point, while reading, I started to cry. There's a single tear waiting to fall from my eye, and I let it go. I read the entire message twice and then I delete it from my phone because I don't want to be tempted to read it again, and I don't want Rowe to see it. I know there's a chance she'll realize what she's done eventually, but I will never bring it up. These words were private—not even meant for Josh. But reading them was just the slap in my face that I needed.

Before I can stop myself—maybe before the sense has enough time to settle in my head—I sprint from the ball fields, through campus, and to the dorms. I take the steps two at a time until I get to our floor, and I'm not even careful or quiet when I pound on her door. Light shines underneath it, so I know I'm not waking anyone; I take a deep breath when I see the shadow interrupt the light.

"Nate, it's okay. I'm not *that* embarrassed. But if you bring it up again..." She's talking through the door, and I can tell she's looking at me through the peephole. I brace both of my arms on either side of the frame and press my forehead against the wood.

"Just open the damn door, Rowe," I say, unable to contain the need building inside of me.

"Nate, I'm leaving tomorrow. Let's just talk when I get back."

"Rowe, I swear to god, if you don't open the door I'm going to break it," I know I'm probably frightening her, and I don't want to. But I need her to act—I can't have her hide, not now.

When I hear the lock twist, I grab the handle and turn it to push her door open before she or I have any time to react and think better of what I'm about to do. She's wearing a dry shirt but the same small cotton shorts, and her hair is still damp and long against her back. Her eyes are wide while she stumbles backward a few tiny steps as I barrel into her room. I scan it quickly to make sure she's alone, not that it would matter or stop me, but she is.

I close the distance between us quickly, and before she has time to protest, I reach my fingers deep into her wet hair with both of my hands, lifting her face toward mine just enough for my lips to touch hers, and I kiss her hard. I can feel her body shake at first, and her hands press lightly against my chest, but they stop fighting me quickly. I suck at her top lip until it's firmly between both of mine, leaving just enough space for my tongue to brush against hers, and when I feel her tongue move against mine, I pull her even closer into me.

Her hands grab at the back of my shirt, almost like she's fighting herself, until finally she submits, and I feel the smoothness of her palms and fingers trail up my back, to my chest, and over my shoulder until she's grabbing my hair, pushing my mouth into hers even harder.

I walk her backward until her body is pressed flat against the wall, and I hold her hands hostage against it, her arms trapped along the sides of her body, while I press kisses along her neck and chin. I don't want to push things, but I need to make sure she feels me, everything I'm feeling. I know I shouldn't have read that message she sent, but I'm glad I did. It was all the proof I needed that there was this opening here, however small, and I need to step through it, crawl inside her heart. Otherwise, she's just going to continue to fight to keep me out.

My body is pressed against hers, and I can feel her aching for me, so I slide my hands along her collarbone, trailing my fingers down her neck and shoulders until my thumbs find the hardness of her nipples. When I touch her there, she moans, and my will to stop nearly dissolves.

"Where's Cass?" I breathe heavily into her ear.

"Out. With Paige." She's panting, her hands digging into my shoulders and her forehead pressed against mine, her eyes closed tightly.

"Look at me," I say, needing to know she's feeling this. I don't want her forcing herself to do something. I want her to *want* to be here, to remember this, to obsess over it until she comes back to me. I want her to want more—more of *me.*

124

"I will wait for you," I say, and her breath catches quickly, her eyes watering almost instantly. "Do you hear me?"

She nods *yes*. Her movement is small, but it is there.

"For as long as it takes. Forever if I have to. I'll wait forever, okay?" Everything base and male inside me wants to lock her door and strip her clothes away so I can taste and touch every inch of her body until I come undone inside of her—but, I know that asking anything more from her would be me being selfish. And she already feels selfish enough for both of us. So I'll wait, just like I said I would.

I kiss her one more time, this time slower and more gently, letting my thumbs brush across her cheeks while her lips quiver under my touch. I step away from her, and see her phone sitting on her desk, so I pick it up and program my number in with her contacts and then hand it to her so she sees.

"I want you to text me when you land...so I know you're okay," I say, squeezing my hands around hers and kissing her knuckles before I back out of her room and go back to mine.

"You get shit figured out?" Ty says when I walk in, his back to me and the light on at his desk while he flips through a yellow legal pad full of notes.

"Yeah, I'm pretty sure I did. I'm just gonna hit the showers. I'll be back in a few," I say, grabbing my clean sweats and the long-sleeved T-shirt Rowe wore the night she slept in my arms.

I pause at the division in the hallway, and I look at the door to her room, the light still shining underneath. I hope she'll sleep tonight, but if she doesn't, I hope it's not because of regret. I walk quietly down the hall—careful not to make any noise that would make her look outside—and I hang my shirt on her doorknob. Then I step away silently until I'm sure the coast is clear. I let out a heavy sigh, and make my way to the showers.

After thirty minutes of cold water, I finally feel calmed down. I shut the water off, dry myself, and pull on my sweats to go back to my room. When I pass her hall, I pause, just to see, and the shirt is gone.

Chapter 17

Rowe

Nate was right. By the third play through, I had all of the words memorized to "Sweet Caroline." The guy sitting next to me even caught me mouthing the words during takeoff and followed along with the *ba ba ba* part in the middle. It made me laugh, and before I knew it, we were soaring above the clouds.

I wouldn't say I *like* flying. But I think as long as my iPod is fully charged, I should be able to survive my trip back to school. However, I would prefer to fly non-stop this time. My parents saved money with this flight, but I had to sit at a gate in Denver for about two hours.

Coming home was strange. I've only been gone for a month, but I feel like so much is different. Maybe it's me. My mom did wait up for me, and we all sat at the kitchen table and ate slices of an apple pie she bought at Kraft's Market.

Sleeping in my bed was strange, too. Before I left for McConnell, I didn't think I would ever be able to find comfort on a strange mattress, in a strange city, with a stranger as a roommate. But I did. And now I think I slept better with Cass snoring a few feet away from me than I did here behind my own bedroom door.

But my best dreams came from the night I stayed with Nate. I wore his shirt to bed last night. I sent him a short text because it was late when I landed, but I think he had been waiting, because he wrote back right away, and said he'd talk to me in the morning.

I sent a text to Cass, too. She told me to take my time coming back, not because she wouldn't miss me, but because she was having a full weekend of sleepovers with Ty. I wanted more sleepovers too, and was a little envious that I wasn't there to take advantage of Nate being alone in his room.

The scent of my dad's eggs and sausage spills down the hall and has me climbing out of bed early. I wheel my suitcase out with me, parking it at the laundry room, hoping someone will notice. When I enter the kitchen, my dad slides a plate my way.

"I see you brought laundry home for me," he says.

"You're just so much better at it than I am," I smile as I douse my plate with syrup for my sausages.

"Yeah, yeah. That's what your mother says, too. I think you two are in cahoots on this whole plot to domesticate me."

"Honey, you came domesticated. That's why I married you," my mom smiles as she slides onto the stool next to me and digs into her breakfast. "Mmmmm, hey. What's this?" My mom pulls at the sleeve of Nate's shirt, and I can feel my face redden immediately. I'm not sure how to explain this, and I'm not very good at lying.

"Baseball shirt," I say, quickly stuffing my face with another bite. I can tell by the way my mother's eyebrow is cocked that she's suspicious, and she waits until my dad's back is turned to drill me a little more.

"It looks like a *boy's* baseball shirt," she whispers. I smile and shrug and keep eating, doing my best not to look her straight in the eyes. That's how she gets me, the eye contact. I think it's one of those skills from being a professor.

"Hmmmmm, we'll talk about this more later," she says, and I hope like hell we won't.

My dad already has my laundry in the works, and my mom has settled into the large recliner chair in the living room with a stack of papers on her lap for grading. Normally, this is where I sift through the channels until there's a movie or a game I want to watch on the screen, but nothing is capturing my attention today. I did bring home some reading, so I open my philosophy book to the chapter on logic and reasoning.

I'm able to concentrate for about thirty minutes, but my mind keeps drifting to my phone, waiting for it to be afternoon Oklahoma time. How quickly my life has centered around Oklahoma time. My mom is completely engrossed in her grading, so when the hour comes I can text Nate in private, I grab my book and head back to my bedroom.

Coming up with the right words seems impossible. All I thought about over the last forty-eight hours was our kiss—and how very much I wanted that to happen again. I can't write that, though. I mean, I guess I could. But being forward like that doesn't feel like me.

How's the tournament?

That's what I settle on. The lamest three words possible—I may as well be a sports reporter. I checked the schedule while I waited at the airport, and I knew there was a break between games. McConnell plays tonight, so I was hoping I could catch Nate during a lunch break.

After five minutes of waiting, I start to get antsy, so I pull out my purse and sift through some old receipts and scraps that I can clean out and throw away. When I stumble on his mom's business card, I decide to check out her website. The first thing that flashes on my laptop screen when I type it in is a series of photos—intricate metalwork in brilliant colors, the pieces all twisted together to form bodies, some human, some animal. I've never seen anything quite like it.

She has three galleries, one in New Orleans and two in California, and the more I click into her pages, the more impressed I am. I could never do anything like this, not with these hands. I'm too nervous, and I question too much. Every single piece she showcases has a story. There aren't any words written with the photos, but I can tell—I can read the story in every nuance and bend of the metal.

33! Miss me already?

Nate's message brings my attention back to the here and now, and the playful tone of his words has an instant smile on my face.

Not yet. Check with me later, maybe I'll miss you then.

I start to rethink my message after I send it. After Nate told me he'd wait for me, I'm not sure he'll appreciate my joke. I'm about to say that I'm kidding when he writes back.

Yeah, I don't miss you either. I do kind of miss my shirt, though. That was a bonehead move—I should have given you one of Ty's.

I'm so relieved he's joking with me. I also can't help but look down at the letters across my chest and run my hands over the fabric that was on his body before it was on mine. It still smells like him, whatever his cologne is, and I want to drown in its scent.

That would have been better. Maybe his shirts don't smell so bad.

I pull the collar up and breathe in deeply while I wait for his response, unable to keep my lips from smiling.

Well, I did roll around in crap before I gave it to you. That could be what you smell.

He's so damn fast with his response that I laugh out loud when I read it, quickly covering my mouth. I don't want anyone interrupting me, and I would be content to lie here for the rest of the weekend and text back and forth with Nate.

I'm kidding. I don't really roll in crap.

I laugh again. I miss him. I miss him a lot, and it feels good inside my chest to feel this way about someone. I wish I had a picture of him, so while I think of what to write back, I Google him on my laptop just to see what comes up. It's mostly baseball pictures, and he's usually wearing his mask, but I can still tell it's him, and my head gets a little fuzzy looking at him.

Me: *I just Googled you.*
Nate: *That's creepy. I might have to report you.*
Me: *Just want to make sure you don't show up in the tabloids with some bimbo while I'm gone.*
Nate: *Just Paige. I helped move some of her things.*

Me: *That was nice of you. No staring at her boobs.*
Nate: *Well, I am a bit of a boob man.*
Me: *Uh, yeah. I know.*
Nate: *You have nice boobs.*
Me: *Oh my god!*
Nate: *Sorry.*
Nate: *Not sorry :-)*

Sometime during our texting, I crawled under my covers to hide. Nate has a way of making me blush in the most wonderful way. My heartbeat is kicking in every part of my body, but the rush is so addictive. I'm not sure what this feeling is, but I like it so very much, and I know Nate's the cause.

Me: *Can you talk?*
Nate: *Dialing you right now.*

He really is, because my phone rings while I'm still reading his words. My heart skips a beat before I answer.

"Hi," I say, biting my lip and burying my face into my pillow. I can't wait to hear his voice, but I'm also scared because I have no idea what to say.

"Boobs." He breaks the ice immediately, and we're both laughing. I miss him even more. "Sorry, just had to one-up you. You know me."

"Yeah, how's that pink room working out for you?" I say back, falling easily into our routine.

"Splendidly, thank you very much. Ty and I are going to add more purple—we think it really POPS!"

"Did you just say *splendidly?*"

"Your issue is with *splendidly* and NOT *pops*?"

Oh my god, I love him. Oh my god! I love him! No, I don't love him. But I could. I want to. Maybe I already do? I don't know him enough. You're supposed to know someone more, have dates and more kisses and hand holding, work up to love. I like him. There, that's it. I like him—a lot. Shit! I'm not talking.

"Where's your head at Thirty-three?" My head is up my ass, that's where it is. I have to get a grip, so I sit up and carry my laptop over to my desk. Right, like a more formal posture will suddenly make me act normal.

"Sorry, I thought my dad needed something," I lie. I hate lying.

"When do you come home?" His voice is suddenly softer, and I can tell we're done making jokes, which suddenly has me sweating.

"Sunday, around three by the time the cab gets me to campus," I say, my heart once again thumping loudly in my ear.

"Can I pick you up? I mean, I don't *really* have a car. But I can borrow one. You know, from one of the guys? I'd...I'd really like to pick you up."

"I'd like that, too," I say, my forehead flat on my desk now. I should not have left the comfort of hiding under my blanket.

"Hey, Rowe?" His voice seems nervous, not like him.

"Yeah?" I'm not like me either.

"I gotta go. But..." I can hear him breathing. I can actually hear him thinking, and I'm with him, on the edge, just waiting for his words to be what I want. What I *think* I want. "I miss you. That's all."

"I miss you too," I say, hugging my body tightly with the sleeves of his shirt.

This...is falling.

My head is trapped with thoughts and fantasies about Nate. We texted a few more times after his tournament Saturday, but nothing as meaningful as the words we exchanged that morning. I let down my guard with him, and it was scary, but I survived. And I want to let him in more. I want to let him in completely.

The Stanton Sunday morning routine is much like Saturday's. My dad has my laundry folded nicely in my suitcase, and my mom and I are quickly polishing off my dad's breakfast, being sure to gush about his amazing cooking abilities. It's part of our shtick, pumping my dad's ego so he'll continue to take care of *everything* in the house. I don't think we really need to do it, because my father is the kind of man who would do anything in the world to see his women happy. But we do it anyway, maybe more for us than him.

"Hey, washed that McConnell baseball shirt last night," my dad says, and my heart sinks a little knowing that Nate's shirt will now smell like Tide and Downy.

"Thanks," I say, standing and moving to the trash to clear my plate. I can feel both of my parents' eyes on me.

"Friend give that to you?" My dad's almost winking at me, and I'm so uncomfortable I want to scream.

"Uh huh?" I ask, doing my best to avoid eye contact.

"They've got a good team this year. Bunch of new kids; some really good ones." My dad is fishing. My mom put him up to this. It has been two years since I have dated a boy. Hell, it's been two years since I've been social with anyone outside of this house other than Ross, my pharmacist, and the occasional run-in with the mailman.

"His name is Nate," I say, rolling my eyes while I turn to face them, over-exaggerating my exasperation so I can act *full teenager.*

"Nate Preeter?" Now my dad is interested. He's a baseball coach, and he's had a few players go on to some pretty great things. Of course he knows Nate's name.

"Uh, yeah," I say, wishing like hell for an exit.

"So this Nate...is he, a friend?" My mom has entirely different interests in the conversation, and the longer we dwell on the topic—the more I want to poke my head inside my own body like a turtle.

"We're friends," I say, holding my mouth into a straight smile and concentrating hard not to let anything else out. My mom lets this sit for a few seconds, waiting to see if there's more, and her slight smile lets me know she *knows* there's more. But she also knows that one wrong word could trigger me into full retreat mode. So she lets it go.

"Good. I'm glad you're making friends, Rowe. I'd like to meet Nate sometime." Her smile is soft. It's that full understanding that happens between a mother and a daughter when they communicate without words, and it's the first conversation we've had like this since those weeks before the shooting.

"I think he'd like to meet you too."

Chapter 18

Rowe

I didn't visit Josh's parents this time. I had to stick to my promise to myself and let him go. My visit is never for him anyhow, and I knew they'd understand. When I left for McConnell, Josh's mom told me she hoped I would find my life in Oklahoma. I think I have, or at least I found a way to start again.

I told my parents I didn't want to come home for fall break, and instead wanted to wait until Thanksgiving. I could tell it made my dad a little sad, but my mom stepped in and reminded him what a huge step this was. I told them I wanted to try to make it longer, to start stretching myself, and my independence. But really, I don't want to leave Nate again.

Because it's early enough, my parents decided to use the airline credit to visit me instead. I helped my dad pick out a few dates that coincided with Nate's second fall tournament. They would be in Oklahoma in a little more than a month. I just hoped Nate still wanted to meet them when the time comes.

"Sweet Caroline" got old after about seven replays, so I switched to the playlist I had made for the first car ride to McConnell. I had sixty songs on that list at least, so every one was something different and a surprise, which made the last hour of the flight pass quickly.

I started looking for Nate as soon as I pulled my carry-on through the gate, but he wasn't there. I didn't think he would be allowed to come that close, for security reasons, but it didn't stop me from fantasizing. I wondered if he would kiss me when he saw me? I wasn't sure how to act with him now. I wasn't exactly sure what we were.

Nate's voice is unmistakable, and it hits my ears and then my heart. He's singing—Neil, of course, in my honor. His tone is deaf, and he's switching keys like crazy, and I'm pretty sure he's making it worse on purpose, just to embarrass me. Then I see the sign, a ginormous pink poster-board covered in glitter and black marker looking for Miss Butstynk.

"What? No 'paging Miss Butstynk' over the phone system? Nate, I'm disappointed. I think you're getting soft," I say, my mouth tingling just thinking about his lips.

He pulls the poster down to his feet and steps in closer to me, reaching his arm around my body to pull me in for a hug. I can hear him chuckling deep in his chest, the best sound I've ever heard, and then he kisses me on the top of my head, and we start walking.

I can't get over the grin on his face, and the way he keeps looking at me every few steps that we take. A few times, he takes a breath, like he's ready to speak, but he never does.

"Flight was fine, thanks," I finally say when we get to the elevator bank, teasing him, but also wanting to end this strange awkwardness.

"Good. Glad old Neil could help you out," he says, holding the door with his back while I wheel my bag inside. When the doors close, Nate steps in front of me quickly, putting his hands on either side of my face and lifting my mouth to his. He pauses for the tiniest second, long enough to check my reaction, and when I smile against his lips, he kisses me completely. It's soft and tender, and he holds my top lip between his teeth for a few seconds while he moans softly.

"Goddamn," he says, backing away and licking the taste of me from his lips.

Two more people get in the elevator at the next floor, and my pulse speeds up knowing they could have just walked in on us. I guess it's only a kiss, and people do that in public all of the time, but before Nate, my only kisses were by lockers, under bleachers, on my parents' porch—and in Josh's bedroom.

"So, Miss Butstynk. Where can I drive you?" Nate smiles at me, tapping his finger to his poster and winking.

"The transplant office. I'm ready...to become a man," I say, and when he closes his eyes to stifle his laugh, I know I've won this round. The duo with us in the elevator looks horrified.

We leave the airport and merge onto the highway for a few miles before Nate pulls off again and stops at a place called Tucker's Onion Burgers. My stomach growls just from seeing the sign.

"Figured you probably need more than the tiny bag of peanuts for lunch. Mind?" He's still so cautious about taking me places, and it makes my heart skip. I smile and nod, putting my hands on my belly to try to keep the growl to a minimum.

Nate takes my hand as soon as we walk to the front of the car, and he keeps it tight in his until we're comfortably seated in a booth in the far corner of the restaurant, our trays weighed down with what may just be the most indulgent hamburger I've ever seen.

"I always wanted to try one of these," he says, pulling the giant burger to his mouth with two hands and taking a big bite. "Ohhhhhh my gawwwwww."

I can't help but stare, and it's different this time, because I know Nate's not pretending to be anything for me. This isn't him playing some game where we talk with food in our mouths—it's just him, being comfortable around me. I'm starving, but all I want to do is watch him eat, so I let him get two more enormous bites ahead of me before I attempt to taste my own burger.

"Oh wow, this is soooo good," I say, knowing fully well that an onion has just slid from my mouth down my chin. I try to catch it, and feel a little embarrassed, though I will never admit that to him, but Nate quickly stops me with his napkin, wiping my chin clean, and then leaning in for a kiss.

"So, my parents are coming to visit in October. They'll be here for the Classic Tournament. My dad, he uh...he's kind of excited to watch you play," I say, taking short glances at Nate while I talk and pick at my fries.

"Oh yeah?" he asks, nodding, his brow a little pinched.

"Yep." It's quiet for a few minutes after that, and I start mentally kicking myself for only saying *yep*, when Nate leans back along the corner of the booth and stretches his arm out so he can look at me.

"I gotta ask. You're not making your parents come here and having them meet me just because you feel bad, are you?" I didn't think of it that way, but I can understand Nate's reaction now. I had some work to do to make sure he knew I was just as ready to take this step as he was.

After taking a long drink from my soda, I push my tray away and drop my napkin on top, then turn my body so my leg is bent in the booth and I'm facing him. "No. I was supposed to go home again for fall break. But that was before," I say, suddenly warm and anxious.

"Before I made you feel bad about not wanting me to meet your parents?" he asks.

"No. Before I realized how much I don't like being away from you," I say, waiting while his eyes stay on mine.

His lips smile, and whisper softly, "Oh."

"That, and my dad Googled you," I tease, just needing to break the tension.

"What is it with you people and cyber-stalking?"

Nate carries our trays to the trash and reaches for my hand at the door. He walks me all the way around to my side, opening the door for me while I get in, and then shuts the door softly, like I'm someone important—important to him.

Nate

I have kissed her exactly three times so far, and she hasn't protested a single one. Once on the head, once in the elevator, and once in the middle of the best-damned hamburger I've ever had.

When she said her parents were coming and wanted to meet me, I felt like crap for making such a big deal out of it. But I really think she meant what she said, and I can't help but feel hopeful that she would rather be here, in a state dozens away from her home, than go back to the place she knows.

There was still so much I wanted to know, needed to know. But I had to be careful how I extracted information from Rowe's head, because so much of it is covered in the scars of her heart. We have an hour of nothing but conversation time, though, so I hope I can get to some of her best secrets today.

"Oh, I should warn you. Ty and Cass...first fight," I say, still pissed that I won't be able to talk Ty into spending the night in Cass's room tonight. Unless, of course, things have changed from how they were when I left.

"You're kidding? What happened?" Rowe asks.

"Well, it's probably Ty's fault. Like I said, my brother's default mode is *asshole* when it comes to women. Cass is really the first one he's been *with* for more than a week, if you don't count his go-to girls."

"Ty has go-to girls? What exactly is a go-to...*oh...never mind.*" Her innocence was cute. I forget how little Rowe probably knows when it comes to things like that, because she can make herself seem so sure and confident.

"Right. Well, they ran into one of the go-to girls at Sally's. Some girl we met when he came down here early with me for summer ball. And, well, you know Cass. She called him on it, pretty much right in front of the girl, and he ended up getting slapped by them both. Of course, now he's all mopey and shit and refuses to go talk to her," I say, glancing at Rowe to see her genuinely interested in Ty and Cass's break up.

"We have to fix things," she says, and I can tell she means it.

"I'm not sure it's ours to fix," I start to say, but I can feel her eyes snap to me quickly, so I stop. "But maybe we can somehow get them to talk?"

"Yes. They just need to talk," she says, pulling her phone from her purse and sending a text that seems to take her minutes to complete. "There. Phase one—done. Now, give me your phone."

For some reason, I willingly go along with whatever she wants, and reach into my pocket and hand her my phone. I'm not a meddler by nature, but for some reason, Ty and Cass being together seems important to Rowe, and maybe her reasons are as selfish as mine—wanting time for us to be *alone.* But I feel like there's something more to it, and if it's important to her, then it's damn important to me, too.

"There. I texted your brother, too. We're having a little goodbye picnic for Paige, and they'll both be there. Paige has a lot of alcohol, so that got them both to say *yes.*"

Of course it did. My brother has endured far worse for cheap drinks. You make them free? There's no keeping him away. "Okay, so where is this picnic taking place?"

"Yeah, about that…" she has a tone in her voice that tells me I'm going to be sorry I asked. "You think you can sneak us onto the outfield, just one last time?"

She's literally pouting with puffy, full lips and sad eyes, inches away from my face while I cruise at eighty along a two-lane highway. I'm at her mercy. I think I was at her mercy the first time I scared her in the hallway. I nod *yes*, and she squeals—one of those girly noises I didn't think she was capable of—she scoots closely to me and kisses my cheek. That makes four.

"So, how did Josh ask you out?" I was feeling brave, all that confidence from her small kiss pumping courage through my veins. But the way she sinks back down into her seat zaps it all away. "Sorry. Should I…not go there?"

She's quiet for a few seconds, and I feel like an ass for pushing her. But I know Josh is the big elephant in the room. No matter what she said in her message to him, I know it takes more than just saying you're done with someone to be done with them totally. I even thought about Sadie from time to time—granted, it was usually when I was drunk and trying out the Ty Preeter brand of post-break-up therapy.

"No, it's okay. It's funny, actually. I asked Josh out, ultimately. He sent me a note once, in class, saying he liked me. I had liked him for a while, and I used to pretend to wait for my dad after practice just so I could watch him pitch. He was pretty good. I mean, I don't think he would have played college or anything, but you never know."

I can see the pain flash over her face, but she pushes through it, so I don't stop her.

"Well, the note came and went, but he never really *did* anything about it. He never asked me out. There was this other girl that liked him. Trisha Harvest, I mean, her name sounds like a town festival, right?" She scrunches up her nose from the memory, and I can't help but laugh at seeing this catty side to her. It's not annoying. It's honest and real—and I adore it.

"Anyway, Trisha was sitting on the bleachers next to me one day, and I knew it was, like, do-or-die time. When he walked off the field, I pretty much boxed her out, like old-school Celtics basketball, and just blurted out asking him to the Spring Fling dance. And he said *yes*. And we were together for more than a year."

When she's done, she just smiles, but there's an edge to it, like the memory of it hurts. I want to ask if she thinks they'd still be together. But I already know the answer to that. So I don't bother causing her any more pain. Instead, I dwell on the fact that she just told a love story like an ESPN commentator.

"I cannot believe you just referenced—and accurately, I might add—both the NBA and the fundamentals of basketball in that story," I say, putting the palm of my hand over my heart and sparing a quick glance at her. "God, I love you."

Oh. Shit! I don't know where those words came from. They weren't even in my mental queue, but damn if they didn't just roll off my tongue. I look back to the road quickly, then I glance down to the radio to start flipping through channels, doing my best to play it off like what I just said was the same as the rest of our normal banter. I didn't see her face for long, but I was on her long enough to notice her eyebrows shoot up to her forehead.

I've thought those words a few times, but usually they're future tense—as in "I think I could love her," or "I might love Rowe one day." But that's a bloody lie. I love her. I love her right now. I loved her when I read her words to Josh, and I hoped for everything she said because I'm a selfish bastard who wants her all to myself. I loved her when she busted my heart with that business about not meeting her parents. I loved her when I held her in my arms all night.

I was done the moment I saw her.

But goddamn if I wanted to tell her that right now! Right now, when I'm guarding every move and word I say for fear of chasing her away. I need to fix this.

"I uh...I meant that, like, you know...rhetorically," I say. I'm not even sure if rhetorically is the right word. I check to see if she's still looking at me in shock. Thankfully, she's moved her gaze to her lap, where she's picking at the edges of her fingers.

"Yeah, Nate. No...it's...it's no big deal. I got that," she says, moving her face to look out her window. "I know you didn't mean it."

But I did. And I do. And seeing her now makes me wish like hell I didn't take it back.

Chapter 19

Rowe

After Nate took back what he said, I became hyper-focused on fixing Cass and Ty. I was a little hurt at first that I had to find out about their fight from Nate, but Cass said she thought it was going to just be a nothing thing that would blow over. Unfortunately, when she went to talk to Ty about it a few hours later, he told her he thought they should take a breather, and maybe they were getting too serious.

It wasn't even my relationship—I wasn't even sure if what I was in *was* a relationship. But the thought of running away for fear of being too serious made something inside me snap. Cass and Ty had to try, because how was I supposed to navigate being with someone if those two couldn't figure things out?

"Girl, this better work," Paige says as she walks by me quickly in the hallway, her tote bag filled with *way* too much alcohol. Paige brought two of her new sorority sisters with her, which made me a little nervous, because I knew Nate was putting himself out there sneaking us out on the ball fields again.

"Seriously, they can't tell anyone about this. And no more people," I whisper to her in the elevator. Paige just winks at me and pulls her bag in against her body.

Nate and Ty are waiting for us downstairs, and we all start walking across the street. Just as I planned, Nate dials my phone from his pocket a few seconds into our walk, and I pretend it's my parents calling.

"Yeah, I filled that out. No, I promise I did. Uhhhg, hold on," I say, pretending I'm having a conversation about financial forms with my mother. Nate reaches into his pocket to end the call, but I keep the phone to my ear and hold up a finger to my friends.

"Hey, guys. I'll just meet you there in like five minutes. I have to run up and check something for my mom," I say, turning to jog back inside quickly. I hear Ty offer to wait for me, but Paige steps right in and throws her pretend tantrum—which is so accurate to her real tantrums—and explains that she can't be standing around campus with a bag of alcohol. I look back once I make it to the lobby, and the group has all started moving again.

Cass got a different version of the story. I knew she would be working out tonight, so I told her I would just wait for her to come home, and she and I would walk together. And somehow, all of my dominos have lined up today, because she's back to our room right on schedule.

Her shower is fast—another trait opposite of her sister—and we're walking over to the field maybe twenty minutes behind everyone else. I text Nate to let him know we're coming, and I feel my pocket buzz when we get to the outfield gate.

Ty is three shots in. You better hurry!

I manage to keep Cass distracted long enough for her and me to get deep into the outfield before she notices Ty, but she freezes as soon as she does.

"Oh fuck no," Ty says, tossing whatever was left in the cup in his hand into the grass.

"Rowe, did you know he was going to be here?" Cass looks heartbroken, and I feel sick. I shrug and start rethinking any good idea I ever thought I had. When Cass turns away and starts to leave, I grab her hand and I pull her close to me. I look Ty right in the eyes.

"No, Cass is my friend and *I* want her here," I say, keeping my eyes on his—a staring contest I have no intention of losing. And I don't.

"Fine, whatever," Ty says, turning toward Nate to talk privately.

I'm pretty worried this isn't going to work, but then Nate raises his arms over his head in a long stretch and yawns, and as Ty turns to look away, Nate holds both thumbs in the air and winks at me.

Drinking is the focus for the next hour. I'm careful, sipping slowly on my cup of rum and Coke that Nate mixed special for me. I've never been drunk. Just one more thing in that long line of rites of passage I missed during the *homeschool years.* The more the others do shots and play games though, the more I understand why Paige picked the sorority she did. The two girls she brought with her—I think their names are Lindsay and Angie?—could not be any more like her if they tried.

"Dude, are you sure these two aren't your twins?" Ty asks, making a joke after we all endure a ten-minute long recap of their trip to the department store makeup counter.

"Uh, I'm pretty sure that would make them triplets, dumbass," Nate says.

Everyone laughs—everyone, but Cass. I feel horrible, because she has sat with Nate and me for the last hour, just staring at Ty. I know she wants him to come talk to her, and when I tried to encourage her to go to him, she shot me that look that was more than a warning.

"Yeah, uh, this has been nice, but...I kinda think I'm gonna go. I have a test tomorrow...or something," she says, brushing the small bits of grass from the back of her shorts while she stands and hands me her still-full cup.

"Oh, Cass. Please...stay?" I say, knowing she won't.

"I...I can't," she says, looking over my shoulder to where Ty is busy entertaining Paige and her friends. I could kill Paige for bringing distractions.

Cass walks over to her sister and gives her a hug, and says something that makes them both laugh, and then she starts the long walk across the outfield grass.

"Well, crap," I say to Nate, taking a bigger drink from my cup than I have all night. It makes my belly warm and burns my throat a little, like old cough medicine.

"Hold on, give it a minute," he says, threading his fingers through mine, and pulling my body in closely against his. He nods in Ty's direction, and I look up to see him following Cass with his eyes. Within seconds, he hands his cup back to Paige and looks over at his brother and me.

"Yo, dude. I'm taking off, too," he says.

"Yeah you are," Nate says, his knowing smirk taking up every bit of his face.

"Yeah, yeah," Ty says, holding up both middle fingers.

"Holy damn. That worked!" I say, my heart speeding up with adrenaline to the point where I almost feel like running. And I might, except my head feels a little bit like it's floating away from my body.

"Whoa, slow down there, slugger. I think you've had enough," Nate says, taking the cup from my hands.

"Awe, I barely even finished one drink," I say, seriously thirsty for more, and liking the small tingles firing away along my skin. I was buzzing for sure, but I think I was more affected by the way Nate was holding me, and the warmth of his leg and side and chest along the right half of my body.

"I know, but I just got you home. I don't want to spend tonight watching you lose your onion burger in the dorm bathrooms," he says, his eyes lowering to look at my lips. His breathing changes, and when his teeth tug lightly at his bottom lip, I can't seem to stop myself from leaning in to kiss him, completely forgetting the fact that three other girls are out here with us.

As soon as my lips hit his, I'm sunk, and when his hands reach for my face, I move to my knees, sliding one leg over him so I'm straddling his lap, our lips never breaking. He sits up taller when I do this, letting his hands trail down my shoulders and arms, reaching around my waist to the back pockets of my shorts, pulling me to him even tighter.

This is desire. I have had sex exactly once in my life, and it was awkward and uncomfortable, just like a teenager's first time should be. But that was planned and orchestrated and coordinated to go along with Josh's parents' work schedules. Everything running through my mind right now is impulsive, and there's a part of me, a raw and hungry urge, that wants Nate completely.

"Good god, get a room!" Paige's voice breaks through our kiss, and Nate pulls his lips from mine, his eyes focusing on nothing but my eyes and mouth.

"That's probably a good idea. Ladies, I trust you can find your way home," Nate says, standing with me wrapped around the front of his body, and quickly moving his lips back to mine. He carries me that way all the way to the ball-field gate while

Paige whistles behind us. "If Ty is in my room, I am kicking him out," he says, his voice almost a deep growl in my ear.

"If Ty is in your room, *I* will kick him out," I say, moving my hands to his face and continuing our kiss once again. Nate carries me all the way to the main road across the street from our dorm building, and then he lets my body slowly slide from his until my feet touch the ground. His grip on my hand is tight, and I can feel my heartbeat in every inch of my body, the *thump-thump* growing faster and stronger the closer we get to Nate's room.

Thankfully, there's no need to kick Ty out when we get there, and Nate pushes the door closed behind us seconds after we enter, locking it before coming back to me. I tug at the long-sleeved hooded T-shirt he was wearing, and he helps me bring it over his head, quick to find my lips again once it's off. He's backing me toward his bed, and we're both working to kick our shoes off, tripping over one another and laughing when our feet get tangled.

Once I feel the back of my legs rest along the edge of his mattress, I sit back, my hands resting on either side of me, waiting for Nate to push me completely on my back. But when he reaches over and presses the switch on his desk lamp, my body drains of every feeling, and panic replaces it.

"Don't turn the light on," I say, my voice breaking while I struggle not to completely succumb to the tears I feel just under the surface. "I...I don't want you to *see* me."

Nate

Her voice is fucking heartbreaking, and it stops me cold. She's the single most beautiful girl I've ever seen, and the thought of touching her like this and not being able to see her—not just her body, but to see her face, her lips, her eyes flutter closed—is torture. But the way she asks, begs me to keep us in the dark, is about something bigger.

"You're beautiful," I say, stepping back enough to let my fingers graze along her cheek and chin. She leans into my palm, her head heavy as she closes her eyes.

"No, I'm not," she says, moving back in my bed until her back is against the wall. She draws her knees into her body and brings her hands to her face next, then begins to cry.

I hate that she thinks this about herself, and I hate that she lost two years of her life to fear and obligation. But she *has* to understand how beautiful she is. I crawl up next to her and pull her into my lap, locking my arms around her so she has nowhere to go, and she melts into me.

This...*this* is what I meant when I said "I'll wait." I don't need all of her, not all at once. I am willing to wait for whatever pieces she's willing to give. And if I have to help her make each piece whole first, then so be it.

I wait. I wait while she slows her breathing down and stops her eyes from watering. I wait while she chews at the edges of her fingernails, her eyes entranced into nothingness while her mind sorts out whatever roadblock is standing in her way. I wait for her to finally look at me, breathe deeply, and tell me her secrets. And I would wait forever. But I don't have to tonight, because she's looking at me, trembling, but ready to face her demons.

"My body..." she starts, but pauses, moving from my arms to sit in front of me, facing me. "I live with this constant reminder of what happened. It's...it's why I don't shower when everybody else does. It's why I wear clothing that covers me just enough. And even when they're covered...I know they're there. I can *feel* them."

She's hugging herself again, and I'm starting to understand that this isn't just something she does when she's nervous. It's something she does to remind herself of that day, of Josh—to punish herself when she feels guilty for forgetting.

"Show me," I say, my voice almost a whisper as I keep my eyes to hers, willing her to trust me, to love me.

"You'll think I'm ugly," she says, the tears once again threatening to come.

"Never," I say.

She leaves her eyes on mine for minutes, and I never break. I won't break. And I will wait—for as long as it takes. Her squeezing of herself loosens, and eventually her hands find their way to her lap, and then the bottom of her shirt. She lifts and pulls the first layer away, but I keep my stare locked on her eyes. I don't want her to feel frightened or ashamed, so I won't look. Not until she tells me to. She's still wearing a tight black tank top, but once she discards the first shirt on the floor, she begins to pull this one over her head too, her eyes telling me just how terrified she is.

Rowe is the bravest person I know. I still don't know what it is she's hiding from me, because I won't look until she tells me to. But I can see this struggle playing out in her eyes while she talks to me without talking. All I can see from my periphery is the thin, black strap and lace edge of her bra, but I know other than that, her top is completely bare. Her breathing comes in fragments—almost as if she's drowning. But I don't stop her. I know if she had to, if she wanted to, she would stop. She's testing herself, to see if she's strong enough. And I have to let her see if she is.

She reaches for my hand, and I give it to her, still maintaining our gaze while she pulls my fingers close to her. She kisses my knuckles and lays her cheek along the back of my hand, closing her eyes, before she slowly moves my hand to her side until I touch her. Once my palm is flat along her skin, she places her hand on top of mine and looks back to me.

"This is me," she shrugs. "I will have these...forever."

I'm careful when I swallow and mindful of my breath, because I don't want her to think I'm afraid to look at her. I don't want her to misread a single movement I make. I reach up with my other hand and run my thumb over her cheek, drying the last of her tears, and then I let my eyes slide slowly along her shoulder and arm until I finally settle and look at the body she calls "ugly."

The most noticeable one is deep and red—a line that runs at least eight inches along the side of her body, and I'm almost certain it's a surgical scar. It's surrounded by others, some small, and many deep, proof that bullets and metal did in fact penetrate her body.

She lets go of my hand, but I leave it there, careful not to move it too quickly. I can feel her eyes burning into me, just waiting for me to run. But I'm not going anywhere. I've never been more positive in my life of somewhere I'm *supposed* to be. I slide my fingers slowly over the rough skin, letting my thumb trace the long line up to the middle of her ribcage, and then I peel my hand away with caution. Her body jerks a little from losing my touch.

"Shhhhhhhhh," I whisper, touching my fingertips to my lips to kiss them and then pressing that kiss back to her beautiful, scarred skin. When I do, she shivers, so I tilt my head and spare a glance at her face to see her eyes full of tears. I lean forward and kiss them away, and pull her head to my lips, carefully working her body back along the bed until she's lying beneath me.

I hover over her, kissing her neck first, then the line along the strap of her bra. Her body rises up, arching into me when I come to the rounding of her breast, and I savor the moment, and let her just feel human—her body, for just the slightest instant, reacting to her needs and desires instead of her fears.

I kiss along the soft material of her bra, letting my lips and cheek feel the peaks of her nipples beneath, and I let my hot breath soften them before I continue to kiss between each, slowly inching my way down her body until I feel her tense up at my arrival at her scars.

"Beautiful. Every. Single. Part of you," I say, letting my lips fall to the long callused line first, taking note when her breath hitches. I continue to glide my hand along each mark, covering each with a kiss before moving on to the next, until I have cherished every inch of her.

When I come back to her face, her cheeks are sopping wet with tears, and she's no longer trying to hold in her emotions. Reaching my hands deep into her hair, I bring her forehead to my mouth, and I hold her against my lips. And again, I wait while she quivers and breathes—deep, labored breaths in between sobs—until her body calms, and eventually she's sleeping.

This...is love.

Chapter 20

Rowe

Waking up in Nate's arms was like beginning a brand new life. In the last two years, I've gone to bed without the aid of sleeping medication only a handful of times. Usually, I'm sick with something like the flu and that's why I can't take my medicine. But not when I'm with Nate. He's my placebo.

He was staring at me when my eyes finally focused. He said he had only been awake for a few minutes, but I have a feeling he had been looking at me for longer than that. I didn't get to shower at all yesterday, and I feel a little grimy now because of it. But I also don't want to wash away Nate's kisses. I know it seems juvenile—the thought of actually savoring a kiss. But I want to.

I slipped back into my room before class and was able to dress in the closet without waking Cass and Ty. I watched them sleep for a few seconds, satisfied at my good work, and then jogged to my first class, making it there right on time.

Next semester I was going to have to rethink how I organize my classes, because having philosophy this early in the morning is a challenge. My brain isn't ready to think this hard, and I'm pretty confident that I am going to fail the quiz I just turned in. I have learned one thing from this two-hour block class I take every Monday and Wednesday—I am not going to major in philosophy. I like it, bending my brain and forcing it to think about things differently, to see reasons behind actions. But it doesn't feel like something I want to do forever. But art—not necessarily the making of, but the appreciating of— that was something that I needed to explore more.

My mind has clearly wandered, because when the desks start shifting and my classmates start standing to leave the lecture hall, I snap from a trance. Yeah, this is another chapter I'm going to have to read twice having missed every word of today's lecture.

I'm the last to make it out of the class, and when I see Nate sitting along the small wall by the bike rack waiting for me, there's worry on his face. But when he finally sees me, he kicks away from the wall and comes my way with long strides, kissing me the second he's close enough.

"Are you okay? You looked upset?" I ask, my inner voice falling into its natural pattern of doubt and self-loathing. Of course I think he's regretting last night, rethinking what he saw and how he feels, but I'm quick to tamp those feelings down. They ruled my life for way too long, and I'm not letting them ruin this.

"I just didn't see you. Got worried, that's all," he says, completely capturing me all at once.

"What's this?" I point to the paper bag in his hand that looks to be saturated with grease. Nate just grins, his dimples deep when his eyebrows move up and down.

"Lunch."

"You brought me lunch?"

"Yeah, well, you packed that sad little lunch the other day when I found you eating before your art class, so I thought I'd surprise you. I don't have to be to algebra for a while yet," Nate says, grabbing my hand and pulling me with him until we're nestled between two trees in an area of the park where I can see everything.

I know what it is the second he rips open the bag, and my mouth begins to water for the Sally's burger. He also filled the bag with fries, and I start stuffing my mouth with those before he even has a chance to unwrap our burgers.

"Wow, piranha!"

"Sowwwwwy," I say, my mouth stuffed with fries. I cover my face with my napkin so I can talk more clearly while I chew. "I didn't eat breakfast, so I'm kinda starving."

"I figured," he says, holding a fry out for me to take. I bite it from his hand quickly, and he jerks back. "Okay, I am going to have to throw a ball in a few hours. Let's not bite my fingers off?"

"You knew the risk," I smirk.

"Yeah, I did," Nate says, his tone serious now as his eyes settle on me. His attention makes me blush, so I unfold my napkin and hold it up in front of me, like a curtain. But Nate reaches for it and tears it from my hand with a chuckle. "Hey, no hiding. Why do you do that?"

"I don't know. I just get embarrassed, that's all," I say, taking a big bite from my burger so I have an excuse not to talk any more.

"Well, I like to look at you, so you're going to have to get used to it. Here, let's practice." Nate moves his burger and wrapper to the side and lays flat on his stomach, propping his chin up on his hands and elbows close to me while he stares with his eyes wide. He doesn't blink for the longest time, and I do my best to hold my laughter in, just eating slowly, and dabbing the corners of my mouth with my napkin.

"The human female in her natural habitat is a unique creature. This one, barely from her parents' den, has yet to learn how to hunt, so she relies on her gathering techniques."

Nate is putting on what I *think* is supposed to be an Australian accent, though when mixed with his Southern drawl it doesn't sound quite right. I finish the last bite of my burger and pull the water bottle from my backpack so I can take a drink to wash it down, fighting to keep my lips from curling into a smile and giving me away.

"Finished with her feast, the young lioness prepares herself for her daily mating rituals. She must find herself a lion, but to do so, she must also ward off the competition from the other members of the herd who have recently come of age. She will need to do something to stand out if she wishes to pair herself with the King of the Jungle. And the lion is waiting..."

Before he can get out the rest of his commentary, I pour the entire contents of my water bottle down the back of his shirt, and I finally let my laugh escape my lips.

"Ooooooh shit! That's cold!" Nate says, jumping to his feet quickly, and holding the back of his shirt away from his body while he hops around.

"What do you think? That *stand out* enough for you?" I ask while I twist the cap onto my now empty bottle and tuck it inside my bag. Nate wrings out the dampness from his shirt a little, and then flicks drops of the water from his fingers at me, making me giggle and flinch. Then he climbs over me, straddling my waist with his knees, pushing my back down along the grass while he tickles my sides.

"Oh, you stand out, all right!" he says while I fight, albeit not very hard, to remove his hands from my sides. He loosens his grip soon, and sits up, pulling me with him and cupping my face in his hands.

"You have to get to algebra," I say, not really wanting him to leave but knowing he can't miss class. He just sighs, his eyes piercing me before he leans in for a long and gentle kiss.

"Did you get to go to your prom?" His question is so out-of-the-blue.

"No, that was...a school activity," I say, trying not to let my insides twist like they usually do when I think about things I missed.

"Right. This weekend, I'm taking you to prom," he says, standing completely now, and unwrapping his burger to take a large bite before he has to go to class.

"Oh, that's...you don't have to do that. I wouldn't know what to wear," I say, not really sure what he means, or how he could take me to a high school dance that doesn't even happen until the spring.

"No excuses. It's my birthday. My wish." Dimples. Smile. Accent. I'm sunk.

I knew his birthday was coming up, but I forgot it was this weekend. I have to get him something. I should get him something, right? What do you give a guy like Nate? With Josh, it was easy—I took him to a game and just splurged on nice seats for the Diamondbacks. Maybe Nate would like something like that?

I pull my phone out while I walk to class alone, and before I can talk myself out of it, I flip to the webpage I had saved—his mother's gallery site. I hit the contact tab and type her a message. Foolishness settles in the second I hit send, but it's too late, so I put my phone back in my pocket and join the others filing in to the lecture hall for art history. When my phone buzzes in my pocket minutes later, I almost fumble it to the floor just getting it out.

My email alert is on, and when I open the tab, there's already a reply from Cathy Preeter.

Rowe, so good to hear from you! I just called Dave, and he said he does know someone with season tickets in Oklahoma. I'll email you the name and number later, and I'm sure Nate would love that for his birthday. Send Nate my love. – Cathy

I'm almost more excited to have such a kind email from Nate's mother than I was to get a message from Nate in the first place. I'm not good at making impressions on parents—I've had so very little practice with it. And with Josh's parents, they knew me as coach's daughter long before I was the girlfriend. I wonder if that's what I am to Nate's parents? The girlfriend.

The lights go out, so I push my phone back into my pocket and pull out my notebook to make notes on today's set of slides. But every now and then I let my pen spill over to the margin, where I doodle hearts.

Nate

The week dragged by, probably because I couldn't wait to get to Friday. I know there's a lot Rowe missed, and her senior prom is probably just the tip of the iceberg. But this is also one of those things I can fix—I may not be able to bend time, but I can fill in the memories.

Taking Sadie to the prom was probably my last great memory I have of her. She was tall and toned, like Rowe, and she wore this deep purple dress that hugged her body down to her feet. It's the only picture I have left of us in my wallet, and I should probably throw it away. But something always kept me from tossing it in the past. I think it was the nostalgia, of being able to pull it out and remember *us* like *that.*

The last time I looked at it, I had just bailed from some girl's apartment during summer ball at about five in the morning. I woke up, hung over and naked, and for some reason that picture was poking out of the edge of my wallet on the floor when I crawled to my feet. I didn't miss Sadie, but I missed having *someone.* And my new pattern wasn't about finding *someone.* It was about finding *anyone*—anyone that would do. But seeing the picture of me with Sadie reminded me what really being with someone felt like. So that was the last girl I had sex with, despite the world of crap Ty gave me over it. I was going to just focus on baseball—baseball and nothing else until the right girl came along.

Rowe just happened to show up really fast.

She has tried to back out of what she is now calling the *Nate Preeter Prom Experience* all week long, but she's been trapped in her room with Cass and Paige for the last two hours, and I saw Paige walk in with garment bags and hair products. I honestly thing she's more excited about this whole thing than Rowe is.

"Did you seriously get a limo?" Ty asks from the hallway as he makes his way through our open door.

"Yes. I told you, I'm not messin' around. Prom is serious shit, and when you throw a prom, you do it right. Now come fix my damn tie," I say back, untying my fourteenth attempt at the bow.

"How are you my brother? I mean...seriously, I'm starting to think we need to give up on all the Barbie shit in our room, because you're making estrogen. You've become an estrogen factory, like women should come visit you for donations for hormone replacement. Wait, show me your legs." Ty is loving this, and as he reaches down to grab my pant leg to roll up the material, I kick at him.

"Dude, don't touch my leg. What are you doing?" I say.

"Just checking to see if you've started shaving your legs. Your razors aren't pink, are they?" he snickers.

"No, jack-ass. And this is just important, so cut the crap," I say, shoving the ends of my tie in his face so he can help me.

"To whom? To Rowe? Because I was in that room an hour ago, and she was not a happy camper having Paige's hands all over her face and head," he says, tugging and pulling on the tie until it's finally even on both sides.

"I know, but that's just her style. She doesn't like the attention and the fuss. But she likes the experience, and everyone needs to have a prom to remember. She missed out on hers," I say, slipping my jacket on and dusting the sleeves.

"I don't know, bro. I didn't have a prom experience, and I turned out fine," Ty says, winking as he turns away and reaches for the remote to flip on the TV.

"That's because you left prom—and your prom date—after fifteen minutes, to sleep with some college chick waitress you met during the dinner," I fire back.

"Oh yeah, that's right," he laughs. "Ahhhhh prom. A'right, go make your own memories."

"Shithead," I say as I tuck my wallet into my jacket. Ty blows me a kiss when I leave.

It was so much like prom—the knocking on the door, and standing in the hallway, feeling like an asshole while I listen to the girls giggle on the other side. I was actually sweating, I was so nervous. That all stopped the second Cass opened the door though and Rowe walked around the corner.

Her dress was white—innocent and delicate and incredibly girly. It fell down the side of one of her shoulders and soft layers of fabric hugged her body, but then ended in a blunt cut along the top of her legs. It was the shortest thing I have seen her in, and I know her legs are the only things anyone who comes in contact with us tonight are going to see. I can't take my eyes off of them right now.

"Daaaaamn," Rowe says, putting her fingers in her mouth to whistle. My tomboy, always trying to beat me to the punch line, steps back and holds her hand to her chin admiring me, like I'm the one out of the two of us worth admiring. "You wore a tux," she says, and a genuine smile curves on her lips.

"All part of the *Nate Preeter Prom Experience*, babe," I say, holding my arm out to escort her.

"Ewww, don't call me babe. It feels so...I don't know...*Goodfellas!*" she says, reaching for my arm and letting me guide her through the door and down the hall.

"Got it, babe," I say with a wink, just to be an ass.

156

"You have her home by morning, you hear Preeter?" Cass yells down the hall after us. I just hold my hand up with an *okay*.

When we reach the elevator, I hold the door with my back as she steps in, and that's when I see how far down the material scoops on her back. *Ohhhhhh fuck me!* The silk sways along her lower back with every shake of her hips, and I find myself rooting for it to sway just a little more, because I swear if it does I'm going to see her bare ass.

Two more guys get in the elevator with us along with a few girls, and I notice everyone looking at the back of that dress—at Rowe's bare back. Most guys would get all kinds of protective from this and want to cover their woman up, but not me. I know what it means to Rowe to be out in something like this, to show parts of herself she normally keeps hidden. And I never want her to feel ashamed again. Rowe is hot as hell, and I want everyone to get a good look at the girl that will be with me all night, and the rest of the weekend, and the rest of the semester and...well, pretty much as long as she'll have me.

"You seriously rented a limo," she says when we walk up to the parking lot curb where the driver is waiting for us.

"Damn straight I did," I say, opening the door for her to step inside. "Oh, and I almost forgot." I reach into my pocket and pull out the small yellow wrist corsage I picked up from the town florist. It was a last-minute order, so she didn't have time to make me anything fancy—but seeing the way it makes Rowe's face light up when she lets me slide it over her hand, and she smells it along her wrist, makes me think this simple flower was the perfect choice.

Putting together a prom night wasn't easy, and there really wasn't a way I could get her to a formal dance, so I did the next best thing and put together all of the silly things that go along with the prom. Our first stop was the Olive Garden, because that's the kind of place you think is a fancy restaurant when you're in high school. Two pasta bowls and two basketfuls of breadsticks later, Rowe and I left to climb back into the limo, sleepy from the carb overload.

"Okay, I'll admit it. That was pretty fun," she says, crossing her long legs in the car and completely putting me in a trance. "So, what's next?"

"Huh? Oh, yeah..." I shake my head.

"You were gawking," she says, pulling the edge of her skirt up a little higher on her thigh just to tease me.

"Don't start something you don't intend to finish, Rowe. I can put up that privacy glass anytime I want," I say, my eyes moving quickly from hers back to the newly exposed flesh on her leg.

"Well, isn't that part of the *Nate Preeter Prom Experience*, too?" she teases. I slide my arm around her to tug her close to my body, and I spend the rest of the short drive torturing her while I kiss her neck and slide my fingertips along the temptingly high hem of her dress.

I knew the next stop would get to her. I had to come up with something that would serve as a *prom*, so when I saw the Friday-night square-dancing notice posted at Sally's this week, I jumped all over it.

"Uh, Preeter? I'm pretty sure this is not what a high school prom is like," she says as I hold her hand and help her from the car to the curb.

"Really? 'Cause I was trying to be authentic to Arizona, and that's how y'all dance there pretty much, ain't it?" She slaps at my side with her small handbag, and I swing my arms around her and lift her into me, spinning her around until she giggles. God I love that sound.

"Wow, you really did your research on my home state. I suppose after this we're going to meet up for a shootout, and then take our horses down to the waterin' hole?"

"Don't be silly," I say, opening the door to lead her inside. "Everybody knows shootouts only happen at dawn."

I never would have expected it, but the square-dancing nights at Sally's are actually pretty happening. Granted, Rowe and I are the youngest people in the building by about forty years, but everyone thinks we are so sweet that they teach us new formations, buy us drinks and appetizers, and even make a special crown for Rowe to be named queen. We leave after two full hours of dancing, and I actually worked up enough of a sweat to have to lose the jacket and undo the tie.

Rowe kicks her shoes off in the car, and I pull her feet onto my lap to rub them. It's all I can do to keep my hands from running completely up her leg to the small, white panties I keep catching a glimpse of, and if she weren't looking at me with those eyes, making that face, I probably would.

"Thank you," she says softly, letting her face fall to the side along the headrest of the car.

"For what?" I say, my fingers pressing into the arch of her feet.

"For caring about me so much," she says, and her words cut into my heart completely.

"Rowe," I say, carefully setting her feet down on the floor and sliding myself closer to her so I can touch her face. "I would do...anything."

She leaves her eyes on mine for a long time, and I just keep stroking the side of her face as we pull back onto the main road to campus. "Anything?" she says, finally.

"Name it."

"Hold me again tonight?"

"Done."

Chapter 21

Rowe

Nate's dad came through with the ticket hook-up, and when I called his business associate, the man turned out to be a huge McConnell baseball fan, and he gave me the pair of third-row seats for free.

When I gave them to Nate after our *prom* experience, he was thrilled. There isn't much in the way of professional sports in Oklahoma, and the Thunder has a huge fan base, so good seats are tough to come by. Now, I just need to work up the mental stamina to be able to sit in a full arena for three hours— without having a panic attack. And I have six more hours to do it before tipoff.

"Hey, he's talking to you," a voice behind me whispers and jolts me back to attention.

"Huh, oh...sorry," I say, startled to have someone talk to me during art history, or in any class. My circle of friends hasn't really expanded beyond my dorm floor, and I haven't really made an effort to be social in class. I look up to see the professor tapping his pen on the side of his podium, waiting for me. Crap! I have no idea what the question was, and judging from the look on his face, he's been waiting for my answer for a while. I swallow hard and shift my posture in my seat, pretending to work to get a better look at the slide showing on the screen.

"He wants to know why yellow was the dominant color," the voice behind me whispers. I owe that voice!

"The artist was trying to depict the ugliness in human nature. He used yellow to signify greed and arrogance. And the lone figure, painted in blue, is there for hope—that humans can redeem themselves," I say, my voice coming through a little unsurely. I read this chapter last night, knowing I zoned out during the last lecture. I just hope I remembered things correctly—and I hope like hell that's really what the professor asked. If not, then the voice behind me might just be trying to make me look stupid.

"Perfection," Professor Gooding says, flipping to the next slide and picking on someone else now. I sink down into my seat, relieved.

"You're welcome," the voice whispers again.

"Thanks, I owe you!" I whisper back. Just then, an arm leans over my shoulder and shows me thumbs up, which makes me laugh silently and smile big.

As soon as class is over, I slide my notebook and textbook into my backpack, swinging it over my shoulder before heading to the main exit.

"I don't know about you, but I'm a big Diet Coke drinker. Forty-four-ouncer sounds mighty nice right about now." It's the voice, the one from behind me. I was so much less intimidated when I thought it belonged to the thin, awkward, geeky guy who usually sits there. I've seen this guy before, because, well, I'm not blind. He's not Nate, but he's pretty damn good looking. Blond hair, broad shoulders, and now I know he has green eyes to go along with the complete package. He always wears tight T-shirts, and I'm pretty sure he does nothing but lift weights—because I can see every ab muscle through the cotton of his shirt.

"You don't really *have* to buy me a drink, you know. I was happy to help," he says, leaning in toward me with a wink. His eyes run down my body once, but quickly. I don't think he wanted me to notice, but I did, and it makes me feel a mixture of heat and uneasiness all at once.

"Well, I was just heading home, but if you don't mind stopping at the snack stand on my way, I'd love to treat," I say, instantly wondering if this is flirting. I don't want to flirt. But he's cute, and he did something nice for me, and I am pretty sure I seem like I'm flirting. *This is not flirting!*

He smiles at me sideways while we walk toward the center of campus, squinting slightly when the sun cuts through the line of trees on either side of us. "All right, I'll take you up on it," he says, the unmistakable grin on his face confirming that yes, this is in fact flirting.

We stop at the small snack bar near the library, and I order us both large sodas. I give him his, carefully, so our hands don't touch during the exchange. Why am I even thinking about this? Worrying about things like hands brushing, and smiles, and the fact that he's looking at me like that again?

"I'm Tucker," he says, reaching his hand in front of us while we start to walk again. Shit, I'm going to *have* to touch him.

"Hi. I'm Rowe." I take his hand quickly and regroup my focus on my drink—also trying not to freak out over the fact that I'm pretty sure Tucker is now walking me home.

"Rowe. That's a cool name," he says, once again glancing at me sideways, this time holding the straw in his perfect, white teeth while he smiles. He's cute. No, scratch that—he's McConnell frat-boy-calendar hot. And a different me, a version without any issues, a me without a boy that I am pretty sure I want to love for a really long time, if not forever, would revel in the fact that hot-man-on-campus Tucker is obviously interested in me...*in that way.* But instead, all I keep thinking about is how I can lose him before we make it all the way to my building.

"Well, Tucker. Again, thank you *so* much for the help in class today," I say, reaching to shake his hand before I cross the street to my dorm—like a business deal. He just laughs lightly while shaking his head, then shakes my hand back and pulls his backpack up on his shoulder.

"You got it, Rowe. Hey, I'll see ya in class next week," he says walking backward and leaving his eyes on me. "And thanks for the drink! Next one's on me."

"Sounds good." *Sounds good?* No, it sounds awful, awkward, uncomfortable, stressful, unfortunate, and pretty much like the last thing I want to have happen. But the *walk* sign is now blinking, and Tucker has turned around, so I pick up my step and head for the front door to the dorm before he can see where I'm headed.

"Who's mister hottie?" I hear Cass say as I round the corner to the front door to the lobby.

"Ahhhhh, okay. Uh, I need to have a serious talk with you and Nate about scaring me. Honestly, I'm thinking of making you two wear bells." I keep my pace up and head to the elevator bank, but Cass is right in step with me.

"Right, got it. Won't scare you. Now spill it about mister pecks and abs," she says, pulling her sunglasses down on her nose to give me the full effect of her raised and suspicious eyebrows.

"How did you even see him?"

"Oh, easy. I was walking in with Nate, and he saw you both across the street. Then I stayed to watch for a while longer...pretty much because I'm *super* nosy, and I wanted to see what had him so pissed off. I get it now. That guy's hot."

Uhg. Nate witnessed that. I'm pretty sure I ceased any and all flirting immediately, but still. I wouldn't be happy if it were Nate walking home with the female equivalent of Tucker. There's a small piece of me that likes that Nate is jealous. We don't talk about our feelings much, and I know that's partly my fault. We talk about my fears mostly, and we've broken through so many of them. But we don't talk about how he feels about me, and how I feel about him. Not really.

There was that brief moment, where he told me he loved me in the car on our way back from the airport, and when he said those words, my entire heart filled up with a joy I didn't know existed. But then it left me just as fast—when he said he didn't mean it. And I'm too afraid to open up that conversation again. Because I don't know how to be in a relationship—when you're not sixteen, and in high school, and going on dates that require you to be home before ten on weekends.

I told Josh I loved him almost immediately. We both said the words while making out in my driveway. But I know now we didn't really mean them then. I meant them eventually, months after we'd been dating, when I realized how important and special he was to me. But I must have said them a hundred times before, and every time they were empty. I think that's why I'm so afraid to say them to Nate, because I don't want him to say them back just because he thinks he has to—like lines in a play, a reaction to my action. I don't want this to be like when I was sixteen.

"So, I'm pretty sure you're going to have to deal with that conversation with mister hottie," Cass says to me as the elevator slides open, and she steps outside. She sees Nate waiting outside our door first, and when I step out and see him, shivers run down the length of my entire body. He. Looks. Pissed!

The closer I get, the more he tries to force coolness, but I can see there's something simmering underneath. He kisses my cheek quickly, then sits backward at my desk chair, his legs wrapped around either side, and his knees bouncing up and down, just teeming with jealous energy.

I toss my backpack on my bed and pull my shoes from my feet before crawling up next to it, getting out my notebooks. Cass, obviously feeling the tension, just smiles at Nate with a nod and then leaves our room, actually shutting the door behind her. Oh god.

"What time do you think we should leave?" I ask trying my best to pretend like everything about the atmosphere in our room is normal.

"I don't know, it takes an hour to get there, so five-ish?" His knees are still bobbing. I can see the motion from the corner of my eyes.

"Okay, I don't need to do much to get ready, so we can still eat something before we leave."

"I'm not that hungry," he says.

Oh.

And now we have silence. I'm busying myself flipping through pages of my notebooks, pretending to look for something, just to avoid eye contact, and Nate's knees are still jumping, and his eyes are still on me, and there's still this awful awkwardness. And then suddenly they stop, and Nate stands.

"All right, just come by when you're ready," he says before quickly escaping through the door. The second it shuts behind him, I flop down on my back. What the hell? Cass comes back in a few minutes later.

"Girl, what did you do to that boy?" she asks.

"Honestly, I have no idea. He just sat here, silent, but edgy. I mean SUPER edgy. And then he left."

"Awe, jealousy is cute on him," she says, crawling up next to me and laying her head next to mine. I just look at her with my eyes wide. "You should use this. I bet you could get him to do anything you want right now."

"Okay, when did Paige take over your body? Bring back Cass," I say, standing to change into a comfortable pair of jeans and a blue shirt for the basketball game.

"Hey, we are twins. Some of those characteristics are genetic," she winks.

Shaking my head at her, I pull on a clean shirt and work my hair into a loose ponytail, suddenly wanting to make myself as plain as possible—so no other boy notices me *ever* and Nate can start acting normal again.

Nate

"Dude, what crawled up your ass?" Ty asks when I shove through our door, popping the handle with enough heat to lodge it against the opposite wall. I pry it loose and close the door again behind me, then I let my head fall forward against it.

"Ohhhhh you know, just lost my shit a little seeing Rowe with some bodyguard-looking dude," I say, rolling my head to the side to look at Ty with a raised brow.

"Ha. You're jealous. That's funny," Ty says, going back to whatever he's working on at his laptop.

"Uh, it's not funny. And I hate it. And I'm pretty sure Rowe doesn't like me like this either."

"Yeah, well, then maybe she won't go hanging out with...what did you call him? Bodyguard-lookin' dudes?" Ty's not quite teasing me, but there's a little bite to his comment.

"He was just big, that's all," I say, not really wanting to go into how good-looking he was, knowing that would just send Ty into fits of laughter.

"The girl practically got you floor seats to the Thunder game, and she's over here more than she's anywhere else. You've got nothing to worry about, unless...have you closed that deal yet?"

Silence. I keep my back to him while I pull out my sweatshirt.

"You're kidding me!"

"She's different, Ty. This isn't some girl from summer ball that I'm using to forget about Sadie. She's...more," I turn back away from him, hoping like hell I'm going to get serious-Ty and not the asshole that also inhabits his body. When he doesn't say anything for a while, I start to relax.

Ty doesn't say another word, and when Cass comes over, the two of them sit quietly, studying. Rowe comes about a half hour later, and despite all of the sense I've talked myself into since I left her room, the minute I see her, my selfish, king-of-the-jungle, pound-on-my-chest instincts move right back inside my body.

She's wearing a pair of tight jeans, black Converse shoes, and a thin, blue T-shirt. I know she's going to get cold later, but I don't want to tell her, because I want her to have to wear my sweatshirt—something of mine. And I want bodyguard-guy to run into us while she's in it, so we can clear that shit up right then and there.

"You look nice," I say, doing my best to push the beast that wants to pound his chest back inside. She leans into me, and I kiss her cheek, pulling her close to my side. Her hair is pulled back, and all I want to do is bite her neck.

"Okay, look for us on TV," she says to Cass, and I reach down to hold her hand again. My teammate Reece was nice enough to let me borrow his car again so I could drive us into the city. I was starting to think I needed to bring my car up from home just so I didn't have to rely on others so much. It wasn't a big deal when it was just Ty and I, but now that I want to do things like take Rowe places, it just seems to make sense. I think Ty would like it if I had my car here, too. It's modified so he can drive it.

Rowe is biting at her lip when we get in the car, and I can tell she's nervous. I know the crowd is going to be a big deal for her. I tried to talk her out of coming, but I know she wants to prove to herself that she can do this.

"I'll be right next to you, the entire time," I say, reaching for her fingers again as I back out of the parking spot. She just smiles nervously.

For the entire drive, we talk about nonsense. Rowe tells me stories about spending Thanksgivings at her grandparents' farm up North, and I talk about our non-traditional ones with my parents, where we order in a bunch of things that have no relationship to turkey whatsoever. She likes the rambling stories I tell, and I think it's setting her mind at ease, so I just keep talking. But inside, all I'm thinking about is that asshole that walked her home, and how I want to ask her about him. But I know now is *definitely* not the time—it wouldn't come out right.

The parking lot is packed, so we find a spot near the roadway. We have to walk far, but at least the exit is close, assuming a line of traffic doesn't block our car in when we leave. The closer we get to the entrance, the tighter Rowe is holding my hand, until eventually my knuckles are actually turning white.

"Rowe, we don't have to do this. I would be just as happy spending the next hour driving home with you, and then we can stop to get Sally's or something," I say, my heart breaking from the terrified look in her eyes as we stand along the sidewalk while hundreds of people pass us. The crowd is so thick, people bump into our shoulders, and Rowe closes her eyes every time it happens.

"Come on, what do you say?" I ask, urging her, almost begging her, to let us leave. Her mouth opens slightly, and she's about ready to speak, when a voice fills the space behind me.

"Nate? Preeter? Is that...you?"

You have to fucking be kidding me? My heart has just lodged itself into that uncomfortable place in my throat, the spot that makes it hard to talk or breathe. The look on Rowe's face has shifted from terrified to confused, and in a split second I see the suspicion take over her face—and she's right.

"Sadie. Wow," I say, turning to fully take in the all-too-familiar vision in front of me. She's wearing a pair of really short black shorts and black heels. She's my height, maybe an inch taller than me in those shoes; while I see in her eyes the girl I gave my everything to in high school, her body is different—older, more...*fuck, I don't know. Just more.*

"What are you doing here?" she says, reaching for me to give me a hug. I let go of Rowe's hand to hug her back, but when I reach for Rowe again, her hands are stuffed deep in her pockets. *Shit!*

"Oh, it's...well, a late birthday celebration, I guess? We just came for the game," I sound like an idiot. I'm too panicked to even think straight, and I wish like hell Rowe would give me her damn hand again. "Mom and Dad said you're playing for OSU?"

"Yeah, it was just a really great opportunity. That's what I'm doing here tonight. They're announcing us at halftime—some publicity something or whatever," she says, her eyes drifting over my shoulder every few seconds while she talks, and eventually my brain gets the message.

"Cool. Oh, this is my friend Rowe. We met at McConnell." I know they're the wrong words the second the sound of my own voice hits my ears, but it's like an avalanche—I pushed a rock from the top of the mountain, and now all I can do is watch it tear down the snow in its path. The two girls—the only two I have ever cared about—are shaking hands in front of me, and the one I love is giving me a glance that says I just broke her heart.

"Well, I've gotta go catch up with the girls. Maybe I'll see ya again," Sadie says, reaching to give me one more hug. I don't know what to do with my arms, and all I can think about is how I can signal to Rowe that this—that Sadie—is meaningless, despite the massive mess that just spilled out of my mouth.

"Let's go get our seats," Rowe says, brushing past me and following in Sadie's wake. On the bright side, her fears seem to be gone. There isn't a trace of the nervous girl I was worried about just a few minutes ago. But something cold has definitely filled her space, and it's my damn fault.

We get to our seats, and I notice Sadie is sitting across from us with her team. She waves at us, and I hold up a hand to signify that I do in fact see her too. Seriously, universe—not cool. Not cool!

Rowe's arms are covered in goosebumps, and I know she's cold, so I offer her my sweatshirt, but she just shrugs me off and says she's fine. She doesn't even fake a smile. She shivers through the entire first quarter, just to prove a damn point.

"Rowe, please. Just take my sweatshirt," I say, pulling it over my head and handing it to her.

"I would kind of rather die," she says, her smile a tight flat line. *Fuck.*

"I'm going to get something to drink. You want something?" I say, standing, almost ready to run I'm so uncomfortable. Rowe just shakes her head *no* and crosses her legs in the other direction. I let out a heavy sigh and make my way to the aisle. At least she seems comfortable with the crowd.

While I wait in a line that literally wraps around the building's insides, I pull out my phone to text Ty.

Me: *You're never going to believe what happened.*

Ty: *You ran into Sadie.*

Me: *Uh, how'd you know?*

Ty: *I'm watching the game with Cass. They did an interview with the OSU coach before the game, and the team was in the background.*

Me: *Super.*

Ty: *I'm guessing it didn't go well?*

Me: *I'm pretty sure Rowe wants to choke me. Or punch me. Or both.*

Ty: *Should she?*

Me: *Probably.*

Ty: *Tell her I'll hold you down.*

Me: *Thanks.*

Ty: *Hey, that's what brothers are for. Oh, and Sadie looks hot.*

Me: *Not helping.*

Ty: *Didn't say I was good at helping. Just holding you down for beatings.*

Me: *Thanks...again*

Ty: *Anytime*

I order a large soda and some Red Vines and make my way back to our seats a few minutes before halftime. Of course, just to make sure I feel the full brunt of the universe's punishment for me, when I turn down our row, Sadie is now sitting in my seat—talking to Rowe.

"Oh, sorry. I was just waiting for you to get back. Really nice to meet you Rowe," Sadie says, sliding past me and kneeling in the aisle while I take my seat next to Rowe. "I wanted to let you know my parents are coming up in a couple weeks for our home match up with Oklahoma. They'd love to see you I'm sure. Just...if you can make it."

"Thanks, I have a few fall tournaments coming up, so I don't know if I can make it. But...we'll see," I say, trying to be polite. That's the problem—I'm too damn polite, and I can tell I said the wrong thing again by the way Rowe's weight shifts next to me.

"Okay, well, hope you can make it." Her legs are almost in my lap when she stands to walk away, and I notice Rowe's eyes grow wide just looking at them. Sadie is extremely attractive, and she's confident. Hell, she used to intimidate me. But she's nothing compared to Rowe. I just have to make Rowe understand that.

"I'm sorry. I didn't think she'd come talk to you while I was gone." My voice sounds pathetic and meek—it's not enough.

"She's nice," she says, her eyes so goddamned sad. Rowe won't even look at me, and when I offer her a Red Vine, she just sighs and holds up a hand.

They introduce the OSU team during halftime, and the announcer does a brief interview with Sadie and a few of the other players. She looks my direction a few times, and I can tell she wants to make sure I'm watching, but this time I keep my hands in my lap and my attention anywhere but her.

"I think I wanna go home early. Is...is that okay?" They're the first words Rowe has said to me directly in almost an hour, and I react instantly.

"Whatever you want," I say, pulling my sweatshirt back over my head and putting my hand along her back to guide her out through the aisle. When we get to the stairs, she shirks my touch, and it stings.

The first half of the car ride is filled with more silence. I smile at her quietly, and she gives me a fake smile in return, but I know the truth behind her eyes. I hurt her, and being there in front of Sadie made her uncomfortable, and I didn't handle it well. I just didn't know how to make it better.

"Look, Rowe. I'm really sorry we ran into Sadie. I...I don't really know what to say. It was just really awkward." She laughs once, rolling her eyes and looking out her window. "I know, I should have just ignored her or cut the conversation off quickly, but I'm not good at being an asshole."

"I don't know, Nate. I think you've got asshole down pat," she says, her eyes on me for the first time all night. She's pissed, but she's talking to me, so I'll take it.

"Yeah, you're probably right," I say, taking in another deep breath. "I'm really sorry."

"You called me your *friend*, Nate." She's actually yelling now. We're pulling into the lot at school, and all I want to do is stay here in this car and figure things out, but the moment I put it in park, she opens her door and slams it in my face.

"I know. I just panicked. I didn't want to hurt Sadie's feelings, flaunting my relationship in her face," I start, but Rowe spins around to face me, her hand flat on my chest to keep an arm's distance between us.

"You didn't want to hurt *her* feelings?" she says, letting out a breathy laugh that's laced with tears. "You didn't want to hurt your ex-girlfriend's feelings—the girl who cheated on you with your best friend. The one you told me you fell out of love with and never looked back. That's...wow. That's truly amazing and kind of you, Nate...to think of *her* feelings like that."

"There's a history there...and I just froze. I haven't talked to her in months, and I just didn't want to make her uncomfortable." Shit! I'm making this worse.

Rowe starts walking away, laughing loudly now with her arms in the air. I'm a good ten paces behind her—my feet glued to the sidewalk with guilt—when she turns around one last time at the door.

"Well, good for you, Nate. I'm glad you were able to spare *her* feelings. But man...you sure fucked-over mine." She's through the door in an instant, and I just let her go, because I need time to figure out how to say the meaningful words Rowe needs to hear—the things I desperately need to say but can't seem to articulate. Clearly, my brain needs recalibrating because it has done nothing but make the wrong move for the last two hours.

Me: *Home early. Wanna grab a beer at Sally's?*

Ty: *Be right down. Saw Rowe in the hall. I'm guessing you'll fill me in.*

Me: *Yeah, it's gonna take a few beers to fix this.*

Ty: *You're buying.*

Me: *Naturally.*

Chapter 22

Rowe

"Well, last night could not have gone any worse," I say while Cass finishes getting ready for her Friday morning class. She's half the girly girl Paige is, but she still takes a while getting ready every morning.

"Okay, walk me through this again. So you two ran into his ex, and he said you were his *friend*," Cass peeks her head around the corner while she holds her hair up on her head, poking a pin in the side.

"Yep, that's pretty much it."

"Well, I do date his brother, and they can both be pretty stupid. Honestly, I wouldn't worry about it," she says, leaning back in to look over her hair in the mirror.

"Right, okay. I won't worry about it. Poof! Look at that, I'm not worrying. Suddenly, I have no troubles. Good advice," I'm being a little bitchy, but Cass isn't really feeling the seriousness of what I'm saying.

"Well, now you're just being mean. I'm going to class. Try to fix your attitude before I get back so we can go to his game tonight. Your parents still coming for the tournament tomorrow?"

"Yeah," I sulk.

"Hey, why don't you go to the gym or something? Get your mind off of things since you don't have a class this afternoon," she says, pulling her backpack from her chair.

"Maybe," I say, still not willing to be cheery.

"Whatever, I'm done helping you. See you at four." I love Cass's brand of tough love, and in most ways, she's the perfect friend for me. But right now, I just want someone to want to help me spread rumors about Nate on the Internet.

After Cass leaves, I try just kicking my feet up at my desk and watching TV. I used to watch soap operas with my mom. I was really into *Days of our Lives*. What's amazing is how I haven't watched it once since I've been at McConnell, yet here I am, able to tune in and know exactly what's happening in the storyline. Jack is dead...or is he? Jennifer is dating some doctor. And Hope is looking for someone on an island. Yep, all caught up.

Maybe Cass is right. Maybe I should check out the rec center. They had some great tennis courts, and it looked like they had pick-up games going on a lot. Maybe I could get back into it...just a little.

It takes me a while to pull my racket out from the bottom of my trunk. It's still buried under the thick winter coat I have yet to use. I haven't swung it seriously in two years, but I could still beat my dad. So maybe there's still something there.

I change into a pair of cotton shorts and a thin T-shirt, then grab my iPod and lock up. If no one is there, I'll just put my racket in a locker and try out a few of the machines. Nate's been gone since early this morning. I know, because I waited outside our door for his to crack open, and then I hurried inside before he could notice. He lingered in the hallway for a while, which made me feel...nice. But it didn't last long; that unsettled feeling moved right back in again.

"Oh good. I guessed right. I was about to give up," Tucker says from the bench outside our dorm building. He looks like he's been running, and the fact that he's waiting here—for me—suddenly has my stomach churning.

"Wha....were you waiting for me?" I'm a little freaked out, and I can feel my left eye starting to twitch.

"Uh...I...yeah. I was. I'm sorry. That's creepy isn't it? I was out running and then I sort of found myself here, and then I started to think, 'huh, I bet she lives here,' and then next thing I know I'm sort of sitting here for a while playing with my iPod. Sorry, I...hmmmm. Yeah, just sort of did this. I don't know." He looks nervous and embarrassed, which actually sets me a little at ease.

"It's okay. I was just surprised by it. I'm heading out...actually?" I scrunch my shoulders, trying to feign disappointment. I don't want to hurt Tucker's feelings, but I also don't want him hanging around my building. And I *really* don't want Nate seeing him hang around my building.

174

"Oh, yeah. I mean, I was just running by. Where you headed? I'll head back with you."

Great. "I'm just going for a quick workout. Try and get a few swings in," I say, holding up the racket.

"Need a partner?"

He's persistent. But I don't think he's really threatening, and I *do* need someone to volley with. I was dreading the idea of working in with a group of strangers. I'm not sure how much Tucker knows about tennis, but I'm willing to give him a try. And it will get us moving out of here, away from my dorm and farther away from the ball fields I know Nate is at for most of today.

"So, what made you pick art history?" He's making small talk during our walk to the courts, and I'm grateful he's carrying the conversation, because I can't think of a single thing to say.

"Well, I'm one of those big *undecideds.* Duh duh duh," I sing dramatically. "Anyway, I took a variety of electives this semester to try to figure out exactly what I want to do. I really like art, but not necessarily the creation of it. I'm more into the appreciation—and I think I can tell a story from a work of art. You know, sort of help interpret what the artist meant for the masses? God, that sounds arrogant, huh?" I have been leaning toward a degree in art history though, and I even went so far as to look into internships with the Oklahoma City Museum of Art.

"Actually, I think that sounds amazing. Your answer the other day? That was awesome. I'm a second-year art history major, and I've been helping out in Gooding's class, trying to earn brownie points. I think you'd fit right in," he says. I watch as he rolls up the cord on his iPod, tucking it in his shorts, and then I realize I'm staring at his very toned arms for *way* too long. Our eyes make contact for a brief second, and I recognize that flash of flirtation in his gaze again. *Oh god. No, this is NOT flirting!*

"So what are you hoping to do when you're done? Run a gallery or something?" I ask, doing my best to steer the conversation back to those moments before his forearms and my gawking.

"Me? Galleries? No, that's not really my thing. It's going to sound awful, but...I like the money behind art," he says, wincing a little at his confession.

"Yeah, that does sound bad. Like, a thief? Or, what...you want to run auctions or a pawn shop?"

"No," he chuckles. "More like appraisals and high-end art dealing. I like that fact that art *is* a commodity. And I think it would be a fun business to be a part of—that's all."

I take in everything he says, and when he puts it that way, it does make sense. The only reason art is something I could major in is because of the value it brings to the economy. It's all well and good to think that we appreciate the arts for their intrinsic value, and I truly do. But I wouldn't be able to if someone somewhere didn't pay for it.

"Okay, I'm down with your career plan. As long as it funds mine," I smile big and hold out my fist. Tucker just laughs and then gives me knuckles.

"Deal," he says, holding the gate open for the tennis courts. "All right, so take it easy on me, okay? I'm more of the lift-heavy-things kind of athlete. I might not be too much competition right away, but I'm a quick study."

"Sure. I'll take it easy," I say, winking at him as I pull my racket from its zipper bag. And damn...I'm flirting again.

Tucker wasn't as bad as he said he was. I did win every set, but he took a few games to deuce, and they weren't easy wins. An hour of playing had me exhausted, but my head was finally starting to clear up, and now all I could think about was getting back home so I could get ready to go to Nate's game tonight. I needed to see him, and I needed to talk to him after his game—tell him how much he meant to me, whether or not he said it back.

"Right, so you kicked my ass," Tucker says, pulling his shirt up to wipe the sweat from his brow. Instead of looking, I focus on my racket and my barely untied shoelace—anything but his bare stomach and abs.

"Nah, you held your own. You have nothing to be ashamed of with that performance out there," I say, feeling my cheeks burn at how my words came out. I sound like I'm gushing.

"So, what's on tap for the rest of Rowe's day?" he asks.

"Oh, not much. Just heading over to the baseball game tonight with a few of my friends," I say, instantly regretting it.

"Yeah? They play this early? I didn't think the season started until spring." All I want is for some great fix to land in my lap, but there isn't one. And I've already established that I'm crap at lying.

"It's a tournament. They have a few in the fall, just to keep the athletes prepped," I say, trying to stand and signal that I'm ready to leave through my body language. I'm stuck somewhere between wanting to be polite and rude; I think this whole thing would be easier if Tucker weren't so damned good looking, and if Nate were really my boyfriend—like the kind that says he loves me, and introduces me to his ex-girlfriend as his *current* girlfriend.

"Cool. Well, maybe I'll see ya there later then," he says, unrolling the cord on his iPod while he backs away. All I can do is nod, smile, and wave goodbye.

Cass thinks it's hilarious when I tell her I may have accidentally invited "hottie-ab-man," as she calls him, to Nate's baseball game.

"Rowe, Nate's literally going to shit himself. Like, I mean, he's going to walk out there on that field, turn around and see you talking to Ab-man, and then shit his pants. And then he's probably going to climb up into the stands and pummel this guy," she says, and I know she's sort of right. But I can't really do anything now. I don't even have Tucker's number, and I don't know his last name to look him up.

"What's all the fussy fuss," Ty says as he enters our room. That's Ty's new favorite term for my issues with Nate—fussy fuss. I'd feel offended if it weren't an absolutely spot-on description of it all. Fussy fuss. I am sick of fussy fuss.

"Rowe invited that dude, that makes Nate crazy, to his baseball game," Cass blurts out before I can stop her.

"Oh, damn. Rowe? Not cool. I mean you're fucking with baseball again. Not cool," Ty says, turning his back to me, and shaking his head with his arms out. I look at Cass, hoping for backup on this one, but she's quick to take Ty's side, too.

"Yeah, Rowe. I'm with him on this one. Not cool," she says, sticking out her tongue at me and laughing. She's finding this whole thing terribly entertaining, but meanwhile, I want to dig a hole, a really deep hole, and push my head inside and cover it in dirt. I'd be content to hide there, eating dirt, for the next two hours.

"Well, let's go get this over with. It should be interesting," Ty says, waiting for me at the door.

"What if I don't go? I'll just hang out here. If I don't go, Tucker won't see me in the stands, and then he'll just go home," I say, starting to really like this idea.

"That's a terrible idea. First of all...wait, did you say this guy's name is *Tucker*?" Ty asks.

"Yeah, why? You know him?" I say, hoping like mad that this situation doesn't get any worse.

"Nah, Tucker's just a pussy name. That's all," he says, and Cass smacks the side of his arm with her bag. "Ow! Anyway...it's a terrible idea because Nate's going to be looking for you. And if he looks for you, and you're not there, he's going to play like shit. And he can't play like shit."

"But what happens if he sees me sitting next to Tucker?" I ask, not really sure how that's any better.

"Yeah, you got me there. If he sees that he'll play like shit. Huh...well, let's get a move on then. I don't wanna miss my brother's crappiest game since little league when he was twelve," Ty says, flinging the door open in his wake and waiting for me in the hall.

I stare at the door for a solid five seconds, weighing my options—weighing everything Ty said. And in the end, I know I'm going to his game. Not because I want to be there for him to see, but because I want to see *him*. Because I need to see him. Because I need to tell him I love him and end the fussy fuss.

Nate

178

My head is not completely in the game. It's a crappy Ivy League team, so I know the competition won't be too tough. If ever there was a game not to be fully invested in, this was it. I just needed to show up enough to make a good impression on coach, not make him regret bringing me in and playing me over his senior catcher.

I keep looking in the stands, waiting for Rowe to be there. But there's still thirty minutes before game time, so I try to distract myself with a few rounds in the cages.

"Hitting with a little extra heat today, huh Preeter?" Coach Morris has been trying to get me to unleash my swing during the last few exposition games. He's right—I've been swinging timid. And Rowe was right, too—I've been dipping my shoulder. I started working on that last week, and I've been striking the ball better ever since. I was excited to show off in front of her today, but now all I'm excited about is seeing her here period—knowing she doesn't hate me.

"I've been working on it, yeah," I say between grunts and swings.

"Good, well...whatever it is you're doing, do more of that," he says, going back to the charts on his clipboard before laughing and adding under his breath, "That's what they pay me for. Coaching wisdom. *Do more of that.*"

Coach Morris is half the reason I'm here. He's one of the best hitting coaches in college, despite what he says. And if I can come out of here with a halfway decent swing, I might really have a shot at catching in the majors.

I take a few more rounds, then my pitcher calls me out for warm-ups. Even though I tell myself I'm not going to look, the row of seats right behind the dugout is the first place my eyes go to when I jog out on the field. Ty's always the first thing I see—probably because my eyes are trained to look for him after so many years of having him come to my games. But then they fall immediately on Rowe. She can't see my eyes clearly through my mask, so I take this opportunity to really stare— long and hard.

God, I'm an idiot. If I could get one redo in life, it would be to go back to that moment outside the Thunder's stadium—in that very second when I realized it was Sadie standing behind me. I wouldn't even bother to turn around. Instead, I'd just grab the sides of Rowe's face and kiss her, like one rude show-off in front of my ex-girlfriend. And not because I give two shits how it would make Sadie feel. Actually, I don't like the idea of making her feel bad. But if it would wipe away all doubt in Rowe's mind and make her realize how much she means to me, then I'd kiss her for hours right in front of Sadie just to prove my point.

"Preet! You ready?" Cash is tossing the ball, playing with his grip, ready to warm.

"Yeah, sorry. Just waiting for someone to show up. But it's all good. She's here," I say, sliding the mask up on top of my head so we can throw for warm-up.

"Which one, that sexy little blond thing next to your brother?" he asks, and I smile and shake my head.

"No, that's my brother's girlfriend. But feel free to tell him you think his chick is hot—he likes that. Mine's the other girl, darker hair, long-ass legs," I say, waiting for him to throw back to me so I can turn around and take her in one more time.

"You mean the one that dude's hitting on right now?" he says, and I just hold up my hand to halt his throw. What. The. Fuck?

"Oh, you have to be kidding me," I grit through my teeth. Cash walks up next to me, putting his elbow on my shoulder.

"So, I'm taking it—he's not supposed to be here?"

"No. And in a few minutes, he won't be breathing," I say, tossing my mask from my head, and dropping my glove to the ground before I break into a jog.

Rowe doesn't see me coming at first, but Ty does. I make eye contact with my brother, and mouth a few choice words, but he just shakes his head and laughs. Without even hesitating, I hop the small wall in front of the seats and climb up the two rows to the dugout row where the big bodybuilder man is now sitting *way too fucking close* to my girl.

"Hey, who the fuck are you?" I ask, unable to stop myself. I passed civil and polite twenty yards ago, and I've gone straight to crazy.

"Nate!" Rowe says, her arms out like I'm the one who's out of line here.

"Dude, I'm sorry...I was just visiting with Rowe. I'm Tucker," he says, reaching out a hand, which I slap away instantly.

"Tucker? You know what rhymes with *Tucker*? I yell, igniting a round of laughter in my brother.

"Nate! That's enough," Rowe says, standing in between her new friend and me. "Tucker, I'm sorry," she says, showing me her back while she talks to...*this dude!*

"No, it's okay. I get it. I've got things to do, so no worries. Just thought I'd stop by. I'll...I'll just see you Monday," Tucker says, pulling his hat a little lower on his brow. The dude is big—I mean, *wide!* And I'm already feeling like an ass from the scene I caused, but he's leaving, and that's what I really wanted. "Nate, man. Heard good things about you. Really, nice to meet you— maybe next time it'll be in better...well, circumstances," he says, reaching his hand out toward me again. I just look at it and laugh once before looking away.

"I'm sorry," Rowe says quietly to him again as he leaves.

"What the hell, Rowe?" My entire body is tingling with adrenaline, and I'm still pissed as hell, so yeah, I'm taking it out on her.

"Nate, go play your stupid game, or I'm going home," she says, sitting back in her seat and pulling her knees up, her feet propped on the top of the dugout. "Go on. Run along," she says, waving me off. I'm so pissed; all I can do is run my hand over my face to keep myself from saying a slew of more things I'll undoubtedly regret in the next twenty minutes.

"Shut up, fuck nut," I say to Ty as I walk by and flip his hat from his head. "Your head looks stupid in that hat. It's too big."

"Whatever makes you feel better, bro. I can take it," he laughs. And he keeps laughing the entire time I walk back out to the bullpen.

"How'd that go?" Cash asks, nodding to the girl I just pissed off beyond recognition behind me.

"Not well, Cash. Not well. Just throw the damn ball," I say, pulling on my mask and squatting, an extra bit of juice still coursing through my veins. I was going to hit the ball hard tonight, but like hell if I ever wanted to get pumped up with something like *that* again.

Coach was pleased. Two triples and a homerun—I'd say it's a personal best. I swung like I was taking my bat to Tucker-fucker's midsection, and I ran like I was hunting him down. I am not a jealous person, or at least, I've never had a reason to feel like this before. And I don't think I like it.

As the game wore on, the reality of my behavior really started to set in, and by the seventh inning, I found myself afraid to step out from the dugout in Rowe's view. God, I didn't even want her to look at me, I was so embarrassed. But I know if that dude shows up again, I'll be right back in crazy mode.

"Yo, your brother's out there waiting on you," Cash says, throwing his dirty towel at me.

"Thanks man. Hey, nice arm today."

"Ha, only half as good as that stick you're swinging. See ya tomorrow," he says, holding the door open and giving me a glimpse of Ty out in the hall. I shove my equipment in the locker and slip my feet into my sandals, my socks, pants, and undershirt completely saturated with the dirt from the field.

"Hell of a game, bro. Glad to see she didn't completely fuck up baseball," Ty says, holding his knuckles out for me. I pound them with mine and then lean against the wall.

"I kinda *used* it, I guess you could say," I admit.

"Yeah you did. That homer went a good four-twenty," he says, tipping his hat down on his forehead, just to remind me that I was an ass to him, too.

"Sorry about the hat thing. It fits your head just fine," I say, my eyes squinting while I look up at him sideways, feeling every bit of shame on my face.

"Nah, don't worry about it. You're right—I have a tiny head. But hey, it's big where it counts!" he says, making me break into a small laugh. My brother's arrogance is the world's greatest depression elixir.

"Rowe go home?" I ask, honestly not knowing when or if she left. I hid from her sight for the last forty-five minutes.

"She's still here. Right where you left her. Said she wasn't moving a muscle until you apologized or some shit like that. But I don't know, dude, I think she's the one who owes you an apology bringing a dude like that out here and waving him under your nose," Ty says, and I know he's wrong, but I just smile and pat his back while I head down the hall for the most awesome begging-display of my life.

"Yeah, probably. But I'm gonna go apologize anyway," I say, turning around and walking backward with my arms out. Ty turns to face me, his hands clasped behind his neck.

"Pussy," he teases.

She's still fuming. I can tell by the way her legs are bent, perched on the dugout in the exact same position they were when I walked away a few hours ago. Her hands are folded neatly in her lap, and her eyes are zoned out, looking at the field in front of her. I walk over to her slowly, and I stop when I'm two seats away. I sit down, putting my feet up like hers, and we both sit there silently for several minutes, watching the grounds crew work to ready the field for the two teams playing early in the morning.

I'd like to be the first one to speak, but I don't know what the hell to say. There are so many things I need to tell her, and so many massive fuck-ups over the last twenty-four hours that I need to make amends for—I don't know which one takes priority. So I sit there, patiently waiting for her to give me a sign, to tell me what she needs to hear first, what she needs to hear most.

"You called me your *friend*," she says finally, and my heart squeezes tightly. She still won't look at me, her eyes following the two men on the field who are pulling up bases and re-chalking lines. I need her to see me. I still don't know what I'm going to say, but I know the words will come as soon as I can get her eyes on mine, so I get up and hop on top of the dugout so I can walk over to where her feet are resting. I sit so my legs are straddling her feet, and then I wrap my hands around her shoes, mostly to keep her from kicking me.

"I think we both know that you and I were never *friends*, Rowe." She shifts her eyes to mine quickly, holding my attention with this silent stare for even longer minutes.

"What *are* we then, Nate? What is this...*this, whatever we're doing*? What are *we* to you?" All I want to do is move her goddamned legs out of my way so I can get to her mouth and kiss her, but she'll run if I rush this.

"I can't tell you what *we* are Rowe. I can't tell you that, because that entirely depends on you. But I can tell you what *you* are to me. And it's not the word *friend*. It's so far beyond the word friend that I'm scared shitless right now to say it out loud, because I'm afraid you don't want to hear it. *You* are the first thing I think about in the morning and the last thing I think about at night. You are the face in all of my dreams and the smile I see when I close my eyes. Your voice when you sing in the shower late at night, when you think you're alone, is like music to my ears—and I know, that's totally weird that I listen to you, but don't interrupt my flow, we can get back to that later," I say, holding a hand up to stop her.

"You've got me all twisted in here," I say, running my palm over my chest. "I don't know what to do, how to act, and what to say. Clearly, I don't have a fucking clue what to say! It all comes out like garbage, because there aren't any words that are good enough. And I worry—God, Rowe, I worry all the time that something I do or say is going to break you. And I can't have that, because you've come so far, and you've come this far with me. And it's such a gift, the way you've trusted me, given this part of yourself to me. And I know, I was kind of...well, shit, Rowe...I was crazy when that Tucker dude was over here, because I see how he looks at you. Hell, it's the same way I look at you. It's the way you deserve to be looked at—admired and adored. But I'll be damned if I'm going to give up everything just because I'm afraid. Because I know the second I walk away, a hundred Tuckers, who all probably deserve you more than I do, will line up to take my place, and I will hate every last one of them. And I'll hate myself for giving up."

"What are you saying, Nate?" Her eyes haven't moved from mine the entire time. I don't even think she's blinked. But I can see her heart on her sleeve, her eyes just waiting to let the tears fall. She's so afraid I'm going to break her right here, right now.

"I love you, Rowe. That's it. I love you. I love you. I love you!" I stand to my feet and shout those words, getting the attention of the grounds crew, who all whistle and mock me—as they should. I jump down and swing her feet sideways so I can kneel in front of her, my face pressed flat against her lap while I speak. "God, Rowe—that feels so good to say. I love you, and I meant it the first time I said it. I never should have taken it back, and I should have said it sooner."

When I look up into her eyes, the tears are threatening to fall even more, and she's breathing in deeply through her nose, just trying to stay strong. If she runs from me now, it will kill me. It will absolutely slay me. But it would still be worth it. Just getting the chance to tell this girl I love her once would be worth all the pain in the world.

Rowe leans forward until her head is pressed against mine, and only then do the tears fall from her eyes, landing on her legs in front of me. I reach up and rub my thumbs gently under each eye, and she leans into my palm, her eyes slowly opening to look at me, her heart pounding so hard I can feel it in every part of her body.

"You didn't dip your shoulder," she says, and my lungs fill completely with relief and hope—and so much goddamned love for this girl that I can hardly stand it. I bite my tongue, but I can't help the enormous smile pushing up the corners of my mouth.

"No. I didn't," I say through small, breathy laughter, reaching down to grab her hand in mine and kissing it. "Anything else you see wrong with my swing...coach?"

"No," she says with a small quiver, letting one last tiny tear fall through her smile. "Well, maybe the follow through. Oh, and your feet are a mess. And your head moves a little...a lot. But, other than that..."

"God, I love you," I say, pulling her face close to mine and pressing my lips to hers so hard, she can barely squeeze out any more words. But she does.

"I love you, too, Fifty-seven."

Chapter 23

Rowe

This is living.

It was like I was born the moment I told Nate how I felt. Coming here, to McConnell, was a breakthrough for me. But loving Nate—letting myself be human and feel something again...that was breaking free.

My parents will be here in the morning, and my belly is full of nerves over it, but they're happy nerves. I don't know how I'm going to introduce Nate, but I know my mom and her intuition, so I don't think I will have to say much. I just hope they love him as much as they always loved Josh.

Josh was a part of our family, almost from the very beginning. He spent time with my father without me. Sure, usually talking baseball. But there was a love there, a connection. I desperately want them to feel that with Nate.

"There, smell better?" Nate says, coming in his room after showering. His hair is wet and twisted in all directions. I love the way the ends are golden from the sun.

"It'll do," I tease, causing him to toss his wet towel from his hand at me.

"I'm pretty sure you're staying here again tonight. I think that's the real reason Ty wanted us to make up," Nate says, slipping one of his McConnell baseball shirts over his head. I'm a little disappointed that he does, because if anything is going to happen tonight, Nate is going to need to be the aggressor. I'm too...I'm just too *new* at *all* this.

"Yes, I bet he's glad to end the *fussy fuss*," I laugh.

"Oh god, I swear, him and *fussy fuss*! He used to make fun of me when we were kids with that damned phrase. He'd punch me, steal my ice cream, and then tell Mom I was making a fussy fuss."

"That's mean."

"Right? I'm such a victim," Nate says. He sits next to me and folds his hands together and leans forward to rest them against his knees. His smile is shy and uncomfortable, and it's sweet.

We both keep stealing glances, then looking away as soon as we're caught. It's funny how putting your feelings out in the open can add this whole new layer to your world. We both seem to be sort of stuck, not knowing what to do with one another or how to act. And I wish like hell he'd just kiss me and keep going.

"You wanna get him back?" I say, just trying to erase the awkwardness in the air.

"Huh?"

"Ty. You wanna get him back? You know, for the years of abuse?" I raise my eyebrows, and Nate stands up with a big smile.

"Uh, yeah I do. What'd you have in mind, Prankmaster?"

"Oh, so you acknowledge that I am in fact the master now, do you?" I say, standing and poking at his chest. He pulls me in for a quick kiss.

"You had me at pink," he winks, and I roll my eyes.

"Okay, Jerry Maguire."

I spend a few minutes looking around Nate and Ty's room, pulling open a few drawers and looking for just the right point of attack.

"He has a Playboy in here. We could pull some pages out and glue them into his textbook so they show up in class," I suggest.

"No, Ty would actually like that. In fact, I think he's done that before," Nate says, joining me to flip through drawers and look under Ty's bed.

I'm about to give up, when I get to the bottom drawer and I move a few balls of socks to the side. "Uh, Nate? What...is *this?*" I ask holding up the small, brown teddy bear with two mismatched button eyes.

"That's Cookie!" he says, taking it from me and squeezing it once. "Unbelievable! I can't believe he still has this thing...and he brought it, to grad school!"

"Nate...we have our target," I smirk, taking the bear back from his hands and tucking it in the bottom of my purse. "This bear is being held hostage, and Ty is about to be our bitch for the next few days."

"I LOVE it!" he says, laughing and picking me up in his arms and swinging me around. "You...are a genius! An evil genius—an evil, sexy genius!"

He kisses me with a little more force, still holding my legs off of the ground, and the more he kisses me, the more I can tell his mood has changed. I don't even hesitate with he finally sets my feet on the ground and begins walking me backward toward his bed, all the while his lips on mine. I pull my shirt over my head, and he follows with his. It was only on him for minutes, and I'm so glad it's off again.

Things get *real* when he reaches for the button on his jeans, unsnapping and kicking them from his legs. And all of the absoluteness—the sureness and confidence I had felt moments before—starts to wane. Nate is not Josh. And I'm glad he's not, because Nate is who I love *now.* But he's not some sixteen-year-old inexperienced boy. It's clear in the way he looks, in the way he moves and in the way he's touching me now.

"We don't have to do this, you know," he says, sensing my nerves. How could he not, I'm pretty sure my entire body is shaking. But just the thought of stopping—of not getting to have him completely—makes my heart hurt, so I shake my head quickly before he can change his mind.

"No, I want to. I'm just...a little out of practice." I feel stupid saying it, but I want Nate to know what he's getting.

"We're here...together. You say stop if we need to stop. And *I* will be *fine* with that. Okay?"

"Okay," I say, nodding quickly and closing my eyes. I take a deep breath and lose myself in the feeling of Nate's kiss on my head. When I open my lids again, my view is of his lower body. He's wearing a pair of black boxer shorts, and nothing else, and all I want to do is run my hands over every inch, every muscle along his back, stomach, sides, and...

Nate pulls on the front snap of my bra, pulling my chin up with his fingers to look me in the eyes, making sure I am okay with his every move. "Yes," I whisper, my eyes falling hooded as my body tingles under his touch. He pulls the straps from my shoulders slowly, letting his fingers trail down the length of my arm. I've been this way in front of Nate before, when I showed him my scars. But this time is *different*. He doesn't see my scars at all, he only sees me. And he wants me.

I crawl onto my back, lying on his bed while he hovers above me, brushing my hair from my face and splaying it out on his pillow. "Can I just kiss you...for a while?" he asks, pressing his lips once to my forehead, and then my lips, and then my chin. I nod *yes* slowly and feel his breath against my neck, each tantalizing pause before he kisses me somewhere new. His tongue finds my jaw next, and when he runs it down the length of my neck to my collarbone, I can't help but squirm. He looks at me again to make sure I'm okay, but I'm squirming because I want him to go farther, to touch me more.

"I'm okay. I promise," I say, and he smiles softly, looking down the length of my body to my breasts.

I can't help but watch in anticipation as he kisses each one slowly, circling around the peaks, but never fully taking them in. The want and need overwhelms me, and I let out a moan, arching my back, urging him to be more forceful.

"What do you want, Rowe?" he teases, his lips blowing cold air across my nipples, bringing them to a painful point.

"I want you to kiss me...there," I say, barely able to get the words out through my panting.

"Where?" he teases again, making my entire body blush. I pull his pillow from under my head and put it over my face; I'm so embarrassed. "Here?" he asks, grazing the tip of his tongue lightly over one nipple.

"Oh god! Yes, there," I say, biting down on his pillowcase to keep myself from saying more.

Nate continues to circle and tease each peak for minutes, until my back is actually sore from arching into him and begging him to take them completely. When he finally pulls my nipple into his mouth, biting lightly at first with his teeth and then sucking it painfully hard, I groan.

"You cannot make that noise if you want this to go on any longer," he says, pulling the pillow from my face and smoothing my hair out once again.

"Sorry," I whisper, wishing I could hide the redness creeping up on my face.

"Never be sorry. That sound, your sound, is so goddamned hot. It's just going to take me some time before I can handle it without..." he pauses and smirks, and I smile, bashfully.

Nate kisses me again, this time his lips rough against mine, and he works his body so he's lying next to me. His hand grazes down my neck and shoulders, and his thumb circles each breast, pinching and pulling just long enough that I can feel the pressure building between my legs. He moves his hand lower, running the tips of his fingers under my waistband a few times, and I can tell he's testing me, making sure I'm okay with him touching me...*there.*

After his hand pauses flat, resting over my bellybutton, I lift my hips and reach down to unbutton the top of my pants, pulling them down with my thumbs until my legs can kick them free completely, and Nate just watches, his eyes moving from mine to my newly exposed hips and skin.

"Are you sure?" he asks, swallowing loudly.

"I'm so incredibly sure," I say, looking him right in the eyes and holding his gaze until I know he believes me. Without pause, Nate moves his body so it's resting totally on mine. His weight is immense, but the warmth of his skin against mine is the most amazing feeling I have ever had. Something as simple as his shoulder against mine sends shivers throughout my body.

Cupping my face in his hands, Nate kisses me tenderly now, his elbows holding his chest up above mine. But all I can focus on is the hardness that's digging into my center below, and the only barrier between us—two small layers of cotton. I wonder if I would look like a slut if I simply ripped them away.

Nate backs away from me, until he's straddling my knees, and he keeps his eyes on mine when he puts the tips of his fingers in the top of my panties, pulling them down the length of my legs, achingly slowly.

"Can I kiss you...here?" he asks touching his finger to the very edge of my pubic bone, so very close to where I desperately want him, and need him. My eyes go wide at his question. I've never been kissed...*there.* And I can't mask my worry on my face that I won't be...*good...down there.* "Please?"

he asks again, the most unbelievably sexy smile stretching over his face. Dimples. I nod *yes*, and once again pull the pillow over my eyes.

He teases me at first, kissing the inside of each knee, and then my thighs. When I feel his hands push my legs wider, I start to think about shutting them, but then I feel the pressure of his tongue on my very center, and *oh my god!* It's like nothing I've ever felt before, the way he tastes me and teases in just the right spot. Once again, my hips arch into him, and he lets out a faint chuckle, pressing the warmth of his palm flat against my abdomen.

When I feel his finger push into me, I pull the pillow from my head, reaching down to grab the strands of his hair, unable to stop the sensation taking over. I'm so full of need and want—I have become someone else entirely. As Nate stands back to his feet, I sit up at the edge of his bed and pull his boxers down completely, not wanting to wait any longer. I wrap my hand around him, and am bold enough to look. I want to know, no, I need to know how large he is, because I'm nervous, but not so scared that I want to stop. I. Never. Want. To. Stop.

"Let me just get something," Nate says, walking over to his dresser drawer and pulling out the small foil packet. I watch as he puts the condom on, and I shift back in his bed so my head is once again on his pillow. Nate climbs back on top of me quickly, his hand holding himself so he can guide things to just the right position.

"I have to ask, one more time. Are you sure?"

"Nate, for the love of God, if you don't have sex with me right now, I'm going to take care of myself," I say, slapping a hand over my mouth I'm so shocked at my boldness.

Nate grins, and dips his head, kissing the top of my breast with his smile and laughter. "While I also wouldn't mind watching *that*...I think I'd rather participate," he says, kissing me gently as he pushes slowly inside me.

The stretch hurts at first. My body isn't used to this, and I wouldn't say my last experience was long—or enjoyable—but I want it to be different this time. I want it to be more, to be the way it's supposed to be when you're almost nineteen and in college.

Nate is slow and tender, never pushing into me completely. My eyes are closed tightly, and I'm sure I'm not making a pleasant face when he runs his fingers across my cheek, his lips brushing against the side of my face. "Are you okay?" he whispers, his forearms, biceps, shoulders—every muscle in his body fully flexed to hold himself back.

I say, "Yes," with a short, fast nod, parting my lips, taking in a sharp breath. "Don't hold back," I say, cupping his face in my hands and looking deeply into his eyes. "I just need to take things slowly. But I want this, you...all of it."

Nate's eyes search mine, waiting for any hint of reservation as he lowers himself into me again, this time moving in deeper, until he reaches a point where he can no longer move inside me. The sensation makes him suck in a quick breath and close his eyes; my body ignites at the power I have over him. When he rocks back slowly and moves forward again, my hips circle with him, forcing him back in just as deep as he was before. "Jesus, Rowe," he says, his teeth biting lightly at the skin on my shoulder.

We continue to move together, our rhythm slow, but growing with comfort every time we connect, until I finally feel something begin to build—a pressure, the most pleasurable pressure I've ever experienced. It's almost like an itch, and every time Nate moves back from me, I'm overcome with this fear that if I don't chase it—it will be lost. Need takes over, and I have to satisfy it, so I pull my knees up on either side of him and thrust my hips up to meet him. When I do, Nate pushes his hands deep into my hair and looks at me for approval.

I kiss him so hard the roughness of his stubble scratches my lips raw as he continues to push into me faster. I guide his hand from my face down the side of my body until he reaches my hip and the side of my leg. When our eyes meet, I nod yes again, begging him to be rougher with me, and he digs his fingers into the side of my flesh, pulling my leg up into his body, wrapping me around him completely. That feeling—the feeling of falling—is so close, and I keep stepping over the cliff, wanting to fall into everything, completely. I hold my breath and run my hands down the length of his stomach, then sides and back, until I'm pushing him into me with force, no longer able to contain the small whimpers leaving my lips.

"Please, Nate. I need to...I don't know, just please. Don't stop, don't stop, don't stop," I repeat over and over until it's barely audible, and my eyes are literally rolling back in my head. My grip on him loosens, and I let my arms fall above me—over my head—feeling every nerve ending inside me fire and pulse and squeeze to the point of pure exhaustion. My body is covered in a sheen of sweat as Nate continues to move into me, his hands roaming up the sides of my body, roughly over my breasts and neck until he finds my arms above my head. He holds them together, his fingers woven with mine, and his strength pushing me deeper and deeper into the mattress. I'm unable to move—not that I want to—and I stare at his face until he finally thrusts one last time, letting out the sexiest breath I've ever heard.

We're a pile of arms and legs and chests and bare skin, tangled in a pink Barbie sheet; I've never felt more alive. My hair is damp with sweat, and Nate looks like he just walked off the baseball field. He's so beautiful, and I'm lost looking at the line of muscles and tendons that begin at his neck and run down his body to his inner thigh. My god, I can't believe this is my boyfriend. The thought makes me giggle inside, and eventually I let it out.

"Hey, you know that *being scared* thing you don't like?" I nod, still laughing lightly. "Yeah, well, guys don't really like laughing after sex."

I suck my lips in and shrug my shoulders quickly. Oh god! I didn't mean that. "Sorry, I was just...happy," I say, letting a full smile take over my face, and I bury it in the crook of his neck to hide, my cheeks once again burning.

"Okay, well...be happy. Just don't laugh at a naked man. It hurts our feelings," he says, nudging his nose against my jaw.

"Nate, that was...*oh*. Don't freak out, but I've never fully, oh god..." I tuck my face back into him.

"Was that your first orgasm?" he teases, but sweetly. I nod *yes* again quickly, keeping my face hidden—I'm so goddamned embarrassed. "Wow. I'm...honored. You know what, you laugh all you want. I feel like I just won an award. I might even make up a T-shirt that says I gave Rowe Stanton her first orgasm."

"Nate! Don't even joke..." I start, but stop when he starts to tickle my sides, making me laugh uncontrollably.

"Oh no. I'm doing it. And I'm making hats, too. And...oh yeah! I'm going to make one for Ty that says 'My brother gave Rowe Stanton her first orgasm!'"

"Not funny!" I laugh, knowing he's just teasing me for fun. This is our thing; we've been comfortable with each other like this since the moment we met. And my heart is soaring knowing nothing has changed. Even though *everything* has changed.

"Hang on, I need to log onto that website, where you can make your own shirts. I'm doing this today," he says, trying to sit back up before I pull him back down on top of me.

"You know what, that's a good idea. You can wear it when you meet my dad tomorrow. In fact, I'll tell him you ordered him one, too!" And...*checkmate*. Nate's smile falls flat; he lies down next to me, pulling the blanket up over us and tucking me deep within his arms.

"Okay, point made. You win with the dad-move. Now I'm pretty sure I'm not going to be able to look him in the eyes after what I've done," he says, and I can detect the truth behind his joking.

"He's going to love you. So is my mom," I say, squeezing him tightly before I get him with one last zinger. "And when I tell them you gave me my first orgasm—"

"Okay! I get it!" he says, kissing me just to shut me up.

Chapter 24

Nate

Maybe I would have been nervous anyway, but ever since Rowe made the joke about me giving her...*that*...and telling her father, well? I've been sweating a lot today, and I haven't taken the field at all yet. Her parents are in the stands sitting with her. Ty sent me a text—with a picture. They look nice.

"Hitting cleanup today, Preet," coach yells over the sound of the balls cracking off bats. There's something therapeutic about being in here, in the cages, with five or six guys all hitting at once. The noise is constant, distracting—I guess that's why some people like wind chimes. I tip my helmet and nod, then take another swing, careful to watch my shoulder and my follow-through. It makes me smile every time.

After a really solid round, I grab my gear and head over to the bullpen to suit up. When I'm done, I walk over to the entrance and look to get a handle on where they're sitting. Rowe's waving at me to come over, her parents standing on either side of her, so I prop the mask up on my head and jog over, the entire time reminding myself not to make an ass out of myself in front of her father.

"Hey," she says, her voice warm and perfect and *God I want to kiss her mouth.* But I don't, because her father is right there, looking at me, like fathers do. And he should. Because I am the guy—the one who *did* things to his daughter last night. *I'm so going to fuck this up.*

"Hey, thanks for coming," I say, catching her in an awkward hug as she leans over the wall to kiss me. We end up in some weird half-embrace, kissing each other's cheeks like we're French. I feel pretty lame, and it just gets worse when I catch her mom chuckling.

"Nate, nice to meet you son. I'm Tom Stanton, and this is my wife, Karen," her dad reaches out to shake my hand. I'm sure to grip him hard, but not too hard, and after we shake, I feel relief that at least I passed one tiny stupid test. Only a million more to go.

"Nice to meet you. Thanks for coming out today." I'm squinting a little because the morning sun is behind them still. It's hot for late October—and I'm already feeling the weight of the gear.

"Pleasure's all ours, Nate. I'm excited to see what you can do out here. I've heard great things about you," he says, and I'm not sure if he's talking about things he's heard from Rowe or just baseball in general. I'm just glad he used the word *great*, though, so I move on.

"I hope I can deliver. I'll try to hit you a foul ball," I laugh, lightly and nervously, while inside I kick myself for being such an idiot.

"Oh, that'd be exciting. Do we get to keep those?" Rowe's mom says, and I smile, stifling my laugh, when I notice Rowe rolling her eyes behind her.

"Yes, ma'am. Part of the payoff for getting hit with a ball, I suppose." Karen just nods, and I stand there while the rest of the conversation dives into a really uncomfortable silence.

"Right, well, I better get back to the bullpen. I've got a pitcher to warm," I say, turning to look at Rowe and give her a look that hopefully conveys *I'm sorry I'm such a tool wagon.*

"Pitchers are prima donnas, Nate. You walk slowly. It's good for them to realize they can't throw until someone's there to make them look good." I like Rowe's dad. "We'll see you again for dinner, okay?"

I turn around to walk backward to answer him, doing my best to fall somewhere between fast and slow with my walk because, hell, I don't want my pitchers *hating* me. "Looking forward to it, Tom. I'll see you at sex."

Motherfucker. I just said sex. I said *sex*...to Rowe's dad! And there is no mistaking it, and he knows it's what I said, and Rowe's eyebrows could not possibly be any higher on her forehead. Shit, shit, shit, shit, shit. I pull the mask down—thank god I'm a catcher—and turn around like I did nothing wrong. Maybe he'll think it's all in his head. Either way, that was easily the worst win-over-the-dad move ever. I better play well today for this man, otherwise I might as well just hand over the bat and let him hit me with it at our sex-o'clock dinner.

One walk and three doubles against one of the best teams in the country is a pretty decent showing—I just hope it was good enough to erase my blunder. We lost by two, but Florida State is coming off of a College World Series year, so I feel pretty satisfied.

I shower and pack up my stuff, then head out to catch up with Ty. My only saving grace is the fact that he wasn't there to witness while I put my foot in my mouth.

"Nice game, yo. Burgers? Sally's?" he asks.

I pull my phone from my pocket to check the time and notice a message from Rowe. "Yeah, that works. I wanna eat light though. I'm going to dinner with Rowe's parents tonight," I say, keeping my phone in my hand so I can remember to read Rowe's text.

"So, what does *light* mean? You gonna order some salad or shit?" Ty asks; his brow all furrowed like I just told him I wanted to eat dirt.

"No, I'm just saying let's eat now, early. And I'll skip the fries," I say, shaking my head at him.

"Ah, okay. Order fries anyway. I'll eat your fries," he says, pushing ahead of me to the crosswalk. "Oh, and hey. What's *this* shit?"

Ty hands me his phone while we cross the street, and I swipe the message screen open to see a picture of Cookie with a ransom message. I almost bust a gut with laughter right then and there, but I manage to hold it together.

It reads: *If you want to see me ever again, you'll be sure to wear the tutu waiting for you in your mailbox on Halloween.*

Rowe...is a genius. What she doesn't know, though, is that my brother will totally wear that tutu. He'll fucking own that tutu and rock it with a full on ballerina leotard to prove a point. But either way, I'm going to *love* watching it all play out.

"Beats me," I say, handing the phone back to him.

"It's Cass. And Rowe, I bet. Those two better be sure they're ready. I'm going to *rock* this ballerina shit! And when I get Cookie back, I'm going to pay them back *so* hard."

He can't see me laughing behind him, but my brother is dead serious. To see a twenty-two year old deliver a message so earnestly—and utter the word *cookie* in the same breath—is something only Ty Preeter can pull off and still look like a man. Barely—but still like a man.

I trail behind him a few more steps so I can check my message from Rowe.

Rowe: *Sex?*

I wince at first, but then grin.

Me: *Is that an offer?*

Rowe: *No, dumbass! It's the very last word you said to my father.*

Me: *Yeah...about that.*

Rowe: *You were free and clear! What the hell happened?*

Me: *Do you think he noticed?*

Rowe: *Let me play the scene out for you after you walked away. Dad: Did he just say sex? Me: Uh, I don't think so. Mom: No, I'm pretty sure he did. He said sex. Dad: Yeah, that's what I thought I heard, too, but I wasn't sure. I'm glad you heard it. Me: *dying, looking under seats, hoping there is enough room for my body.* Mom: I can see where you could make that mistake. Six, sex, six, sex, six-sex. Yeah, it's a tricky slip... shall I go on?*

Me: *Sorry.*

She doesn't write back right away this time, and now I start to feel like an even bigger asshole. I am single-handedly self-destructing this whole damn thing—I'll be lucky to make it to dinner. Ty and I exit the elevator and head to our room when I feel my phone buzz in my pocket and I pull it back out, hoping like hell it's Rowe with some witty comeback.

Rowe: *Waiting.*

Huh?

It buzzes again, this time with a photo, and I can tell she's not wearing anything because I can see her bare shoulders, the smooth skin of her neck and her lips, which are *seriously sucking on her finger? Oh. Hell.*

"Hey, I'm gonna go hang with Rowe instead," I say, turning away from Ty without even looking.

"Dude! I'm hungry!" he says.

"Then go eat," I say, knowing my brother would do the same damn thing to me in this situation.

Thank god for baseball. I'm sure I'm not the first to think those very words, but I truly mean it right now because for the last thirty minutes, I have been absorbed in an intense baseball discussion with Rowe's father, and he seems to be rapt by everything I say. If I can just stay on the topic of baseball for the rest of their time here, I should be able to come through this thing with Tom Stanton having a good opinion of me—despite my very serious attempts at self-sabotage.

"I'm really looking forward to seeing how you all handle LSU tomorrow. We should be able to watch most of the game before we have to leave," Tom says. I feel Rowe's hand squeeze mine under the table, and when I turn to her, she smiles—that soft, reassuring, proud kind. I've somehow come back out on top. "Curious why you didn't decide to attend LSU...being from Louisiana and all?"

"I almost did," I admit, and I feel Rowe's hand tense up against mine. It's amazing how close I was to not coming to McConnell, and then I never would have met Rowe. "But I was really interested in finding a good fit for both me and my brother. Ty, well...he's my best friend really. We don't act like it sometimes..."

"Oh no, you definitely act like best friends," Rowe inserts with a laugh, and I reciprocate.

"Yeah, most of the time we do," I say with a fond smile. "Ty's always been there for me. He's my *number-one guy*. We sort of have this crazy fantasy of being in business together—baseball of course. If things go just right, he'll be my agent. Or if I don't make it..."

"You're going to make it," Rowe interrupts, and I love her—the way she looks at me. Like I really am something special.

"But *if* I don't make it," I smile, "we sort of have this crazy dream of going into sports management on our own. Preeter Brothers Sports Management, or something like that. I don't know...it just sounds like pipe dreams when I say it out loud.

But Ty—he's so smart, a real head for the business side of things. Me, I'm more of the PR, the talking-to-people part."

"That's probably for the best," Rowe says with a laugh.

"Yeah, I guess so," I say. For a brief second, I forget we're here with her parents, and I lean in and kiss her cheek quickly. When I sit back, I realize what I just did and my eyes flash wide and I mouth *sorry* to her.

"Nate, it has been..." Rowe's mom, Karen, begins to talk, but she sits back and looks at her husband for a few seconds mid-sentence, taking a deep breath. The smile on her face is the kind that looks like it could switch to tears at the drop of a hat, but she manages to hold it in place when she looks back to me again. "It has just been truly a pleasure to meet you. Tom and I are *really* glad you and Rowe...well, we're just glad she has someone *here*."

Rowe looks embarrassed by her mom's statement, but I appreciate the sentiment. I don't know how much they know *I know*, but there's a sort of feeling I get from her parents—I can't put it into words, but I get a sense that they trust me. And they should. I would walk through fire for their daughter. Hell and back—without even questioning it.

"Well, there's been something on my mind...our mind, actually," Tom begins, and Rowe sits forward on her seat, her face covered in concern. "Nothing's wrong. Nothing at all."

He smiles back at his wife, and they both look nervous, like this is something they've rehearsed.

"Rowe, your mother and I. Well...we haven't...gosh, I'm not sure how to say this," he says, looking to Karen for help, and she just squeezes his hand on the table and nods with a smile. "Well, since you've been gone to college, that's really been the first *alone time* we've had...in a couple of years."

Her dad is doing his best to dance around the reason Rowe has been home, probably at their side, for the last two years. It makes me wonder how often, if ever, they have talked about the shooting and what it did to their daughter.

"Are you guys getting a divorce?" Rowe interjects suddenly, her palm sweating instantly in mine.

"Oh, honey! God no. No," Karen pipes in, once again exchanging that strange, nervous glance with her husband. "It's...oh boy. There's no easy way to say this, so—your dad was given a *huge* promotion at work. It's a good thing. It's...it's a *great* thing actually. But, it means we're moving. To San Diego."

"We're moving to San Diego?" Rowe asks.

"Yes. And you'll love it there—you know, over the summer? And I was able to pick up a contract with San Diego State, teaching economics." Her mom looks nervous, the way she's sitting perched at the edge of her seat, just waiting for her daughter to smile, congratulate her, and tell her she's excited. But Rowe's fidgeting in her lap—and I can tell she's lost.

"But, what about our house...in Arizona?" What she means to ask is what about Josh, and her memories—however tragic they may be. And I know this is what has them concerned the most.

"Well, that's the thing. Your dad starts at his new position the first of the year, so we'll be getting the house ready to sell, and hopefully it will go quickly. And part of the promotion was also a vacation—your dad sort of won this trip...to the Bahamas. And, well, we have to go, over Thanksgiving."

Rowe looks like she wants to throw up, and I don't know if it's all of the change being thrown at her at once, fear of having to travel to a place like the Bahamas over Thanksgiving, in a plane, over water, or the fact that she will lose one more connection to Josh. "Can Rowe come home with me?" I hear myself saying it before I even have time to think it through, but when I feel her hand thread even tighter through my fingers, I know I have to keep going. I'm her life raft right now. "I mean, for the holiday. Like you said, you guys haven't had much alone time. And...it might be nice to have a vacation, you know...on your own? And well, my parents really would love to have her come. And we don't do anything very formal. I'd like her to come. I...I'd like it a lot."

I don't know who looks happier about my idea—Rowe or her mother, who has actual tears developing in her eyes. She looks at Tom and nods, signaling her approval, and Tom turns to his daughter with his shoulders scrunched and his brow pinched.

"Rowe? Would you be okay with that? I mean, we don't really do anything formal either, and your grandparents aren't coming over this year. It would just be the three of us anyhow," he asks.

Rowe looks from her parents to me and then to her lap, her lip tucked between her teeth before she finally looks up at me, her eyes reaching inside to my heart and squeezing. "Are you sure it's okay? I mean, that your family would *want* me?"

"We want you," I say, leaning a little closer and whispering the rest. "I want you. Please, come home with me."

"Okay," she says, a slow smile taking over and dispelling the nerves and worry that were just battling against her. Then she turns quickly to her mom. "But, can I see the house? One last time—before you sell it? I mean, if someone buys it before my semester's done, can I come home just once to say goodbye?" Rowe swallows hard, and her mom reaches across the table to take her daughter's hand while she nods *yes*.

Rowe

My home is gone. My home is gone. My home is gone. I have said this in my head, over and over, all night. I don't know what it means other than the fact that I can never go back. And I don't really want to go back...do I?

There's a part of me that feels like I have been in a fantasy world, playing dress up like I did when I was a little girl. I'm *playing* college. And when I'm done with this, I'll go back to what I was before. Except that was never the point, was it? I suppose what I'm going through is no different from the other thousands of students walking to classes, living in apartments and dorms, and calling their parents on the phone less and less as months turn into semesters and then into years.

But those *other* students don't have pasts like mine, with scars covering their bodies and their hearts—and a first love that has dominated their every thought for almost a thousand days.

"Are you okay?" Nate asks, his thumb gently tugging at my chin while we lie in each other's arms in his pink bedroom—just one more scene in my fantasyland.

"Yes. No...I'm not sure. Is that...bad?" I ask, tucking my head under his chin to feel safe.

"Yes. No. I'm not sure," he says with a light chuckle. I don't know if he really understands, but he pretends well enough. "I'm glad you're coming home with me for Thanksgiving. I'm selfish."

"I'm glad I'm coming home with you, too," I say, and most of me *is* truly glad.

"San Diego really is nice. They have beaches," he says, and I smile against his skin.

"I love beaches. Or, I think I do. I don't know. I've never actually seen one," I say almost laughing.

"You're kidding?" he says, pulling back a little to look in my eyes, and I just shake my head *no,* confirming for him.

"There's a lot I haven't seen or done," I say, my face flushing a little remembering the last *first* that Nate gave to me.

"So it would seem," he teases, but his teasing is short. "We should make a list. I'd like to be a part of more firsts."

"Okay," I say, doing my best to force my brain to focus on anything other than my old bedroom, and my old boyfriend who lives only a few blocks away. "I can't drive."

"Wha?" Nate says, the sound of his voice soothing as his neck presses lightly over my ear.

"Never learned. Then, just sort of never needed to get anywhere. Permit expired, and ta da! I'm a lame teenager," I say.

"Yeah, you're pretty lame," he says, unable to hold in the small laugh that vibrates in his chest. "Good thing you have a cool boyfriend. I'll teach you...over Thanksgiving."

"Thanks," I say, not really meaning for the driving lessons.

"You're welcome," he says, pulling me tighter and flipping out the light; I know he's not talking about driving lessons either. This is love.

Chapter 25

Nate

I am going to play like shit today. I don't sleep well when Rowe is with me. It's not because I'm uncomfortable or she snores or anything like that. It's just that I can't let myself relax, like I always need to keep my eyes on her. I'm afraid she'll disappear.

Ty woke us up early, and I had been asleep for maybe a couple hours before he came barreling into our room looking for his razor and grabbing a change of clothes. I told him about Thanksgiving, and he seemed genuinely excited. And for a while, I thought he might want to ask Cass to come, too, but he never fully went there. Maybe it's because Cass has her sister. Or maybe my brother's afraid.

When I walk out from the dugout, there's a man leaning against the third baseline wall, and at a quick glance, it looks like Rowe's father. I head that direction in case it is, because I know Rowe's parents had planned on coming to most of my game before they had to leave for their flight. I confirm it's him as I get closer, and when he recognizes me, he pulls his sunglasses off and tucks them in his shirt pocket.

"Mister Stanton, thanks for coming out again today. I sure hope we can pull of a win for you," I say, reaching to shake his hand one more time. "I'm sorry, Rowe's not here yet. She said you guys were coming right at the start of the game, so she's probably still getting ready."

I feel like he can see through my lies, like he knows I spent the night with his daughter, and only left her an hour or two ago.

"Oh, thanks, Nate. Yeah, her mother will come with her. I wanted to get here early," he pauses, and it's strange.

"Oh, more tips for my game? You know, your daughter has had a few things to say about my swing," I laugh, trying my damnedest to lighten what is quickly become a very serious mood. Tom laughs in response, but it's a forced one, and I can tell his mind is elsewhere.

"No, actually...I was hoping to catch you before your game," he says, his eyes focusing somewhere over my shoulder until he takes in a sharp breath and looks me right in the eyes. "How much do you know...about Rowe?"

"I know enough, sir," I respond quickly, and I realize my reaction at first sounds a bit defensive, so I add to it. "I mean...she told me...about what happened, the shooting."

Tom nods, his eyes full of this un-maskable sadness. "Did she tell you about her best friend? Betsy?"

"Yes," I say, my stomach heavy.

"And...Josh?"

"Yes," I say, looking down—out of respect. When I look back up, his gaze is once again distant. But I know he has more to say. It's like he's stuck—and the longer we stand here in silence, the more the pressure of...of whatever it is he needs to tell me eats away at us both. "Sir, what's going on?"

His eyes close when I ask, and when he opens them again, looking at me, they're red from his efforts not to cry.

"She's different here. Rowe?" he says, and all I can do is nod in return. "She's...better. God Nate, you have no idea how scared Karen and I were, how afraid we were that Rowe would never...*ever*...get better. She was like a zombie that first year. You know, she didn't even talk for the first six months."

I wasn't aware of that, but I don't say a word. What Rowe wants me to know and what her father wants me to know need to exist in two separate boxes. And I need to be strong enough to keep them apart.

"Therapy every day. And for the first year, we couldn't get her out of the house. Then one day, she asked us if she could go visit Josh. So we drove her there, just happy she wanted to get out of the damned house, you know?"

He's crying now, and seeing this man—six-foot-plus and in his late forties—cry, has me wanting to as well. But I don't. I take in a deep breath, and nod, needing him to continue.

"She sat in their kitchen, rooms away from him, not wanting to *actually* see him, but just wanting to see where he was. Be near his family. Josh couldn't hear her anyhow. He couldn't talk or open his eyes. He was just lying there with tubes and machines and a live-in nurse that the state paid for as part of a settlement for his parents. Ha! Like that's supposed to somehow make it better. They were at school, Nate! That's supposed to be the safest place in the goddamned world!"

I let him pause for a minute and breathe. I can't even imagine what it must be like to be a parent in his situation, let alone Josh's parents.

"I'm sorry. I just get so damned angry when I think about it."

"I understand," I say, not wanting to interrupt more.

"Anyway, we drove her. And then she wanted to go again the next day. So we drove her again. Every day, for six months, we drove her to Josh's parents house, and she sat in their living room and kitchen, talking to Josh's mom, or just reading. Sometimes she just went over there to do her homework. And then one day, she didn't want to go any more. She said she felt stuck, and then she had this awful panic attack where she couldn't breathe, and she started vomiting. We told her therapist."

"Ross," I say, having heard Rowe mention him before.

"Right, I'm glad she's talked about him. Well, we told Ross, and he said that Rowe was trying to grow up, move on. But she had guilt. So Ross talked to her about college. We talked to her about college. And every day we talked about college a little more. And then she shocked the hell out of Karen and me, picking McConnell. But we wanted her to go, and the distance...frankly, the distance was a blessing. She needed that distance, Nate. She still needs it."

"This weekend, we see glimpses of our little girl. She's *living*. And I know it's not just because of you. I give her more credit than that. But Nate, I have to thank you, because I know you're a big part of it," he says.

"I love her, sir," I say, just needing him to understand how deep my feelings really are. I don't want him thinking that I am just with Rowe because of her situation, because I feel guilty, or that I'm taking advantage.

He smiles at me and reaches for my hand, shaking it once, and covering the back with his other hand to hold it tightly. "I know you do. We can tell you really do," he says. "We talked about this all night, Nate. And Karen…she wasn't sure I should come talk to you this morning. But…we need your help."

And suddenly my stomach drops again. Something's wrong. Something's wrong with Rowe…

"Josh passed away. Just a few days ago." As soon as he says it I know why he's here. This will destroy her. Rowe loves me, and I know she loves me. But Josh has her heart. Not like a boyfriend, but like a memory. He has her heart trapped—trapped in that day, trapped in what they were, and trapped under a mountain of guilt over everything they weren't.

"What do you need me to do?" I'll do anything. Hell. And. Back.

"It's true—about the job. And we're selling the house and moving. But the trip? That part we made up. We were just going to take her on vacation for the holiday. But thank you for saving us from doing that. We want to be gone before she knows. It may not make sense to you, and I know I sound like the worst man on earth for doing this, but I can't let my baby girl go back—she'll get stuck, Nate. And I just need to make sure there's no way for her to get back in, back into that past, when I tell her. I just need you to be there for her when I do. Because it is going to break her."

"I understand," I say, my skin suddenly tingling with panic. I know so much…so much more than Rowe. But it's her life I know about. And I have to keep this new information in that other box, the one that I don't mix with things just for her. And I am going to have to lie to her.

Tom Stanton pats me on the back, pulling his sunglasses back out of his pocket before reaching forward to shake my hand one more time. "Like I said, Nate. Karen and I are so glad Rowe met you. You've been good for her," he says, stepping up a level into the stands. "They'll be here in an hour. So, this…just between us, okay? I came out here to watch your swing."

"Yes sir," I say, my mouth in a hard flat smile as I push the mask over my eyes and hide how I really feel from the world.

Chapter 26

Rowe

Ever since my parents left, Nate has been different. I don't know how to explain it—he's still with me, still physical, and still says he loves me. But he seems to go somewhere else entirely sometimes, like he's in the moment, our moment, and then suddenly he's not.

"What about this one?" Cass asks, holding up a nurse's outfit from the costume rack at the Goodwill in Oklahoma City.

"Kinda slutty," I say with a wrinkled nose. My response gets Paige's attention.

"Oooooh, lemme see," Paige says, taking the naughty nurse outfit from her sister and walking over to a mirror to hold it up against her body. I'm pretty sure her boobs won't fit in it, but then again...maybe that's the point.

We've been shopping for Halloween costumes in the city for an hour. Paige's sorority is throwing a huge party at their house off campus, and when she invited Cass and me, I actually felt excited. Maybe it's just the idea of dressing up and pretending to be someone I'm not. Somehow, that makes it easier to be in a crowd—like hiding out in the open.

"What did you pick?" Cass asks, still sorting through the various costumes piled on the floor.

"Ghost," I say, holding up the sheet I found for ninety-nine cents.

"That's lame. You can't be a ghost," she says.

"She's right. I'll pretend I don't know you if you show up in that crap," Paige says over the curtain of the small changing room. She steps out in the nurse's outfit, which she has crammed her tits into, and Cass and I just look at each other and try not to laugh.

"I think I'm getting it," Paige says, pushing the halter up to make her boobs even more the main focus.

"Good call," I say, and when Paige ducks back into the curtain to change, Cass and I let out a silent laugh.

"Okay, so not a ghost. What should I be then," I ask, throwing the sheet back on the shelf nearby but keeping an eye on it, just in case. I watch as Cass sorts through a few more costumes and then her eyes light up.

"I got it!" She holds up what looks like an old-time woman's baseball uniform, and it's actually not half bad.

"Hmmmmm, maybe," I say, walking over and holding it up in the mirror.

"You'll need to tart it up a little," she says, tucking the shirt into itself to show what it would look like with a crop.

"Uhhhh, I don't think I'm at belly-shirt confidence levels yet," I say.

"Right. Sorry, I forgot. Well, then we'll just have to take out a few buttons at the top. And I have this really great bra you can borrow," she says, looking the outfit over while chewing on her fingernail.

"I thought this was Paige's thing—makeovers and dress up?" I say, wondering when Cass got so girly and creative.

"Oh, it totally is. I'm just good at sexy dress-up. I do it for Ty all the time," she says, like it's no big deal.

"Ohhhhh my god. I don't need to know this."

"What? He likes it, and we're adults," she says, then goes back to the pile of costumes, still looking for something to wear. I hold the outfit back up against my body one more time, pushing up my boobs, trying to imagine myself. "And I saw that!" she says. I blush, and put the outfit down in my lap.

Cass settles on a cheerleader outfit, which I thought was pretty predictable, but she seemed happy with it. We take the shuttle back to the campus and spend the rest of the afternoon getting ready for the party. I told Nate I would just meet him there since he had late afternoon workouts, and I kind of wanted to surprise him with my look, especially since he's been acting so strange lately.

Before we left, I spent minutes standing in front of our mirror with Cass's lacy black bra peaking out—*way out*—of the baseball jersey I had on. My hair was pulled into two pigtails, and black mascara smeared under each eye. Cass was right—

210

the look was sexy, and I was going to get a lot of attention. I just wasn't sure if I was ready—or wanted that.

Walking through campus was the hardest part, because most of the people staying at school were dressed normally, and I felt the heat of every stare from every male I passed. And while at first it made me feel a little uneasy, the more it happened, the more I sort of liked it.

"Yeeeeaaaawwwwww!" The scream was followed by a whistle; a convertible Camaro, packed with five guys, slowed as it passed us while we walked along the road. Paige was eating the attention up, even going so far as to blow kisses while the car drove by.

"If she keeps this up, they'll make her their queen," I say to Cass while we step up to the lawn of the sorority house.

"Are you kidding, she's already their queen. You could be, too, in that outfit," she says, fanning herself. I smile and put my head down, still not quite ready to believe that I'm anything *hot*. I may be cute, and sure, with my boobs flirting with the public in this bra, I was something to look at. But I wasn't quite ready to label myself *hot*.

"Thanks, but I'll settle for ruling Nate's world," I say.

"Then let the reign begin," she smiles and spins me around, pushing me to a group of guys standing around a large bonfire. Nate's back is to me. He's wearing a football jersey, and the helmet is dangling in his hands.

"Rowe Stanton," Tucker says a few feet away from me. My heart skips a beat, and not the excited kind. More of the nervous kind—of a girl who doesn't want her boyfriend seeing her talk to Tucker while she's dressed like...well, like a sporty hooker.

"Tucker. Hey..." I trail off.

"You look..." he doesn't finish his statement either, but his eyes can't seem to make their way all the way up my body to my face.

"Like a women's baseball player from the forties?" I try to steer clear of any compliments, but Tucker wants none of that.

"Rowe, if that's what the girls looked like back in the women's league days, then I'd run home right now and build myself a time machine."

Well damn. I have to admit, that made me feel pretty nice. "Thanks," I say, my smile tight and my face blushing.

"So, where's that boyfriend of yours? Not sure I'm in the mood to get punched tonight," he says, only half kidding.

"Yeah, I'm sorry about that. We were sort of working through some things. We weren't really official yet, if that makes sense," I say, suddenly feeling sick to my stomach having this conversation.

"I'm guessing you figured things out?" he says.

"Yeah," I laugh lightly. "Speaking of, I should go tell him I'm here. He was waiting for me."

"Right. Well, I'm going to head inside for a refill," he says, tipping over his empty red cup. "I'll see you in class? I hope you're thinking about that art history thing."

"I am. And you will. Have a good night, Tucker," I say, finally breathing right, now that we were separating. Unfortunately, we didn't part quickly enough.

"Yeah, I'm pretty sure I hate that guy," Nate says, walking a little past me and letting his gaze completely follow Tucker into the house. Nate finally turns to face me when Tucker's totally out of sight. "So, what'd you end up pick—"

And now, I feel...*hot.*

"You like it?" I say, spinning around once slowly, but knowing fully well that it's the four missing buttons on the front of the shirt that have him stammering for words. When he holds his hand up against his face and rubs his temple, his eyes almost bulging from his head, I start to heat up significantly.

"You are going to get a lot of attention tonight wearing that," he says, a guilty smirk starting to spread across his lips.

"Well, I was kind of hoping one certain southern gentleman might notice me tonight," I say, slinking up to him so the only places he has to look are my eyes and the expensive black bra.

"I think you're pushing the limits of the word *gentleman*," Nate says, not even hiding his arousal, pulling me in close to his body, dropping his helmet on the ground so he can almost touch me places he shouldn't in public.

"That's exactly the reaction I was hoping for," I tease, stepping up on the tips of my toes to kiss him lightly. "I hear I'm easy when I'm drunk," I breathe against his lips. Nate just tilts his head to the side and looks at me for a few seconds, one eyebrow raised.

"You…ever *been* drunk?"

"Well, not *technically*," I say, my seductress side starting to fade, foolishness moving into its place. "Okay, no. Not at all." Hanging my head, I start to back away from him, but he's quick to pull me close again.

"It's okay. I'm actually glad that I'm here for this. It's one of those *firsts*, you know? And frankly, I wouldn't trust you getting tipsy in an outfit like that around a bunch of assholes like the kind taking up at this party," he says.

"But *you're* at this party," I tease.

"Yes. But Tucker the Fucker's here, too."

"Nate! Stop that," I say, pushing him lightly. I'm slightly serious, but I'm also careful not to make Nate jealous, because I know how that feels—I had the same feelings when he was talking about Sadie, and I would never want to do that to him. "I'm sorry that's how you had to meet him. He's actually a nice guy."

"Yeah, probably," he says, grabbing my hand in his and pulling me up the front steps into the house. "But that doesn't mean he has good intentions when he looks at you. Especially in *that*."

"How do you know?"

"Because I'm a man, too, Rowe. And my intentions? They're nowhere near good right now. They're not even in the same language as the word *good*."

"Oh yeah? What are they, Mister Preeter?" The sexy coed once again taking over my brain and body, I take a large stride and step in front of his path, stopping him in a room full of people. Nate pushes his forehead to mine and walks us backward a few steps, his arm around my body, keeping me close.

"Come on. Let's go get you drunk, and we'll find out."

Being with Nate made everything easier. I dared more, and every day I felt more and more like the person I was supposed to be—the person before everything was stolen from me. Months ago, I never would have imagined me sitting here at a table with a dozen drunken college kids, screaming out obscenities and daring the girl before me to drink more, but here I am.

When it's my turn to play, Nate stands close, caging me in between his body and the table in front of me, his breath hot against my neck. He's been this way all night—possessive. And I think if this were normal, I'd fight it a little. But I know he's just making sure everyone's clear whom I belong to. And I like belonging to him.

"Okay, here's how it works. You take this ball," he says, handing me a small orange Ping-Pong ball. "All you need to do is get it in that cup on the other end. Do that, and that guy down there will have to drink the beer."

"Got it. I think I can do that. It's what? Like, three yards away?" I hold the ball up and squint one eye, lining up my shot. "What happens if I miss?"

"He gets to toss to your cup. And if he makes his shot, you drink," Nate says, his hands sliding to my hips until he lets go and steps back, giving me enough room to throw. "Come on, baby! You got this!"

Seems silly to have someone cheer for you in a game like this, but everyone else is yelling, too. I make the mistake of looking down, and when I do, I realize just *how much* beer there is in front of me. All I can really compare it to is a Coke can, and it's bigger than a coke can. And that's...what...twelve ounces? This is maybe sixteen...maybe more. I swallow once, and take in a deep breath, raising my arm and lining up my shot. I feel like playing the bounce might be the best way to go, so I take a few practice swings with my arm, and then finally I let one go—and rim it off the edge of the table, about two feet wide of the cup.

Well, shit.

Turning to Nate, I shrug, and when I turn back, the guy on the other end is rolling up his sleeves, readying himself for his shot. Everyone behind him is yelling "Cash! Cash! Cash! Cash!" When they do, I realize I recognize him. He's on the team with Nate. He's a pitcher, which means he's probably pretty good at aiming for things. And two seconds later, my hunch is confirmed by the small orange ball that's taunting me from the bubbles in the center of my cup.

"Drink! Drink! Drink! Drink!" It feels like it takes me minutes to get up the courage to pick up the cup and bring it to my lips, but when I finally do and tip it back—feeling the sharp tang of whatever cheap beer filled it—I down it fast.

"Wooooooo!" I say, lifting the open collar of my shirt up to my mouth, wiping it clean, my insides burning a little from instant alcoholic fullness. "Okay, I wanna rematch. You! Yeah—you're not getting off that easy. Let me see you do that again!" I was feeling brave...and probably a little drunk. No, I was feeling a lot drunk. But who cares. My boyfriend was hot, and I was in college, and nothing else mattered. This. Was. Awesome!

Nate

I knew better. But she looked so damned cute when she asked for another cup of beer. And she seemed like she was holding it together well. I was careful to make sure she was pacing herself, drinking water in between. But then we started playing a game. Fucking drinking games.

Rowe might be good at hitting a ball with a racket, but she was shit at throwing a Ping-Pong ball into a cup. And by the end of the night, I was just happy she hadn't ripped the bra from her body and gone skinny-dipping in the pool.

She still looked hot as hell, but I was going to have to convince her to bust that outfit out another time, because there was no way she was doing anything other than passing out or throwing up tonight. Probably both.

"Nate, your girl can't hold her liquor," Paige says, walking over to me with a very Jell-O-like Rowe slumped around her shoulder. "I love this girl. But if she throws up on me, I'm dropping her."

"I got it," I say, reaching in quickly and pulling Rowe up in my arms, keeping her body close to mine.

"Snuuuuuuuuggle," Rowe slurs, rubbing her face against my chest like a cat.

"I got ya," I say, gearing my muscles up for the long walk home. I pass Ty and Cass while I walk through the front porch. "Hey, I've gotta take her home and get her to bed. We'll be in our room, that okay?"

"Yeah, whatever. Just don't let her puke on my bed," Ty says, waving me off.

"Right, because it'd be a shame for something to happen to your princess sheets," I laugh over my shoulder.

"Malibu Barbie, douchebag. Don't disrespect!" he says, fluffing the ruffles of his tutu.

"I still can't believe you wore that thing—over boxer briefs. Pink ones. You know, that's going to give me nightmares," I say, doing my best to avoid looking straight at my brother's junk since the tutu is all fluffed up in the front of his lap.

"You hold all the power, right there in that pretty little drunk package you're taking home. You convince her...and *this one*," he says, pointing to Cass, "to give me back my Cookie, and I'll put pants on. Until then, this is your view pal."

"What's...*Cookie*?" Cass asks, her brows tilted while she looks at Ty with suspicion.

"Yeah, yeah. Nice try, sister. But I know you're in on this," Ty says, making me chuckle, which stirs Rowe in my arms.

"Cookie is his itty, witty teddy bear, and big ole Tysie wysie can't sleep without him," she slurs, her lips pouting in the most fucking adorable way ever.

"Yeah, you go ahead and play this out, Rowe. We'll see who's laughing about Cookie at the end," Ty says as we walk away, and I can tell by his tone that he's a little embarrassed. I almost feel bad, too. But then I remember all the times he punched me and told me not to fussy fuss, and my smile comes right back to my face.

"You little evil genius. I *love* you for this," I say, kissing her head as her eyes fight to stay open.

"That's the only reason you love me?" she asks, her lids finally closing completely as she pulls in tightly against my chest.

"Sweetheart, your pranking skills are merely the tip of the iceberg," I say, kissing her head and swinging her up in my arms for a better grip.

She dozes off for most of the walk home, but the elevator ride somehow registers with her, and by the time we make it to our floor, I have to rush her to the bathrooms. "Just a few more feet, hang on," I say, rushing into the women's restroom, hoping like hell no one is in there. Thankfully, the floor seems empty for the night, so I rush her down to the big handicapped stall at the end and get her to the toilet right in time for pretty much everything she drank tonight to come rushing out.

"Ooooooh god, this...this is awful," she says, laying her face on the rim of the toilet.

"I know. That's another first...maybe I should have warned you. Your first time getting drunk is usually followed by your first post-drinking vomit-fest," I laugh, looking under the stall door to make sure the bathroom is still empty. "Hang on, I'll get some wet towels. And you should probably not put your face on that...I doubt it's clean."

"Yeah...but I sorta don't care," she says, her voice barely able to project.

I pull the paper towel dispenser open and grab a good handful from the metal before pushing it closed again. I run them all under cold water and carry them, sopping wet, back to Rowe, who has somehow slid down to completely lie on the small-tiled floor.

"That's one of those firsts I don't care to repeat," she mumbles.

"Yeah, I know. I said that too. But then, I did it again," I admit, as I lift her up into my lap and smooth her hair away from her face. She's covered in a light sweat, and I can tell she has the chills by the tiny bumps all over her arms and neck. "Here, let me see your face."

She tilts her face to me, but her eyes are almost glued shut. She's seconds away from passing out, and as bad as this sounds, she's beautiful—even like this. I take a handful of the wet towels and run them over her forehead, cheeks and neck, trying to cool her and make her feel less like a speed-race of bile just cleared her lips.

"There, that any better?" I ask, and she moans, her mouth too weak to fully frown. "You think you need to do *that*...again?" I lean my head toward the toilet, and Rowe cracks one eyelid open long enough to see before closing it again. She shakes her head *no*, bringing her hands to her mouth to wipe again. "Okay, come on. Let's get you to bed."

Rowe's legs are sexy as hell, but carrying them drunk has me wishing she were five-foot-two instead of the extra six or seven inches she is. Lifting her body from the floor is tough, probably because she's not helping. Like...at all. I nearly jar her head into the doorway of the women's shower room as we leave, and when the small mousy girl from down the hall exits the elevator and catches us, she blushes.

"She got a little carried away tonight," I whisper, and she smiles and rushes back to her room.

It takes me a few seconds to get the keys from my pocket and unlock our door, but I finally do. Rowe manages to sit up at the edge of my bed, and I pull her shoes off first, then the long baseball socks she had on with her costume. "You want one of my shirts?" I ask, working the buttons of her shirt off until I get to see the entire bra that has been teasing me for most of the night. Well fuck. This night could have gone *so differently*.

"Can I have your green one?" she asks, and I head to the closet to begin sifting through my hangers.

"You mean gray? I don't have a green one," I say, finding the long-sleeved shirt she usually sleeps in and flipping off the light before I shut the closet door behind me.

"No, the green Boston one...with the Red Sox logo on the front," she says, pulling her arms from her bra and laying back against my sheets, letting out a big breath while her body sinks deeply into the blankets scrunched up around her.

"Yeah, I'm pretty sure that shirt is in your head. Come on, give me your arms—I got your favorite gray one," I say, lifting her body enough to pull my shirt over her head and down her arms and body. I tug her pants from her legs, and she crawls up to the head of my bed after I drop them to the floor, gathering the entire blanket up in her arms, squeezing it tightly, her face buried and her hair a tangled mess.

Once I flip the light out, I kick off my pants and shirt and slide in between her body and the wall, doing my best not to shake her. She moans a few times, and I know she's still feeling dizzy and sick, so I start to stroke her hair, trying to tame the wild mess she's managed to create.

"I hope you find it, Joshy." I pause, my breath held and my hand an inch away from her head, frozen in my *almost* touch.

"Find what?" I say, the knot in my throat impossible to swallow.

"The Boston shirt. It was always my favorite. I hope you find it." And that's the last word she utters before her breathing turns heavy and her throat gives way to the tiny vibrations of a snore.

Joshy. Not Josh, or I was *thinking* about Josh's shirt, or sorry, was just *thinking* about Josh. But *Joshy*. An intimate pet name, full of all kinds of...shit, I don't know what the fuck it's full of—but that one word. That goddamned name! That name I can't even hate because Josh is dead. And Rowe has no clue. And clearly *Joshy* is still alive and well in her subconscious.

For the next hour, I stare at her, watching her small movements while she sleeps. Every flit of her eyelid makes me jump, just waiting for her to tell me she needs to go back to him, or find him, or talk to him, or see him. And she can't. Not because she let him go, but because he's gone. And whether I like it or not, I'm competing for the girl I love...with a ghost.

Chapter 27

Rowe

"Come on, just one more party...before you leave me to go home with my boyfriend *and* yours." Cass has been dropping little hints ever since the Halloween party about not going home with Ty over Thanksgiving, but Ty seems to be pretty good at ignoring them.

"Why don't you just tell him you want to come with us? I'm sure he'd love you to be there," I say, pulling out my oversized sweatshirt and leggings to change for an evening of finals studying. Cass pouts when I do, knowing she's probably lost her battle to drag me to a party tonight.

"Because..." she says, letting her lips flap while she flops on her back on my bed behind me, her face still in full-sour mode.

"Because you're afraid you like him more than he likes you?" I ask, wondering when I got so bold with my questions for others. These kinds of things seem funny coming from the girl who barely woke up from a two-year social slumber. Cass is staring at me, not saying anything, but her eyes flash with a brief moment of sadness before she rolls her head to the other side, and she starts picking at the corner of my corkboard.

"No. Yes. I don't know," she says, pulling her knees to her chest. "Come do Pilates with me."

I lie back next to her and let out a similar lip-flapping breath. "I'm pretty sure this isn't Pilates," I say, holding my knees into my chest and rocking slightly like Cass is.

"I know, but I like to pretend it is. It's really just wallowing, but it makes me feel better...you know, if I call it Pilates?" she says, pulling her face tightly to her kneecaps, masking the small tears I see forming.

"Yeah...it does," I say, pulling my knees to my chin and turning to look at her with a soft smile. "Tell him you wanna go."

She shakes her head *no*. And I don't blame her. I was afraid once, too. Still am. We both rock slowly, keeping our eyes locked so we can talk silently, like I'm trying to pull her sadness out of her heart and cure it for her. I think Cass would be content to lie here like this next to me in our small safe cocoon for the rest of the night, but the soft knock on the door wakes us from our trance, and Cass sits up quickly, heading to the mirror to finish straightening her hair.

"Hey, study buddy," Nate says, walking in with his heavy backpack loaded with probably every book he owns. "Can I crash your big night-out plans?" The grin on my face is probably making my response obvious.

"Gah! You two are cute, but when I want to be pissy—you kind of make it tough. I'm heading to Paige's party. I'll be home late," Cass says, stuffing her phone, wallet and keys in the back pocket of her jeans.

"Ty's wearing...an interesting T-shirt," Nate says, biting his cheek and smirking knowingly at me. My latest bribe to him was that he had to wear this special shirt Nate and I ordered for him. It reads: "It's past my bedtime, and I want my milky wilky and my widdle teddy weddy bear named Cookie. Wah!" When I sent the *ransom* text a few days ago, I told him he could find his next party shirt in his mailbox, where we left it.

"Oh great! I better get something out of this little grudge match you three have going on. You know, in this scenario, I'm the one who's *with* the guy with the embarrassing shirt," she says, and Nate and I both seem to get the same idea at the very same minute. And it only takes Cass a second or two longer to catch up with us. "Oooooooh no! You two are *not* pulling me into this! No getting creative ideas to make shirts for me!"

"Oh, but come on, Cass..." Nate starts. "You know you want a shirt that says something like 'I'm with Teddy Bear man'..."

"Or 'My boyfriend wears tutus,'" I pipe in, barely able to finish my words I'm laughing so hard. Cass, on the other hand, has her arms crossed while she stands at the door looking at the two of us, cracking ourselves up.

"Are you done yet?" she says, her lips pulled up to the side, and her face irritated. This only makes us laugh harder, and Cass rolls her eyes and holds up her hand. "Good night, *children!*"

It takes us almost fifteen minutes to settle down enough to actually open up books on my bed and dig in for some studying. We both have big final exams the week we get back from Thanksgiving break, and I have an essay project due for my art history class. I really want to finish it early so I won't have to focus on any homework while I'm with Nate.

At first, I was a little anxious about going to his parents' house for the holiday—worried that I was intruding, and maybe missing, just a little bit, the traditional thing I always did with my parents. But the closer we got to break, the more excitement bloomed in my belly. This—and just being close to Nate, period—was making it extremely hard to study tonight.

Somehow, I'm able to read two chapters, and my brain seems to retain most of what I read. Nate is sitting on the opposite end of the bed from me, his legs stretched out next to mine, and every so often he nudges me with his toes.

"Keep your stinky feet to yourself," I say, pushing his socked foot to the side, which of course only makes him drop it completely on my lap and kick it around under my nose.

"Oh, I'm sorry. Am I...*in your space?*" he teases. I pick up my heaviest book and open it, resting it on his ankle, pretty much trapping his leg in my lap. He chuckles, and folds his book closed, laying back a little and resting his chin in his palm, his elbow holding up his weight. I can feel him staring at me for several minutes, and I'm no longer even coming close to paying attention to the words on my pages. I close my book and turn to the side, my face flat against it like a pillow—and we lay still like this, quietly studying one another, for several minutes before either of us talks.

"Do you still think about him a lot?" I'm not surprised by Nate's question, but it causes my pulse to race, and my stomach to twist tightly, nevertheless. He's chewing on the cap to his pen, his face so kind and regarding. It's not a jealous question—not like how he is when we joke about Tucker. No, this question is one of genuine interest, of wanting to know me that much deeper, know how my insides work, and how my head routes the thoughts of everything that happened.

"Yes." I can see a hint of sadness color his features when I admit this. "But not as much as I used to. It's a little less...everyday."

More silence settles in, but it's comfortable. We're still for several minutes, and then Nate reaches his hand for my foot, and he pulls it into both hands in front of him, digging his thumbs into the bottom for a massage.

"Is it bad that I don't think about him as much as I used to?" I ask, and Nate's hands pause. He takes a slow deep breath without looking at me, and I can tell he's really thinking about my question, putting himself in my shoes.

"Honestly? I think it's human," he says, his thumbs circling my foot again. "Either way...I think it's okay."

We don't talk about it anymore, and after a few minutes, Nate picks up his books and hauls them back to his room. He has early workouts in the morning, and we're leaving for his parents' house later in the day, so he said he wanted to let me really focus to finish up my paper. And in my gut, I felt a little pang over him leaving, like there was something else, something unspoken. He didn't want to be here. But I also didn't fight to make him stay. That small conversation put something in both of our heads. And I was thinking about Josh tonight...more than I wanted to.

Plane rides were definitely better *with* Nate. It took about three hours to get to New Orleans, and another hour or so to get from the airport to Nate's parents' home in Baton Rouge. Their house isn't large, but it's old. The grass out front seems to stretch forever until you get to a porch flanked by white posts and stretching the entire expanse of the home. It's yellow, like sunshine, and with the sun setting behind it, I swear I've stepped into a postcard.

"I love your home," I say, and I realize it comes out kind of corny, like the thing you're supposed to say to be polite. But I mean it—I really love his home. It feels like I fit here. I keep that part to myself, though, because *that* sounds crazy.

"Yeah, I guess it's nice," Nate shrugs, lifting our bags from the back of their family van. Nate's father picked us up from the airport, which made it nice since there were three of us. Nate pulls Ty's chair from the back and unfolds it next to the van; I watch as Ty lifts himself into it. The move takes seconds, and I wonder how long it took before it was easy.

"Your mom ordered pizza; I hope that's okay," Nate's father says as he pushes Ty's chair up the sidewalk to the ramp at the side of the porch. It's the only time I've ever seen Ty not push himself, and when I realize I'm staring, I shake my head and look away quickly, hoping nobody noticed.

"It makes Dad feel good to do it sometimes," Nate whispers into my ear. I just mouth *oh* and smile.

Pizza was the *perfect* idea after our trip, and maybe I was just starving, but the slices were gone from my plate in minutes. With dinner done, Nate pulls our bags to the bedrooms down the hall, and he gives me a quick tour of his family's home. The living room and kitchen are one big room with a giant stoned fireplace and a TV mounted to the wall above it. The floors are long, wooden planks, and every wall is adorned with a collection of family photos or art. I notice a few paintings in the kitchen—signed by Nate's mom, Cathy; I wonder if the others were done by friends.

"I like these," I say, running my finger along the bottom of an ornately carved frame.

"Thank you," Cathy says, coming up behind me, her hand on my shoulder in a way that feels nice—like acceptance. "I painted them in college."

"What about these?" I ask, motioning to the ones I know are done by someone else.

"Those," she starts, but pauses, her face sliding into a large smile. "Those are Ty's."

"You're kidding!" I'm unable to mask my surprise. I get closer, and I can recognize the signature now, and I'm blown away. The paintings are oils. Abstracts, but full of color, the shapes almost making something recognizable, but always not quite—they remind me of dreams.

"He still paints sometimes. For fun," she says, turning to look at Ty who is lost in some basketball game playing out on the TV while he talks with his dad. "My boys are full of surprises. I'm pretty sure I haven't seen everything they're capable of yet." She watches him with pride in her eyes for a few seconds before taking a quick deep breath and turning her attention back to Nate and me. "Come on, let's get you settled in your room."

The Preeter home is one big circle, with a hallway that starts and ends in the family room, looping around to four bedrooms—all with views of the big yard and giant trees that surround the back of the house. My room is next to Nate's, and I can't help but wonder if he'll sneak in to see me at night. I sit down on the full-size bed, and I can tell the lavender quilt was washed recently, the smell of fabric softener still strong in it.

"This is lovely," I say, wondering where this sudden formal version of myself is coming from. Nate mocks me behind his mom, mouthing the word *lovely* and holding his hands up to his face with wide eyes. I glare at him, and he laughs silently.

"I'm glad you like it here," she says, reaching around me and hugging me to her side, filling my body with even more warmth. I notice the stare she gives to Nate as she leaves, like they have a silent conversation about me, but I look away when Nate comes toward me.

"Oh, Mrs. Preeter, your home is simply divine. I *must* have your decorator," Nate jokes, putting on his ridiculous, high-pitched girly voice.

"Oh my god! I do NOT sound like that," I say, shoving him into my bed.

He raises his hand and holds his thumb to his index finger, measuring an inch. "You kinda do. But just a little."

"Shut up. I want your mom to like me. And it's really nice of your parents to have me here," I say, actually feeling a little bad that he made fun of me. Nate can tell, and he grabs my hand, pulling me to his lap and hugging me tightly.

"I'm sorry. It was nice of you to gush. And for the record, my parents freaking love you. Just like I do," he says, his smile warm against my cheek. Within seconds, he's kissing me, and he keeps kissing me until we hear Ty clear his throat in the doorway.

"Yeah, you can't do that shit at the Thanksgiving table. I'll get sick," he says, pushing into the room and lifting the corner of the blanket to his nose. "Damn. Mom actually washed your blanket. Did she wash yours?"

Nate shrugs, and Ty backs out of the room, heading to Nate's. We follow him in there and he pulls Nate's blanket to his nose then quickly tosses it back down. "All right, this is *bullshit*! Mom, what's up with everyone getting dryer-sheet bed but me?" He's down the hall and moaning to his mom within seconds.

"Dryer-sheet bed?" I ask Nate, laughing lightly.

"It's a Ty thing. He likes the way they smell. It's kind of like Cookie," Nate says with a small shake of his head. "Ty likes what he likes."

"Oh! Speaking of...look what I brought," I say, leading Nate back to my room and unzipping my small travel bag and pulling out my teddy bear hostage. "I thought maybe we've taken this far enough."

Nate nods, leaning against the doorframe and grinning while I start to tuck it back into the zipper bag. "You wanna win Ty over forever?" Nate asks, and I pause, pulling the bear back out again. "Come with me."

Nate leads me to a small door near the back porch, and I realize quickly it's the laundry room. We toss Cookie into the dryer with a fabric softener sheet and let it spin for about five minutes. When it's done, we pull it out, and I write a small note in all caps that says: "NO MORE FUSSY FUSS, OKAY?" and we tuck the note and the bear in the top of Ty's blanket for him to find at bedtime.

Nate

I like having her in my house. She feels...permanent. But there's this constant ache scratching at the back of my mind every second. It's the secret I'm keeping, and I know if I tell her, she'll leave. And I would understand. She should leave—she should have known all along, and had her chance to say goodbye. But she can never get that back. So I guess the only decision now is what happens moving forward, and maybe her parents are right. Maybe, to move forward, Rowe just needs to keep moving. And maybe knowing this will hold her back, mess with her head during finals, ruin her great start. But I can't help but think it might all just backfire, too.

Her parents haven't sold their house yet. But the last time she talked with them, right before we left for our flight, they were mostly packed. I wonder if they really went through with taking a trip—a vacation for just the two of them—or if they're just at home, pretending.

We spent the night curled up with one another on the couch, watching the end of the Pacers and Miami game with Ty and my dad. Mom busied herself in the kitchen, prepping for our un-traditional Thanksgiving tomorrow. Mom made Lasagna and eggrolls, and Rowe actually seemed excited by it, which only made me love her more. Every little thing—sometimes the tiniest things—makes me love her more, and I'm in so deep now, I know I won't make it back out whole.

Stretching out every moment, I hold her body close to mine along the sofa. My dad, per tradition, has dozed off in his chair, and Ty is busy dropping sunflower seeds in his hair, one at a time, which makes Rowe giggle, and makes me hold her tighter—*loving her more.*

"All right, kids," Ty says, brushing his hands of the salt from the seeds while he backs away from my dad's chair. "This face needs its beauty sleep. And I told Cass I'd call."

"Good," Rowe says, her voice a little forceful, and it actually surprises Ty *and* me.

"I'm sorry, did I miss something?" Ty asks, his eyebrows pinched as he scratches the darned-near full beard he's been growing for two weeks. Rowe looks up at me with her eyes wide; clearly her tone surprised her as well.

"Sorry, that...that came out harsh," she says, pushing against my hip to sit up in front of me. "I just meant you should call; she's missing you." Her words have a strange smile on Ty's face, and if I didn't know any better, I'd swear he was blushing. "You should have invited her to come too, you know. She wanted to come."

Ty just nods at her, his lips tight and his face reverent. "Yeah, I probably should have. I'm...kind of new...at *this*?" Ty shrugs and we all sit still, sort of soaking in what has suddenly become a strange serious environment for the three of us, which Ty, of course, is the first to break. "Anywho...gonna go see if she wants to have phone sex. So, goodnight all."

Ty is gone for about fifteen seconds before he's back, gently tossing Cookie in one hand, a sinister chuckle crackling in his chest. "Well, look what we have here," he says, looking down at the small bear in his hand before he brings it up to his nose to take in its scent. He laughs a little louder when he does, and finally looks up at me, and then to Rowe, pointing at her. "*You*...you just got lucky there, sister. The dryer sheet...yeah. That was a nice touch. Might have just saved you a *world* of hurt," he trails off, turning around and going back in his room where he closes the door.

"Your brother's weird," she says, leaning into me slowly.

"Yeah," I say, kissing her cheek lightly. "But he likes you. And that's not easy to do." She shoves me, kinda hard, and I realize what I said. "I mean...getting *Ty* to like you. No, liking *you* is easy. Ah, fuck...I hate grammar. It's always screwing me over."

Rowe giggles, then slides to my lap and kisses me, and soon her lips—and the rest of her—is all I'm thinking about, and I'm pulling her from the couch, quietly tiptoeing away from my father, and the murmur of the television, to the lavender room—that she's supposed to stay in alone, but to hell with that.

Chapter 28

Rowe

Eggrolls for Thanksgiving are my new awesome. Seriously. Awesome. I'm usually a sick kind of stuffed on this holiday, and it's normally from mashed potatoes. But today, it's eggrolls. The lasagna was good, too, but I think there's a chance I may try to marry those eggrolls.

After our early dinner, Nate took me on a tour of where he grew up—driving us by his little league field, grade school, high school, and first girlfriend's house. He even showed me the tree where he first carved into the trunk NATE LOVES STACY, and then came back a few weeks later and scratched it out with a pocketknife. Stacy, apparently, did *not* love Nate. He was twelve, and bitter.

After the tour, he gave me my first driving lesson in three years. I wasn't awful, but I wasn't *good* either. I stayed a good fifteen miles per hour under the limit and stuck to the side streets. At this rate, I should be driving by age thirty-five.

We spent the rest of the night watching old Christmas movies, like *White Christmas* and *It's a Wonderful Life.* I got excited when *Home Alone* came on, and when Nate admitted he had never seen it, I forced him to watch it with me. I caught him laughing a few times.

At almost midnight, we're the only two left awake in the living room, so Nate pulls a few logs from the pile in the corner and builds us a nice fire. I snuggle in between his legs as he sits on the floor with his back against the side of the sofa, putting us right in line of the fire's warmth.

"Thank you," I whisper, reaching my hands around his forearms, which are wrapped around me, and dipping my head to kiss his skin.

"For what?" he whispers back.

"For letting me have this...today, this trip—this time here with you. I don't think I would have liked the Bahamas over Thanksgiving, and being here has sort of made me forget all about how my mom and dad are selling the house." Truthfully,

I haven't thought about it once, and even talking about it now, it doesn't hurt as much as it did when my parents first told me.

"I'm glad you're here," Nate says, squeezing me tightly to his chest, and resting his cheek on the top of my head. He holds me there for several minutes while we both stare blankly at the fire.

"Hey, guess what?"

"What's that?" he asks, his lips brushing against the side of my head in the sweetest way, I almost forget what I wanted to say.

"I'm picking a major when we get back. I'm meeting with my advisor," I say, actually excited about my future.

"Astrophysicist?" he asks, turning my chin to look at him so I can see his serious face, just before half of his mouth curls into a sarcastic smile and he winks.

"Yes, I totally want to work on rockets, despite my absolute detestation for math. And science. And fear of being lost in space," I say, and Nate laughs but then stops quickly.

"Fear...of...being...lost in space?" His eyebrows pinch.

"Yeah, I can't watch those movies. Like *Apollo 13*? I get all freaked out," I say, and he laughs. Hard.

"That's...a strange fear," he says, still sporting his perfect grin—dimples and all. "And, you know *Apollo 13*, that...that really happened."

"I know, but I like to pretend it was just a movie. Swear to god, freaks me out. Lost in space?" I snuggle back into his arms and relish the low rumble of the chuckle in his chest.

"So what do you want to *be* then? When you grow up," he asks.

"A curator. Like in a museum. I'm going to be one of those art-history nerds," I say, the smile on my face one of excitement. Nate is quiet for several long seconds, and I start to wonder why, so I turn in his arms so I'm facing him, and he smiles, fast. "What do you think?" I ask, really wanting his acceptance.

"Sorry, was just thinking of funny art-history jokes." He looks proud of himself, so I nod my head toward him, encouraging him to let me have it. "Okay, so...how do you get an art-history major off your doorstep?"

"I don't know. How?"

"Pay her for the pizza," he says, with a loud blurt of laughter afterward.

"Nice, Nate. Real nice."

"Wait, I have one more. I was trying to decide which is better," he says, and I sigh into him. "What are the first two Italian words an art-history major learns?"

I sigh again before I respond. "What?"

"Venti cappuccino," he laughs, and I roll my eyes in response. "Get it? You know, because you'll be working at Starbucks..."

"Yeah, got it. Thanks," I say, not really liking the jokes.

"Oh, come on Thirty-three...I was kidding. Honestly? I think that's the *perfect* thing for you to do. You seem to really love art. And my mom would totally help you, you know."

I stare at him, then finally speak. "I love it when you call me Thirty-three. You pretty much had my heart the first time you called me that," I admit.

"Good. That's the first time I wanted it. And I like getting what I want," he says, pulling me into a deep kiss that lasts until the old grandfather clock propped up on the mantle begins to ring out twelve times for midnight.

The fire is starting to spark less and less, but I don't want to leave this spot. For some reason, looking at the flames has me in a trance. And after a few silent minutes, I get an idea—more of an urge really—and I squirm out of Nate's hold, getting to my feet. He looks up at me and starts to push himself up, too, thinking I'm ready for bed, but I hold up a finger; he sits back down. "Be right back," I say, rushing to my purse in the guest room.

It doesn't take me long to find the pictures of Josh, because I stuffed them in my purse when I packed for this trip. I wanted to explain them to Nate more, and then I wanted to get rid of them because I was tired of holding on. But for some reason, being here—with Nate, in this perfect moment—has put things in fast-forward for me, and I'm prepared to fully let go...of everything.

When I come back to the living room, Nate is sitting with his elbows propped on his bent knees, and when I come close, he leans back, welcoming me back into his embrace. "Does this gate thingy open?" I ask, pulling on the small wire frame that covers the front of the fireplace.

"Sure. Why, you want me to throw another log in?" He crawls up on his knees and opens the gate a little, but before he reaches for another log, I stop him.

"No, actually...I kind of wanted to throw something *in*?" The few photos I've kept, I now hold in front of me like a poker hand; when I do, Nate stumbles back on his legs.

"Your pictures...of you and Josh," Nate says, and I nod slowly to confirm. He pulls them from my hands, flipping through them slowly, pausing for long seconds while he looks at each one, until he's seen them all at least twice. Then he piles them into a neat stack, but keeps them grasped firmly in his hand. "I don't know, Rowe. I think you should hang on to these."

"I don't want to anymore," I say, and my conviction stuns me. I reach to take them back, but Nate leans away from me, pulling my photos to his chest and then moving them behind his back. "Nate, I know what I'm doing. Please?"

"Rowe, I..." he starts, but then he looks down, pulling the photos in front of him, looking at the corners poking through his closed fist while he shakes his head. When he looks back into my eyes, there's an unmistakable sadness there.

"Nate, you're not making me do this. I hope that's not what you think. It's something...something I've been trying to do...for months. For years! This isn't about you. It's about me. I promise," I say, reaching forward again. But Nate only holds them tighter, his eyes flicking between his fist and my eyes, until eventually he stands and pushes the photos into his back pocket, and reaches down for my hand to lift me to him.

"Tomorrow," he says, pulling my chin up gently with his thumb, and then reaching around to sweep my hair behind my ear with his other hand. He leans in and brushes my lips lightly with his, sliding both of his hands up until they cup my face. "If you still want to throw them in the fire tomorrow, I'll build you one, just for that. But just do me a favor...wait until tomorrow. Just to be sure?"

My eyes are closed, and our lips are still breaths apart, but I can tell this is important to him, so I nod slowly; I feel his body release and exhale when I give in. Maybe he's right, and maybe I should be sure. But I don't think my mind will change, and feeling so certain—feels good enough for tonight.

Nate

I can't do this anymore. No matter how this plays out, Rowe is going to hate *me* at the end. Not because any of this is really my fault. She'll hate me for lying, but I think she'll forgive me for it eventually. The long hate—the kind that's going to last— will be the misplaced kind. The kind she needs to place on someone because her heart is broken. And me not telling her— me putting this off—is just dragging things out. It's selfish, because I don't want her to hate me yet. I love her too much. But if Rowe needs to hate me to get through life, I'm willing to be that person for her.

She whispers in her sleep. I watch her lips move every time we sleep together, like they're telling the universe secrets. Tonight, I can't help but feel like they're trying to tell me something, like they're begging for me to be a man.

I got out of bed hours ago, and I've just been sitting here, in this chair by the window, torturing myself with her beauty. I've counted every freckle on her arms, memorized her eyelashes and the way they cast perfect shadows along her pink cheeks. I've watched her lips for so long that I anticipate when they're going to open to breathe. I won't sleep any more tonight. I can't, because as soon as she wakes up, I'm going to tell her, and then I won't have any more time with her, *like this.*

Every time she pulls the blanket in close, or rolls to her other side, I hold my breath. And finally, the thing I've been dreading happens, and she stretches out her arm and feels that I'm not there next to her. Her eyes struggle to open at first, and I hold my breath, the voice in my head wishing—begging them to close again. But they don't. And in minutes, this will all be over.

"Hey," she whispers, her lips giving way to a yawn. "Are you okay?"

"Uh huh," I whisper back, unable to push my lips into a smile. I'm sad. I'm so unbelievably sad, and I can't fake it any more.

"You're not...I can tell. What's wrong?" Her voice is so fucking sweet while her fingers rub the sleepiness from her eyes.

I can't get my voice to work at first, and all I can do is stare at her, which only makes her more suspicious. "Nate? Tell me...are you sick?"

"No, baby. I'm not sick," I say, my chest crumbling around my heart. Everything inside me hurts right now. "I'm okay. It's fine..." I almost try to convince myself to play this off, to abandon my plan. But that wouldn't do me any good. Everything would still be waiting for me in the morning. I understand Rowe's parents, and I know her dad had the best intentions with everything. But I hate them for putting me in this position.

"Tell me," she says, her voice a little louder now, and I can tell she's fully awake. "You're kind of scaring me."

She sits up, the blankets pooled around her, and the only light in the room is that from the half-moon reflecting off the clouds outside our window. "I love you," I start, just needing that to be said, needing that to be the first thing she hears.

"I love you too." She says it back quickly, and I can tell she's full of worry now.

"Rowe, I know something. Something that...God, I wish I didn't know. And I'm not supposed to tell you. But I *have* to tell you. Because, if this were the other way around, you'd tell me, and I'd want you to." I'm talking in circles, and I'm sure none of this is making sense to her. But I can almost see her eyes working the puzzle out, the tears already forming in the corners.

"Tell me," she says, almost breathlessly.

234

"Before your parents left, your dad came to see me. It was before my game, before you and your mom got there. He…he told me something, and Rowe…it's killing me. I hate that I know this, and I hate that I've lied to you."

"Tell me!" She's crying now, gripping the blanket close to her with one hand while the other covers her mouth, and her body is starting to shake. "Just say it. Say it!"

"You're going to hate me," I say, and in that moment, our eyes lock, and I know that she will. This is that time—there's no going back from here. "Josh died, Rowe. A few weeks ago."

Her eyes are locked open, dripping tears down her cheeks, while the rest of her body remains rigid, frozen. I lean forward from the chair, making a movement toward the bed, but she reacts quickly, almost scurrying backward away from me. "No! Don't!" she yells, and my heart literally rips in half. "How? Why?"

"I don't know, Rowe. Your dad…he didn't want you to find out until the semester was over. He was afraid this might set you back. He only told me because he wanted me to be here for you when you found out. But I just can't know *this* and not tell you. You deserve to know…"

"You shouldn't have," she bites back. "You should have kept this to yourself!" She's not looking at me any more, and her stare is wide, and off somewhere else entirely. Her knees are pulled tightly to her body, and her arms are wrapped completely around herself.

"Rowe…" I begin, but I don't know what to say, so I just sit there and wait for her hate to grow.

"I was better off not knowing," she says, her voice an angry kind of calm. Minutes pass before she speaks again. "Are they even selling the house?"

"Yes, that part's true," I say. "But the trip—" I'm unable to stop myself, and the second I say it, I know I shouldn't have let out so much. But it's too late. Her eyes are on me like lasers.

"There's no trip." Her face has gone through so many emotions in the last few seconds, and the one looking back at me now is full of anger. All I can do is shake my head *no,* and when I do, Rowe is quick to get to her feet, and she starts shoving all of her belongings into her suitcase, not even taking time to change from her pajamas.

"Rowe, you can't go back," I say, reaching for her arm, but she jerks it away from me.

"Watch me." She's so angry, and I know I'm going to get the brunt of it, so I close my eyes and take a deep breath, readying myself.

"I'm coming with you," I start again, but she cuts me off.

"I don't want you to," she says, her fingers already dialing her phone.

"Rowe, you need to process this. Stop. Just wait until morning, and then we can call your parents and figure out what to do."

"Ha! Don't you think the three of you have figured enough out for me? ...Hi, I need a cab," she's says, snapping her fingers at me suddenly and holding the phone away from her ear. "Address."

"Don't. Do. This," I whisper one more time, pleading with her. I reach to touch her arm, but everything about her is cold. I may as well be touching a statue. She looks down where my fingers wrap lightly around her arm, but her stare is blank, and Rowe...Rowe is gone.

"Address," she says once again, her voice seething, and her eyes narrow, and so very angry. Everything about the way she's looking at me right now is killing me, but I take it. Because I know as soon as she's done being angry, she's going to be destroyed. And I guess I'd rather see her mad at me instead.

"Seventy-four seventy-one North Meadow Drive," I relent, then listen to her repeat it to the person on the other line. I sit back and let my head rest against the window while I watch her make her arrangements to leave my parents' home—to leave me. I'm helpless. I could bully her, because I'm stronger. I could physically keep her from leaving. But then what?

This...this...has to happen. My only hope is somehow, in the end, she'll come through her broken heart completely. And still want me.

I watch her wheel her luggage down the hall, and I stand several feet away from her in the foyer, just watching her pull her jacket tight from the chill. I would give anything to be able to close this gap, to put my arms around her and let her cry on me for hours. But I'm not the one she needs right now. And unfortunately, the person she does, is gone—forever.

Chapter 29

Rowe

Flying angry makes flying easier, too. Maybe it was because I hadn't slept much, or because it was six in the morning when my plane took off. Whatever the reason, I barely even registered the five hours it took me to get to Phoenix from Baton Rouge. I charged the American Airlines ticket, and it was pricey. And my parents would pay it. They owe me that much.

I was ready to walk through this door and rip into them. I pushed my key in, my face showing everything I'm feeling. But then nobody was home, so I started looking around, and all of my verve completely deflated.

Boxes take up places where furniture used to sit. The walls are empty, dust and dirt on the walls outlining places that used to showcase family photos. Even the simple things are strange—like the fact that the cord from the lamp that used to sit behind our sofa is no longer taped along the floor to the other side of the wall. Everything—*everything*—is gone.

I take a trip upstairs, because I like torturing myself. It feels good, takes away the other things I'm trying not to let simmer to the top of my mind. I'll be angry about *this* instead. My room is nothing more than a pile of boxes, stacked neatly in the middle, and labeled "North Room 2." My parents' room is pretty much the same, except there's a tattered looking air mattress with a few rumpled blankets sitting in the middle of the room. The move, it seems, is happening very soon.

"Hello?" my mother's voice calls from downstairs, and my heart starts thumping fast again, my hands naturally forming into angry fists.

"Rowe? Are you here?" my father calls out now, and I exit their room, charging down the stairs. "Oh, honey. You're home," he says, opening his arms, expecting me to hug him. I can't come near him—I can't come near anyone!

"What were you thinking?" I growl, rushing beyond their reach to the foyer, where my bags are still dropped by the door.

238

"Nate called us, told us you were coming home." My dad's voice is calm, and I don't know why, but it only makes me angrier. I don't like being coddled. This is coddling.

"Stop it! Just...just stop this! Both of you! Quit pretending this...*this*...is normal!" I shout, turning slowly in a circle, my hands gesturing to the packed house and the darkness that seems to be settled everywhere. "None of this is normal! And I don't need you to feed me make-believe!"

"I told you. But you wouldn't listen," my mother says under her breath, walking away from my father and pushing through the kitchen door. My dad stares after her, his face pained. He's upset that my mom is upset, that this situation is upsetting *her.* But what about me?

"Hey! Here!" I say, snapping at him and forcing his focus on nothing but my face. My dad is speechless, and all he can do is cover his mouth with his hand and shake his head. "You don't get to feel bad that she's angry. She's right! This was a bad idea, keeping this from me. You stole *everything* from me! *Everything*! Josh is dead! And it should have been me! I get to live, but he died. And I didn't even see him!"

My dad is still frozen, staring; I can feel my mom coming back behind me. Her fingers are on my shoulder, and I jerk, but she holds on, and I jerk again. "Rowe, honey..." she says, and somehow my cage cracks the tiniest bit, and my lungs stutter with one big cry, but I bite my lip quickly, doing my best to hold it in.

"I didn't get to say goodbye," I say, my voice softer now. "I didn't get to say goodbye. He didn't know I was there. He was alone. I left him...alone. And I didn't even say goodbye..."

My eyes are flooded with tears now, and I can no longer stop myself from feeling. Anger can only carry you so far, and mine has run out. Now, I am only devastated. I collapse to the floor, and my mom collapses with me, pulling me to her body and rocking me in her arms while my dad still stands in front of us—his hand to his mouth, and his eyes crying just as hard as mine are.

I cried for a solid hour, and I don't remember breathing. My mom managed to find a box with towels and pulled one free for me so I could take a shower. I feel like a zombie—not as ugly as the *Walking Dead*, but as animated. I pull a clean outfit from the top of my suitcase, a purple sweater and a pair of jeans, and then run a comb through my tangled hair.

"I packed the dryer. I've just been towel drying," my mom says behind me.

"That's fine," I say, scrunching the ends of my hair until the dripping stops. I turn to face her, and she reaches up to my face, holding her hand to my cheek, and I close my eyes because I don't want to pull away. But I'm still so angry. "When do the movers come?"

"Tuesday," she says, her hand still there. It's making my face feel hot. "We meant well, Rowe." And just hearing her say that starts a new chain reaction through my bloodstream. I breathe in long and deeply, forcing the boiling inside back down to a simmer.

"I know," I say, but it comes out cold. I can't say it any other way. I know they meant well. Everyone *meant* well. But it doesn't make me forgive them, not yet. I still can't forgive myself. "I need to go to his house."

"I know," my mom says. We stand there in this face-off for several seconds, and in that time, I play out everything I'm walking into—so I'm prepared for it, prepared for everything I'm about to feel. "They're expecting you. I'll take you when you're ready."

My mom leaves, and I spend the next few minutes putting on eyeliner and lip-gloss, and then twist my hair up into a clip. I look like that girl...the one from two years ago who used to get dropped off at Josh's house for movie night. It feels right to go there looking like this.

My dad doesn't talk, but he comes along for the car ride with my mom and me. We pull up to the Andersons' home; I notice the For Sale sign planted in the yard, and it makes my eyes tear up again. I remind myself to *breathe, just breathe*, and then I put my hand to the car door, still not convinced if I can do this. "Do you want me to go in with you?" Mom asks.

"No, I'm okay," I croak. One last inhale, and I pull the handle and step to the curb. Everything here looks the same—the same black door with the gold handle, the same bench sitting off to the side, and the same pillows stitched with owls on the front. I can almost visualize Josh sitting there, pulling his cleats from his feet and banging them together to get out the chunks of dirt.

The door opens before I ring the bell, and Josh's mom, Patty, is smiling softly. Not the happy kind, but the understanding kind—the kind full of words without speaking. She's older, even though it's only been four months or so since I last saw her, she's wearing years on her body and face. Everything about her is tired.

"Rowe, it's so good to see you," she says, and seeing her glassy eyes make mine sting as well. I step into her arms, and she hugs me tightly, her hand gripping the back of my neck. "Come on in," she says, holding a hand up to my parents who are still out in the driveway. She doesn't ask if they want to come in too. There's no need. Everyone knows what I'm here for.

I follow Patty to the kitchen where she has a plate of cookies and a glass of milk already prepared. She always had snacks for me—even when I came to visit when Josh was under their care. She pushes the plate at me, and I pull a cookie into my hand, not really hungry, but not wanting to be rude.

"I didn't know," I start, and I can feel the burn in my eyes instantly, so I suck in trying to keep it together. "I would have come. I would have been here. But I didn't know."

I put the cookie down on the table and look down to my lap; Patty reaches across the table and puts her hand on mine. "I know you would have, sweetheart. I know," she says, just holding her hand there for a few minutes while I sob softly.

"Where's Mr. Anderson?" I ask, doing my best not to notice the small things that are familiar around me. This place is more familiar than my own home at this point.

"He had to work. He sends his *hellos* though. He's sorry he didn't get to see you," she says, and I nod in response.

"Was it...I don't know...fast? I mean, that's stupid..." I fumble through my words, and the more I talk the more my gut hurts. "I guess I mean, did he suffer? At the end?"

"No, Rowe," she says, the faint smile coming back to her lips, and I know she's being honest. "He went in his sleep. He had been failing for months. It was his time."

I nod again and look back to my lap, doing my best to swallow the lump choking my throat. I reach for the milk and take a sip, then pick up my cookie again, breaking off a small piece and eating it. Like everything else, it's familiar, and it floods my mind with a dozen more memories, so I put it back down.

"Rowe, you know you couldn't have done anything, right?" Patty asks, tilting her head down to force my gaze up to hers. I shrug, because even though I know I couldn't have, I feel like I should have tried, or at least been here. "Rowe, my son was gone the day that madman entered the cafeteria. These last two years...while he was here, it wasn't really *him*, you know? He was alive, but his mind was gone."

"But I should have said goodbye," I say, unable to stop myself from full-on crying now. Patty moves her chair close to mine and pulls me into her arms, her hand rubbing up and down my back while I convulse into huge sobs. "He died, and he thinks I forgot him. That I didn't love him. "

"No, don't you for once ever think that, Rowe," she says, squeezing me tighter. "I'm convinced, the last thing my son remembers is that last day here on earth with you—talking about summer, and the end of the school year, and your date that night. I like to believe he died playing that memory over and over in his head, the best memory of his life. He wasn't even aware of anything after."

"But I never saw him. I couldn't do it. I was too...too weak," I say, rubbing my eyes with my balled-up fists.

"I'm glad, Rowe, because you can have that last memory, too. The same one Josh had. His dad and I, we weren't as lucky. And if I could have chosen never to have seen my son like that, the way he lived...barely...for the last two years—I would have," she says, lifting my chin to look at her and taking a soft towel to my cheeks.

"I don't know," I say, feeling ashamed for being so afraid.

"I do. I know," she says, forcing me to keep my eyes on her. She studies me for several seconds, then she stands and reaches for my hand. "Come with me. I have something for you."

Patty leads me down the hall to Josh's room, and my anxiety grows with every step we take. "It's okay," she says, over her shoulder. "We've boxed up his things and the hospital bed is gone. It's not the same. You'll be okay."

I love that she understands, and I hate that she has to understand. She pushes the door open, and the windows are all open, the room sunny and bright. It's almost a guest room, as if he never lived here at all. She slides the closet door open and kneels to the floor, pulling out a hatbox and bringing it over to the bed. She pats the side next to her, and I come over to sit.

"I saved some things, and everyone has a box. I made one for us, one for Josh's grandparents, and one for you," she says, sliding the box to my lap and pulling the lid off, like she knows I won't be able to on my own. The first thing I see is the picture of Josh smashing cake in my face at the baseball banquet. Betsy took this photo, which makes it even more special, and I can't help but smile looking at it. I pull it out and set it in the lid, moving on to the next thing. There's a stack of letters, and I realize they're all notes that I wrote to Josh—notes that he saved.

"Don't worry. I didn't read them," she says with a gentle laugh. "I wanted to...but I figured there wasn't really a parental reason to do that now."

I smile and clutch the papers to my heart, letting a tear slide down my cheek. I set them in the lid with the photo and move on, pulling out the invitation for our homecoming dance, more photos of Josh and me at various baseball games, barbecues and parties, and then finally his old baseball jersey, still dirty from the last time he slid on base. I put everything back inside and close the lid, full-on weeping now, holding the box to my body in a hug.

I mouth *thank you*, unable to get my voice to work, and Patty pulls me into her arms for another hug. "You're welcome, Rowe. You're welcome," she says, letting me stay right there for as long as I need.

Several minutes later, I finally make my way back outside. I never ask them about moving or putting the house up for sale, and I don't ask about where Josh is buried. Because everything I need—the things that I need to move forward, but remember—are in this small box.

Once I'm back in the car with my parents, I set the box next to me on the seat, keeping my left palm flat along the lid, just to make sure nothing escapes. When my mom starts driving, I reach forward and put a hand on my dad's shoulder; he sinks under my touch before reaching for my fingers and squeezing. I hold his hand for the few minutes it takes us to get back home.

Nate

It feels like the first day of school again, even though Ty and I are only coming back for a few days for finals before leaving again. It feels like the first day because it feels like everything from before was a dream. Rowe isn't here, and I wonder if she'll come back for her finals.

I've sent her a few texts, but she hasn't written anything back. I hope she's not angry that I let her parents know she was coming, but I wanted to make sure she got home safely, and that someone was there for her. Her dad sent me a text when she arrived, so I know she landed. But that's the last word I received.

Ty filled Cass in for me, and if she's heard anything from Rowe, she's keeping it a secret. She comes in while Ty and I slide our bags next to our beds, and all I can do is laugh when I look around at this stupid pink room. She's gone and painted herself everywhere I look—there's no escaping. I lie back and laugh harder, because she's all over my bed, too.

"Are you having a breakdown on me?" Ty asks, flipping my foot from my bed.

"Yeah...I think I am," I say, my hands pressed to my eyes, trying to block everything out. "You hear anything?" I ask, looking right at Cass now.

"Nothing. I sent her a text yesterday and this morning. She has to take her finals, though, right?" Cass asks, and I just shrug. Rowe doesn't *have* to do anything. I pull my phone from my pocket and check to see if she's sent me anything, but my message alert is empty. "Fuck!"

I don't do outbursts, but all I want to do right now is scream. Days ago, I had everything, and now the only thing I feel is sickness and regret. If I just knew she was okay, that she wasn't back to being lost... I think if I knew that, I could get through this.

"I'm going to the cages. I'll be back...I don't know...later," I say, pulling on my ball cap and pushing it low over my eyes so I don't have to look at anyone. I hear Ty and Cass talking softly behind me when I leave, talking about me, I'm sure, but I don't care. My state right now is something to talk about, and maybe they'll come up with some answers for me.

During my walk to the batting facilities, I pull out my phone and text her again, because something has to get through. *Are you at least taking your finals?*

There—a truly simple question. She can send me back two or three letters—*no* or *yes*—and I would be thrilled. I push the phone back into my pocket and jog across the street. A few guys are already hitting, so I go to the locker room and pull out my gear, getting my helmet and gloves on. I'm not really dressed for much of a workout, but there aren't any coaches around, so I just stay dressed in my jeans and long-sleeved baseball shirt—Rowe's shirt, because I like to torment myself.

I nod to a few of the guys, then take the cage at the end, flipping the switch and watching a few of the pitches go by before I step in and swing. *Crack!* The first one stings. I'm hitting like shit, not concentrating. I'm hitting angrily. I step back and watch two more go by and take a deep breath before stepping up to the plate again. I line the next four balls, some of the hardest swings of my life, and then completely miss the fifth. This isn't working. I don't know why I thought it would. I shut the machine back to *off*, kick the balls to the end of the cage, and flip my bat to the ground.

Pacing doesn't get me anywhere either, and after a few long breaths with my hands clasped behind my head, I clean up my failed batting session and return to the locker room. When my phone buzzes, I almost drop it in my rush to get it out of my pocket; my heart goes from feeling high to the pit of my stomach in a fraction of a second because the message is from Ty.

Ty: *Dinner. Sally's. Cass is buying.*

Me: *OK. Be there in 20.*

I slam the locker shut, and pushing my lock back in, I nod to one of the guys walking in as I leave. I almost wish I never met her. But that's a lie...because even those few weeks, months, were worth it all. I'm approaching Sally's when my phone buzzes again, and I pull it out to tell Ty I'm there, when I stop cold. It's her. *Yes.* That's all she says. *Yes.* She's taking her finals. She's not fully gone. She isn't quitting—at least not completely. She will be here—in our building—for at least one day. My girl isn't gone. And she hasn't completely shut me out. Three letters, the three greatest letters ever. That's all I needed.

Chapter 30

Rowe

The hallway is empty. Most of the rooms are locked up, the students already gone for the holidays. My mom called my advisor and was able to get all of my finals pushed to the last two days in my professors' offices. It wasn't going to be easy, but I was pretty prepared before I decided to change my plans mid-Thanksgiving break. For one, all I needed to do was turn in a paper, so I wasn't too stressed.

Cass is still here. I ended up calling her to let her know I was coming, and she said she had a final at the very last possible time slot, so she would be here too. I was glad—I didn't want to stay here alone.

Nate's room looks dark though. I didn't message him again after the first time. I just didn't know what to say. The way I left his parents house...I was embarrassed. But I also was still so angry about everything. Whenever I thought about the times he and I were together, all the times he *knew,* I just got madder.

"Yayyyyyyyyy!" Cass is jumping on her bed when I unlock the door and pull my small bag in with me.

"Uh...yeah. Yay," I say, tossing my keys on my bed and dropping my bag to the floor.

"I saw you walking up out the window. I knew you were coming. I haven't really been jumping this whole time. That would be weird," she says, jumping down to the floor. The room smells like nail polish, and she's wearing cotton in between her toes.

"Pedicure?" I ask, gesturing to her feet.

"Oh," she pulls her toes up in a curl away from the floor. "Yeah, I forgot. You like?"

She walks closer to me and wiggles them; I realize she has them painted like snowflakes. It makes me smile.

"Yeah, it's nice."

"I can do yours. You want?" She holds up a bottle of dark blue polish, but I just shake my head *no,* and she places the bottle on top of her dresser. "Hungry? I waited, in case you wanted to eat."

My stomach grumbles at the mere mention of food, so I shrug and pull my purse from my bag. Cass locks the door behind me, and we walk to the elevator bank, my eyes zeroing in on Nate and Ty's door the entire time.

"They left. Had to go home yesterday," she says, brushing her arm into mine. "But he wanted to stay. I...thought you should know that. He wanted to stay."

All I can do is smile and nod. I don't want to talk about him. Not with Cass. But I also want to know how he is, what he's said about me, and what he thinks about everything I said and did. We take the elevator down to the main floor and walk to the cafeteria. The entire school is like a ghost town, and there are maybe four or five other students in here.

"Is everyone gone?" I ask, looking at all of the empty tables and chairs—so different from the last time I ate here.

"Yeah, pretty much. Most people were done two days ago, and they didn't waste any time. Paige left already. Bitch."

I laugh when she says that, and she smiles at me as we grab our trays and slide them along the counter. I pick out a sandwich and an apple and then fill a glass with milk. Nothing sounds appetizing, but I know I need to eat. My stomach is empty, and if I want to do remotely well on my exams, I need food.

Cass's tray is loaded with junk food, and it makes me laugh at the contrast between our two dinners. "Hunkering down for winter?" I ask, raising my eyebrows as we walk to the table in the corner. Cass doesn't even ask; she knows where I like to sit.

"Hey, I have been good all year. But my language final is stressful. I'm stress eating," she says, dropping her tray and pushing the straw into her chocolate milk before tearing open the package of small donuts with her teeth.

"You took sign language," I say, just blinking at her, and she stares back for a few seconds before finally huffing.

"Yeah, and guess what? Turns out, it's hard. Like *really* hard. Like my fingers *this way* means something totally different from my fingers *this way*," she says, contorting her hands into signs I don't know, before pushing an entire mini-donut in her mouth, a few crumbs falling down her chin.

"What does this mean?" I say, holding up my middle finger and doing my best to hold my grin in. It slips out in seconds though.

"Yeah, fuck you too," she says, throwing a donut on my plate. I pick it up and eat it; she laughs lightly.

We both finish our dinners quickly, eating silently, and then we make it back up to our room. I take a fast shower and change into my pajamas. I pause when I walk out of the shower room, lingering in the hallway and remembering the first time we met. I feel a small pang that I'm not wearing Nate's shirt, and not sleeping with him in his room. Cass is already watching MTV when I come back, so I snuggle under my blankets and do my best to get lost in the show we're watching. Some girl is yelling at a guy about dating someone else for most of the show, and it all seems ridiculous after too long, so I pull out my phone and send my parents a text *goodnight*. I also sweep down to the list of messages from Nate, and I go through every one of them.

"Have you talked to him yet?" Cass's voice surprises me, and I flip my phone off quickly and hide it from her view.

"No," I say, letting my eyes fall to the floor while I lay my head flatly along my hands. "I don't know what to say. Everything is all...I don't know...messy?" I look back up and stare at her, and we both just sit in our locked gaze, cheeks against our hands and eyes tired.

"Yeah. But—" she starts, but then pauses, pushing her lips tightly.

"But what?"

Cass rolls to her back and holds her arms and legs up in the air, then bends her knees and draws them into her body, hugging them tightly before rolling back to face me. "It's not like he was trying to hurt you. I mean, I know, you probably feel a little betrayed."

"*Very* betrayed," I butt in.

"Right. I know," she continues. "But he was sort of put in a really crappy position. And he's been a wreck."

I know I shouldn't be happy about that. But I am. Not that he's suffering, but happy that he's feeling. I dreamt about him last night. I dreamt that he showed up in the middle of my final exam and pulled me from some strange office and lifted me into his arms. And when I woke up, I was sad that it wasn't real. I want to forgive him. But I also want to yell at him. And I still see Josh's face in the middle of it all, and it makes everything confusing.

"Hey, guess what?" Cass asks, her cheerful voice a change.

"I don't know...what?" I respond, leaning more over the edge of the bed and letting my arm swing back and forth so my fingers graze the carpet.

"I'm going to tell Ty I love him," she says. I freeze, then let the smile stretch my entire face. Hearing Cass say that, especially after going home with Ty and seeing new sides of him, makes me feel hopeful for a lot of reasons.

"Yeah?" I say, looking up at her. She's biting her lip and soon she starts kicking her legs excitedly, and hiding her face in her pillow.

"Yeah. Can you believe it?" She's still hiding, but peeking at me with her eyes barely above the pillow.

My smile softens, and I roll onto my back and look at the ceiling, then nod slowly. "Yeah, I can." I remember talking to Ty, telling him how disappointed Cass was that he didn't invite her home for Thanksgiving, and I remember the look on his face when I told him. He loves her, too. I just hope he's ready to admit it.

"I'm happy for you," I say, keeping my eyes focused on the ceiling so Cass doesn't see my smile fade. I am happy for her. But I miss Nate. And I'm jealous that she's in her honeymoon phase. Mine was cut short, just like every major milestone in my stupid life. Problem is, as much as I miss Nate, I also miss my box of Josh memories. And I'm not so sure there's room to miss them both.

My exams take most of the next day and the full next morning. By the time I get back to our room, Cass has her luggage packed, and she's almost ready to walk out the door to head to the airport.

"So, this is it, huh?" I ask, looking at her and almost wanting to kidnap her and put her in my suitcase so she can come home with me.

"Stop it. Don't you dare get mushy on me. We're not criers!" She pulls me into a hug, and I giggle lightly, doing my best to mask the tears also threatening to come. Because truth of the matter is Cass and I *are* criers. We just don't want anyone to know.

"Have a happy Christmas!" I say, sitting back on my bed while she pulls the straps of her bags up on her shoulders.

"You, too. And I'll see you...in a month, right? You're coming back?" I nod *yes* and offer a tight smile, but my stomach twists because I'm not so sure. When I fly back, I'll be staying with my grandparents, where my parents are staying through the holidays until they settle in at San Diego. I've thought about transferring, that way I can live at home with them. But that's not really home either.

"Oh, and I have something for you," she says, pulling a folded envelope from her pocket and tossing it on my bed next to me. "I'm leaving now, so I won't get to see you get pissed at me for sitting on that for two days. But I had very specific instructions. And...well...I love Nate's brother, so I sort of felt like I owed him one. You know, by extension? Anyhow, whatever. Read it. I did. Again, get pissed when I leave. Okay, love you. Bye!"

She's out the door with a barrel of noise and activity, her bags hitting every wall on her way out and down the hall. I hear the elevator ding, and when I know she's gone, I turn my face to look at the envelope, my heart pounding so heavily I'm convinced if I looked down I could see it beating through my sweatshirt.

Swallowing hard, I pick up the envelope, which has clearly been torn open, and I can't help but shake my head and smirk at Cass's confession. The need to know is so strong that I don't hesitate long, and I pull the folded sheets of notebook paper out. It's written in pencil, and some of the lines have smudged, probably from my nosey roommate, but his handwriting is familiar, and just seeing it has me smiling.

I miss him. I miss him. I miss him. I unfold the pages and smooth them out in my lap, pulling my legs up crossed in front of me, and begin to read.

33,

And begin. I've written the first line of this letter about a dozen times. Ty says I'm wasting paper. Every opening line sounds desperate and cheesy, so I'm opting for that one. Now that I'm this far in, I think I can keep going.

I love you. I also wanted to make sure that was said up high, should you stop reading. I hope you've read this far. Have you read this far?

I pause and run my arm under my eyes while I laugh. I can actually hear his voice while I'm reading, smooth and deep, and I miss him more.

I'm sorry. That's the other thing I needed to make sure was said. I wasn't sure what should come first—the 'I love you' or the 'I'm sorry.' I took a gamble and went with love, mostly because it's happier.

Now, I also want to make sure you're not angry with Cass for not giving this to you right away. I wanted to make sure you finished your exams first, and she had very specific instructions. Did she cheat and give this to you early? I hadn't really thought about that until now. I guess there's nothing I can really do if that happened.

Right, so what's the point of this letter? Rowe, I'm so sorry I lied to you. Your dad was so concerned, and when he told me what life was like for you, right after the shooting, I didn't want you to go back. But looking back on it, I think I was maybe being selfish. I didn't want you to drift back into depression, because I didn't want to lose you. I didn't want you to become so distraught that you couldn't be here any more, and the fear of that was strong enough to convince me that not telling you was the right thing to do. But I lost you anyway, didn't I?

When you almost threw those pictures in the fire, it's like my trance was snapped. I realized how selfish I was being. And I couldn't let you get rid of those memories; not knowing they were all you had left. So I told you. And I'm sorry I didn't tell you sooner. I love you so much it makes me selfish—greedy for you. I want you all to myself.

Since you walked out of my parents' house, though, all I've been doing is thinking about Josh. And I've come to a realization. I think Josh loved you just as much as I do. And if he's the kind of man who can love you this way—see you for all the things I do— then he sounds like he's probably a pretty great guy. And maybe I'm all right with sharing your heart with a guy like that.

I have another confession. I know you wrote to him sometimes, on Facebook. I know because you accidentally sent a message meant for him to me.

I stop when I read this, my heart rate speeding up and my stomach feeling as if it's full of rocks. I pull my phone from my purse and open my Facebook message to see, and when I go to my string to Nate, it's there...the last letter I ever wrote to Josh. Nate read every word. Re-reading it makes me cry, remembering how hard it was to want to let Josh go, and how painful it was admitting to him—even in this way—that there was someone else. It takes me several minutes before I can put my phone away and open Nate's letter again, but I finally do.

I'm sorry I didn't tell you that sooner. I probably should have. But you were opening yourself up, and you were falling for me. And Rowe, I just didn't want to stop that. I told you I'm selfish. I wanted you to fall. And I wanted to catch you.

But since you left, I've been thinking about that message you wrote. I bet there are more. You don't have to tell me; those words are private, for you and Josh. But Josh hasn't been able to write back. And the more I thought about you sending him messages, and not getting anything in return, the sadder it made me—for you.

So while this isn't Josh writing now, and while I don't have the memories of you at sixteen that he did, I do feel slightly qualified—as someone who loves you just as much—to speak on his behalf. You didn't get to say goodbye, Rowe. But neither did he. If he did, I'm pretty sure these are the things he would want to say:

Dear Rowe (he would be more formal than me),

You were my first. And you were my only. And I am blessed because of that.

My last great moments on earth were with you, just as I would have wanted them to be.

Kissing you for the hundredth time is just as intoxicating as kissing you for the first.

You will always be the only girl I want to dance with.

I can't believe how big your heart is, and how strong, for being able to carry me in it for so long.

Thank you, for caring so much for my parents and for me.

I'm proud of you, for fighting through what life handed you. It wasn't easy, and for many it would have been impossible. But you're a fighter, a beautiful, brilliant, funny, witty, kind and loving fighter. And the world needs you. So thank you for coming back to it.

And it's okay to keep me in your heart. I talked with that other guy...Nate something or other. And he doesn't mind. Like, at all. (Okay, so he probably wouldn't say this, but you get the point.)

I won't say goodbye. And you shouldn't either. Because what we had is permanent, and goodbyes would only erase that. So instead, let's say good beginnings. The best beginnings—first loves. I hear your second one is pretty crazy about you, too. (Yeah, that last part is totally me.)

Yours. Forever.

Josh

And Nate

Chapter 31

Rowe

Maybe I'd already forgiven him. But reading his words, seeing his handwriting, and knowing his touch was on that paper—scribing out every raw emotion coming straight from his heart—had me turned upside down.

What was I giving up? I'd come so far. After two years of nothingness, somehow I'd come to this place, this place where he was, and I'd met him, gotten him to love me, and started to breathe again! I couldn't go back to life before; I didn't want to. This place, here on this floor, this hallway, this room and his—this was my home now. And next semester, it would be my home again. And next year, I'd find my home wherever he was, wherever Cass was, wherever my friends were. This was living. And I wanted life. Josh would have wanted it for me.

I called Cass from the airport and left her a message, knowing she was probably already on her flight. She texted back later that night, giving me Ty's number. And I sent Ty a text, begging him not to let Nate know. He was the only one who could help. I hoped he would have that same sense of obligation Cass had when she helped Nate.

I had two weeks. Nate would be in Arizona right before Christmas for the Pac 12 invitational baseball tournament—an official kick-off for the season. The games were played all over Arizona at various ballparks. But I would drive—I didn't care how far it was. I would come see him. And when I did, I would give him everything he asked for, I'd give him my heart. I loved that he was selfish for me, but I also loved that he was willing to share my heart with Josh. And as crazy as it sounds, part of me can't help but feel that somehow Josh sent Nate to me.

There really wasn't a way to practice putting myself out there. I was just going to have to leap. Just like I did when I stepped out of my parents' car months ago and hauled my things up to a dorm room a thousand miles away. I'd have to find that courage, and more, for what I wanted to do. But for Nate...for Nate, I think I can do it.

Nate

I'm sure she's read the letter. Cass told Ty she gave it to her, and Ty's been reassuring, oddly reassuring. He likes Rowe, though, so I hope he's not just willing it all to work out. I hope he really truly believes.

I was hoping she'd text by now though. I wanted to let her know I would be in Arizona. Maybe she found out. Maybe she'll see it somewhere. Maybe she's here? That's stupid. But maybe...*maybe*?

"Come on, Preet. Warm-up time," Cash says, slapping the top of my helmet while he passes me in the locker room. I shut the locker on the rest of my gear and grab my bag of equipment, heading out through the long hallway to the field. These tournaments are the real deal, and there's something cool about playing on a spring-training field. I can't help but imagine being here—*for real*—sometime down the road.

There's a decent crowd outside, and the air is cold for Arizona. I guess it's nighttime, and winter. I just always thought of Arizona as hot and dry. I pull the sleeves snug on my undershirt and pull my mask down while I drop my gear in the bullpen and then start throwing with Cash.

I love playing catch. It sounds stupid, but this is the best part of this game. This simple act—throwing a ball back and forth with someone—it's so numbing, and wonderful. Of course, all I can think about is Rowe, and how she's only miles away. I should text her. No pressure, just to let her know I'm in town. Maybe she'll want to come to a game, bring her dad. I hope he's not angry that I told her. He seemed to understand when I called to tell him she was coming home. Okay, maybe playing catch sucks—because all it does is give you time to think.

Cash and I are warm after about fifteen minutes, and then I pull the spare gear from my bag for the bullpen catcher and head back to the dugout with him. Ty's coming, but not until tomorrow, and it feels weird to play a game completely on my own. My brother hasn't missed many, and I like it when he's here.

256

We're playing Washington. They're good. But we're better. There are a lot of scouts in the stands. They come early, before spring training, and they like watching these tournaments. I'm not expecting anything, but I just hope I make an impression. I'd like to be on their list, someone they'll remember when they come to watch next year or the year after.

"Mister, mister," I hear a kid's voice say, and when I look down, I see him pulling on the leg of my pants. He has curly blond hair and a McConnell baseball hat is mashing most of it down. I kneel down and pull my mask off to look at him, and he's holding a pen and a ball. "Can I get your autograph?"

"Sure," I say, unable to hide the smile this puts on my face. This is the *first* time anyone has ever asked for me to sign a ball. This is awesome. I write my name, clearly, and my number and hand the pen and ball back to the kid. He tucks it in his back pocket so it sticks out, and it makes me chuckle. He hangs around our dugout for a few minutes until someone official-looking comes to get him and leads him over to the home plate area. He must be throwing out the first pitch, or yelling "Play ball!" or something.

The rest of the team finishes warming, and soon the dugout is crowded. Gum is popping and seed shells are being spit everywhere. The announcer goes through the lineups, and there's enough of a crowd here that there's actually applause. I wonder if anyone travelled from McConnell for this? I bet it's mostly boosters or alumni. Once they get through the announcements, everyone climbs the steps, and we all take our spot on the third base line, caps held to our chests, my mask held to mine.

The music fires up, and I expect the same recording of the *Star Spangled Banner* that I hear every game. But tournaments must be special, because after the flowery intro, someone starts to sing.

She starts to sing. I know it the minute the first word leaves her lips. I would know that voice anywhere. It's the voice I imagine when I'm going to sleep every night, and the one I listened to silently, hiding in the dark, while she sang in the shower when she thought no one was there to hear her.

Rowe is singing. In front of at least two thousand people...maybe three. And she's not missing a beat. She's hitting every note, and it's perfect and beautiful...and she's *here*, within reach—touchable. The longer the song goes, the more I can hear her nerves coming through, but she keeps going, her voice just as pretty as the first note, just not as strong. If I knew I wouldn't get booed for interrupting the ultimate act of patriotism, I would break formation and run to her right now, but I wait.

When the second verse hits, the video screen switches from a slideshow of fireworks to her—*it's her*! She's holding one arm around her waist and the other hand is clutching the mic, her eyes closed, just trying to survive this. I can't believe she's doing this, and I know how hard it is for her. This is light years ahead of what she thought she was capable of, and she's doing it for me. I feel Cash lean into me at my side, and when I look to him, his eyebrows raise.

"That's your girl, right?" he whispers.

"Yeah...that's my girl," I whisper back, rapping my mask against my leg just waiting for the song to finish so I can run to her. Her hair is long and wavy, tucked under a McConnell headband, and she's wearing jeans and a McConnell sweatshirt...*mine*! Ty! Ty must be here. He's the only one who could have given that to her. I turn my head without fully looking, and I can see him by the dugout.

Our national anthem is long. I mean, like, stupid long. I'm sure Rowe is thinking the same damned thing right now as her voice quivers for those last few lines. The crowd can feel her losing her nerve, and everybody starts to join in, even the guys standing next to me. As soon as she's done, as soon the word *brave* ends and there are no more syllables for her to sing, I drop my mask and I run.

It takes a while for the crowd to notice what's happening, but when I get closer to her, a few people start to cheer. Her arms are trembling, and she hands the mic back to a guy wearing a shirt and tie, and she looks like she wants to pass out. She doesn't see me coming until the last second, and when she turns to me, her eyes grow wide and she bites at her bottom lip. I don't give her a chance to explain—I don't waste another second. I cup her face in my hands and pull her to me, kissing her so hard that I have to bend her backward and hold the arch of her back in one hand.

The cheers are unmistakable now, and there's whistling, too—lots of whistling. But Rowe just grabs my face, clinging to me, her hands making their way into my hair as her kiss grows stronger and deeper. After several long seconds, I finally break—because we both need air, and I'm pretty sure any longer will earn my team a delay of game.

"You're here," I say, pulling her close and kissing the top of her head. "I can't believe you're here."

"That was some letter," she says, her lower lip once again finding its way between her teeth.

"I meant every word," I say, looking her right in the eyes, making sure she understands. "There's room enough for both of us. And I'm willing to share."

"I know," she says, standing up on the tips of her toes, and pressing her lips to mine, her hands soft on either side of my face. "And thank you...for understanding how Josh fits in my life. He'll always be important to me," she pauses, her fingers flirting with mine while she thinks. "But...I really think he'd want me to give *this*," she says, putting her hand flat on her chest, small tears forming in her eyes, "to you. You have it all— I just needed an angel to tell me I was ready."

I hug her once more. I hug her because telling her I love her and saying thank you isn't enough. And I hold her tightly, because it's been too long, and because I want more, but for the next three hours this will have to be enough.

"I came here with your brother," she says, stepping back, but leaving her fingers locked with mine. "And my dad. You know, more swing analyzing," she winks, and I'm done. I love her; I love her so fucking hard.

"Right, well...maybe when we're done going over my swing we can play back that recording. You know, look for those parts where you're a little pitchy," I wince, playing it off seriously, but she just jabs me in the ribs under the catcher's guard, and I can't help but laugh.

"Screw that. I wasn't pitchy, you ass," she says, her eyes glaring a challenge. She wins, of course. She always wins. I'd paint my whole damned house pink, and run up the white flag if she asked, she has me so wrapped around her finger.

"No, you weren't pitchy. You were perfect," I say, kissing her quickly one more time before I have to rejoin my team.

"I'm not perfect, Nate. I'm a work-in-progress. But this is me...this is me, trying," she says, our fingers dropping apart as I back away. I smile and turn, just letting her think she's right. But she's already perfect. She was perfect the moment I laid eyes on her—perfect for me.

THE END

Don't miss Ty and Cass's story in book 2 in the Falling Series!
Here's a little sneak peek at *YOU AND EVERYTHING AFTER*,
coming late 2014!

Prologue

Ty

Here's the thing about a really good dream. No matter how hard you try to stay in it—eyes closed, hands gripping the sheets, face pressed deep into the coolness of your pillow—you always wake up.

Always.

My dreams are always the same. I can feel the pull of the bat in my hands, swinging it around my entire body, the pressure on my thighs as I push my weight back on my right leg, my hips twisting, the bat cracking against the ball. Then I'm running. *I'm really running.*

I can feel it all.

Sometimes, when I can hold on long enough, Kelly is there after I round the bases. I feel her weight in my arms, her hands along my ribs, reaching around my back as she curls her legs up around my body and I lift her. It's all so effortless. I kiss her, carry her, touch her—breathe her in.

And then it all just stops.

The buzzing of the alarm is harsh, everything about my *now* a painful contrast against the dream I was just forcefully removed from. I spend the next few minutes grieving. I have to get it all out of the way here and now, because I can't make my goddamned useless legs anyone else's burden. And I have to get up. I have to pack and get my ass on a plane back to Louisiana to make sure my brother follows through with college. I know if I go where he goes, we'll both make it through—through life.

He doesn't know this, but I need him, probably more than he needs me. But I'm the strong one. And Nate's the gifted one with the big heart. That's our roles in life; I was crowned at birth by being born first. I take care of Nate, no matter what. Even if I'm fucked up and broken.

"Hey, you're awake." I barely register the half-naked brunette exiting my bathroom. It's all a bit of a fog. There was a party, and there were a lot of underclassmen there, and I remember the flirting. Huh—I must have been charming last night.

I force my typical smile to my face and push my body up so I'm sitting on the edge of the bed, still wrapped in my sheets. Reaching for the T-shirt half hanging from my dresser's top drawer, I indulge in a quick glance at the back of her naked body while she's facing the other way. She's hot. Super hot. But she's not my type. Nobody is.

"Hey, sweetheart." I hate calling chicks that, but I have no idea what her name is. "Thanks for last night, and I hate to be a dick, but...I gotta go," I say as I pull myself up to the chair and bend forward to grab my jeans.

"I know, you told me. *'You don't do girlfriends',*" she says, making air quotes with her fingers. Good, glad I was with it enough to have that conversation with her before anything else. "You planning on coming back to Florida next semester though?"

And there it is. She knows my deal, we had the conversation—but they always want more. "Sweetheart," I say, her name's still a total blank. "I'm probably never coming back to Florida again. And if I do, it will be in my private jet as CEO. Now, I have a flight to catch in just a few hours, and that towel you're in? I need to pack that. So..."

She looks like she wants to punch me, and I don't blame her. But I never make any promises I can't keep. I'm on the hook for too many promises as it is. Promises to my parents to "be strong for my brother" and to "do something *big* despite my disability." I'm good at playing strong—sometimes I even believe it myself. But other times...hell, I'm just fuckin' tired.

"In case you change your mind," she says, handing me the corner of some paper she just ripped from one of my magazines. *What the hell?* I turn it over and see her number and, ah...that's right—Beth.

"Yeah, thanks," I say and toss it in the trash right in front of her. That pretty much seals the deal, and she's gone seconds later, giving me the finger on her way out. I deserve that. I probably deserve a lot worse. But Beth is better off without me, and as selfish as it sounds, I need to keep all of my energy in reserve to get through the things I want in *my* life. I don't have the capacity to share with anyone else. I lost that the moment I dove off that cliff.

Finally alone, I stop everything for a few minutes, pushing myself to the window so I can watch everyone going about their lives outside. Pressing my forehead to the windowpane, I watch a couple say goodbye; the guy picks the chick up and swings her around, and then they kiss like they're in love. You can tell the difference. My kisses are all about using and avoiding. They're great in the moment, but I don't taste anything, except maybe vodka or Tequila or, sometimes, smoke. I don't feel anything, other than my need to get off. But that kiss—the one happening two stories down from my window—is so foreign. It's about love and happiness and the future.

My phone buzzes on the bed, so I snap myself out of my torture and put on my mask. It's Nate. "What's up, man?"

"Hey, I'm picking you up from the airport. Parents are staying put," he says. "Anything special you want since you're getting in late?"

"Yeah, to hit the strip club on our way home," I say, half kidding.

"Right, so a bunch of singles then. Got it," he says, without even as much as a laugh. We're playing this straight, like we always do. I love my brother. He's my best friend. But Nate's not strong enough to bear the weight of everything that happened to me, so I finish making plans with him on the phone, and when I hang up, I spend the next two hours packing the rest of my things, a job that would take anyone else fifteen minutes.

Before I leave, I push myself back to the window to watch my life that *should have been* happen outside, but only for few more seconds. With the heaviest bag on my lap and the roller behind me, I make my way to the hallway and ask another student to help me wheel the roller to the taxi out front. Once the door is shut and we're on our way to the airport, I forget it all—the dream, the scene out my window, the last four years at Florida State; it's all meaningless. And so is everything that's to come. I'm just going through the motions. You know...being strong.

Whatever.

Chapter 1: The Last Day of Summer Ball

Ty

"Come on, princess. Get your ass up! It's time for workouts. Early bird gets the worm, and all that shit," I practically sing to my brother, whose head is buried under two pillows. He's still nursing himself a little after our late night. Nate's not used to my schedule. I've never needed much sleep, a side effect of constantly waking up in pain—however real or not it may be. I pretty much filled my undergrad years with party after party, and I still finished with a three-point-eight GPA.

"Gahhhhhhhhh," Nate bellows, his voice muffled by his mattress as he throws the top pillow at me, hitting me in the chest. "What are you, part robot? How are you not tired?"

"I'm just that awesome. Awesome people don't need to sleep as much as you mere mortals," I say, tugging the blanket from his body to really piss him off.

"Alright! I'm up, I'm up," he says, pushing his fists into his eyes and rubbing like he did when he was a kid. He's still that kid to me—probably always will be. "The team doesn't even start workouts until nine anyway, asshole!"

He's complaining, but he's still getting dressed. I push Nate. I push him because he takes it, which means he secretly likes being pushed. And I push him because the kid is seriously talented. I was good...before I got hurt. I maybe could have played college ball, probably for some junior college back home. But Nate, he could go all the way, as in big leagues, and stay there—for years.

"Hey, that's *awesome asshole*, thank you very much. Now get your shoes on so we can get our miles in," I say, pushing out into the hallway to wait for him.

We go six miles every morning—Nate takes the treadmill at the gym, and I work the hand cycle. My body, at least what's left of it, is something I can control, so weights and fitness has kind of become an obsession. School has always been easy, which is probably why the partying never seems to get in my way. But throwing myself in the pool and making my arms pound the water for a mile or two is a challenge—I need those challenges to remind me that I'm still alive.

"You're like this happy little morning elf, and I hate you," Nate says, throwing his workout towel at me before turning to lock up our room.

"Dude, it's not like I'm the one putting the hard stuff in your hands. You know, you can get drunk on just beer, bro. You don't have to do shots and shit like that. That's why you're always so tired in the morning," I tell him.

Nate was a goody two-shoes in high school, always hanging out with the same group of guys and his girlfriend. The switch flipped when he found out she cheated on him. Thank God I was home when that happened. He left the party, came home to me, and we shared our first bottle of Jack. Damn, maybe it is my fault—I should've started him out on something weaker.

"About that, man...I think I'm out," he says, pausing right before the doorway leading out of our dorm.

"Out of what?" He's lost me on this one.

"Out...of this partying and trolling for random chicks thing we're doing every night. It's...it's just not me," he says, and I can't help but laugh. "Fuck off, I knew you'd make fun of me."

"Sorry, sorry dude. That was just..."I have to pause again to try to keep a straight face. Tucking my big-ass grin into the side of my arm to hide it, I force myself to take a deep breath—and to take my brother seriously. "I'm sorry. I guess I just don't see the down side."

"You wouldn't," Nate says, walking ahead. My smile's gone at that—he's right, I wouldn't. And that stings a little.

Workouts go the same, and when Nate heads off to join the team, I put in some extra time. There's a posting for personal trainers that I've been looking at, I just haven't had the balls to ask about it yet. But today's the day. There's a cute girl working the main counter, so I hit her up first.

"Hey, Nike!" I call her Nike because that's what her shirt says. She looks down and smirks and then looks back into my eyes. My grin makes her smile and bite her lip, and I know I've got her. "Sorry, didn't know your name."

"I'm Sage," she says, leaning over the counter just enough to give me a nice view of the frilly white lace trim on her bra.

"Sage, nice name," I smile, falling right into my routine. "So I was checking out the posting for the personal trainer. That filled yet?"

"Nope," she says, her smile bigger now. "You interested?"

"Yep," I say, playing off of her flippant answer. She's oblivious though.

"Hang on, I'll get the manager," she says, pushing back from the counter with a skip and heading into a back office. I allow myself a glance at her tiny shorts and perfect ass while she walks away.

The manager wasn't as charmed by my dimples and good looks, so I had to win over all six-foot-four of him with my skills. After six years of physical rehab, I know my stuff, so he was happy to hire me to work with freshman students who were just looking to stay in shape.

I type Nate a text on my way back to the dorm, making our now regular lunch plan for burgers at Sally's. I think it's our dad's fault, but Preeter boys like their routine. I think maybe only two or three days have passed that we haven't eaten at least one of our three meals at our new favorite hole-in-the-wall.

I have a good hour to kill before Nate's practice is done. Alone time. At least during school I can sink my mind into something for one of my classes; I usually end up working ahead just because I can't stand being idle. But there's not much to distract me now. Even *Sports Center* is lame in August. McConnell is not known for its football team, so like hell am I going to get into *that.*

It's a bad idea—it always is—but my phone is in my hand and my fingers are typing and hitting send before I can stop myself. It's been three weeks since I've talked to Kelly. She had the baby two months ago. That was a slap in my face, a reality dose I probably needed. That's why I broke up with her in the first place—so she could have these things. I did it because I loved her so much I wanted her to have it all. But damn did it hurt seeing her live her life and move on from me so effortlessly.

Kelly stayed with me after the accident, through high school and the summer before we both left for college. We were going to go to the same school—that was always the plan. But I could tell by the look on her face, the one that she wore more and more every day, that she was forcing herself to go through with it all. She wanted out. But she loved me too much to hurt me. So I pushed her away instead.

My phone buzzes back with a response, and I hover over the screen for a few seconds, afraid to open it. I just asked her how things were going at home with Jax, the baby. We've managed to remain friends for four years. *Friends*—even though every conversation with her is like driving a stake through my heart. Last year, she got married, and a few months later, she told me she was pregnant. And I died a little more.

Swiping the screen, the first thing I see is a picture of tiny feet nestled inside Kelly's hands, the diamond ring on her left hand like a banner waving in my face. Her husband, Jared, tolerates me, but I don't think he'd mind at all if Kelly and I just stopped communicating completely. I have a feeling he'll get his wish one day—distance and time, they do funny things to the heart, they make you...forget. Or at least want to forget.

He's beautiful. That's all I can say.

Thanks. That's all she writes back. And I know we're near the end, and I feel sick. I'm getting drunk tonight, with our without Nate as my wingman. Hell, I might just pull up a stool at Sally's and join the regulars who plant themselves there all day.

Cass

"Oh my god, you literally brought your entire life from Burbank to Oklahoma, didn't you," I huff, dragging two extra bags on top of my own trunk along the walkway toward our dorm.

"That was the deal. I would come *here*, but I still get to be me—and I like to have my things," she says, prancing ahead of me with the lighter bags. Paige is a full minute older, but you'd think years separated us with the authority she holds over my head.

When it came time to decide on a college, Paige's choices narrowed down to Berkley and McConnell, and Berkley was definitely her preference. But for me, it was always McConnell and only McConnell. They had the best sports and rehab medicine program in the country, and that's what I wanted to do—what I was destined to do. But my parents wouldn't support me moving thousands of miles away without someone around to keep an eye on me. Supervision—the word made my skin crawl I had heard it so often. *Supervision* and *monitoring,* words bandied about so often in conversations about me, but never in conversations with me. God how I wished just once someone threw in the word *normal.*

So, as much of a pain in the ass as my sister is, she's also a saint, because she picked McConnell, and I'm the only reason for that. And I owe her—I owe her my life.

"Okay, so here's the deal," Paige starts as soon as we get our bags, mostly hers, loaded into our dorm room. "I want this bed. And I'm still going to rush a sorority. Mom and dad don't need to know that I won't technically be living *with* you."

"Works for me," I say, already unzipping my bag and flipping open the lid on my trunk. I feel Paige's purse slam into my back suddenly. "Ouch! What the hell?" I say, rubbing the spot where the leather strap smacked my bare skin.

"The least you could do is pretend to miss living with me," she says, her eyes squinting, her smirk showing she's a little hurt.

"Oh, Paigey, I'll miss you. I just hate that you have to be my babysitter—*still!*" And I do hate it. I think that's the worst part about being a teenager with MS; everyone's always waiting for something to go wrong.

It started in the middle of my freshman year—I would get this pain in my eye. It would come and go, weeks between each occurrence. When I couldn't ignore it any longer, I told my parents—and we went to the eye doctor. My vision was fine, and he told them it was probably stress from school and the running in soccer leaving me dehydrated. What a simple and succinct diagnosis. It was also complete crap.

The fatigue hit next. Again, easily summed up with too much soccer practice, which of course led to truly uncomfortable fights between my parents—my mom wanting me to quit completely and my father saying I just "need more conditioning." It was because of these fights that I hid the tingling from them. That went on for months, until it was summer. And then one day, I couldn't walk.

I could stand from my bed, get to my feet, but that was it. The second I attempted to move toward my door or drag my feet toward my closet to get dressed I wobbled and fell. I felt like the town drunk without the benefit of the booze and a paper bag. I screamed for Paige and my parents, and I knew by the look on their faces that my life as I knew it was done.

The fights continued, and my parents separated for a while. After the MS diagnosis, my mom insisted I quit soccer. And I got depressed. My dad supported my wishes to play again, of course under strict circumstances and with limited workouts. And everything pretty much sucked for the next year.

It was a series of med trials, seeing how certain combinations affected me and finding out what side effects I could handle. I also got really good at giving myself a shot—three times a week for three years, until they came out with the pill version last year. I didn't mind the shots, though. What I minded were the constant questions and lectures from my parents. "How are you feeling?" "Are you fatigued?" "You should rest, stop working so hard."

Paige never lectured. Through it all, she just stayed the same. True, she's terribly self-absorbed, and there were moments that she resented the attention I got because of my disease. But it was more about the attention, and the fact that it wasn't on her. And I liked that.

We made a deal with my parents, coming here as a package deal. We fought for it for months; my mom really wanted to keep me at home. But that's the thing about MS. It never goes away; it's always with me. And the shots, drug trials, therapies—they don't fight the disease. They only slow it down. Like the front line of the Pittsburgh Steelers, except nowhere near as effective. Maybe more like the front line of the Miami Dolphins. So in the end, I got my way. Now that I'm here, I'm not going to let MS be a part of any conversation. I'm just Cass Owens, and my story ends there.

"Hungry. Now," Paige says, snapping her fingers at me. I smile out the window, not offended in the least. I'm free.

"Let's go eat greasy, fried crap," I say, grabbing my purse and blowing right past her, ignoring her eye roll and protest and impending whine about needing a salad with low-cal dressing. Freedom!

Ty

I'm two beers ahead of Nate by the time he walks into Sally's, and I can already see the lecture building with every step closer he comes. He's doing that thing, where he cracks his neck on one side and looks down, shaking his head at me in shame.

"Save it, bro," I say, picking up my glass and finishing off the last of my second beer while he sits down and admires both empty mugs.

"You called Kelly, didn't you?" It's not really a question, so I don't answer. "I don't know why you torture yourself. It's not like you can't meet other women. Damn, Ty—that's like your best skill. You meet women every five minutes, and they're in love with you after six minutes."

"Yeah, but I don't love them. No one is Kelly," I say, feeling every bit of my self-loathing settle over my body.

"No, but maybe…just maybe, someone could be better, you know, like *different* better. If you'd just give it a damned chance," Nate says, stretching his legs out from the booth and pulling a menu out from the rack on the wall. I can't help but watch his muscles stretch and hate him, just for the smallest second, for being whole. I don't really hate him, but sometimes it's hard to be so damned positive all of the time. "Order me a cheeseburger and chili fries. I'm hitting the head," he says, pushing out from the booth and walking to the restrooms in the back.

Our mom always says that Nate's the romantic one. Me, I'm all numbers and practicality and logic. But I don't know, I think my romantic side is alive and breathing—it's just tortured. It's this sliver of my soul that feels certain that there's only one girl out there who could ever love me, and her love wasn't meant to last forever.

"Hahahaha! You are sooooo not the sexy one," a chick's voice squeals from behind me so loudly that I'm compelled to turn around. That, and she said the word *sex*, pretty much an automatic for me. I glance over my shoulder, and at first all I can see are two blondes. I can't quite make out their features though, but if pushed, I'd say they were both probably pretty damned sexy. When they pass me, I breathe in and the air smells like the ocean. One of them is taller than the other, lean but built, clearly a runner. The other one is curvy, and she's wearing a sundress that, if I had to guess, was hiding no bra and probably a pretty sexy pair of panties.

"You're, like, predictable sexy," the tall one says, and I hear a bubble snap from her gum. "I'm like ninja sexy."

I can't help but smirk at what she says. This chick's funny. And I'd have to say, that might just give her the edge on sexy. I keep my gaze forward, pretending to look at something on my phone screen on the table, but I notice the pair of them slide into a booth across the room.

"What'll you have today, Ty?" Cal says, pulling the pencil from behind his ear to write down our order. I don't know why he bothers asking. Four weeks we've been coming here, and I'm pretty sure we've ordered the same thing every time.

"Cheeseburgers," I say, nodding to Nate, who's now standing behind Cal and waiting to slide back to his seat.

"Oh, hey Nate," Cal says, writing down our order and putting the pen back in its spot somewhere within his mess of hair and the mesh Budweiser hat he wears every single day.

"I'm starved, man. Today's practice was brutal. It's just...so damned hot," Nate says, pulling his own phone out and looking at the screen. I'm glad he's only half paying attention to me, because my focus is dedicated to the booth about twenty feet away.

"Do you have any low-fat dressings? Like, at all?" the curvy blonde says, a strand of her hair wrapped around her finger when she asks.

"We have Italian," says the older woman taking their order.

"Yeah, but is it just oil? That doesn't mean low fat. Is it fat-free or low-fat?" This chick is high maintenance.

"It's...Italian," the waitress says. A small chuckle escapes my lips and the other girl, the *ninja*, looks my way briefly. I don't know why, but my heart kicks a little at getting caught.

"She'll have the Italian. Just put it on the side," the ninja princess says, and the waitress walks away.

"Good thinking. It's low-fat if you put it on the side," the diva says, and my ninja princess just stares at her, watching her pull out a mirror and check her lipstick, and then flips her gaze to me. This time I don't panic, instead just lifting the right side of my lip in a tiny grin to let her know I'm with her—hell, I'm *so with her.* She shakes her head at me in disbelief and then returns her gaze back to her friend.

"Putting the dressing in a different bowl doesn't change its chemistry, Paige," she says, and I smirk again.

"What's so funny, dude?" Nate interrupts, but I shake my head and hold up my hand against the table.

"Hang on, I have to hear this out," I whisper, and he bunches his brow before turning to look at the two girls behind him who have me completely rapt.

"Then why the hell did you make me get it on the side, Cass?" she asks, and I commit that name to memory the second it leaves her lips.

"So you could use less," Cass huffs back.

"That's stupid," Paige says.

"Yes, I see that now," Cass says, stepping out from their booth to head to the restroom area. She gives me one last smile before she leaves, and I hold up my empty beer glass to toast her—the sexy ninja princess with the patience of gold, and the next girl I want to get to know in Oklahoma.

274

Acknowledgements

This book was just begging to come out of me. I dreamt pieces of it, and scribbled other parts down on notebooks, receipts and napkins that I stuffed into the depths of my purse while in the strangest places. I think I jotted down Nate and Rowe's names on the back of an ASU baseball ticket. And when I pulled everything together and sat down to write, it just poured from my fingers. Thank you—seriously...thank you, for reading it.

This Is Falling is in many ways about those *other* stories that I never got to tell as a journalist. I covered the tragedies, and sometimes, as a reporter, would go back to revisit things on anniversaries. When enough time has gone by, things become newsworthy once again. Looking back at it now, I'm not sure why that is. *This Is Falling* is about the people those tragedies touch but whose stories don't make the paper. The dominoes of aftereffects from a school shooting don't all fall down in a straight line. They scatter and touch everyone. And Rowe Stanton embodies this.

I must thank my amazing editors, Tina Scott and Billi Joy Carson, for their work on this final product. And I would be lost in a world of doubt and second-guessing if it were not for my beta readers—Shelley, Bianca, Jen, Debbie and Brigitte. You ladies rock!

Lastly, *This Is Falling* is my fifth title. Being an author is my dream, and it is only true because of my readers and the power of the book blogging community. I have connected with the most amazing readers and bloggers, and I cannot thank you enough for the time you have spent on my words. Ty's story? That one's for you!

About the Author

Ginger Scott is a journalist and writer from Peoria, Arizona. A proud Sun Devil, she is a graduate and associate faculty member of Arizona State University's Cronkite School of Journalism. When she's not typing feverishly on her MacBook during the wee hours or reading in the dark on her iPad, she's probably at a baseball diamond somewhere watching her son or her favorite team, the Arizona Diamondbacks, take the field.

Books by Ginger Scott

Waiting on the Sidelines
Going Long
Blindness
How We Deal With Gravity
This Is Falling
You and Everything After, coming late 2014

Ginger Scott Online

www.littlemisswrite.com
www.facebook.com/GingerScottAuthor
Twitter @TheGingerScott